Menta-Life

Written By: Avery Nunez

"A real adventure! It starts you off right into some amazing action and continues with plot twists and turns that are hard to figure out until the very end. A great Sci-Fi novel for people who want something original yet straight forward. A must read!"

—Austin P.

"This futuristic world is beautifully put together. The twists in this book were completely unexpected and I enjoyed every word."

—Amazon Customer

"Vanessa Pheros is a renegade type of character that was so fun to fall into from the beginning. The action kept me engaged and ready to figure out what troubles she would get into next. I'm ready for a sequel."

—Destiny W.

"An interesting book which looks at future tech and it being implanted into people's brains. Sci-fi fans I think would enjoy it. I would recommend it."

—S.K. Gregory

Series Sequels

Desertion

Defiance

Deception

How many sides to the story?

#housementalife

To further support the fight!

www.averynunez.com

Visit my website for updates on new releases, social media links, special promotions, author biography, and other written works.

Registration Number: TXu 1-963-190

This is a work of fiction. Names, businesses, characters, places, events and incidents are either the products of the author's imagination or used in a fictitious manner. Any resemblance to actual persons, living or dead, actual events or products are purely coincidental.

No part of this book may be reproduced in any form or by any electronic or mechanical means including storage and retrieval systems without permission in writing from Avery Nunez.

All Rights Reserved

Copyright © 2015 by Avery Edwin Nunez

Editing by Nanda Olney and Belisa Brownlee

Cover Design by FlowerXl

Contents

Prologue: The Corporation...I

Chapter 1: Van...1

Chapter 2: Home Stretch...13

Chapter 3: New World 2086..22

Chapter 4: Welcome Home..36

Chapter 5: Meet and Greet...50

Chapter 6: The Threat...67

Chapter 7: Finding Equility..83

Chapter 8: Socialite Ball...103

Chapter 9: In the Dark..119

Chapter 10: Deserted..130

Chapter 11: Background Check...136

Chapter 12: Normal Work, Abnormal...150

Chapter 13: Secrets...170

Chapter 14: Three Sides, One Coin...192

Chapter 15: Plan A..205

Chapter 16: Rules and Guidance..221

Chapter 17: Plan B..240

Chapter 18: Wake Up, Van...259

Desertion Preface..281

Acknowledgments...I

Menta-Life

Prologue: The Corporation

Menta-Life was born in the year 2072. A corporation that lets citizens live lives through a mass server as a means to rebuild what the human race destroyed. Mentally extending the human lifespan. In order for the server to work, placement of a "microdot" onto the brain's analytical portion is required; a device about the size of a single hair follicle. An intricate piece of art. From the start, surgical placement costs five thousand aers. Serving as a connection to the intranet. Then connection of the intranet synchronizes directly to brain stems. After the operation, the microdot is slowly reeled inward by each thumping pulse. Taking two days to reach the analytic center.

With placement and a link to the simulated outside world, the brain decelerates into thinking, but not believing, it's living regularly during Life; this allows slumbering users control over themselves while others around them live as *normal* beings. Upon returning, staff settles the client into a secure location. A necessary, comfortable, quiet environment to initiate a medically induced coma. Assure an uninterrupted sleep for three days; the amount of real time taken to live a ninety-year Life from admittance to passing. Shorter stay, dependent on age and transpiring events. Keeping a client under and providing nutrients while comatose costs fifteen thousand aers per visit.

Dreaming begins; Life begins. The mental world is fully based around shared internet data streams. Clients in their mental Life have complete access to everything the world has to offer, regardless of choice to access it. If a real-world traffic accident occurs near a dreaming client's location, they will experience horrible traffic conditions once information is uploaded to the internet. If close enough, they will witness the accident as described. The occurrence and all surrounding data are implemented as a Rapid Major Event. Past sub-events are also in place to keep the mind flowing with old and new information, spreading over duration.

If a citizen chooses to make their online social media profile publicly available, a client can unintentionally access it; possibly meet the digital citizen, getting to know the stranger as rivals or becoming the best of friends. Then gainful opportunities. Shared online courses are made available, transforming Life into a handy tool for those openly seeking knowledge. Clients can achieve astronomical certification in one day's real time, dedicating an adequate number of years to the demanding effort required of that position. In turn, a criminal can work up to status of crime lord.

No being in Life is real yet information and reactions are as real as can be. If the client pushes someone, that someone could push back based on their online persona. Be it with force or informing officers. On that note, ignorance to law does not excuse a client from consequence and repercussion. If someone commits a crime, law enforcement responses are arranged by distance and calculated pursuit time, followed by culprit apprehension to the best of their ability. Those with fetishes, like sadists, love the Life server. They go through their mental Life, harming as many citizens as possible, before getting cornered and going down with a fight. Once the client is deceased, they awaken, and their server time is concluded. The connection must stay linked for three consecutive days unless the client passes on during their Life. Unknown side effects may occur, if woken otherwise. Predictions more mentally violent but similar to waking a sleepwalker.

A brain can only withstand the server for a full seventy-two hours. Not a minute longer. If multiple visits are made before a two-day rest period, the body will begin to gradually shut sense perceptions. First stage being the ability to walk. Basic motor skills. Of course, relearning isn't impossible. Experimentation on additional stages were never trialed due to safety concerns for test subjects in an already scarce humanity. Two additional safety protocols about the Life server: no one can regress younger than their current age and it's impossible to access a Life within a Life.

The corporation is sworn, by written statement, to privacy. Language stated on contract and signed at the initial screening process. Citizens continually returned. Menta-Life is the leading corporation, becoming addiction after going public with a free Life trial offer. Soaring higher at the media takeover which they basically had an indirect hand in reestablishing, along with most of the New World itself. Regrown populations take to Menta-Life as a symbol of hope, crowning their inexperienced rulers with branches existing at the five city's hearts. More than well-funded by its clients. Since citizens can do as they please in their mental Life, crime rates declined drastically; reforming inhabitants with clean histories. The corporation has done well by the people, single-handedly aiding rapidly increased technological efforts. Far surpassed achievements collectively with the digitally manufactured safe space for those to educate themselves and invent within. Thriving in external expansion. Elderly have shared knowledge of the past; researchers share knowledge of the active present; prodigies theorize potential futures. Menta-Life has changed the world for everyone…

Chapter 1: Van

    The world grows, yet my prison cell's still horrid. A space the size of a walk-in closet; twin bed, sink, toilet paper and toilet to match. For the likes of me, an ideal home. A toothbrush delivered and shipped after each meal. Brief individual showers between twenty-four-hour intervals, at conveniently chosen times; steaming two minutes of stood relaxation.
    One repetitive highlight is in progress; sitting. Snug in a form-fitting, blue jumpsuit. Mocked by the bright shade. Occupied in my brown hair. Twist here, twirl there. Not lengthy like model women in holographic magazines and billboards but keeps my upper back warm. A forced style since chopping it shorter isn't allowed. The two-year old, broken-in mattress aches my… glutes. Alternatively, circling my cell today killed my legs. These thin blue slip-ons socks do my feet no justice on concrete, either. Lying in bed aches my back. Killing time

exercising will ache all the above. Springy mattress is the winning option, beating concrete ground any day of the week.

Nothing else to do, I spend a lot of time thinking outside the box. My prison title is 22641-0B8. A name of zero sense so guards call me "Inmate." Beyond these walls is yet another. My name is Vanessa Pheros and I am a skilled smuggler. The last isn't pronounced with an S at the end, keeping as silent as I've been since my arrest. I grew up minorly in England.

Although my country was destroyed during the last war at age seven, my accent didn't crumble too hard with it. My mother died the day I was born, giving birth. My father died in a war he wasn't fighting; brilliant researcher, or so stories told. Didn't know much about his occupation nor do I care. His legacy carried on with him. He left me on a shuttle with our neighbor to revisit his lab, retrieving some research data meant to aid life after the war settled. I watched from the rising shuttle's window as the bomb struck. In a flash, he was swallowed whole by a cloud of smoke. The last glimpse caught of my father was a sprint toward an office building. Then the shuttle caught turbulence and departed.

Both sides lost the war and so did the planet. A global nuclear fallout. Centering survivors to the safest zone in the United States; Kansas. Not long after, my prior ill neighbor passed. I welcomed an angry life of delinquency. Counting orphanages, foster homes, group homes, mental homes, jail, and prison, I've been in captivity longer than alive.

The year is 2086. I believe my birthday was a couple of months ago in November. A healthy twenty-four, although time is frozen without clocks and windows. I stopped accurately tallying days, too many months ago. I'm just assuming my second prison anniversary already past. No cake and candles and singing. No guards swing by with happy birthday reminders; an available perk I swiftly denied. Constant loneliness. Preference dating to childhood.

People are annoying, mostly expressing interest in ridiculous fashion trends and gossip. Overall, containing no relation to illegal efforts. Pheros policy: No friends inside or out, and always stick to self. Many women tried to socialize. A couple even sprouted attitudes at the rude rejection. Expected reaction that I purposely goaded. Their attitudes didn't last long after having sense knocked into them. I'm always stopped before fully warming up. Word spread, and everyone stays away.

Everyday repeats in this sterile prison: three meals, six hours total in the I.Y. per day. An option between group therapy or educational services for two hours, not both. To decline both is open also, opting for two additional hours in a cell. My workout times.

Signifying dinner is ready, the prison bell blares. Couple of loud beeps, followed by cell doors sliding open from left to right on my side; right to left on the other. Without fail, my first thought is *freedom*; a longing sight too good to be true. However, it's not so simple. Inmates aren't hostile enough to riot, discouraging my joyous thought. Without fail.

Automated defense turrets are set to attack escapees with nonlethal shock pulses, one minor detail keeping inmates terrified. The turret is a square box about one-and-a-half feet at base and height with a barrel for spewing pulses. Essentially, a glorified taser that can shock someone unconscious for an hour. Generally used for breaking up fights, which I am familiar. Fortunately, what doesn't kill makes me stronger, knocking me out only half the hour. Always alert, my body built a tolerance against unwanted sleep years ago, pre-prison. I can't exactly track time, but unconsciousness feels more like a doze than power nap.

My cell slides open. Two digital lines zip left. Women sneak peeks at me, casually sauntering by in the line's pursuit. Observing the animal in its natural habitat. I rise from my bed. Step out and merge between the lines as a copycat. Cautious not to cross the outer yellow border. Distance is spaced for one person to walk in front of another, oddly not promoting reform and unison. I did run quite a few times. Once an obvious blue target crosses the border leading to the chow hall or I.Y., a single wail blurts. Offensive operating commences if the target isn't back in formation fast enough.

The prison's highest letter block is H. Mine is B. A long hall of extremely thick cell doors. Three floors high with metal staircases reaching each. Steel gates barricade upper level railings to prevent prisoners from committing suicide. No windows, no exterior yards. No outside contact, other than receiving mail.

Across the block, a custodian is wiping a cell's thick glass door. A lucky someone shipped out between returning from the I.Y. and dinner. Two black-uniformed guards idle near the worker. Button-up shirts tucked; "ORI" stitched on the chests. Untouchable arrogance displayed proudly. Armor or brandished weapons to protect themselves isn't necessary when there's faith. Full faith in the turret targeting system. One shot and guards earned thirty minutes to dump a prisoner wherever. Cell, warden's office, solitary. If turrets were stationary, situations would stack differently. They slide freely on metal rails along every wall. Every corner. Every floor. Able to surf the entire prison at rapid speeds upon threat detection, vanishing through numerous holes at each end when the last occupant exits. Either housing or accessibility to the remainder of the prison.

The yellow line guides into a single metal door centered on the back wall. Into a bright white hallway. The prison stays illuminated. Eyes already well adjusted to this pale gleam. Lots of white doors facing off, yet no windows to see out or in any rooms. All that's visible are the doors' sliding pulls and near-flush seams. No metal rails above for traveling nuisances. Whatever's behind those doors, turrets may not have rail access to. Something I bear in mind.

Facilities have peaceful names, I'm just too criminally minded to use them. Ori Prison, not standing for anything in particular, at least not to my knowledge. I.Y. for Interior Yard. The chow hall is called Dining Delight. How can I describe it? Warping dimensions to an executive limbo? Still bright. The back wall curves a half-circular design with a dome ceiling. A mellow instrumental plays faintly, meant to bring serenity and works based on many humble expressions. Who doesn't it work on? Crème-colored tables clutter the center in rows to sit for a meal. Crème-colored benches loop the outer perimeter for comfort during social mingling. Dispensed food cycles on trays via conveyor belt, served before looping into a second gap in the wall. A gap too small to fit the human body. But workers must be reloading the conveyor. The food doesn't taste bad; honestly, my favorite thing about Ori. An hour in the chow hall, and it's back home. I start eating. Staring into the light green tray's swirl design as I chew.

Many Ori inmates were reformed on arrival; short sentences due to menial misbehaviors like skimming to gain greater financial standing.

Many didn't completely adapt to the New World; sentenced for worse crimes like bootlegging, robbery, and murder. Smuggling is where I fit. Few have been waiting to leave since before a New World prison was established; trickled down to the worst crimes. The kind committed when the world was Survival of the Fittest. Their bad behavior here ends in banishment. In a prison where no one can do harm, peace conquers all.

A reason why I hate it here and stay to myself exists, but I can never remember. My gut tells me not to trust anyone. When does it hurt to listen? There isn't a reason to watch my back. If there was, inmates are probably friendly enough to watch it for me; smiles and chatty behavior. It's unreal. I pictured prison being different, with angry women fighting throughout the day and the occasional shanking. I'd read about that in the library's historic archives. If an opportunity arose, they'd revert to savages in a heartbeat.

The bell blares on the hour mark. Dinner concludes. On our way back, I glare into a few cells dappled in little decorations. Hung letters, reminders of someone special waiting. Holographic pictures of family and friends. Homey feelings. A holographic picture uses a small projection dot that spouts a still image a couple of inches from itself. My cell can never be mistaken because its still image is as plain as moving day. The sliding door seals. I accompany my bed nowhere again. Slink into thoughts like usual.

Most nights, mild exercise comes after dinner. Usually taking two split nights a week to give myself a break. And this is one of those. A way of barely keeping time. Lights go dim, but not out, when all inmates are secure in their cells. Indication that my lights need to be out. I lie on the uncomfortable, springy mattress. My twin lids break from another day.

The next morning, my lids reopen. Blurred pupils focused at the ceiling. Feeling rejuvenated and hungry. Without a clock or window, I can never tell how long I've slept. Eight hours, as recommended to children? Ten for hard-working adults? One elongated blink for the insomniac? Routine waking trained my senses. My index finger accuses the ceiling.

The breakfast bell blares. Every block gets mandatory time in the I.Y. and, since two meet at once, someone is eating breakfast late. Ready, I stretch to the sliding cell door. Usual dull; no angry faces, no new arrivals, no one stepping outside the line. I linger until most settle and eat. As if selections altered, I select a breakfast tray from the conveyor. Stroll toward a far table where I eat alone. An inmate twists away from a table, bumping my shoulder hard enough to slip the plate from my tray. Frustrated about missing the main course, I drop the entire tray. Crashes echo the domed room. Silencing patrons. A warning alarm wails once as an indicator that the action was noticed and is being monitored.

The woman politely speaks, "I apologize for my clumsiness, please allow me to—"

I spank the unfinished tray into her face. Instantly, a sharp pinch hits my shoulder. Shrouded in darkness. I wake. Chest flat on concrete. Underneath the bed looks just as bland as every other portion of my cell. I roll over and greet the ceiling. Those turrets glide rails entirely too fast for their own good. The hot pinch is charring my shoulder like barbeque. I sit up to the cell across. A woman's sincerely disappointed expression is aimed, no doubt wondering what my problem is and why. I don't break eye contact, sterning my expression and waiting for her own business to be minded. The woman wanders away.

Why does missing meals hurt so much? My quick temper is somewhat satisfied, though not worth it. I reel my shoulder forward and drag my jumpsuit down from the neck. The dark reddish burn on my pale skin is easily noticeable. I haven't seen sunlight in too long; the hallways, chow hall, and I.Y. are all the shine available.

Footsteps sound outside. Quick successions of pats from heavy boots. One pair. That occurs in solo formation when a guard delivers mail. I sit on the bed. Listen to the approach. Shift closer to watch the guard pass. She strolls into sight, wielding a letter-sized envelope. Performs a sharp pivot in front of my cell.

Her lips move, "Mail."

For me? I've never received mail, not ever in my life. And am not interested. It's probably a bargain arrangement for a magazine subscription anyway... which couldn't happen in a prison. Involuntary investment rears its head, wondering a bit. A slot of glass retracts outward, about the height of four webbed fingers, flapping down in sections until it hangs stiff. I witness this when my three opposing neighbors receive mail; appreciated weekly highlights. I spectate the envelope's heroic entrance. Then the guard's swift departure. Landing paper scrapes the concrete. The mail slot flaps upward in sections and slithers home. "Vanessa Pheros" is written on the envelope in black ink. No return address, nor thickness like holographic pages. It's a regular old sheet of paper. Curiosity swallows me whole. Although just meeting, I lean forward and squint like we're significant rivals. Who would write me? And about what? I stretch my bruised shoulder and pick it up. Unwelcome reading material in hand, I tear the envelope's end carefully and remove the paper. Unfold the top up and bottom down. Small words on a big sheet. An address and message:

"Urgent that we meet at this location. 8 o'clock tomorrow morning. Someone will await your arrival. Do not be late."

Dates with me are demanded in writing now? I flip the paper. No signature from a sender. Who sent this? Who'd want to meet me? Aware of my incarceration, how? I ball the letter and hoop it in the toilet, refusing to waste another second solving a riddle. Locked in the New World's prison, where no outside contact is allowed, I'm expected to schedule a meet and greet. Maybe if I ask nicely.

An alarm whines in spurts, sounding messier than typical blares before cells open. I snap at the door. View opposing cells for confirmation of sanity. The women rush to their doors and scan what they can. Is something going on in the hallway? Lights darken, powering down loudly. Palms out, I dash at the door. Both hands mash the pitch-black glass. Not a slit of illumination present, as if my eyes are shut.

Emergency lights activate, glowing a sluggish red. Alarm blares discontinue. A more familiar, singular blare initiates, soon repeating too quickly to count. Then cell doors begin opening. Left to right, right to left. Pasting my face to the glass, I watch inmates on my level and one level above vigilantly exit their cells. Drenched in confusion. The toilet letter telepathically directs my eyes, going over the situation and evaluating connections I'd decided didn't matter moments ago. Is this coincidence? Or a related power outage? Intensity of staggering blares drags answers to the last thing I should care about. A terrible Samaritan could be handing out freedom passes and I'm not losing mine.

A guard sternly demands over intercom, "Return to your cells immediately! I repeat, return to your cells immediately!"

I cling to glass again. What's happening out there? I can't see the start of either side. Inmates on my right stare further toward the I.Y., forming a speechless alliance. Finally achieving unison around here and I'm missing it. Guards continue warning that action will be taken if inmates don't comply. Inmates instigate an offense with the nothing we were given; clashing noises speak of a bare-fisted battle against an approaching force. Since guards always brought and took toothbrushes, we had no means to manufacture weapons. The future is rough for criminals. I am grateful others aren't obeying. Escaping alone would be next to impossible. With downed power, turrets are inactive, helping substantially.

Civilization fell apart as soon as the lights died. What was a peaceful sanctuary is now an open arena for long time criminals who've yearned freedom's air. Shorter-sentenced inmates remain in their cells. But not enough. Without turrets as backup, guards aren't trained or equipped to handle this problem; New World hires versus old world veterans. And me.

My door begins sliding. Impatient, I squeeze out. Hook a right toward the I.Y. which has more entry points, unlike the dead-end chow hall. Seeking exits there is a better bet. Turmoil is aggressive in both directions. Reinforcements enter the block wielding stun batons; black rods about forearm's length, juicing fifty thousand volts. The batons don't have handles. For operation, users must have a specialized glove to avoid cooking their own hand. A good defense if lost. Relieving a conscious guard's glove is doable but tougher when sauntering in pairs.

Oncoming reinforcements clash, shocking resistant inmates unconscious one by one. I race into chaos, dodging every situation.

An unavoidable guard challenges my bravery. The horizontal baton swipe instigates my drop and slide; feet crashing into another's leg, causing a flip and flop. I rise, closer to the cracked double door. Dodging unfriendly and foe until shoulder bashing inside. This hallway isn't brightly lit like usual because of the power outage. Whipping around to shut the door, I realize I've been too closely followed. I slam it anyway. Half his body becomes a doorway obstruction to a cracked position again. Head smashed also, painful groans dribble, as he waves the baton wildly and exhibits tremendous effort. Allowing the door space to swing open, he stumbles in. I thrust a foot at his hip. Surprised and wounded, he stumbles back into the cell block. My hands slam the door shut.

Rioting is a faint clamor now. A metal bar used to block doors rests behind. I make sure it doesn't go to waste, and not a second later, immediate bangs start. Hands pleading entry. You snooze, your sentence increases. I jog along the hallway. Skip unnecessarily tall stairs and burst through the next double door without a second thought.

The interior yard is a massive octagon-shaped room. An indoor replication of an outdoor courtyard. Hundreds of inmates can comfortably admire plant-life within and enjoy another dome scenery. Tactic of the rehabilitation process. The grass and flowers are fake, though appearing exceptionally real. The rectangular structures housing plant-life are high enough to lean and sit. When power is active, the yard is illuminated with the same color white as every other area. Eight double doors connect each block to the yard. A to H. Then diagonally across to my right, a single ninth door. No guard or inmate ever comes in or out. I jog toward the courtyard's center to cut across.

Meters before, an impactive *BOOM* rains from the ceiling. Hard enough to cause vibrations. The hollow space makes it sound everywhere at once yet holds an obvious origin from a wide radius of sunlight. I freeze and spectate. Shield my face for a clear view of what struck. More than just a huge chunk of debris crashes, throwing me onto the ground; into a hurried crawl behind the closest plant structure. Watching dust settle.

Coated is the back of a white and black Alpha. A killing machine about the size of a quaint two-story house; two legs, four arms, and equipped with the best arsenal of weapons-grade armor that aers can't buy. Two upper arms are customized weapons that end with a barrel; two lower arms are basically long pincers. "ORI" initials painted on, though not the manufacturer. Proving ownership. Lastly, standing between my possible exit and I. Sunlight would make the Alpha's night vision a liability. Nowhere near a hefty benefit but better than nothing. The mech turns in my direction. I catch a vivid glimpse of slanted yellow eyes during a shift into cover. Avoiding its cone of sight and staring at where I came from. No way I'm going back.

The mech commences patrolling. Heavy and slow pounds on the ground. Fading away, for what little that's worth from such a huge machine. If guards commanded an Alpha here, specifically, something worth protecting is behind door nine. I find it strange that no further back-up has shown to assist with troubles in my block; must have full hands on every end, unless ORI's understaffed. What's happening in other blocks? If anything at all. Stun rods against unarmed inmates shaves fractions of time off my escape. Stealth is still logical. I rise to a crouched position. Stick to the wall and ease to the rectangular plant enclosure's end. Hands braced for extra support. I poke an eye out.

The Alpha is circling the courtyard center. Moving silently will be easy with these light shoes, as long as it's a fast act. When its back is turned, I speed at the next enclosure. Then the next, realizing greed set in. Over-throttled momentum causes my accidental smack against the wall. Not painfully hard but prying ears hard. To the mechanically enhanced presence, I just played a concert. It abruptly halts. My eyes close. As if the problem will suddenly go away.

Jeez, Van.

Total silence remains. No movement from either predator. Unable to even hear my nostrils exhaling. Am I breathing? Lack of sound makes me nervous. If fully alert, it would've been trying to smash my head in already. It will wait me out. Batteries lasting much longer than mine. Once my stomach rumbles another concert, I'll be caught. No other choice than to run. When control is regained, my cell will eventually be occupied. And not by Vanessa Pheros.

After a brief time, in which I sit forming a plan, power reactivates. Brightening with that popular white gleam. The damaged ceiling area is flickering. Did light affect the mech's perception? Maybe I could wait it out now. It may assume something mechanical made the sound. Wait…, the power is on? My wide eyes focus on the corner at the closest turret gap. Hoping none arrive. One spouts out the hole and takes direct notice to me.

I irritably grunt to myself, "Jinx."

The turret doesn't hesitate firing shock pulses. I dart toward the rail, which circles the upper perimeter. If its targeting and my momentum are accurate, we'll intersect. I physically feel the Alpha join in chase, spewing heat pulses from an upper arm. I vault an upcoming rectangular structure and use the walled structure to pounce as high as I can. My empty hands latch the turret's shell, zipping me away. These turrets cannot look directly below themselves, searching blindly. Unable to detect I'm still present? The Alpha doesn't let up. But the turret is moving fast enough to evade the barrage of harmful red pulses. Another turret emerges from the opposite side and instantly fires shock pulses. Aid from another angle. My ride is approaching the mystery door fast. Time for departure. The move must be flawless to avoid many trailing pulse rounds. I release the turret. Land just before the door and bash through. In a falling spin, it slams shut behind me. Pulse rounds peck the sturdy wooden door until a sudden stop. Much too close for comfort.

Keep moving for the exit.

A hallway like one linking the chow hall; same bright white and door pulls, absent windows and turret rails. One could feel confused, especially with the ending double door. The chow hall was never closed; no stairs descending to a cell block. I trawl the hall.

Quarter way, a threatening bang startles me stiff. No way an Alpha can fit? My body hesitantly turns to the recently damaged single door.

A second and louder bang bulges the door and wall. And my chest. That thing's crazy. Got to hide. I slide the nearest door open and enter, closing it. A lunchroom with a small table. Former occupants were in the middle of a nice dinner and card game when the riot started. The cards are blue-hued, digitized to the table itself for easier playing and no cheating. A long window to my left gratifies caste suspicion that guards watched through two-way mirrors.

Louder than the last, a bang snaps perspective at a destructive following. The single door meets the ground in a tumble. Chunks of wall ricochet, breaking into smaller pieces. Another bang shakes the hall itself. Is that thing trying to fit in here? Cement dust seeps underneath my door and breezes past the window. I bend under it, sneaking a peek from the tiniest corner. Obviously, the Alpha did this. With advanced hardware, I can't risk it possibly spotting me through the glass. Also, can't see doorway damage from this low angle. Don't hear any more movement on that end of the hall. I scoot to the door. Pull the handle away, staying behind it. Nothing happens. The Alpha could have gone to look elsewhere. I use care stepping out. My eyes heighten at the demolition work.

A giant hole where an innocent door lived. The wall is completely broken at the sides and top, left kindly revealing sunlight from outside. Unintentionally sweet enough to create a shortcut. I tiptoe toward the hole. Press myself against destroyed wall. Venturing closer to the cracked opening. The Alpha appears to be gone from the courtyard. Where could it have gone? Where'd the turrets go? I shimmy between the broken wall. Take in outside prison air.

Chapter 2: Home Stretch

    My eyes adjust to natural light, faced at a concrete wall extending left. Warmth. The roof between interior hallways; housing for unnecessarily tall sets of stairs. By count through blocks A-H, seven more of these long structures should decorate this roof. All attaching to the gigantic dome. Out of the V shape is an enormous gap about a half-mile long. Gap, hallway, interior yard center; interior yard center, stairs, cell block, chow hall. Interesting layout.
    A city rests in the distance, precisely twenty-seven miles away. Skyscrapers and the clear dome surrounding can be seen. Gharis City, my past home. At the gap's end, over the chow hall curve, I glance left. Blinded by the setting sun nearing desert horizon. Confirmation guards have been fooling us with the time. No way I was running that long. The breakfast bell only rung about two hours ago. Heat from the concrete burns through my shoes. A sign to keep moving. The hallway I exited has no door to get back inside.

Great, now what?

No reason to gander over the edge. The chow hall curve seems to match well. Nothing less than death should lie over the side. Just for kicks and clarity, I inch close. Stare past the tips of my feet. A concrete slope leads to another drop. A steep drop. The concrete can be cleared with a careful spider crawl. What's beneath will be the bigger, steeper problem that I don't mind not unraveling the equation to. The slope is circular to the left and right; I'm marooned on a waterless island.

Over my left shoulder, one difference from this hallway exterior is a roof access structure above. Maybe leading to air transport? The double door at the end must have stairs inside. Likely to a platform for prisoner transfer. Jackpot! Flying isn't my strong suit, or any other suit in my arsenal, but if an aircraft is the only way, today's training day. How hard can it be? I'm at freedom's doorstep, and for the life of me, someone's going to answer, or else the house is coming down. I take a couple of lengthy steps back, spinning and rushing the return trip.

Very lightly, the prison shakes. I freeze. A shock? A tremor? A quake? Not once since the war. Above to my right, the Alpha is breaking air from a jump over another hallway. Within a second, crashing downward through the outer wall ahead. I leap and roll left, avoiding airborne debris and metal from a now destroyed staircase. During landing, the Alpha slides nearer. Reaches out with its pincer to snatch me. I jump toward it. Land flat on the ground and scurry between thick, metal hooves. It takes a step backward in turning. Almost crushing me as I throw myself away from the impact. Behind it, I hurriedly bolt for the broken wall. Intent to reach the helipad diminishes on sight. The stairs are too badly damaged. Mechanical joints are moving. My waist twists to lock eyes. A spark from the shoulder weapon oozes a rocket. Unable to avoid it, I twist into a slouched position and cover my face. The rocket voyages at the damaged wall. Strikes. Demolishes any climbable remains and forces me backward into a temporary hover. From the explosion, I am breathless. A tumble onto my stomach stops me. Ears whining. Can't clearly see. Struggling to maintain steady breathing; missing that meal isn't working in my favor. Should have bitten the lunch in the break room. With destroyed stairs, I'll need a new way up.

Heavy vibrations approach. My blinking eyes aren't visible. I haven't moved, hoping to feign unconsciousness. Air from the hoof gusts through my hair at the halt. Pincer reaching down, I quickly roll under. It lifts a leg. I spring to my feet. The slamming hoof misses. It lifts the other. I cartwheel into a backflip behind the mech before another slam. Its right leg sticks straight out, rotating its entire body on the left's ankle joint. A back handspring dodges the fast-swinging hoof. Then a wide squat dodges the next. I can't run laps with this thing all night. How can I escape something this size outside?

Dumb ideas arrive fast; measures of survival instincts kicking back on. Armed or not, no one can take an Alpha. Perhaps, a pretend escape over the ledge will make it go away? Abandoning logical options, I swoop a broken metal step and sprint toward the slope. Severe vibrations rock the prison, as the mech follows, firing more rounds. I hop off the ledge and swing the stair under myself. Ride the slope like a sled on snow. Behind me, in pursuit, the Alpha storms out too. A clear underestimation by how it attempts to catch itself. Then stumbles into an uncontrollable barrel. Pieces of mech begin breaking off. Falling in the only direction gravity will allow. Hands gripped at the step's sides, I tilt and shift, trying my best to avoid huge chunks of scrap. Failing, big pieces flop around and over me. Dodging with my actual body becomes necessity. The slope is coming to an end. The mech digs pincers and hooves at the concrete, now scrounging chunks of rock. Minorly slowing itself. If I don't manage to slow more, I'll plummet to my death. I shift the step diagonal, attempting to brake. Not working. Nor for the wildly digging mech with parts just too smooth to hold. I carefully leverage upward like I'm surfing and dive toward the mech. Land on its foot and savagely climb to reach its head. The mech's feet reach the edge first, gradually sliding off. I clutch one of the thick wires connected on its leg, holding myself in place. Somehow wedging the ledge, I am left dangling from the wire. Science doesn't have to tell me we're going over any second. The Alpha has no fingers to maintain steady grip. Pincers are inching. I gaze below, like an idiot, at the stupid choice's result. The slope has been replaced by a drop of about eight hundred feet, into a small outreach of concrete. We did not appear this high from the top. I instantly regret this decision.

Instead of hoping for wind to blow us up, I climb toward the ledge where my life would be in my own hands. On its back, before I could jump, the Alpha loses what little hold it had. We sink fast. The mech is wall carving and digging to slow itself; thriving, until a hoof gets caught in a dug piece with nothing to grab. Unintentionally falling away. Wind breaks harshly against my back. The Alpha is rotating slow enough for worry. On the wrong side of pressure, I'm about to become a pancake in seconds. Hanging for dear life, continuing to rotate backward. Then to a dive, picking up heavier speed. Then almost reaching a belly flop. The Alpha smashes on its chest plate. An awkward landing bashes my head on the mech's back, to a tumble up and off. Darkness temporarily replaces my eyes. Returning to bouncing off the mech's arm and hitting the concrete on my side. Instantly losing sight again.

Sounds of sparking wires wakes me. Need to lie still for a moment. Make an effort to regain full focus and conscious. Vision clearing, I'm lying on my back facing sunset. I wasn't unconscious too long because the sun is still setting. A single shade darker than earlier. I try to sit up, ceasing in a cringe at the throbbing ache in my left arm. It took a bad hit when I crashed. A multicolored scrape rests on the same shoulder. Mixture of blue from the cloth, my pale skin, dirt, and light blood. My arm isn't broken, and the ache is… bearable. I use both arms to fully sit. A tickle on my forehead that feels like thickened sweat attracts attention. I wipe the back of my hand across. Blood but not much. It's going to be dark soon.

Gharis lights like a beacon at night. On such flat land, anyone can find it for a hundred miles out. Come one, come all. Not getting there tonight isn't an issue. I'm concerned with lack of nourishment. A twenty-seven-mile journey through desert with no food or water. I refuse to make the headline:

*"Woman Dies of Starvation, After Fantastic
Prison Escape and Besting Alpha! Ha-ha!"*

Someone will investigate. A vehicle and hijack possibility. Also possible, an escort of prison guards or Regulators present to search for the winner. Underwhelming odds. The broken Alpha is sparking. Down, but maybe not out? If I can get it active, using it would be a faster way to reach Gharis alive. I start by inspecting damage; horrible condition, more than just a few screws got knocked loose during the tumble and chest plate plummet. Luckily, not on its back where the circuit panel is. Don't see myself rolling this boulder over to gain access. In this heat, anyone would faint at the initial push. Wouldn't stop my attempt either. I stretch minorly to work out my own body kinks first. Then mount for repair labor.

Smuggling days as a Runner granted some wiring experience. My mind can't picture this being any harder than hot-wiring a vehicle. Simply pair things together until results spark an action. Mostly survival instincts. Of course, vehicles don't have weapon systems and kill orders, but it won't be all strange. I trace wires to proper areas I'd prefer to function, keeping locations in mind. Rip burnt wires. Disconnect a huddle of wires from what I believe to be the tracking and targeting system. Reroute to replace burnt ones. Use my last good wire to power the green circuit board. Conclude with a couple more remaining. Toggle every switch from left to right to left. Finished.

The Alpha automatically powers on, springing to its feet and throwing me off. I hit the ground hard, winded again, taking a defensive stance in recovery. The fall has me broken, nevertheless I can't recuperate while being confronted. The mech spins around. Points its left and right weapons at my face. No dodging that. I unleash a deep sigh. The targeting repair didn't work, so to speak. I don't have firepower to battle this thing head on. No one does. I gradually raise my hands just above my head until another terrible plan emerges. It won't take excessive action during surrender. Calculating current conditions of the threat, me, shouldn't trigger response. It starts circling to my left; assessing and analyzing. I don't make sudden moves, not even with eyes watching the machine. Losing peripheral sighting, I tilt my head a touch. Focusing ears on movement. Zzz psh, pause, Zzz psh, pause, Zzz psh, pause. Thus, concludes a full circle, to the exact initial step. Complete assessment. Analysis. My eyeballs raise, curious as if its acute shaped head could change expression and provide positive or negative feedback. Accepting of a minor headache by lifting my brows too high. It faces right, away from the sun. A panel on its leg slides up to reveal a pulser rifle and pulser pistol. The Alpha stands in place.

A loud, dramatic sigh. Opened mouth and chest exhalation purges. The repair worked. An assessment to check if I was armed or a threat, which I'm not. I approach and grab both weapons. Place the rifle at my back. A cyber strap appears, attaching the weapon to my torso. From over right shoulder and under left rib. Meeting at my chest and fitting tightly. An ultraviolet colored strap that utilizes itself when a weapon is at specific body parts and angles. Secured, and detaches when the specific user reaches and touches the weapon for quick, untangled use. Effective in combat, by comparison to primitive models that hung loosely, dangling the weapon dangerously and freely. Every pulser has one, able to toggle a cloak for tactical purposes upon connection. I place the pistol at my thigh. Deactivate both ultraviolet glows by simply tapping the strap.

The mech places a pincer forward. Handshake goodbye? Does it know I need a ride? I approach. It lowers the pincer to my feet. I board, walking toward its shoulder. Being raised at its waist. I climb and take a seat next to its head. Can it comprehend verbal instruction?

I delay a command, "Gharis… City?"

The Alpha begins a rapid walk across the open gap. Concrete for about sixty feet from the prison wall, sprinkled with gradients of blown desert. Then becomes the full entree. This is going to be a long ride. I know for certain Alphas can't return communication, but other classes can. The more deadly of two, and overall soldier of four. Half an hour out of prison and my first ally is the most dangerous creation in New World existence; for now, a travel ticket. Who knows what else could be done with this thing? Says a lot about my character. Questions and a problem will arise, marching to the southern gate perched on an Alpha mech's shoulder. I'd have to ditch it beforehand.

"Can we go any faster?"

The Alpha excels past request of just *faster*. I brace tight, almost falling during the speed boost. Grip the shoulder plate with both hands and pin to it. Face beaten by the breeze. Forcing the lowest possible squint, barely seeing where we're going. Brushing through desert sands quick enough to kick whirlwinds. I patrol our surroundings.

Eyes widen, relaxing at the prison. A faint shine is over the roof. Higher than I was. Glistening like sunshine on a rippling ocean. Unstable. Moving and getting brighter? The light shifts sideways, unmasking an attack helicopter. Swinging hastily in our direction. I doubt it's ironic. A bad situation already casting where it's not wanted.

"We've got company!"

Its head spins completely backward. Not a beat skipped at sprinting. The helicopter nears, suddenly spouting artillery from above. Dangerous tubes that go boom. The Alpha makes evasive maneuvers against incoming missiles, keeping up at a turning pace. Guidance systems collaborating. Could be tailing heat signature. Armaments in a machine like this produces plenty. Alphas have no proper seating in event of a bumpy ride, or tense situation with missiles exploding in proximity. I concentrate forward and spot a distant grove, left of Gharis City's southern road. I've been through it enough times to memorize how to get lost. Not close enough yet for worry to vanish.

"We can try losing them in the grove!"

As it won't fit, by *we*, I mean me. Likely at maximum capacity, the Alpha maintains speed. The pilot is desperate. Shooting gunpowder bullets and missiles in unison. I drop forward into a spin. Cling onto the damaged chest plate. It can't avoid the aerial assault with a visitor hanging on, clutching me with supportive pincers. Loads of piercing bullets and a couple of missiles make contact, resulting in a drastic speed decline. I feel heat. The Alpha is critical. Struggling to maintain the run, and extremely close to the grove. My only means of helping are heat rounds; more lethal than shock. New-tech rifles and pistols use both in smaller doses, compared to the Alpha, as not to be fatal. Heat ceases bleeding, external and internal, by burn. Intent to immobilize, preserving a target's life. Dialing back, the helicopter fires another missile.

"We got one more incoming!"

Another hit, and the blast could also kill me. Even surviving, a run from here without getting cut off doesn't scream possibility. Would an attempt to detonate the missile do good? I'm not using gunpowder bullets, but heat rounds may suffice against the outer shell. Oozing a spiraled smoke trail in passing, the missile is rapidly closing in.

I release one hand from the chest plate. Firmly clutch tighter with the other. Equip the rifle and aim over the Alpha's shoulder. Rest for controlled spray, incapable of steadying with rhythmic bouncing. Tug the trigger. Small heat rounds purge the barrel. Thanks to necessary galloping, accuracy is very off. Multiple punctures do nothing. Too close for comfort, an urge to bail advances. The missile explodes. Success brightens the dim sky and my day. Blending with the sunset until black smoke expels into an expanding circle.

Excitement oozes from me, "Yes!"

The explosion shelters the sky between us and the helicopter. Sucking the dark cloud's center inward, a second missile pierces. My defense is pointless against an unavoidable impact. Only yards from the grove, a run will happen regardless.

The Alpha scoots a pincer under me and springs forward, shooting me outward at the sea of trees. A forceful push causing dizziness. I feel the rifle depart from my hand but not my back tearing wind. Listening to it in my ears but deaf to the explosion in my eyes. A soar between grove trees. I hit the ground, tumbling wildly over grass. At risk of breaking a bone, unwilling to halt myself. Perception resumes with bad timing. My body abruptly stops when my back smacks a tree. So hard my ears articulate the sound. So loud I can't hear the painful exhale. Am I broken in half?

Ahead, the fire-wrecked Alpha glows. Far enough away to not spark a bigger fire. Close enough to be beautiful. Not shattered into tiny pieces; unsalvageable for my proceeded use and not going anywhere by itself. Alphas are nearly impossible to destroy, perhaps being the first recorded in history. If not riding passenger, that attack helicopter wouldn't have stood a chance. It buzzes away, slashing through air high above. Giving up so easily? Belief the explosion engulfed me? Deceived behind the smoke cloud, naked eyes didn't witness the pitch.

Now I have to walk. Bummer. Once the noisy helicopter fades silent, I recover. Dust the thin, distressed bodysuit. Feeling a pulsated back ache. Easing tension, response with light massage. A transfer of hurt spreads body wide.

Fight it, you're too disobedient.

Eventually Regs will arrive to examine wreckage for my corpse. A good idea to be much farther when they do. I limp the grove toward Gharis City's dome.

Chapter 3: New World 2086

No wildlife resides here. Hasn't been an observation, not even a stray bird, since war resulted in widespread radiation throughout the seven continents. Mute trees. Only healthy patch for hundreds of miles and projected beyond that. The grove is an ongoing migration test. Never a buzz. Never a chirp. Never a slither. Always a failure. Limp footsteps and occasional ruffling leaves are all that sound.

Coolness swaps perks with the sunken sun. A twelve-hour light, now on the Old World. Vast darkness broken by a glowing guide. City lights hue over the trees. Gharis is illuminated by electronics. Literal power to fry what's left of the United States if an accident with the main power grid occurs. My stature heightens the dome through treetops. Still growing with incoming vision. Sixteen hundred feet high. Lights deflect, attempting escape but trapped. Every New World city is protected; sanctuary from the old world by domes. Allegedly thick enough to withstand every known natural disaster. Fortunately, none have been experienced by the post-war generation. A small world run electronically, eliminates natural disasters caused by worldly comforts. An unimportant reason is the population's mostly upper class. Upper class citizens must look perfect. No one looks perfect drenched in rain, makeup dripping down their faces, or with dirt picking up on their cruiser.

I reach the main road. Realize my limp ended. Winter chills attack what this prison jumpsuit doesn't cover. Continuing toward the steel wall of a gate along the lone path. Paved the same method as pre-war and remaining perfectly paved - people don't drive on roads anymore, since cruisers hover. Transport trucks are the exception. A couple of cruisers pass over my view of the early midnight sky. This day and age, cars are electric and equipped with a switch that sets high, medium, and low gravity. A new title of "cruiser." Gravity ranges from zero to seventy-five to one hundred and fifty feet. Specified safe distances for gravitational patterns to avoid interruption, not causing accidents between travelers merging onto different planes. Distribution decreased accident rates by ninety-eight percent of whatever the previous pre-war number was. Allowing additional options to reach destinations in a safe and timely manner. Cruisers look like curved-surface cars. Wheel cover caps give the appearance of absence. Generally, wheels should only touch pavement when parked.

The south gate is ahead. Standing maybe forty feet in height. Enough head room for Alpha access. At the checkpoint, cruisers must drop to street level and be greeted by guards. After occupant identity confirmation, vehicles are granted entry to the purified city.

Not having the cleanest legal reputation as a smuggler and recent escapee, waltzing in isn't on the table. I delivered city to city. One civilian driver and passenger, preferably a couple seeing each other socially to not spark suspicion. The couple would drop the smuggler and product on this road. Smuggler would navigate the grove to an underground passage that exits at an inconspicuous location within Gharis. A secretly controlled route; west of the south checkpoint, about a mile inward. Where I need to be. Avoiding capture and imprisonment.

The guard duo is too busy to notice my left swing into the tree line. A figment just that. Count fifteen minutes to a mile. Vigilant of an open area with two loving tree stumps idling side by side. A watchman is always nearby monitoring activity. Best off expressing caution of spooking them. To my surprise, no guards. No footsteps, whispers, or life presence. This tunnel is the only illegal way in. Is it operating? Slow day at the office? I approach the stumps. Face the tree where the hidden entrance lies.

A twig snaps, drawing only my ears. No chirps. No growls. Someone is watching. Due to no occupying species, a snap typically means that person knows they're caught. An amateur skulking watchman. My hands sluggishly raise halfway for the second time today. People, armed with pulser rifles, emerge from separate hiding places to meet. Bushes, behind trees and in them. Surrounding the bullseye. Dressed in black, blended with the night. Two in front, one in peripheral. More feet lightly pat behind, too lightly for an accurate tally. Punctual on the pistol draw in defense if the moment called.

I facetiously enquire, "Little much for one person, don't you think?"

A man behind me voices disinterest, a veteran tone almost matching mine, "You're armed."

I clarify without looking, "It's a pulser pistol."

"What're you looking for out here?"

A familiar voice, carrying uncertainty. I'd done countless jobs with someone who was just as skilled of a runner as me. Second best, but skilled enough to brag about. This man sounds like him. I casually spin one-eighty to reveal my face and sneak a look. His focus implies recognition.

Calling my nickname, his weapon eases, "Van?"

I immediately match face to voice. He removes the knit cap to further reveal himself. Still has that struggling ponytail. Dayio is a young man of Asian descent. I believe we're the same age, based solely on appearance. We ran jobs for Trex, pronounced treks, *Ruler of the Tunnel*. I guess Dayio's talent is now wasted babysitting. Any normal day, a watchman guards the entrance alone in shifts. No one should need these many weapons to protect a single tree.

Dunking my hands, I return a greeting, informally, "Dayio."

He commands the crew, "Weapons down, everyone. She's clear." Dayio shakes my hand, speaking with a joyful and curious mixture, "Where've you been?"

"Prison."

Dayio places the rifle at his back, scanning my blue ensemble, "No kidding? It's been two years since anyone's seen you through here. Surprised you remembered how to find the entrance."

I observe unnecessary reinforcements, "What happened? This used to be a one-man operation and you weren't part of it."

"Trex's former made a mistake one day on watch, so I took the reins for a bit. And he thought it'd be good for me to take on trainees for when I have a run."

"Doesn't seem to be working. Whoever stepped on the branch handed their position away."

"A crucial element of the team distraction. Someone snaps a branch opposite the intruder, we get a view from all angles when they turn and get the drop on them. No one was there afterward. Though the master was clever enough to give herself up."

Dayio's always been a great tactician. I'm okay, but much less subtle. My impatience and attitude reel more trouble than normal civilians can handle. Usually, my plans begin immaculate, until I deviate off course with wonderous curiosity. The rest is a downward spiral of chaos on simple pick-ups and drop-offs. Dayio became dominant planner.

I ask, "Trex still running things?"

"Never giving it up. And he won't be happy to see you after being M.I.A. all this time."

"What a coincidence. I was never happy to see him."

He smirks and issues an order to his crew, "Everyone stay here."

Dayio approaches the side of a regular-looking tree. Opens a secret panel and presses buttons I never bother memorizing or look at. Familiar with the entry, I wait in front of it; a disguised tree trunk that's actually a small double door, able of fitting one person at a time. Dayio joins me as the split door tilts outward. Revealing the well-lit, blue underground passage. A darker shade than mine. He enters first, marching downstairs. I shadow, distantly, in case of mistrust. Warmth shields me.

The passage hasn't changed. Widening six feet at the bottom. Never was a fan of blinding deep-water blue. A half mile stretches, before officially entering Gharis City through a bakery's basement. There are two rooms within this stretch: an office and the opposing lunchroom. Trex's entire operation is run down here. Safer than topside where Regs can successfully caste suspicion on his inactivity amongst the populace. For him, this is home. Essentially, off the grid. Only the most loyal smugglers are granted passage access, ensuring no outside problems drift in. I was one of the initial few. Now, seems I'm lost within a half-dozen. The approved list makes the runner a regular for city to city transport, since so few are aware the tunnel exists. Those claiming a tunnel does exist, won't think to check a bakery basement or an entire grove. Where dueling rooms face off, Dayio enters to the left.

Trex is seated behind his desk, punching and jabbing the padded keyboard for his digital computer. An early forty-something year old man from the Islands. Dark-skinned. Always wears his dreadlocked hair in a ponytail. Living and breathing this passage, twenty-four hours a day. Office lit the same color blue as the passage. I glance at a twin bed a few feet from the desk, unable to deduce the last time sunlight embraced his skin. On no occasion seeing him outside of this office - ever.

Trex questions, "What's up, Dayio?"

Before Dayio answers, Trex ganders up. Drawn to me. Stops typing, hovering fingers over digital keys. Staring me down, not violently but viciously. There's that mistrust. I view from the door. In a moment, the pecking of keys continues. Dayio expected this reaction or else he would've answered the question: *"Your good friend Vanessa is here!"*

Trex's deep voice and islander accent interrogates, "What're you doin' here? Come to pay off the debt you owe?"

Technically, I don't owe a debt. Two years ago, the run went sour after civilians he set me up with, set me up. I couldn't explain since this tunnel doesn't have a postal address and mail slot overhead. On the other hand, I could've considered other means, like sending to the bakery. Needing tunnel access now, kind of feels like I should have. What am I saying? Receiving was the only option.

I enlighten him, "I just spent two years in prison for you. A bow and *'How are you?'* would be a better greeting."

"I'd heard a whispered-around rumor that you were locked away. Didn't believe for a second. We both know you ran with my package and spread those rumors."

"Why would I do that?"

"Because you can't be trusted. And you're smart."

I riposte to myself, "Not smart enough."

"Wait…"

He steers the power wheelchair to me and reads numbers on my form-fitting jumpsuit. Then looks at my face, obviously not feeling foolish about his two-year accusation. But his eyes do show belief.

With joyful surprise, he laughs at my expense, stating, "You really were in prison! What's with the jumpsuit?! You break outta Ori?!"

"Yes."

The laughing transforms to snooping worship, "Seriously? How? Ori is aerial access and like two hundred feet off the ground."

"Does it matter? Run the prison number or check my IDN for proof. I need tunnel access, if you want your stuff back. First, I need clothes and food. Then I'll find the couple who stole the package from me and deliver it to you."

"You're two years too late. The package is useless now, and the couple disappeared. No trace. However, if you're as sharp as you used to be, you and Dayio can do a run. Tonight."

Dayio lightly elbows my arm, "Like old times."

"Can we start with food? I'm starving."

Trex approves, "Go on next door. I'll give Dayio specifics."

"Perfect."

Trex calls out, before my start toward the door, "Hey. My steak's on the right holder. Don't touch it."

I raise my eyebrows once. Pass six feet into the opposing door. The lunchroom is a little bigger than Trex's office. Blue glow, full bathroom, cabinets, tables and chairs. The highlight, glowing brighter in my eyes and singing a delightful song in my ears, a foodie box. A rectangular food storage, like the classic deep freezer but less wide and doesn't freeze. The center button tilts the lid upward, freeing a chill I don't mind being hit with. Wheels rise; two right, two left. Rested on metal holders, full meal selections peek halfway out. Teasing. I hold the right button to turn the corresponding wheels, revealing other meals keeping each holder company. Then the left button for the next wheels. Watch more choices revolve.

At first sight, a steak dinner wrap seductively connects with my brain. Trex won't realize until I'm gone anyway. The box seals on my way to the table. Starving, and don't feel like taking ten seconds to warm it, I dig in. The stomach relief is extraordinary, admitting it would taste better hot. It's been at least fourteen hours since my last meal. That thought increases my hunger. Finishing, I return for another something. Devour that too. Keeping great shape, I'm not worried about laziness silently striking after overeating. Dayio strolls into the room without his rifle.

He examines the clean plates and comments, "Someone filled a hole."

"You have no idea. I haven't eaten since last night."

That isn't exactly accurate. My last night was his this morning; an irrelevant topic. I'm ready to work.

He commands, "Pulser stays here."

I detach and leave it on the table. We resume the half mile to the passage's other end. Is everything arranged for myself and the job?

I ask, "What about clothes? I can't roam the streets in my prison outfit. And probably have no aers on my revoked IDN either."

Aers are the new form of digital currency that synchronize with the IDN; abbreviation for Identification Data Network. Using the human body as an I.D., everything that has anything to do with the individual is accessible. People in every domed city have an IDN, usable anywhere to prove citizenship and spend aers. Deeper access by Regs show criminal records, debts, and everything else. An IDN is almost impossible to live in a city without.

Dayio addresses my concerns, "Trex is working on that as we speak. For now, I'll use my IDN to get new threads. He should have your new IDN created and in the system by the time we get back."

I comment with relieving enthusiasm, "Nice. What's the job?"

"There's a courier delivering a package that Trex needs intercepted."

"You mean stolen? We're stealing for Trex now?"

"Not exactly, Trex wants to know who the courier is. They found a way to smuggle without using the tunnel. He wants to know how. In addition, we're procuring the package and doing the handoff ourselves."

"So we're stealing for Trex now?"

Dayio smiles, "Securing clientele and eliminating competition. How sharp are your running skills?"

I boast, "It's been two years for the best runner that ever was. I'm always top shape. What about time?"

"Trex has eyes on the courier. We prep you, get in position, and wait for the call."

We ascend an equal-number of steps, entering the bakery's basement through automated floorboards in the back-left corner. The basement is lit blue from the passage, otherwise, dark. No one ever tends storage. The floorboards are gradually closing. Remaining light helps guide us up stairs centered on the wall ahead, before sealing perfectly. Obscuring light from anyone who may wander down here.

The basement door is outlined by slits of yellow-ish light. Our ears hone on a classical melody seeping from underneath. Doesn't surprise me.

Socialite ball. A large gathering of guests are mingling in the bakery's ballroom; an area the size of a small mansion's first floor with no walls. Very fancily decorated. Striped red and yellow carpeting in huge rectangles, stretching across the entire room, including upstairs. Two wide, sparkling chandeliers hang. A long table with delicious looking hors d'oeuvres. I lead the way, merging and scanning for Feegle Tolen.

Guests are dressed colorfully: bright green suits, bright yellow dresses, bright purple robes with bright orange sandals. Gharis' fashion sense has never been of interest to me. Why I always manage to stand out. At this moment, it's more Dayio. Wearing all-black clothing that masks well in the grove. A differing outcome indoors. My blue prison jumpsuit somewhat blends, minus the black numbers and lack of flowy elegance.

Needless to say, a lot of eyes are on us unhurriedly surfing the room. Holding attention for minor seconds. Not a peek from MechCi guests, which will bring trouble if they read the numbers. My arms fold, blatantly covering high. We stop. Observe small groups parting a path for the bright pink suited Feegle. An older Caucasian man. Thin, trader style mustache. Blonde hair. Chubby, not exactly overweight for his height. Standing low at almost a foot shorter than me. I'm five-seven so that's saying something.

Feegle's heightened voice very politely approaches, "—me. Pardon me, thank you. Excuse me." His slicked-up hair maneuvers the crowd, reaching us with a stern demand under firm breath, "You, follow me!" He leads toward stairs at the back wall, politely acknowledging guests, "Excuse me. Apologies. Thank you."

Word travels fast. For how long it's been, I would expect more of a happy reaction, from him, to see me. With my long hair and his stress over judgment, perhaps recognition hasn't processed yet. Feegle always held a soft spot in his heart for me; one I don't even hold for myself. We ascend the tall, semi-circular staircase. I glance over the railing at guests enjoying themselves, without distraction, again. Socializing over serene classical music. Their weirdly bright clothing makes the main floor look like a herd of rainbows at a disco. Some have matching colorful hair.

Mechs able to communicate in a formal manner like humans, are called MechCi; Mechanical Civilian. Built and sold as counterparts, becoming what personality the buyer molds. Integrating perfectly amongst civilization. MechCi are purchased as male or female and in the form of adult or child upon buyer's request. Originally, purposed as assistants. Others more kind-hearted split ownership as business partners. Friends to share life experiences. Children they can't give birth to. All manufactured with a chip that prevents initiation of any illegal action. Few owners with criminal intent attempted dismemberment of purchased MechCi, removing the chip. In hopes that illegal action could become an available option. Unfortunately, the chip is needed for models to function and fries upon exposure to outer elements; destabilizing its environment. Expensive mistakes.

Feegle unlocks the second door on the left, quietly rushing, "Come on. In. In."

Voice lightly toned as if he is shy. Not a day was I ever fooled; this man is quite a chatterbox. Feegle shuts us all in the bedroom. A moderate size for a famed baker. During reconstruction, it was an easy choice over sacrificing space elsewhere. Adoring social life required accommodation for big social circles and then some. Ballroom crowned monarch, meeting predicted occupancy, whereas the remaining interior hardly grazes standard.

Compared to where I live, the bedroom is comfortably livable. Queen-size bed, nightstand on both sides, armchair right of the bed by the balcony, vanity with a simpler chair babysitting between myself and the closet. Bathroom, balcony, and closet beyond closed doors.

Feegle shares thoughts with minor agitation, "You know, I truly wish Trex would conduct counsel *so much* further in advance before deciding to send—" Recognition chucks his attitude and breaks words, spawning an amazed expression, "Miss Pheros?"

Wondering what great feat I accomplished, I half-smile at the facial strangeness, "Yes, Feegle?"

He excitedly greets with a tightened embrace, "Oh my dear, how are you?!"

From childhood to now as an adult, Feegle's always been fond of me. *Perceiving my beauty outside, and inside*; whatever that means or wherever that is. And from late teens into adulthood, I would occasionally do the favor of accompanying him to events around Gharis or here. Doused with coats of makeup and fitted for fancy dresses. Elegant styling for those with curves. Sauntering about on his arm, as a platonic date or eye candy, for profit. Extra pay, if I further sold elegance using a full English accent during conversation. Feegle Tolen's the man to know in Gharis City, gathering an overload of popularity. A lot of wealthy men and women love his outgoing personality. I'm biased.

He loudly queries, "Where have you been, my dear?! Skipped on to another city without so much as a goodbye?" He reverses into a frowned expression, "And, gosh, what is that awful aroma permeating from you?! And what are you wearing?!" He swipes my hand and pulls me toward the closet, "Pee-ew. Come here my dear. We will get you sorted in—"

Dayio leans against the nightstand, smiling while watching me get dragged. I would entertain this, if actual relaxed-wear were stored. Feegle's idea of *sorting* has no relation to coziness. More dresses, and being generous, wedges.

I retract my hand, "Feegle, this isn't a social visit. We need your help."

"Darling *help* is precisely what I am trying to do."

"We're on a job. I need to lay low for a while so Dayio can get me a *comfortable* change of clothes and I can clean the permeation." I face

Dayio and request, "Can you get an outfit from Lynn's shop? Just tell her it's for me. She'll have a go-bag."

"Got it. Be right back."

Dayio departs. Alone with a happy Feegle. I go to his balcony and relax at the rail. Chill air. Gharis becomes interactive at night. Numerous lights flashing on and off make moonlight seem nonexistent. Electricity going twenty-four hours a day. Shops managed by an owner's MechCi while said owner is away doing things; like attending a social gathering at a certain bakery. Below and above, cruisers drive through the sky; hovering to be technical. On sidewalks, humans and MechCi stroll together, conversing en route to their destination. Blinding advertisements do deactivate during daylight hours. Then everything is still. A calm normality of corporate warfare and errands. The New World's alive in Gharis.

Feegle joins with a question, "Is it as you remember?"

A low pitch exits, "Same flashy nonsense? Right on the nose."

"Why do you abhor this city so? There are too many attractions and wonderful citizens, present company included, to detest such a fine place."

"Apparently, you've never been underground with the Deserted."

"My dear, why on Earth would anyone want to go down there?"

"A taste of what the rest of your *fine city* has to offer."

"Deserted migrated underground because it is where they want to be."

Sarcasm touches my tongue, "Oh right. Groups of Regs with rifles had nothing to do with that."

"Deserted are welcome to rise and join us civilized inhabitants whenever they so choose. They choose to stay underground, happily sulking in their own malevolence and kindly leaving us peaceful folk alone. Ugh, I despise them all."

"And the despise is mutual."

"Well, it is good they continue committing meaningless atrocities below ground, amongst themselves, instead of causing turmoil above ground, yes?"

I agree to shut him up, "Yes, Feegle."

"I will tend to my many guests. Please, feel free to help yourself to any facilities, Miss Pheros."

"Thank you."

His head bows toward me. A middle ages gesture of departure. I watch pleased people below. Deserted were citizens, still legally are. Deemed too unstable to reside above ground amongst a *normal* population. The city is not wrong. Inhabitants forced underground have, literally, lost their minds. Suffering from some undetermined mental condition or plague. Feegle would be pissed to know I live underground too. Why is that home? Without direct contact, Deserted are no harm. *Normals* pester too often to see that. Pestering is something I don't do unless profit is involved. There are lots of theories and rumors. Following either is looking for a problem that someone will be tempted to keep buried. And I don't solve problems... unless profit is involved.

I leave the balcony. Strip my prison outfit and pick out a new pair of underwear from the closet. For women Feegle dolls and flaunts, he stores varied supplies of spare clothing. Catering most sizes. A guest experiences a spill, replacing won't be hard, likely providing an outfit better than what they arrived in. I enter the bathroom, sparking a nice hot shower. Determined to enjoy it longer than the two minute prison schedule permitted.

Dirt, sweat, oil, blood; all seeped onto one lone person. Not smelling what Feegle did but won't expose my armpits for proof. I step into the shower. Rinse as scorching water streams onto my semi-bronzed skin. Snatch a pair of scissors from the sink and blindly chop away unwanted lengthy hair. Watch each chunk waterfall into a nasty combination of liquids at my feet. After sloppily chopping a couple inches above my shoulders, I wash it. Then let it sit while scrubbing my skin rigorously. So rough it should be peeling off.

A knock demands my response over thumping water, "Yeah?!"

Dayio's tone mimics, "I have your gear stacked on the bed!"

I thank him. Rush a conclusion to the shower. Wipe fog from the small mirror above the sink and examine a rejuvenated Vanessa

Pheros. It's been so long since I've last spectated any mirror. Kind of forgotten what I look like. Light skin. Hazel eyes. Brunette hair. Small lips. An unbroken British accent would mesh perfectly with a high-class background. Bruises demean the appearance a bit.

    I exit the steaming bathroom. An experiment emerging from tanked preservation. A woman reborn. My clothes are placed on the bed, neatly folded on top of each other. Instantly, recognizing the leather jacket. Dayio got the correct stuff. Lynn accepted a commission once, complimenting my personality and habits. Love defined since the first time worn. It's time to feel my version of normal again; to feel home.

Chapter 4: Welcome Home

Walking to my clothes, I scan the room. No one's lingering who's not supposed to be. Yes, I'm out of prison; pending freedom to do anything, of legal precedent. But I still don't know who sent that letter. Don't know who cut power so I can break free. Don't know who expects my presence at a responsible hour of eight in the morning. Unlikely for good intention, someone in Gharis wants me to find them.

I pull up the black slim-fit jeans that stretch perfectly over my hips. Black tank top. Dark yet obvious green leather cropped jacket. Black knee-high boots, specialty designed to match "running" habits, not fashion. Last items are a pair of fingerless leather gloves and an Econ; abbreviates "Ear Connect." A mobile device for the ear. It rests inside like an earpiece, capable of accessing anything by tap of the only button and request. Gloves and Econ will be necessary for climbing and keeping in touch with goings around the city. I slide gloves on and earpiece in. The vanity mirror examines. My jacket is cropped a little higher than the tank top and has three-quarter sleeves, not because I lost height and gained reach in prison; checked box for style.

No longer carrying the battered prisoner appearance, it's time I rejoined civilization and began my work-release program: Paying off false debts to Trex. I exit the bedroom. Join Dayio against the rail beholding fancy life beneath. False irony.

Without turning away, I ask, "Wishing you could be like them one day?"

"Just counting colors. Wouldn't be bad living the easy life. I bet most of them don't even like each other, though."

Dayio sticks behind me toward the stairs on our descent to Feegle. The social affair is a success. We approach through multiple small groups. He is having a laugh with some guests in a larger caliber; probably about another guest in attendance tonight. No, Feegle isn't the type. Conversing with him is a safe space. Loving this New World and respecting everyone in it. We wait for dwindle and our chance to freely speak.

The guest's attention draw Feegle's to my words, "We're taking off."

He passes a smile with acknowledgement, "Okay, dear, and do try not to stay absent for so long."

A smile and conclusive comeback, instigates my leave, "Prison will do that to you."

Nearby guests express subtle amusement. Safely assuming his dissociation with such crowds. In belief, Feegle isn't amused. His laugh isn't meshing in my ears. Dayio and I create a path through more guests. Passing the basement. Servers are lined at the right side of the shop's door. We enter the bakery's business portion. In width and length, it's a few feet bigger than my cell was. Feegle's male MechCi is behind the display counter. Babysitting the storefront and greeting later arrivals.

It turns to us and articulates, "I do hope you have enjoyed the revelry. Have a fantastic evening, citizens. Goodbye."

We ignore the mech, exiting curbside as I ask, "Where's the courier hiding out before the meet?"

"Not too far from here."

Dayio treks inland; north. Streets are lit with white overhang lights. Bright enough to blind someone, nonetheless very tall to avoid doing so. Take about nine of me from head to toe and we got a centered overhang from a building tall enough to illuminate quarters of city blocks. Blocks packed full of friendly folk, properly dressed in colorful garments. Same nightly faces I'm certain I'd recognize if I paid enough attention. Nothing ever changes. Repeats and constant loops. Day in and night out. Gharis gets richer and other cities continue working for the rich to afford a decent living.

I've been a smuggler since age sixteen. What made me great back then was no one anticipated my arrival. Nobody in their right mind suspected a teenaged girl with a backpack to be transporting packages for undesirables. I tried making it a full-time thing, but every foster parent expected me inside by curfew and on time for school. Once returned to the group home for disobeying, restrictions left zero work. Many clients didn't need delivery from door to door. That, and no employer, meant extremely little work. Big prizes and demand were in city to city delivery. At seventeen, I was of legal age to fend for myself. Workload barely increased. Second year smuggling solo, I met Dayio. Inside Feegle's shop. It took some stalking and the theft of a package, but impressed, he made the introduction. I'd known Feegle long before then and never knew an underground passage was right under my nose. From then, I went straight to Trex for bigger, city to city jobs. His fee was a small price to pay and worth it. At twenty-two, he sent me on a job with a couple who acted as travelers. My ride to and from the deal location. The great betrayers. They parked outside while I went in. I accepted blame for dead bodies in a rundown, middle of nowhere house. No ride to escape incoming Regs. I could never explain to Trex how everything happened. Since Dayio wasn't commanded to attack on sight, I can safely figure Trex knew. Forgiven so easily, I suppose that package is mine to make up for. A new identity tacked as a bonus. Dayio stops at an outdoor restaurant where a lot of people are seated and eating. Perfect place to blend.

Dayio states, "We'll wait here."

A small table for two. Dayio scoots his chair closer to my right side, facing across traffic. Not too far in the crowd to spy, not too far out the crowd to be noticed. A MechCi server approaches.

Dayio quickly demands, "Two tap waters to start please, and thank you."
The MechCi hurriedly whirls with confirmation and treads away as I investigate, "You know what the courier looks like?"
Dayio shares vague info, "Nope, but I know he or she will be by themselves and carrying a bag."

Suspicion would less likely be caste on a MechCi. Why not use them? These perfect smugglers aren't allowed to accept payment of any kind for services rendered outside of a shop. MechCi can smuggle if sending parties trusted recipients to transfer aers after receiving merchandise. Most parties do. However, MechCi aren't allowed to exit city limits without their owner or manufacturer representative. Those big jobs. One we're here to ruin.

Dayio sparks off-topic conversation, "So how'd you break out of Ori?"
"To be honest, I'm not sure. I got a letter with an address inside. Less than a minute later, there was a blackout. Cells popped open and I hauled it."
"Hauled what? The only way off Ori is in the air. That pimple's built little less than a quarter mile off the ground. You found some secret entrance the public doesn't know about?"
"I fought an Alpha on the roof and we ended up crashing down. Fortunately, I came out on top in the fall."

The MechCi serves our drinks and inquires, "Are you ready to view our menus?"

Dayio answers, "No, thank you. We're just stopping in briefly."

The MechCi acknowledges before departure, "Yes sir—" It twists to me, "—and madam."

Dayio faces me and expresses with a smirk, "Wow, let's not downplay how incredible that is. How'd you survive a fight against an Alpha?"

"Wasn't easy, that's for sure. Thing is, I have no idea who sent the letter. Whoever it was wants me to meet them tomorrow morning at eight."

"Someone expects you up that early?"

My face frowns, "Right."

Dayio articulates, "Read message…" He says to me, "Couriers on the move, eyes up." We focus, "I couldn't guess who would have tech to shut off power to the prison from within a city, or in general, but whoever it was wants to meet you bad."

Penalty to the hacker who shut Ori's power down would certainly be a life sentence; guards hurt or killed in the riot and property damage would all fall on said hacker's accountability.

I assure, "Doesn't matter anyway. I'm not going."

Dayio's face shifts to snooping, pursed lips and scowl, "Why not?"

I shrug, "What for? Because they broke me out of prison? It'll take much more than that to control Vanessa Pheros."

"You're not even curious about finding who it was?"

"Nope. I'm free. That's all I care about."

A suspicious man across the street on our right catches my eye. Bending the corner with a small duffel swaying in hand. Speed-walking almost urgently toward an alley entrance just past the building closest to him. If that's not someone involved in something illegal, my retirement party from smuggling should be tonight.

I state, "Dayio, look."

He hones on where I'm facing. The man is alone. Afraid and overly paranoid. Attempting to blend with average citizens by wearing flashy clothing. Walking too fast, or any pace above graceful snail, is a dead giveaway. He's not inconspicuous. To top it off, luggage may ruin someone's outfit.

I ask, "What's the plan?"
"We don't need the package yet; we just need to tail him somewhere secluded. Hopefully Trex can lie his way into the existing client after we get it."

The courier slips into the alley's mouth. Takes cover by the wall. Obviously covering tracks and loudly announcing fear of a pursuer. From how he's acting, there's not a doubt in my mind one exists. He lifts a hand. Looks inside his wrist and triggers something. The clothes gradually change from a colorful flashy ensemble to an all-black stealth suit.

Dayio comments, "That's uh... different."
I stand, ready to go, "We could lose him in that alleyway if he hides. We have to move."

The courier disappears further inside from the wall. We cross, striding wide to catch up. A group of three bend the same corner the courier came from. Shadowy clothing marching fast in our direction. I snatch Dayio's hand and decrease pace. Smiling up at him like we're just having a leisurely stroll. Peering constantly into his brown eyes. Already distracted by escaping prey, this will keep them in pursuit. If not, I'll attack when Dayio does. Failing to find an occupied hand, the trio snakes into the alley where the courier went.

Dayio taps his Econ, "Call Trex." A brief hold, then update, "Trex, the courier has a tail. What do we do? ...Okay." Dayio taps again, "We tail the tail. Anything fails, package is priority."

Dayio swiftly steps to the alley entrance. Sticks to the corner wall and glimpses inside. I stand close. Noticing his head tilt upward as if someone's climbing. An activity I haven't stretched for.

He commands, "This way."

We pass into the alley and jog to a lengthy metal pipe going up the left building. Dayio scales quickly. I don't hesitate, scaling also. Crawling right hand then left foot. Left hand then right foot. Rinse and repeat with ease and prior experience. Reaching the ledge, Dayio pokes eyes just above. Taking in the situation, holding for an opening. I remain underneath. Back hanging out, palms firmly clasped and feet braced. People below haven't taken notice to our dangerous actions. Who would think to? Dayio ascends and dashes east. Climbs the adjoining rooftop. Still behind, though running like he knows where to go. I don't see anyone. We cross a couple more close-leveled rooftops. His momentum is stationed. Preparation for the next big leap. A leap worth timing correct numbers of steps and proper speed, since worse than injury lies below. Someone's head pokes from behind a short structure on the destination building. Very briefly. We weren't careful and Dayio doesn't realize.

Wanting to halt Dayio, I shout, "Wait!"

It's too late. Fully stopping near a roof's edge would only throw him off. He is already soaring across. And lands. Unbalanced, perhaps from my alert. The hidden pursuer reveals. Punches Dayio, causing a stumble backward at the ledge. No, no, no. As fast as possible, my steps match an accurate and powerful push off my foot. Not a jump. A dive straight at a window one floor below the roof. I meet Dayio. My shoulder collides into his chest, before both colliding through the window. Into a spacious living room. The hardwood floor did not even attempt to cushion the landing. Dayio is conscious, out of breath and in pain. There's still a package on the loose.

The tenants, a family of four, observe in shock from the couch where they were watching the news network on a projection dot. The dot harnesses the same technology as a classic projector, no longer needing a huge screen. The tiny device sticks on any surface with an immediate range of image display; like holographic pictures except an expanded and full motion version.

I lie as I dart for the door, "Regulator business, we'll cover the damage."

I ditch Dayio. Exit the apartment to a hallway. A sign at each dead end reads "Stair Access." I sprint to the closer door. Bash through, continuing up the flight of steps into lightened night. The three pursuers have cornered the courier a couple of rooftops ahead. I quickly cross close-level rooftops. Ready to prevent outsider thieves from retrieving my package. Aiding would be the only way to help the courier reach the contact, easily spotting me if I follow again. Dayio shouldn't be long behind. Both covers will be blown. *Package is priority*. The bag is as good as mine.

Lots of shifting and flinching back and forth is happening. Playing an extremely high stakes game of "Keep Away." The courier's eyes lock with mine. Pursuers follow sight and blow my cover. Three of them bare my skin tone and one is darker. All four even more shades darker, because of the glow below throwing my perception.

Opportunity calls. The courier whips his bag back and smacks a pursuer across the head, knocking him out cold. What is in that bag? The remaining two resume flinching and shifting. I rush to the less wrong side. A pursuer spins my way. Ready to fend me off while his partner now plays tug-of-war. I need to stop them fast. Tugging near the ledge, we could all lose, if the bag goes overboard. The pursuer flinches toward me. I throw a high kick. Leaning backward, he dodges. Steps closer and retaliates with a quick right jab. I trap his arm between my left bicep and ribs and turn right. Placing us shoulder to shoulder, facing the same direction. Stealing control and willpower, I twist further, circling him around front of me. Left foot planted, I drag the other into a slant and spring my knee up to contact his face. He flips and plops flat.

Slipping off, courier dominates the game and wager. Plummeting at the sidewalk, he screams six stories. Then a loud crash. Breaking glass, and more hysterical screams instigate in that order. Whoever's cruiser that was won't be happy. The last standing pursuer peeks over the edge. Navigating left, his head begins raising. Eyes strangely following something other than many witnesses. Something ascending?

He rotates with an electrifying shout, "H-T!"

A bright light beams from below, igniting half the street and a segment of alley. An H-T70, Regulator attack ship, hovers high above the roof. It centralizes the spotlight's shine momentarily, dividing into three at fleeing pursuers. I shield my eyes with a forearm for a better look. Sleek, dark aircraft about twelve feet in length and ten wide. Frontal height about two feet, on a gradual incline of three toward the back. An isosceles triangle manually operated by a single person lying on their stomach for proper maneuverability. That person being a Regulator; peace officers. Duties are to enforce and uphold the law, avoiding civilian casualties while doing so. Another automated targeting system ensuring they never manage to endanger civilians or allies with advanced toys. I take a couple steps back. Pursuers escape past me.

The male voice in the ship announces, "Surrender immediately!"

These aircrafts mean business. I dart right, heading east. Leap to the attached roof. The ship's loud but pleasant hum announces motion. A second sound my ears don't want to hear are shock pulses thumping gravel near my feet. I slide behind the wall of a roof access door. The ship ceases fire, zipping overhead extremely fast. I double back to open the door. Locked. Unfair that the one before was wide open. I head north. Humming noises are hunting again. Obstacles in my way prevent a smooth run. I slide under a long pipe. Bump into and fluidly roll over a small wall immediately after. Late realizing it's actually a gap between rooftops and not an extension of the roof. A welcoming alley below that I couldn't see over. I fall into a single roll and land, back first, on an outer emergency staircase. Lying from sudden loss of wind. Not enough loss to violently cough, yet enough to disorient. A bright light shines from above my resting head. I tilt upward to look behind at the ship's hovering. Leveled and locking my position.

I demand so loud that my throat itches, "Give me a break!"

I roll myself downstairs as the ship commences firing shock pulses again. Outer stairs become knocked loose from the brick wall. By the barrage of strays? Pulse rounds don't have physical elements, which means this staircase just has weak structural integrity. The city better expect a complaint from me in the morning. I get to my feet, though unable to maintain balance while stairs are wobbling heavily back and forth. Two by two, more bolts snap apart from the wall. I hurdle sideways through the closest window and a tenant's bed comforts with unbelievable fluff. The staircase bashes the next building. Collapsing into smaller pieces before unifying at ground level.

Despite being littered in glass, this is the most comfortable I have been in two years. I pounce off the bed and rush left into the hallway. Shield my eyes at a sudden surprise of light. The ship is already here. Floating over the street with light dazzling through many glass panels trailing to my right. No other exit I could've taken to avoid confrontation.

More sternly, the pilot demands again, "Surrender now!"

Prison wasn't my favorite place. No chance his wish will come true. I bolt right. This third time around, the officer makes considerably less hesitation firing. Thumping crackles and loudly crashing shards unmute the environment. I can't shake this thing. Got to take it down somehow. Pulse rounds are inching as I draw to the hallway's center on a one-track race. The barrage throws glass over me. I take a short inhale. Entrap adrenaline and thoughts of a dumb idea. Hurdle out the missing panel. Through the threshold, my foot pushes my body higher off the casing. Clear over the incoming swarm that would have devastated me. Stomach first, I splash on the ship. It tilts a bit from sudden weight shift. Rocking forth then back to rebalance. Smooth surface and curved front forces reliance on leather gloves and jacket sort of gluing to the metal. The officer intentionally shifts right to left. I shift left to right, avoiding a drop at concrete more meters down than I'm willing to count. Is the officer going to let me fall? We travel through the district, exiting. Enter another. Halting and looping above an intersection near a tall parking structure. With a safely timed landing, losing it between parked cruisers becomes possible. A circle completes. Quarter before the garage's top level, I push away from the spinning ship. Thrown over a thirty foot sway, crashing on a cruiser. My body tumbles in the continued directional momentum and splats into a neighbored cruiser prior to splashing concrete.

Accepting no recovery, I hide from the adjusting aircraft. It slowly circles. Humming tune hunting prey. I am heavy enough to have knocked a dent in the roof. Just in case, I crawl under the next vehicle. Then the next. Then another. The H-T70 whirs around for a while longer, eventually departing. I continue lying. Relieved and not exhausted. I tap my Econ.

A robotic female voice greets, "Good evening. How may I be of service?"

This Econ doesn't have a start-up greeting like brand new ones should. Dayio must have already programed it; hopefully with his Ear Connect code synchronized.

I command, "Call Dayio."
The Econ alerts, "Connecting…"
Dayio's voice speaks into my ear, "Van? Where are you?"
"A parking structure, relaxing under a very nice cruiser."
"Nearest parking structure is in the Lunor District. How'd you get way over there so fast?"
"Hitched a ride. Bad news: the courier's dead. He fell off the roof and kindly took the bag. How do we go about getting it now?"
"That guy may never walk again but survived. I saw what happened and recovered the bag after the H-T showed. We're good."
A sigh exits my nostrils, "What about the tail crew?"
"Didn't see them. Wanna meet and deliver the package to Trex?"

"No. Think I about had enough fun today. I'm going home. Deliver it asap, to be on the safe side. Who knows where that H-T is off to. Or how the tail even managed to find the courier."

"Be careful then. You're new IDN should be ready by now. I'll ask Trex to confirm. His code's synced to your Econ, if you wanna get in touch. Along with Feegle's."

"Thanks."

"Hey, you saved *me* today. I should be thanking you for tagging along."

"Like old times."

I tap my Econ to disconnect the line. Recuperate a little while longer. Another fatal encounter in less than four hours. Results of freedom, day one:

Shot at three times, check.
Fought an Alpha, check.
Dove off a roof and a prison, check, check.
Watched some poor guy's fatal encounter, check.
Went toe-to toe-with an H-T70, Regulators'
fastest and only ship model, check.

If this wasn't a runner's welcome back party, I don't know what is. I am glad Dayio was able to retrieve the package. Life without an IDN isn't living. Mooching off Feegle is optional but pride will only allow a certain extent. A plus that Dayio's okay also.

I leave the cruiser. No Regs combing to make an arrest yet. No cruisers passing. Surprised and not testing luck, I make haste. The garage's end stairway guides to street level. Safe and inconspicuous. Becoming lost in civilian traffic, I use public transit trollies.

Life is still moving, happily like pulse rounds weren't just beautifully soaring skies. During firefights with an H-T70, crossfire civilians must remain as still as possible, while internal systems calculate each pulse's trajectory faster than firing rate. A user's task is to sternly warn, target criminals, and hold the trigger. With automatic cease and fire, everything else takes care of itself. Civilian safety standards have been upheld tonight. H-T70s only generate shock rounds, unlike Alphas which have heat rounds and a missile cannon.

Smiles surround in transit. Glows of relentless color schemes bounce off their eyes. Close equivalent to brightly sewn wardrobes. My outfit is mostly black, standing out by standing in. Seen yet not paid attention to, assuming low class identity.

Gharis is alike everywhere, carrying different district titles. In five cut fractions, southeast and central have access points leading underground. Eight manholes spread around the outer southeast fraction and two tunnels on the outskirts bordering the dome; east and southeast. I arrive at the closest manhole entrance. Insert my fingers, lifting and sliding the heavy metal cylinder away. Unleashing a rancid smell strong enough make anyone second-guess entry. Not a bother since I've grown familiar over years. Mindful, my prison-tamed nose may relay a false reading. I grab the ladder and step down a few. Press against tubular wall and slide the manhole closed. Shrouded in darkness. The blackest pitch. I carefully descend and follow a small tunnel. Trace my hand along dirt wall until a beige aura navigates entry. Electric lanterns along bounce off-yellow light around, meshing the two.

Underground is a scattering of ragged tents and makeshift structures over solid dirt. Somehow, few Deserted manufactured small stone shelters with raw materials the cave came with. Water flows, creating puddles of lightened mud from intentionally broken piping. City workers tasked with dumping food to nourish, like snakes in a pit.

Deserted don't appear to eat, anyway. Forced here to live peacefully amongst themselves. A handful of them used to be successful. Popular somebodies quite well-off in life. Easily remembered across networks for accomplishments. For some reason, minds got lost; misinterpretation and confusion. Violent toward themselves and others. Like they forgot who they were, roaming aimlessly. Murmuring about things that don't make sense to me. Loved ones were just as confused.

I descend a second ladder into the pit. Carefully tread between mumbling, dirty clothed masses to my aluminum shack. Still standing, despite constructing it myself. Little more square footage than the jail cell but doesn't smell as nice. Tougher bed. Curtain, instead of a door. No foodie box. No windows. No plumbing. Bachelorette pad in a nutshell. The kind of accustoms I've settled with my entire life. Most my time is spent above ground, so much isn't needed here except a bed and change of clothes. Lacking the latter. I'd taken undamaged outfits, thinking I'd wind up in another city for a few days after my run two years ago. For now, I'm stuck with a barely scraped, two-hour worn outfit. Hungry, but more tired. I show my twin-sized bed attention by calling it a night.

Chapter 5: Meet and Greet

Eyes open to rusted ruffles of aluminum roof. An extra layer of blurred scribble clouds the ridged design. Snooze status lower than empty. My stomach growls loudly. Wonder which I didn't get more of: sleep or starvation. No telling if it's day or the next night outside since I'm underground.

I tap my Econ, "What time is it?"
The female voice informs, "The current time is 6:38 a.m. Do you have an appointment you would like to set an alarm for?"
Someone thinks I do, but I won't make it this or any other morning, "Nope, no appointment."
"Very well. Feel free to notify me if you need anything else."
I give a silly farewell, "Goooodbyyyye."
"Goodbye."

The Econ disconnects itself. I've no interest in exploring new, venturous opportunities. Whoever sent that letter wants to meet, badly, although I'm gathering a nagging suspicion someone broke me out for worse deeds... I don't have bold enemies, nonetheless someone with bad intentions could be looking for blood. Maybe a rival of Trex wants me to defect. I'm going to be a no call/no show today.

I've got errands. Food and clothes. Current style is my preference. Like every businessman has a suit and every ninja has a second skin. The shop that makes my suits doesn't deliver down here, nor does anyone else. I pick up multiples from the designer and return with damaged articles for repair. On account of last night, this outfit is in bad shape. I have to pick up new ones after breakfast. My stomach growls again, so loud Deserted should've heard. Champion decided, I concede.

Okay, we'll go eat.

I rise to a stretch. Dust myself and leave the aluminum shack. Outside, Deserted freely roam the area in a daze. Some holding their heads tightly, groaning. Some talking to themselves, incoherently. Some seated, rocking and swaying. Some frozen, doing nothing at all. I maneuver around and up a ladder to the south tunnel. Then accept darkness to a second ladder. I barely push up the manhole, revealing a weak, day-broken sky. I ascend, seal the hole, and mount the sidewalk.

City lights deactivate at seven in the morning. Though bright enough, districts remain unnecessarily well-lit until the top of the hour. Traffic is light. Few cruisers at street level and more airborne. I tour in search of the nearest restaurant. Lights go out. Gharis' 7 a.m. indication. I stumble upon a restaurant.

In entrance proximity, the daily special appears. Displaying an enticing meal offer during my pass. Many retail shops and restaurants use holograms for specials and discount prices to reel people in. A worm for the fish. I find it creepy. The hologram follows like a set of eyeballs on a stationary painting. Clearly tolerated enough suffering, my stomach barks again. I don't want the daily special but will dine anyway. I enter the restaurant. No one is present at the podium to greet. I sit at the farthest back corner booth with a door view. A MechCi server approaches. True definition of *morning people*.

A stiffly warm greeting, "Good morning." It places a small, circular panel on the wooden table, "For you, valued patron, is our selection menu. Unless you would prefer an order of our delicious daily special."
"I'll browse the menu, thanks."
"Very well. May I start with an ice-cold beverage prior to your meal selection?"
"Not yet."
"I will promptly return in three and a quarter minutes to take your order."

The MechCi putters away. I tap the circular panel's centered button. A 3D meal schematic projects upward, displaying layered ingredients. Slow rotation demonstrates every angle. I slide a finger across the panel to display the next selection. Four selections deep, I select a breakfast omelet. Keeping the hologram open so the server can see.

Returning, I dive into curiosity at the haste, "Was that really three and a quarter?"
It responds, confused, "That can't be, I haven't taken your order yet for payment to have been conducted."
I clarify, "I mean for the time you said. Three and a quarter minutes?"
"Oh, I understand."

It instigates a controlled, fake laugh. Functions make MechCi personalities seem real. Friendly to keep people at ease. Making them lovable. May work for everyone else, but not me. I patiently wait for the patronizing machine to stop attempting to appease.

It continues, "You are funny indeed. Of course it was correct. Is the breakfast omelet your chosen option or have you not finished browsing?"

"Chosen option."

"And what shall be your selection of beverage this morning?"

"Water."

The MechCi toggles the digital menu, scoops it and inquires, "Sparkling or filtered?"

I test awful sarcasm on the machine, "Can I have both?"

"Separate glasses, yes?"

"No, same glass."

It instigates laughter again. I smirk and look at my lap for a brief second. Created too lifelike in personality. Like humans without thick flesh and replaceable, jointly connected bones; also, variety of chrome colors and not wearing clothing distinguish them from ordinary men and women.

The MechCi excitedly expresses praise, "You are beyond funny, ma'am! Unfortunately, I cannot approve your request."

"Filtered will fit the bill then."

"Your meal will take approximately eleven minutes to prepare and thirty seconds to serve. Do you disagree with the wait time?"

"No."

"Terrific. I will return shortly."

It putters away. I slide further inside the booth. Kick my feet up and relax against wood panels. Tilt my head backward until stopped. Concentrated breathes in and out, while I wait. No company. No incoming calls, none outgoing. Loner's life of seclusion and flying under radars.

Foster homes, group homes, and cells influenced grudges against those in perpendicular situations. By association, the entire New World became untrustworthy. Anyone can easily trust a friendly person. A humorous MechCi. What happens when every person and thing is friendly? Defensive protection joins shadows. I'd rather be alone and alert than friendly and backstabbed. From an affiliation stance, MechCi carry more trust, to me, than humans. Chasing mutual gain, I do associate with runners. With crooks like Trex and criminals like Dayio, it's expected. Trex is a businessman who would sell anybody under the bus for aers or blind assumption. Just as blame shot when I entered his office. I'd prefer Dayio not cross a line yet I'm not ignorant to the option. One I'd think twice about exacting revenge on.

The MechCi delivers my food and water and asks, "Will there be anything else you require at the moment?"
"No, thank you."
"Enjoy your meal citizen."

Putter away, little machine. The restaurant is empty. I go full carnivore on the defenseless omelet, which is more delicious than expected. Appetite satisfied at the finish line. Prison food was delicious to an extent. Duplicate scheduled weekly meals became nauseating. This omelet is a fresh take on something beautiful. Blowing a huddle of dandelions into a breeze.

The MechCi putters to my empty plate with a pocket-sized scanning machine, "The meal charge and free beverage comes to twenty aers. IDN please?"

I stand and stare at the MechCi aiming the payment scanner at my feet. A device used to process goods purchases with digital currency. A horizontal white line appears. The MechCi leisurely sways up, scanning my entire body.

With aers, no one has to worry about clumsily losing cash or falling prey to masked thieves. There are constant digital trails. Two individuals can transfer aers by request through treasury. Servers would receive a notification to establish a connection between sender and receiver, approved upon spoken agreement. A brave crook can abduct a victim and setup a link, directly tying their IDN to the transaction. Able to disappear far and fast? The recipient's IDN will be blocked; transfers reversed. A useless crime. Food purchases allow a debt limit of ten thousand. Irresponsible users can safely go into debt without fear of repercussion. Being digital, currency earned pays aers owed. Funds earned once debt clears are the user's to spend freely. For responsible, upstanding citizens, going into debt is almost impossible; my debt's begun.

The MechCi finishes scanning with a three beep notification, "Payment has been completed. Thank you for your business and have a wonderful day citizen."

The MechCi goes to the podium as I proceed past adjacently to leave. Next task on my agenda is aers. Check-in with Trex for a package update or maybe additional work. Too bad there's no bulletin board for runners to pick a job; I'm not good at one hundred percent of the legal ones, anyway.
Transit services are free. Trollies for outskirt and inner-city travel. Two routes cut Gharis into four halves. One circles outer, another inner cuts eight; from aerial view, it's a target. At a cost, taxis are also available. I journey the southwest border, using trollies to Feegle's bakery and Trex's hideaway. An outskirt trolley arrives near the south checkpoint. Docked, while passengers interchange. I board and ride. Disembarking a few blocks from the bakery. Arrived, Feegle is working at the counter with his personal MechCi.

I greet, "Good morning, Feegle."
He expresses excitable recognition, "Miss Pheros, sweetheart! How are you? What happened to your clothing?"

Silly me, wandering an upper-class city in torn-up gear. It's morning. After a talk with Trex about jobs, a change of clothes comes next.

I obviously lie, "I had a welcome back party last night. I need to speak with Trex."
Feegle remarks with bland kindness in his tone, "That's a true understatement. Go on through, darling."

Emptiness in the sparkling ballroom is quite soothing. No windows shielded by huge purple drapes occupying the left wall. Intentionally placed décor to make guests believe there are. This room's classiness unlocks imagination of what's beyond; A grand garden. Fountain of chirping birds. Fleet of luxury cruisers. Farmland of white horses.

Good work, Feegle.

I cruise the ballroom. Listen to echoing boots crush hardwood. Look at empty tables lined along the right wall where restrooms are centered. Feegle caters well, and in return, earns excellent business. I veer left and enter the basement. Down dark stairs to the right corner. I reach at the right wall and guess around. Push a false wooden shingle. The hidden door splits in a rise, beaming blue light.

How did a greedy criminal like Trex and a flamboyant baker like Feegle meet? Which decided constructing a smuggler's den in a positive-vibing social hotspot would be a good idea? Not once finding an asking moment. Never hearing them draw breath in the same space, offering casual chances to spring questions in conversation. Must be some interesting tale there, other than *"Trex pays monthly."* I pace the passage and knock on Trex's office door.

Instructions follow, "Come in!" At my entry, he joyfully adds, "Just the girl I wanted to see!" He whips out a digitized page, slapping it down on the desk, "Check that out!"

Trex is smiling immensely. I approach with minor caution. Tap a finger on the page. A news article prints on, including video of an elderly Caucasian man at a podium. Addressing a crowd. Inaudible dialogue. He looks familiar, although I can't place a name, where, or what he does. I spent two years too many forgetting faces to remember some old guy.

I ask, "Who is this?"
Trex excitedly reacts, "You can't possibly call yourself a resident of Gharis City and not know who that is! That is *thee* Gene Archibald…"

A brief pause. Awkward for him because I still have no clue what he's going on about or why I should care. Does he expect me to know who the man is by verbal introduction?

I shrug my shoulders, "So?"

Trex holds expressed excitement, "So, the package you and Dayio took was a delivery for the Menta-Life Corporation! ...Gene Archibald is the founder!"

Another pause. Clearly excited, but I'm not seeing why. We, indirectly, hospitalized their courier and stole their package. Disrupted illegal dealings of the New World's leading authority. He's happy about that? Stealing from a powerhouse like Menta-Life would, in any circumstance, be a massive problem.

Annoyance takes my tone, "Is this winding up to the part where they wanna kill me and Dayio or is this just conversation?"

"Okay, listen. I made some calls and found out the delivery was goin' to Menta-Life. Called anonymous and told them I *'found'* the package. Hired outside help to make the drop and they paid out big! Hundred and twenty-five thousand aers!"

Now, that's more like it. First day out and snagged chunky fish with an even chunkier reward.

I ask, "So what's my take? Forty thousand?"

He sends a reminder, "Don't forget about your debt from two years ago."

I roll my eyes and speak under my breath, "How can I?"

"Minus that, your cut is... twenty-five thousand. Then payment for that clean IDN..."

His incorrect mental math processes in hums. Minimum wage is five hundred aers per week regardless of hours worked or overtime. That last job was a ten thousand aer take, which by his labor split rate, was not a package worth much. In short, he is trying very hard to pinch a lot of aers.

I contend, "With how little my cut was supposed to be for that package, the deal couldn't have been worth more than fifteen thousand. And seeing as you vouched for the couple that took the package, the debt is yours. Now I can forgive you for trying to skimp a full cut or could hop over this desk and start with an arm."

He momentarily ponders options, "Ya know, you're a hard woman to please."

My palms plant firm on the desk, "I'm an impossible woman to please."

"Thirty thousand aers it is then."

A sympathetic sigh exhales. Responsibility became mine when I accepted the package. And he deserves payment for my clean IDN. If not for him, instead of paying at that restaurant I'd have been prime target of a citywide manhunt. Arrested. Shipped to prison faster than time it'd have taken to digest breakfast.

I show appreciation, "Keep half for the IDN and call it square?"

I surrender for a handshake and he swiftly obliges, "Very well, it's been a pleasure doin' business with you, as always. Did you want any work?"

I back away, "Did, but not anymore. I'll just get settled. Explore what I missed for two years."

"Wanna go for a run with Dayio? He usually recons sections of the city durin' the day."

"He still does that?"

"How you think he stays in shape?"

"I saved his skin last night, so someone needs to recommend a new regimen. Where is he?"

Trex presses a button on his retro landline and calls out, "Dayio?"

Dayio's voice exits the speaker, "Go ahead, Trex."

"Van's comin' out."

"Got it."

He presses the same button to disconnect, "Mindin' his post in the grove."

I exit the office and walk to the grove. Dayio's minions are seated in a staggered circle. On break. Wearing black stealth clothing. Many branches and leaves make these shady grove stalkers shadier. Dayio is standing, back to me. Verbally coaching trainees or engaged in small talk. Eyes shift, alerting Dayio to a new presence. One phoned about minutes prior.

Dayio subtly greets as I approach his side, "What's up, Van? Trex tell you about the package?"
"Menta-Life. Big deal I guess."

The war of 2068 ruined more than half of Earth and, considering a third is water, that's speaking volumes. Years after, hope was reachable. What's now the leading New World corporation arose at Gharis City's heart, in all terms. Menta-Life issued direction, scavenging and rebuilding. Gharis developed circular sixty miles around; four smaller cities and Ori Prison are also their claim. To accomplish so much in seventeen years wouldn't have been possible without their Life program, or so I've heard. I don't bandwagon manipulative media. Menta-Life is a big deal for the five domed cities. Period.

Dayio shares thoughts, "That turnout definitely wasn't what I expected. And a major payout, too."
"What was in that package? Something so small couldn't have been worth so much unless it was an illegal relic."
"Some kind of imitation emeralds." He whispers, "Whatever it was about, I'd jump on their payroll in a heartbeat to do it again. Of course, with you around I'd probably get pushed off a roof."
Inside humor forces our chuckles, and my bogus curiosity, "Really? That was my fault?"
His voice returns, "Who else's would it be? It wasn't mine. Anyway, you here to train?"
"What about recon?"
"That can wait. We're about to spark some training exercises if you're down for some schooling. You and I both know you could use it." He addresses everyone, "Let's get warmed up!"
Random Econ notification, "A transfer of fifteen thousand aers has been made to your IDN."

They lead into simple stretches. Then warm-up exercises. Train in stealth, skulking quickly but silently and repetitive tree climbing and balance. A crew of three heads inside for lunch, while the rest break an hour. Train in offensive and defensive tactics, games of Capture the Carrier and open-handed sparring. Three hours have gone by. Second trio will have food soon and my stomach is churning. Training informally concludes. I listen to everyone swap stories. I don't chime personal experiences. When lunch comes, Dayio and a female join. We each grab a meal and dine at the same table.

Sort of impolitely, the female takes an interest in me, "I hear you and Dayio did runs together a couple of years ago."

I confirm while stuffing my face, "We did, jealous?"

She smirks, "Curious, more like. What made you stop?"

No harm intended, she's just blunt, dialing my attitude back, "A prison sentence."

"Got caught on a job?"

"Job didn't even get to start. Apparently, I murdered four people."

Dayio takes watchful interest, while surprise swamps the woman, "Bit dangerous, for a smuggler. I like that. Doesn't mix well in our line of work."

"I am, thanks, but it was truly apparent. The couple Trex paired me with must have jumped the deal before taking me there."

"How come they didn't get you too? Did you get them first before you went down?"

"I didn't. I was in the middle of nowhere and they were gone as soon as I stepped inside. The fall girl. Regs swarmed almost immediately. Got sent to Ori and, two years later, I'm back here."

"Two years? That's it? Please share what amount of good behavior can shorten four murders."

"I think someone staged a blackout so I could escape."

"Trex does breakouts?"

"I don't know who did, but it wasn't Trex. Guy hates my guts. Everything went dark and doors started popping open. I bailed straight into a fight with an Alpha. I jumped on its back during our tumble off the prison wall. The crash left it badly damaged. I was able to rewire it and it brought me to the grove."

Her head tilts and eyes squint, "Anything to do with those explosions yesterday?"

"An attack helicopter pilot doing their job way too hard. It blew up the Alpha and almost got me. The mech pitched me into the trees before impact. I almost didn't survive. Still aches like I didn't."

"That's crazy! An Alpha? Please warn me before I get on your bad side. What are you gonna do now that you're out?"

"Same thing I did to get in."

We all laugh. Finish our small portion of a meal. They seemed very interested in my story. If someone told me what I'd just told them, I would have said they were full of it. A bit of summarizing sped things up, though key points got across.

Dayio asks me, "Wanna go for that recon run?"
"Sure."
He gives orders, "Rejoin the others at your post, do a final sweep and take off. We're heading out."
She acknowledges, "Understood." Then turns to me, "Nice chatting, Van."

I nod at her departure, trailing out next. We walk the passage, cross the bakery, and hit the street. Both immediately scan sidewalks and rooftop ledges. Active runners' reflex.

Dayio asks, "Which direction you wanna go?"
"Which has newer developments?"
"That'll be west. We'll go northeast toward Menta-Life Corp and hit west from there."

He leads to the nearest stoplight. Legal cross to remain inconspicuous, in black clothing. We enter the first building. Dayio greets citizens on the way up like they're his neighbors. For a smuggler and thief, he's got a kind heart. Polite and sincere. We're total opposites. At the roof, our eyes lock northeast. Gharis has a rising effect; buildings mostly ranging from shortest on outskirts, to tallest, which is Menta-Life. Almost doubling height of the second tallest. Then descending in every direction. A sort of staggering pyramid.

Dayio points out, "Menta-Life."

A tall tower that has a half-slant roof. Menta-Life brand etched on all four sides with a crescent Earth logo beneath each. Conquerors putting their name over Earth itself. The skyscraper's top half is all that can be seen beyond blocking buildings.
Miscellaneous businesses are important also: electric company, internet services, magazine publishing, and more.

Dayio points left, "Here's a new piece, Atrio Bank, built about a year and a half ago."

The bank isn't flat-topped like most buildings; demonstrating financial status with a kind of domed presidential top.

My confused inquiry blurts, "A bank?"
"The company released a new piece of technology called DSC, Data Storage Cores. They found a way for people to store aers onto individual storage devices not linked to connected networks."
"Contingency in case some lucky hacker manages to breach IDN security? Seems kind of pointless. Your funds get hacked, treasury just gives you more almost instantly. Digital currency is as safe as it gets."
"True. But wealthy people wanted off shared networks and result are in. Could be for 'off the books' transactions."

On and off public transit and rooftops, Dayio announces more recent developments facing west on the northern path. Our grand tour ends at the southwest corner of Menta-Life's main HQ. Birthed right here from a hut. We storm into a neighboring business building, discussing work-related urgencies like employees; topics everyone ignores us to not be involved in. Ride to one of the tallest rooftops in Gharis' pyramid. A full skyscraper view rests in my eyes.

I state, "There she is. Icon of all icons."

Windows blacked from the second floor up, adoring privacy. It's hard to imagine hordes of offices and computers in there. An abundance of room for nothing illegal to be going on. Ground level has a line of customers flowing and no cruisers curbside. Must be underground parking nearby. A gated delivery entrance closer to the northwest corner.

Dayio asks, "How much you think they rake in a day from their Life program? All those people, that's fifteen thousand per head."

"I'd lose count with numbers that high."

"Ever been inside?"

"Never. All Menta-Life Corps have the tightest security available. Only way in is as a customer. I'd cased the place years ago."

Dayio scoffs, "As usual, one track minded. I meant as a customer. You never wanted to try a Life?"

"No. You?"

"Want to, but… I don't know. I heard it's like living constant forevers and I'm all for it. You can find things in there. Be things. I'd like to be more than a smuggler, one day. What am I gonna do at fifty? Leaping old bones across rooftops for Trex?"

I attempt to revitalize positivity, "How about happily retired? By fifty, we'd have long since figured out how and robbed this place blind without a trace. The Super Score."

"And if that doesn't work?"

"Remember, there are *much* worse places in the world than Ori Prison."

Dayio's head shakes, facing due west and hands bracing hips, "Ready to run?"

I shift sideways where he's facing. Going west, each rooftop descends. Runner reflex already has me mentally calculating routes; high scales, low drops, gaps, fire escapes, open windows. Repurposing structures as mini launch pads. An abrupt *yes* commences the race, cheating into a head start. Patterns reconfirm. I spring off the edge. Cross an X to break wind from my face. Dayio is on a slightly different route, staying close. Still pointing new places while pyramid declining. The almost blinding sun is setting ahead, stopping our race early. Must be around five o'clock. I finish in front. We catch our breath.

Calm, I comment, "Looks like you need practice."
Calm, he denies, "Hardly. Oh, don't forget, you cheated. How did you manage to keep in practice?"
"Like riding a bike."
"I gotta get back. Where're you heading?"
"Grab a bite and home."
"We just ate! Never mind. You need anything, come by. It's good having you back."

Dayio jogs to a drainage pipe and vanishes down the building. I haven't watched a sunset in years, sitting and losing myself to the orange glow. It feels good being embraced by sunshine again. City lights activate, meaning today's done. Forgot again. Go to Lynn's shop for an outfit. Recalling its location and arranging a new route southwest, I cross rooftops until I'm closer. Descend to the sidewalk and stroll fifteen minutes west amongst the public. Flashy clothing's nightly debut has begun.

Lynn's Professional Alterations does not stand out. Bunched between a line-up of various shops. No attention-grabbing hologram. Multiple base colors beyond windows *can* offer friendly welcome. I pass under a single door to bright yellow walls lined with clothing of all types and sizes. A counter in the center, where orders are handled. Where she's seated, reading a digitized page. I approach. Lynn is a middle-aged woman that is a lot humbler and less exciting than most. The best tailor around. She works for exclusive clientele and wishes to remain nameless; dearly valuing free time and peace of mind, not becoming overwhelmed by masses of celebrity copycats. Personal preference of a volunteer pariah.

I pass a plain greeting, "Hello, Lynn."
She looks up, greeting more sluggish and uninterested, "Vanessa, how are you?" She examines me, "Should I have asked?"

"You already did. If you got time, I need new gear."

The digital page meets the counter and the chair slides away. I peek at what she's reading. Paragraphs neatly separated. Many quotes. A scrollable page story book. A psychological thriller? Perhaps, dark crimes? Humorous, if it were romantic comedy.

Lynn lifts and sits a black cloth bag on the counter, "I made two last night after Dayio left. Go change, and I'll have it patched and another two ready tomorrow. Boots are back there also."

"How much?"

"For these two, fixing, another two pairs, and boots, five thousand aers."

Her prices were usually a little steeper, making me question obvious generosity, "That's it?"

Fingers tip the page, slipping it into her hands, "This time it is. Welcome back, Vanessa."

I take the bag. Enter her back room to switch the same outfit. Finished projects are displayed like trophies. Rare masterpieces. Meaningful creations because I see no flashy robes. Work materials neatly scattered on a couple of tables. Strangely neat for a seamstress. I violate the bag. Pull a pair of jeans, tank top, and jacket. Change into fresh clothes, placing my dingy outfit on the table. Good as old.

At the shop floor, bag in hand, I state, "It feels great. Ready for payment."

Lynn swipes the small payment device, scanning from her seat. It beeps three times when finished.

I speak, "Thanks, Lynn. I'll come back some time tomorrow."

She says nothing. Lynn and I have never been on informal terms. Like our personalities clashed, though not knowing what each others are. She seems to not enjoy this city and inhabitants as much as I, so naturally there should be common ground. If not for business, we'd have no interaction. Another person I'd brush past.

I leave the shop. A man is standing curbside of a parked four-door cruiser. About thirty and rugged. Suspiciously under-average attire. Too casual. Passenger door stretched open. Nothing short of creepy. Parked and waiting directly out front, though no one was lingering inside. Doesn't fit the description of a celebrity's sophisticated chauffeur, and an average cruiser that an average person would drive.

The man holds a stare, "Are you Vanessa Pheros?"

Oh good, this stranger's here for me. My eyes shift left. Then right. Conduct an inconspicuous search for any suspicious individuals in immediate view. Surroundings appear fine as far as peripherals can tell, without visibly breaking my neck to be nosy. Maybe he is just a driver for someone. I don't care enough to find out.

Chapter 6: The Threat

Asking by name with the door spread open, this man expects me to get in. An older model cruiser. Black, curved surface in front, but square in back to accommodate rear passengers and luggage space. Not near flashy enough to consider jumping in without question. A limousine would change things. How did he know where to find me?

I answer, "Never heard that name."

He splits his black leather coat. A pulser pistol is living inside the waistband. I'm halted about eight feet away. Close enough to take his weapon before handing a free attempt to use it on me.

He calls my bluff, "I think you have. My employer wants to meet." My arms loosely cross, "For what?"

"To talk."

"I doubt she'd wanna talk."

He reaches fast for the pistol. I zip closer, almost before the yank off his hip. Snatch his wrist. Twist downward and spin him toward the cruiser, claiming the weapon. Stick it under his head while holding pinned against the closed rear door.

Forearm deep into his back, uttered words struggle, "We need your help. You have skills to do things that we can't."

Unintentionally sold myself. Should've known right away that he wouldn't have hurt me. Not that the opportunity was presented. After word passes, this employer will want me more. Who does he work for? If there's an offer, it can be potentially profitable. Yet with how this man is dressed, potentially not. What harm can there be in hearing them out? All I have to say is "no" and worst they can do is attack. Not like they'd be the first to try... or last to fail.

I ask, "Where's your backup?"

"I came alone."

"Then I ride shotgun and I'm keeping the pulser."

Wrist freed, I shove him at the front of the cruiser. Discreetly aiming, observing his loop toward the driver's side. I occupy as passenger. Continue watching movements until he joins inside. An average interior. Well-maintained. Dashboard concealed by carbon fiber panels, unlocking with a correct keypad code entry. Anti-theft features. If not for age, brand new. Rented? The driver door closes. I close mine. The center console keypad appears. Digital. He quickly enters "81402," likely hoping I'd miss it. The battery automatically ignites. Steering wheel slides out. Dashboard panels slide up, revealing average cruiser features. Air condition controls, radio, gear shift. He grabs the wheel and drives north.

I demand, "Take us to seventy-five."

A short glance is thrown my way, before the press of a steering wheel button. A smaller dashboard panel flips between us. The gravitational riser. He triggers a slow rise from street level while automatically maintaining speed limit range. Reaches sixty feet. Then merges upward with parted traffic, matching seventy-five. I still have the pulser held, unconcernedly.

Silence breaks with his question, "Don't you want to know where we're going?"
"Doesn't make any difference. I'll find out when we get there."

He nods, promoting silence again. Easy understanding of my response says his employer is the letter sender who wanted to meet this particular morning. A lackey dispatched because I didn't show. An explanation prepared and denied. They aided my escape for something beneficial. If the price is right, they may have a fresh recruit.

The sun has already fallen over the horizon. Through the windshield, lights from billboards and signs illuminate our pass. Advertisements, products, services, activities. Set thirty feet above each gravity limit to avoid blinding drivers with unnecessarily illumined shades. There are two opposing lanes on upper planes, dependent on an area's structural height. Activity increases and lanes condense on approach further into a higher section. Nearing the inner circle. The driver's hand shifts. Unhesitant, my thumb toggles the pulser's element function. Still rested in my lap, carrying a slight pitch with its quick charge. More peripheral focused, holding my blank face at the windshield.

He hurriedly explains, "We're close, just lowering gravity so we can park."

I don't respond. He switches off gravity. The cruiser slowly descends streetside, merging when traffic clears. Ending soon at Cravanaugh Hotel's valet. Below tall granite steps to the main entrance. A light brown color with many windows and a forever slowly revolving door. Ramps on both sides; one for handicap access, other for consistency. The hotel is about thirty stories. Clear regulation exception. Catering kindly to those who enjoy looking down on others.

I tuck the pistol away as a valet approaches the driver side, "Park for you, sir?"

Mystery man answers, "Yes, please." He looks at me and states the obvious, "We're here."

My eyes drag at him, "You gonna open my door?"

An irritated expression gathers. Then, forcibly calm, he exits. The valet replaces with a heartening smile. I return a false one. My door opens. The driver looks away while doing so. Ashamed at the act. I exit. Pulser concealed in my jacket. Ready to draw at a moment's notice. Itching to burn through fabric.

I sarcastically compliment, "What a gentleman."

I confidently follow by his side. Up stairs and through the revolving door. Cravanaugh's interior is fancy. Marble flooring. Beige walls, almost matching the exterior but touches lighter. Plenty of seating for lobby loitering guests. Marble pillars hold floor two up about forty feet. Three elevators live dead ahead. Two red-carpeted staircases: one left and right of the elevators. Identical development.

Safe around many witnesses, I store the pistol in my inner jacket pocket. Follow directly through the lobby. His employer must've waited all day since there's no reception check-in. The driver smashes the right elevator's call button. It promptly arrives. We step into a fancy golden-trimmed box. Top-level numbers displayed, stopping only at the highest floors; first four exclusionary. He presses button "28". Our ascent is quiet. I detach the pistol's battery and underhand now nonlethal pieces at him. He fumbles them to a leaning catch. Needing to wait for the recharge process before making it dangerous again.

He looks at them, defeated, sarcastically acknowledging, "Thanks."

Without time to ready for use, pieces drift into separate pockets. Adjusting his coat afterward. We arrive at a hallway with art hanging along beige walls. Gold doors lined very far apart. A tacky design that's become an overcompensation. I follow onto red carpet. Surprised armed guards aren't watching the door his employer is behind; whoever, they're not too important. Or not meeting in person.

Less than halfway he approaches door "2812", using a keycard to unlock and enter. More marble flooring under my feet. Bathroom immediately right and an entry area ahead. Gold trim lining on white walls. Chandelier hanging peacefully from the dome ceiling. A small round table in the center, decorated with a vase full of imitation roses.

We approach a group of four men standing; three from last night's courier theft, dressed in average clothing. Don't recognize the nerdy-looking blonde in the sharpened gray suit. I strolled into a trap. My steps ease, keeping distant, in case the driver gets handsy. If they're anything like the man I took down last night, escaping won't be an issue. I halt a few meters away, mentally preparing a physical defense.

The man I fought unleashes some angry barks, "Hey, what is this!?! That's the same woman who made us lose the smuggler's bag!"

He rushes for round two. Having taken him once, I can easily do it again. Other allies, except the suit, hurriedly converge to stop him. I cross my arms and watch the show. Soon ignoring them for the suited man behind who can't be in charge; unless aers course his veins. He's poorly masking nervousness during the struggle. Too well-mannered to tame this bunch of scruffy ruffians. Rectangular frames make him appear hospitable and aiming to please like a secretary or advisor. Also, I doubt someone in charge would appreciate unsolicited hostility. Doing something right, the rooftop failures manage a firmer grasp.

The driver forcefully demands, "Calm down! She's the one he wants to speak with!"

The angry man argues, "She can't be! She stole the package from us!"

The nerdy man chimes, "That is for your employer to sort. Everyone wait outside."

Foreign accent. Broken from years in America, like mine. Maybe German? Still lacking confidence. Confirmed powerless over them and doubts whether or not they'll obey orders. Why not unleash them on me for what I'd done?

The angry man shakes the other two off and sternly states, "I'm fine."

Still frustrated. Seeming to have it under control. Must have a decent salary but the suit's not their employer either. Middleman? The foursome group together and walk by. I can feel the angry man's eyes as I stand with my arms folded, not paying direct attention. Fueling additional anger. The front door shuts.

The suited man expresses sincerity, "Apologies. Last night was an… unexpected occurrence. Can I interest you in a beverage?"
Not going to lie, water or juice would do wonders but there's small matters of trust that guide an answer, "Only if I can pour it myself."
"Certainly. Follow me to the kitchen please."

It's on his right. The hotel room is not all silent. Perhaps to untrained ears; a white noise is itching in the background, as if recording or eavesdropping is in progress. We enter the kitchen. It's gorgeous, like something seen in a celebrity's basic home; before full mansion upgrade. Upper floors must be suites. I wouldn't mind permanent residency. The island counter begins rising out of the floor. He circles the square, opposing and halting. Smart to think of safety first.

I dig into the full-sized refrigerator, "So what do you want with me?"
I grab a gallon juice bottle and set it on the counter during formal introductions, "My name is Hines Aldwich and, well, first I would like to know what happened to the package."
"Got me. I never even touched it. All I know is that super corporation Menta-Life has it."

"What a terrible shame indeed."

Food selection isn't very appealing; set for a trainer's diet. Things I don't even recognize. That's the real shame. I close the fridge and chug pulped orange juice straight from the bottle. Hines watches in disgust, like he's better than I am. Which he may be. Judging this book's cover accurately.

His throat clears and continues, "The package's contents were of great significance to Menta-Life; contents that I had interest in."

I shrug, "Oops... Hey, can you believe they paid a hundred and twenty-five thousand aers for something so small?"

"Yes, I can. And you were underpaid. It contained vital technology my people could have potentially used against Menta-Life. Worth five times that amount."

"Use against them? I thought rich suits like you loved them."

"I'm far from a rich suit, Ms. Pheros."

I smile, "Looks like I've wasted my time coming then."

"Have you ever heard of Equility?"

"Nope."

I chug more juice, "That's good. My people represent change in Gharis City. We want the Menta-Life Corporation to crumble."

"So what're you guys, some kind of terrorists?"

His expression lightly strains, taking offense to my question, "Freedom fighters, Ms. Pheros."

"Menta-Life is the number one corporation, head of the New World, and is more secure than any other made so by armed security, and a government, as rumors state. You believe you and your four pathetic henchmen out there will be able to go up against that?"

"Equility's numbers greatly exceed the five of us. Our mission is to stop Menta-Life before they intentionally abolish the New World they've created."

Hines is being too over-exaggerative for my tastes and very incorrect. The corporation makes too much money off people to consider tarnishing their creation, or anything else for that matter.

I judge this book with a smile and condescension, "You're obviously crazy and I think you and your goons out there should get some help. Besides, I have no interest in Menta-Life or helping the New World. It was such a pleasure meeting you. And good luck."

I place the jug on the counter and walk away from a quick warning, "Everyone is in danger! You're no exemption!"

"They can try me."

He loudly demands, "Stop!"

I stop and turn my head back toward him. Did he just yell? A small part of me kind of respects the forceful tone from such a kindly-spoken person.

His palms point out with plead, "Please, just hear me out?"

I face him. Cross my arms. This is the anticipated recruitment drive I am not interested in. As smart and incapable as Hines appears, the worst he can physically do is petition. Footwork would be in my court. That's why they need me. I have skill, but not enough stupidity to aid an attack on Menta-Life. He seems desperate. It can't hurt to at least hear what he has to say; still hoping profit could be involved…

I answer, "Fine."

"Thank you." A relieving breath sighs, "A little more than a year ago, we uncovered vital information from an inside source who was captured during retrieval. He breached Menta-Life's server from within and directed a heavily encrypted message. It took a month to decode. The information was troubling." Hines begins pacing, "As citizens are aware, Menta-Life utilizes their technology to allow one to live a ninety year Life on connected servers. From what we've gathered, since founding day, technological advancement has shot up three hundred percent and continually ascends. When the old world was defaced in 2068, we lost everything except for belongings survivors had on them. Menta-Life only took a decade to surpass a level of technological innovation that'd previously taken humanity thousands of years to achieve. However, that's not terrible news. Technology is expanding, *yes*. Menta-Life's high percentage in the involvement, is questionable."

I scratch at my head. A bored reflex. He sure can talk. It's not that his words aren't getting through, it's just he's campaigning to the wrong crowd. By scratching, he understands the unsaid message that his speech is running too long.

He quickly summarizes, "We have reason to believe they've been monitoring their client's Lives and stealing their creations."

I know bits and pieces about Menta-Life. One thing everyone knows for certain, mentioned in fine print, is they never invade a client's Life.

He continues, "Now, of course, just stealing ideas isn't enough. Those who see their technology commercialized on networks, billboards, et cetera can come forth, taking a stand. To eliminate that risk, Menta-Life has taken it a step further and breached said citizen's memories, keeping the existent Life for themselves. Follow me."

Suddenly comfortable and trusting, Hines exits the kitchen. I follow, peeping every corner. Toward the door ahead of the entry. An office. Darker shade of brown than outside. Same red carpeting as the hallway. A desk with three chairs; two in front, one behind. Perfect for intimate client meetings with significant others present. Hines approaches the back chair but doesn't sit. Activates a digitized page and twists it around.

"Look at this."

I stare at him a moment longer. Accept genuine concern and approach the page to see a middle-aged man being arrested. Dreadfully attempting to break free from blue uniformed Regulators while shouting inaudibly at the media. Struggling didn't seem to get him anywhere. Regs just hauled him along a crowd of photographers and reporters. The vid loops.

I ask, "Who's this?"

"Liam Reber. He pled a case against Menta-Life, believing something significant was *forgotten* after his most recent Life. Though, there was no way to know. Still isn't. The first to ever publicly come forward. A famed scientist deemed insane. Just like that. Ironic thing is, soon after, he became so. We closely followed reports and realized his mind began to deteriorate. Until he one day disappeared. We think he was secretly cast down as Deserted. The accusation took place in 2079, four years after Menta-Life's public opening. Deserted numbers have increased slowly, inconsistently, ever since."

"You're saying Menta-Life is responsible?"

"Precisely. Handfuls of Deserted were important figures who'd become drawn to potential creative differences. Prodigies, scientists like Liam, citizens of superior intellect who discovered Life can be used as more than just a tool for entertainment and minor progressive technological efforts equating weekly financial gain. Other majority, missing persons. Randoms. Unimportant chaff to stray public eye, stating anyone can fall victim to this phantom epidemic. That was the aforementioned message we'd received. It read 'Deserted' and we instantly understood. We must do everything in our power to stop them before it's too late."

"Too late for what?"

"Menta-Life has branches in every city. I can assure you this is not just happening in Gharis. They will continue stealing memories and we don't know if they'll stop, when, or their true intention. Equility isn't willing to await results."

His theory makes sense based on what I've heard and seen of Deserted before my time in prison. Living amongst them since seventeen, I'd heard but never listened to ramblings and whispers. Cooperating sounds like something I'd risk my life to accomplish. Wondering how much that's worth.

I ask, "How much?"

He pauses then requests, "I beg your pardon?"

"It sounds like I'm going to be helping save the New World from utter destruction, so how much do I get for my services?"

"This cause is much greater than money."

"Gharis and everything around it can burn for all I care, but if it's worth anything, you'll pay. Recent census states at least three million people in this city alone, and abductors demand upwards of a hundred thousand for ransom. Multiply by three million. That's my price."

A baffled tone exerts, "Preposterous! There is no way anyone can attain a sum that high!"

"Then throw out a number and make me happy."

His tone remains high but unforceful, "I unquestionably cannot!"

The white noise is still airborne. Bringing the recording or listening party to the stand might help increase offering odds.

I scan the ceiling and raise my voice, "Then how about you up there?!"

Hines quickly panics, whispering through his teeth, "What are you doing?!"

I answer normally, "Seeing if your boss has a better deal." I raise my voice, "Come on out, I have no problem waiting! What's the offer?!"

An older male voice rains from above, "You are very perceptive, Ms. Pheros."

I add, "And very irritated by that white noise static. You should maybe consult your electrician if you want better eavesdropping equipment."

"Equility is in dire need of your expertise in order to cease operations of Gene Archibald and Menta-Life."

"What do you know about my expertise?"

"I know everything about you. About your time in prison, every jail, foster home, mental hospital, et cetera, et cetera."

"Nosy, aren't you?"

"Ms. Pheros, I am a very powerful man."

I insult, "But not powerful enough."

Hines comes to the speaker's defense, "Ms. Pheros—"

The old voice interrupts, "Mr. Aldwich, it is quite alright." He addresses me, "Ms. Pheros, you will be one of many working to help our effort."

I ask, "Then will you meet my price, *Mr. Powerful?*"

"Your asking price exceeds unreached limits of personal finance mathematics itself."

"I highly doubt that. What do you have?"

"I can't promise much."

Why does this strike as a ruse? Claiming power, yet not having much to give. Contradictory wording. Since his group plans on attacking Menta-Life, massive profit may be over the horizon regardless.

I reply, "That doesn't sound promising. A million aers to start and we'll work the rest later when I see your operation and plans."

Hines declines, "Pre-payment is out of the question."

I reply, "Then be glad it's not a question. That's my starting price. Pay or I walk."

The old voice notifies, "Payment is being sent."

My eyebrows raise and so does Hines' voice, "But sir—"

The old voice states, "We cannot manage to halt Menta-Life operations without Ms. Pheros' help... She has us in a bind."

I chime in, "Glad you understand because Hinesie would've let me stroll out that door."

A voice notification relays via Econ, "One million aers have just been transferred to your IDN."

Wow. I thought the man was bluffing. Apparently they do need me. For a million aers, Equility has me reeled as far as I can possibly go. I could care less about their ideals and accomplishments; as long as I get paid, we don't have a problem.

I admit, "So, seems you people really mean business. Where do we start?"

The old voice answers, "First, Mr. Aldwich will escort you to meet myself and members of Equility, then we work from there. We'll be seeing you soon."

The white noise goes silent, forcing words while itching at my ear, "Finally, that irritable screech is done with. Ugh, was annoying."

Hines sprouts a baffled expression but no words. Thinking I'm referring to his boss as annoying. Doesn't bother me. I stand, staring, waiting for him to make the next move. Hopefully mentioning food because I'm fresh out of fuel.

Broken, Hines asks, "Shall we proceed to the meeting?"
I take initiative, "No. It's been a while since I've eaten, so I'm getting food first."

Every fancy hotel has a buffet and that's exactly what I need. Stupid decisions don't tend to work well on an empty stomach. Hines doesn't know but my gourmet meals will be comped when I charge it to room "2812."

He suggests, "I do think we should make haste."
I mock him, "I do think we should not. Relax, I won't be long."

I leave. The crooks are on guard at the door; two left, two right. Sentries expected on arrival and unexpectedly underdressed. Left toward the elevator. The angry grouch is staring. Being around just makes me feel like pissing him off even more. Living under people's skin and in heads is comforting.

I smile, closed-mouthed in passing, "Looks like you're mine now, pumpkin."

I wink. Then face the elevator. That felt good. To maintain cool, I can't see damage dealt or I'll appear cautious; afraid of being attacked from behind. Paranoia isn't a tough quality. I reach and press the call button. As fast as it arrived earlier, shouldn't be too long. A heavy door closes. Distant. Someone must have gone into the room. Signaled by Hines? The elevator opens to a tired smiling bellman. Forced into existence despite a long day on the job. Hands at ease behind his outfit: burgundy slacks, white button-up shirt, burgundy vest, and burgundy midway cap a bit too big for his head. Tiny brim pulled low, meaning nothing since he's taller. Shiny gold buttons make his vest pop.

I ask, "Where's the buffet?"
"Third floor."

Out of reflex, my body shifts away as he boldly treks by. Rude behavior for an employee working at a place that uses gold doors. I push button "3". A cleared hallway aside from the bellman with eased hands now in front. Strange guy.

The elevator door closes. Stolen sight on a quiet descent. Taking a single step out into a stop. This isn't right. A much wider hallway than the other, lined with gold double doors. A sign above reads "Convention". Numbers above clarify arrival at the correct floor. Stupid bellman doesn't even know where the buffet is... Why is that? Hat unfit and purposefully low, practically shoving by, switching hands after crossing paths. A feeling that something's wrong checks my gut. I slap button "28".

Lowly whisper, "Dammit!"

The elevator can't make its way up fast enough, still much faster than stairs. Hiding his hands should've been an automatic red flag. And I ignored it. *Ping* sounds louder, overreacting to vigilance. A left corner shift as the door spreads. No one enters. My head spies the hall.

A body lies in the doorway I need. Unconscious? Dead? Obvious male but can't identify who since he's faced opposite me. I brace the wall, easing over in a tip-toe silence. Recognize the angry man's clothing. Halt at the door, maintaining concealment from the attacker. Facial confirmation.

Eyes slightly seeing and not blinking. Stiff, motionless, and deceased. Must've opened at first knock, assuming my immediate return. Struck as the bellman entered. Caught by surprise with a knife or pulse round to the abdomen. Clutching the wound before collapsing into fetal. Probably never took a second to ask or peep who was there. A careless action.

Four men are unaccounted for, and an armed killer disguised as a bellman. I peek into the room. Then quickly retract. Nobody fires. Not even a startled shuffle from who saw, deciding to flee. It's safe to enter. I cautiously investigate inside.

Driver is lying in a puddle of glass next to the small table; deceased. Pistol above his head and table upright. Must've been shot upon entry. Collapsed onto the glass, flipping, breaking and scattering on and around him. A second weapon could be in play for the bellman to have quickly shot them.

The body at the door has a pulser pistol. I take it and enter. My eyes catch two small burn markings near the immediate bathroom wall. Driver got two shots off in time after seeing his partner fall. Two inaccurate shots. I scan the area. Pistol ready. Kitchen doorway is clear. Only the retracted counter and partial emptiness. The jug I left behind is gone. The right double door and back office door are closed. I quickly pass into the kitchen, hoping to startle. Check for the bellman or Hines and two missing henchmen. Clear. I return to the entry. Three burn holes live in the office door's center. I push it open from the wall. No startled noise, no pulser fire. So in I go.

Another thief dead at the desk. Seems he was hit through the closed door. Heat rounds are too weak to singly penetrate anything unless it's against flesh. This assassin must be an amazing shot to pierce multiples like that, unless he pressed it against the door. At least three will punch wood this thick. Fourth henchman dead behind the door. Must've shut it when the front was stormed. Took a rapid-fire that killed them both?

Four bodies tallied, but no Hines or bellman. Doesn't appear to have been a tussle. As if he pierced the door and never entered. A goal-oriented invasion. It is possible the bellman saw Hines enter a different room, going straight for him after cornering the cowards. Last unchecked room should be the bedroom. I leave, taking a left and quickly forcing the door open. Check off boxes: bed, end tables, mirror wall, closed window with drapes down. Too high for an exit. No one's here. The bellman could've abducted Hines. Never exiting the only elevator, they could be using stairs. Is there time to cut them off? I flee the crime scene. Impatiently wait for the elevator to arrive; recently used. I rush inside and continually tap "L" until the door shuts. Pistol hidden behind my back, just in case. At the ping, I tuck it under my tank top and slip between the splitting door. Almost powerwalking. The lobby is fully occupied, but no one I need to see. Stairs shouldn't have gotten them far ahead. Descending one floor then taking the elevator is a different case. Someone will report the dead bodies and it won't be smart to get quarantined when Regs show up. I can camp in the cruiser, though. I exit to valet. Same attendant curbside.

I approach, "Sir?"
"Yes, how may I be of service?"
"Can you fetch my cruiser?"
"Yes certainly. Ticket?"
"Oh shoot, it's still in my husband's coat pocket. You're not gonna make me go all the way up there to get it are you? I just need to pick up his sleep aid."
He smiles, "That's not necessary ma'am, right away."

He jogs away. Then I casually search the surrounding area for anything fishy. Few patrons exit; none familiar and nothing irregular. No one being hauled through the street against their will. The valet arrives. I climb in with a *thank you* and pull away. Drive to the corner, U-turn and park. Not secluded but inconspicuous; holding hotel entrance view from a good, unnoticeable distance. Hoping my targets didn't escape, because if so, where do I begin pursuing? Damn. Hines had to have an incapable crew try to protect him. After failure one, he should've rented new or extra help. Without him, I don't know what's next, unless Equility decides to find me. Assuming they don't believe this was my doing. Who was that bellman?

Chapter 7: Finding Equility

After a half hour, fixated on the entry, sirens touch my ears. The rearview mirror tells me nothing. No red and blue flashers, only off-yellow headlights. None ahead. Wailing closes in. A Reg cruiser slinks from above and approaches the hotel. Blocking valet from civilian traffic. More converge from the other street. If Hines nor the bellman have come out by now, they won't for a very long while. I can't bank on Equility knowing how to find me. Still I have a million aers of their money, so I know they will make every effort. Right now, next stop is a decent meal.

I ignite the cruiser and tap my Econ, "GPS to the nearest restaurant."

The female voice alerts, "Searching... The nearest restaurant is located on Sopp and Flounder. Would you like directions?"

Already familiar with the cross streets, I tap my Econ and begin driving. It's not busy tonight. Social gatherings and formal balls don't often happen near the city center. It's mainly crowded during opening and closing business hours. I spot and rush into a restaurant, conveniently on the way. Order the first advertisement from a human server. Not much business here either. A speedy transaction. Food in hand, I add the bag of clothes. Ditch the cruiser. Take local transit back east as I nibble.

Regs will more than likely put an all-points bulletin on the vehicle; likely after me already for that rooftop chase. MechCi synchronize search parameters for wanted vehicles. Citizen data is overwhelming for MechCi, what with an entire carried personality. Too many lawbreakers, but only few cruisers; functions won't be tampered, and employment won't decline. If MechCi spot a suspicious cruiser, Regs would be notified and the vehicle would be tracked. Regardless of ownership, sitting abandoned for a couple of days would make it suspicious.

I board a busier trolley heading south. Many people ride, and I suppose *car*pool, choosing not to buy a cruiser for energy conservation. Traffic increases as the trolley nears an outer perimeter section. I depart. Going to the closest connecting manhole to underground; an alley between a couple of vacant shops. Not every manhole connects, as majority cater to sewage systems. Unfortunately, once this epidemic began, Gharis had to reroute lines around the Deserted's new home. I jerk the manhole open and dump my duffel. Clenching teeth on the plastic bag, I climb in and seal the manhole overhead. My feet pat the dirt. Silence and that familiar smell meet my senses. This manhole entry delivers a straight shot to the ground floor where Deserted roam aimlessly. Closer to where I live.

No one understands, making everyone afraid. I, on the other hand, don't care enough about anyone to be afraid. Initially arriving, I expected a fight to live here. The opposite happened. Deserted just zombie around me like they zombie around each other. Sometimes they get loud, but, unless direct contact is made, no harm will be done.

I don't think anyone is aware except me, which makes underground a perfect place for disappearing.

I sway the sheet to enter my shack. Drop the duffel bedside and sit. Strip my jacket and enjoy my meal, weighing different details for viable options. My face is all over cameras at Cravanaugh, so I'm number three on the apprehension list. Hines set at number two; Bellman set at one. I know nothing about the bellman. Not even appearing familiar from the recollective glance. I have a better chance of finding Equility. They don't know where to find me and, if suspected underground, won't come looking. I need to pass along word I'm searching, maybe drawing them out. They're attempting a fight against Menta-Life and I've got one name: Hines Aldwich. Literally, everything I can use. Getting enough weapons for the fight isn't as simple as it sounds. Needing to be built, stolen, or smuggled. Trex may have an idea where I can start.

After eating, I lie down and embrace a night's sleep. The next morning, my eyes rise to another day; same rusty patterned aluminum ceiling. I look around from the bed to make sure no Deserted wandered in. Coast is clear. I tap my Econ.

The female voice formally greets, "Good morning. What can I do for you?"
A groggy vocal advance, "Call Trex."
"Connecting…"

The Econ goes silent. These devices don't use dial tones like previous model phones. The receiver either answers or doesn't. Then caller is notified if it isn't answered or suddenly greeted by receiver.

Trex's request spits straight out, "Van, whatchya need?"
"I need help finding someone."
"Ya know how much information costs?"
"I know it's cheaper for your favorite smuggler."
"You not and it's not."
My voice welcomes aggravation, "I know the price."
"Then come by so we can chat."

I rid his voice for a while. Stretch lightly into my jacket and grab the bag of trash to-go. Halt outside my makeshift entry and take in immediate surroundings. Nothing new. I turn left. Cut through the maze of poorly constructed huts and tents.

Deserted murmurs flood endless loops of echoes. Nonsense voices over additional nonsense voices. Never once thinking Menta-Life could be responsible for this… loss. Hines made a good point; I'd vaguely recognized a literal few people from networks, billboards, and magazines, despite having torn out their hair or are clothed in old rags. Like spotting a known billionaire at a thrift shop. I can't assume Menta-Life affiliation, though feel Hines knows what he's talking about.

I navigate dark, dirt-walled tunnels to the southern exit. Sun beaming in my eyes on emergence from darkness. Should've checked what time it was. City lights are not active. Streets are empty. Did I sleep well? Can't tell. I ride public transit to Feegle's bakery. Enter to see him behind the counter chatting with his MechCi assistant.

I cruise by, "Hey, Feegle."

Feegle follows closely with a joyful attitude, "Vanessa, dear, tonight is a wonderful evening for a gathering, would you agree?"

First name basis? He wants something. It makes me feel bad to deny such a sweet man but there's aers to be made. He pays too, yet nowhere near as much as my current opportunity.

I trek the fancy ballroom toward the stairs, answering, "I don't really have time tonight. I have people I'm trying to find. Maybe next time."

Feegle begs, "Oh please, Vanessa. I have quite an esteemed guest-list this evening. A few of the best and brightest professors from medical institutes, high-end firm attorneys—"

I mildly whisper, "You know the law and I don't belong together."

Feegle didn't hear me, "—technology developers, Menta-Life representatives—"

I halt and quickly brace his shoulder, "Menta-Life?"

A proud answer, "Yes, the founding capitalists of our new civilization will be in attendance."

"I'll do it free if you introduce me."

"Absolutely, dear. I am not certain what un-pleasantries you have planned this day, nevertheless please return by six so we can doll ourselves up appropriately."

I speak, proceeding for the stairs, "I'm gonna use your shower."

I skip upstairs and hear him agree, "Okay, I'll be at the front end if you need anything."

I reach Feegle's bedroom. Admire his organizational skill thanks to intruding daylight from the opened balcony. Enter the bathroom and run the shower. Take my clothes, gloves, and Econ off. Step in without adjusting the temperature. Chilly, but I'm too focused to fix it. Cycling questions I don't have answers for. I gotta find out what Trex knows, so I scrub down and get out. A purple bruise on my shoulder attracts attention. No doubt, from the night before last over the parking garage. Absent pain but Feegle won't appreciate that later. I put my belongings back on and visit Trex's office.

Trex, eating at his desk, mentions, "I hear ya been I' into trouble."

I approach with a sluggish reply, "Well, you know me."

"Got anything to do with who you're lookin' for?"

"Equility."

He stops chewing and stares. An obvious sign that relevant information can surface. A hesitation dedicated to something we shouldn't be speaking about. He breaks eye contact and resumes chewing. I let him revel in silence, gathering whatever he's going to say.

Shaking his head, Trex swallows and refuses, "Uh, uh. You don't find Equility. And if you lucky, Equility don't find you."

"What do you mean?"

"Equility are terrorists. Been tryin' to destroy Menta-Life's Gharis operation for little over a year. Failed at every turn but there's big numbers on their side and only one'a you. Seen?"

"Any idea why they're after Menta-Life?"

"They get so much dirt thrown on them, it could be anything. Equility's an organized group. Reg chatter says they even have, like, a signature tattoo kinda brand to prove allegiance. Way in over their heads."

I speak out loud to myself, "So, they're terrorists."

"I'd say so. They claim to be revolutionaries. There was something big between them and Menta-Life recently, but it was completely covered up."

Doing their own dirty work, what do they need me for? Maybe more skilled bodies to pull off the job? Tired of piling failures, desperately reaching out. If Equility can shut down a prison, they can shut down Menta-Life right?

Trex continues, "As far as where to find them, no idea. Nor would I wanna know."

"Ever heard the name Hines Aldwich before?"

"Sounds familiar. Hang on a sec."

He faces the keyboard and types away. I fall into my brain, pacing back and forth. Finding Hines won't be an easy task. With my stroke of luck these days, what is? It's not like the bellman will just parade an abducted prize for the New World to see.

Trex swiftly recalls, "Oh yeah, this guy. One'a the executives at Menta-Life."

My surprise steals vocal control, "What?!"

My fingers drag across the holographic screen to activate a second. On the flipped neighboring screen is a picture of Hines Aldwich. Shaking hands with an older man at a podium and smiling at the crowd below. A ceremony? A promotion? It is Hines, but if he's a Menta-Life executive, why betray after climbing that ladder? An inside job *would* make things easier to accomplish Equility's goal. Is that why Hines was abducted? Does the assassin bellman work for Menta-Life? He has to.

Lower ranking members of Equility were killed. Hines, the important target, must have been taken to his bosses. If that's the case, who was the old millionaire?

I ask, "What did you hear about me?"

"Last night a crew was found dead at the Cravanaugh Hotel and you were spotted fleein' the scene. Regs are after questions and arrest for the night before too. Just made a clean IDN, twenty-four hours later, you already in the system."

"I can safely blame that rooftop incident on you." I recall mention of Equility members having special tattoos as brands, "Did you hear anything about who the bodies were? Any mention of Equility?"

"No, nothin' like that. You know media don't advertise murder. They keepin' that entire situation tight under wraps."

"Looks like I have to go see for myself."

I spin toward the door as Trex inquires with confusion, "To the morgue?"

"Yep."

I shut the office door and hit the streets. Take public transit to the east side. My destination is Clomy Morgue. Only morgue in Gharis and only somewhat guarded. Most people nowadays die of natural causes like old age or clumsiness, leaving it quite vacant. But a person's death is still to be kept private. Shame I have no consideration.

Reaching the morgue, I scope from across the street. Five stories high with pillars spaced and bracing the entry perimeter; a sort of roman architectural build and short by regulatory location standard. Compared to neighbors, I'd vote six stories below. An uninviting concrete gray color. Covered by more walls than windows. The front has a courtyard a few feet from the sidewalk. A small border wall, meaning no one can accidentally wander onto the fake lawn with valid excuse. Left face has another building, but the wall appears to continue around the grass. Patrolling, dark clothed security guards have pulser rifles relaxed. Two stationed by the main door and four milk the clock in the courtyard. No way I'm getting through there. A basement window to cremation can work. I circle the block to the right; two guards. The rear is just as covered. For a morgue, it's more fortified than my initial assumption; likely thanks to esteemed new arrivals. Left's more relaxed. Less foot traffic since it faces another building. No sign of a basement window. How can I get inside unnoticed? Cause a traffic accident? Break a window? Subtly plotting a distraction, one of two guards heads inside, using a single side door. With one remaining, skulking around the two decorative concrete squares as cover isn't an impossibility.

I cross toward the narrow alley. Soon as my feet touch grass, I kneel onto it. Out of the pedestrian path, pretending to tie my laceless boot. Idle long enough for civilians to overlook before crouching further toward the side opening. The square structures within are equal height to this perimeter wall; one left and right, standing a few feet high. At my low position, the guard appears from behind the left structure and casually disappears behind the next. I skulk in, taking cover at the far left end. Listen to faint trickles of water above. Not curious enough to peek for confirmation. The corner door doesn't have any keypad or card reader. Mine for opening. The guard's head bobs into view from behind the right structure. Before turning my way, I hurriedly shift to the left side. I should have tracked a pattern first, but the other guard may return soon, making it more difficult to enter undetected. If these rear guards weren't blandly sidewalk scanning, I'd be caught already. Hours of standing takes a toll. I scoot to the further end and peek. Two front entrance guards at their post, faced forward and socializing. Shift again? Hope my guard won't walk over here? I carefully peek above the corner at where I entered. The guard has stopped. Facing the side gap, looking left then right. Instead of waiting for the next move, I make a light dash for the closest pillar. Hide. No one firmly states or shouts stopping orders. I peek again. The guard is still halted in the same spot. I enter and quietly shut the door behind me.

The second guard is in front of me. A young man. Medium build. Cute and appropriately anxious. He grips my jacket with one hand. I swipe it away and introduce my head to his face, staggering him a few backward steps through the small hallway. My hands catch his shirt and swing us at a nearby closed door. On contact, the door bursts open, spilling us into a small storage closet. My back pounds against the wall. I duck low as he throws a cross swing and accepts a harsh stomach strike. Freeing a gasp and hunching from loss of breath. I twist momentum and smash a fist into his face. He collapses behind the door, forming close cornered acquaintance. Unconscious, for now. Changing this to a timed event of finding dead bodies before he wakes. I ease out of the storage room. Shut the door, providing a darkened sleeping environment. Follow short hallways, making the only available right turn then left. Reach an abrupt end with a left and right.

A digital sign appears above that reads: "Check-In" with an arrow pointing right; below that reads: "Elevators" with an arrow pointing left. Check-In will be the main lobby area. I cut left to elevators, pacing with purpose and not looking back. Inconspicuous. Expressed authority by pretending I belong. Out of uniform? A door left of the elevator conceals a stairway, stated obviously by signage. I glance over my shoulder. Two guards are conversing at reception. A rugged blonde male and brunette female. Helping me remain unnoticed by not facing my direction. Wondering what doesn't belong. Arrows point up and down. I press "up". The higher arrow shines green, and sounds. I check again. Both guards drawn my way. Eyes collide momentarily during my turn away. One unwelcome moment too long.

The female guard sternly yells, "Hey! Excuse me! I need to see your credentials!"

I ignore her demand. Wait for the incoming elevator. What's taking so long? Small moments seem like a lifetime when someone has a pulser at my back. Stairs aren't seeming like such a terrible route. Guards aim and expel shock pulses. I pass through the stairway door. Hold it slightly open while continuing to wait. Targetless, they cease fire. The elevator door opens.

Guards' feet beat rapidly on tile as the same female notifies, "We have an intruder in the building! Female, green jacket, west stairway!"

I bolt into the elevator and take cover as the male guard loudly updates, "She's out!"

They shoot inside carelessly. There's a list of buttons from five to one then "B" for basement. I press "4" and "5". The elevator seals a slit. Banging hands of fury fade as I advance. A sharp ascent of about thirty seconds. I don't know where I'm going, spitting in the wind and dreading a shift. Finding out won't be a problem when I can lie low for a second to gather bearings. Each floor should have a directory. I'll search for one on the fourth while guards search the fifth.

The elevator opens. I tap "door close" to hasten the process during my exit. Another hallway. Immediate right door leads to stairs and two more on each side before a left turn. Past the turn is a replica with a huge dead-end window; sun shining brightly. Clomy Morgue seems very understaffed. Then again, deaths aren't in great quantity nowadays. Plenty of vacancies. I jog to the hall's center.

A C-shaped reception area lives at the front-left corner, fitted with basics: Computer, a chair babysitting, and neatly placed page files. The holographic monitor is screensaving, marketing Clomy's company logo and confirming zero floor presence. I swipe a finger across the touchpad to awaken the home screen. Open document files and filter recently accessed. The newest shared section folder contains four files. Each labeled by last name, preceding first. Within each file, a description and corresponding image. This bundle may be what I'm looking for. I slide fingers across the screen to spawn the second holographic. Occupy it with another picture. Two accounted, and I'll assume the rest are. Bottom right corner has a note that reads: "Screening Level 2". Profile wording contains no mention of tattoos. Pictures should at least be present for affiliate relevance. Jeez. How hard can making my job easier be?

A crash causes distraction. Someone just swung the stairway door. I hurriedly scroll different files, searching one with any level besides two. This entry for a dead woman in the basement couldn't be a more perfect distraction. I abandon reception. The nearest door reveals a typical office. Feeling I've been in more of these in the past couple days than in my entire life. My ear braces the wooden door, listening to what's happening outside.

A commanding guard demands, "Check down that way. You secure this corridor."

Another guard calls out, "Take a look at this. An opened autopsy file for one deceased female. Currently awaiting cremation."

The commanding guard concludes, "The intruder could have gotten around us. I want you four to secure this floor, every room, guard the two exit doors and elevator. We need to box her in. You three with me; we're heading to the basement. East stairwell has been cleared and sealed from use."

Footsteps quickly putter away. I move from the door. Circle the desk and inhabit the computer chair. A sigh to relax. One slow spin for entertainment. Four guards are half convinced that I'm not on this floor. Another four, plus backup, will converge in the basement. I need to reach the second floor fast and examine the bodies.

Fourth floor guards are muffling through the corridor. Loud bangs resume from doors being kicked in. No way forward without a fight so might as well prepare. I stand and stretch. Feeling fantastic, like waking from a nap. Initiate a stand-off versus the door. Banging grows louder and louder as guards draw nearer and nearer. A shadow darkens the gap underneath my door; set of heard but not seen feet huddle close. Surrounded by others staggering in place. I slide my right foot back and lean forward.

A guard blunders in, having used his shoulder to bash. What they don't know as their final bang ignites my charge forward. After a second step, I hop and whip a swift kick. Unkindly meet his head. Another guard outside wields a stun baton. Late at realizing it was a mistake to search overconfidently. I ram her stomach and crash at the wall. Slip behind her woozy body and grab her wrist, stealing baton control with a violent tango. My free arm wraps her neck. I manipulate the baton, whipping it at the final approaching guard. Cracking his shoulder. Body stiffens and immediately drops. An elbow to the back finishes off my hostage. A fourth guard is meant to be present; I've only taken three. The last must be waiting to surprise. Waiting is an option, although whoever it is may have contacted backup. I pace toward the same stairway and enter. Unaware of commotion that took place, guard four is staring down in a bored slouch. The opening door and silence draw notice. His face transforms from simple to surprised. I deliver a thrusting kick. His body bounces off the wall, tumbling wildly downstairs. I follow, descending zig-zagged flights to floor two. Then stealthily enter.

Back toward me, a single guard slowly trawls the hall. Blonde bun horribly done, boot laces loose, one pocketed hand and one frontal; real chill vibe. I quietly close the door. Hear only an extremely minor click. Then approach for a fast takedown, not knowing how many other people are working this floor. Close enough to execute an attack, her body tics. Sensing an unknown presence?

My first reaction: duck. Her unseen arm swings around, granting last second notice of a low-leveled stun baton. I fall backward to avoid it. Roll up to my feet and regain posture. She's charging forward with the baton posed near, ready to strike. Controlled range with stiff stopping power. A veteran of the craft. I swiftly, yet cautiously, dodge electrifying touches by reversing a step during each advance. Attempting a rib shot, her arm retracts for a heavy thrust; a one-blow finisher. I spin, allowing the baton space to slide past, and throw an elbow up. Bash her down onto her chest and cause a fumble. A useless opportunity without a glove but certainly preventing another swing-a-thon. Scurrying toward it, I rush to a bend and clutch her ankle, reeling with planted stature. Her palms crazily smacking tiles to pull forward. I respond by pulling excessively harder, finding it an easy task. Her hands release and allow me to yank, rotating and swiping a kick across my face. Knocking me into a slight stumble, yet not enough to free herself. She grabs my jacket, twists her captured leg inward, slides it across my neck, and strains me into it. Underestimated choking technique. I unclench and dreadfully try pushing away to no avail. Air is no longer reaching my brain. My body weakens. Numbing from neck down. Feeling myself blacking out. I tilt back almost a solid inch. Wiggle fingers in-between her leg and my neck and push outward for minor breathing room. Inhaling a forced gasp, barely restoring drowsy senses. Her same leg slides out and strikes. A forceless calf pushing me into a roll near a door.

For an average guard, she has unexpected skill. I've never met a New World citizen mentally or physically equipped to deal with animals like me; somehow, seeming more than capable. Why hasn't a call for backup been placed? Why is she alone? I stand and face the guard for another round.

A sharp exhalation exits my lips like a gut punch, but worse. Taking recently siphoned air. She lifts and rams us through the nearby door. Slams my back onto a desk. My arms snuggle her to strip a pin advantage and she struggles passionately to escape the constricting hold but won't. I breathe steadily. Recuperating. She plants both forearms and drops weight; a position that states a want to pick me up again. Soon as the lift initiates, I release her into an accidental stumble and fall. Roll backward off the desk, observing her hasty rise and dashing return. Anger and humiliation have manifested. No swerve around the desk but a leap straight over. Tunneled vision of fury. This will be a fast end. She dives. I draw the smaller top drawer and swing at her head. Off with timing, bashing a shoulder just as her body crashes onto mine. Delaying my assumed victory. We fall into a filing cabinet. Then onto the floor. I repeat the failed tactic. Quickly rip a bigger drawer from captivity, palm the width, and successfully bash. Impact flips her body off, and it doesn't move. Fully reclined, I catch my breath in deep huffs. Watch her chest heave for proof of life. That was intense.

Who is this woman? Maybe a squad captain? Well… what squad? She's nothing like average security I'd ever seen anywhere. Too young to be ex-military. Regardless, it's a bad idea to stay here. Despite having dead bodies to find, a nap behind this desk sounds wonderful. I limp out of the small office. Cautiously check surroundings. There are a few differences from the hallway upstairs, and one mattering most is the centered double door. Next to them, a small plaque that reads: "Examination." I enter the swaying black doors.

Two rows of four tables with white body-formed sheets occupy the room. Sharp pointed duos at the end of each silver table are obviously feet. All facing my direction. I scan everything else: bright lights, small chrome tables holding up surgical tools, big chrome tables holding up corpses. X-rays and color photos litter walls, showing points of interest. Like tattoos? I approach the closest table and drag the sheet down slightly. This man doesn't look familiar. The table left of it is next until I notice sharpened feet. Doesn't take unwrapping to tell it's a woman. Upper left corner is next. I pull the sheet. It's the driver. Pale, like he's been in a freezer. I step to the nearby table and examine hanging colored photos. Burn entry wounds from the pulser pistol that took his life, but no tattoo.

Maybe I underestimated lethal worth of heat pulses. To avoid shock pulses from knocking someone out, criminals can wear a lot more clothing. Sort of deflecting. Heat pulses come in handy to puncture and immobilize a smart thinker.

Of all photos, one is missing from the collective bunch. A blank space surrounded by stilled life. No sign of the tattoo Trex mentioned. Back at the body, I pull the sheet completely off. Stripped except for a pair of white briefs. A wavy black smear stains his hairy chest. Beside his stopped heart. Morgue attending must be dirty business. On to the next body, revealing the angry man. Pictures are pasted nearby above his skull. Entry wound, and a blank space standing out just like the last. A second missing photo? I fully slip the sheet. Same briefs. And same smear on his right chest; thinking clearer, they resemble more of an ink stain than sludge or grime. Washable tattoo ink? I rapidly approach between two other tables. Rip sheets off, one at a time. Same ink stains on the other bodies and in the same place. Whatever tattoos were there are somehow gone. Both blank photo spaces are present. Too strange to be coincidence. Who would erase these? *How* could anyone erase these?

False tattoos tell a story. These thieves successfully tricked me into thinking they were Equility. Why pretend? I shove the angry man's body off the table and sit down. Posing as Equility doesn't make sense. Why not come clean? I had never heard of Equility until last night. And still don't care about either faction's motives or intentions. Someone went through great lengths to fool me; even shelled out a million aers in the matter of a minute. Menta-Life and Equility are the only true suspects in this game. None answering who these men are in relation to the missing link but narrowing. Hines works for Menta-Life and his four henchmen are dead; maybe the bellman is actually Equility? Opening many more questions, I've moved nowhere closer to a definite truth. I push myself off the table, catching eye of a black smudge where my hand was. Did that come from me? I quickly inspect both hands. Ink is being patronizing from my right; still fresh to leave a mark. Fresh on a dead man's chest… Recently erased? One person was on this floor when I got here and she's unconscious in the office. Did she do this? Why erase the ink? Why steal pictures? She's covering up evidence!

I rush out of Examination to where I left the strangely trained fighter. Undeniably appointing affiliation. She's gone. Another blank space where something should be but isn't; another link to possibly locating Equility slid from underneath. Dressed as a guard and not baring my hair color, she could be anywhere. It's too late for her. Profiles on those thieves might shed more light on their legal citizenship and illegal reputation, sharing what kind of company the corporation keeps and what Clomy chooses not to log. Each examination table has an individual drive providing information on corresponding patients. I can access and safely look them over at Trex's hideout. More back and forth, I snatch a small storage drive from each of the four tables. Return to the hallway. Dash toward the elevator until the ping rings. I stop dead in my tracks and watch.

The door splits to three hastily exiting guards, "There she is!"

Two run toward me while the final stays sheltered, alerting others through earpiece, "Intruder located on the second floor! All units! Second floor!"

For any chance of a successful escape, I must take these guards. The first charges like she plans to ram me down, prepared to pin for an arrest. She lowers and spreads arms for the tackle. An attack with uncountable flaws. Dangerously close, I swiftly shift sideways and leave a foot firmly planted. Our calves touch. I shove her past, an expenses-paid trip and crash. The second approaches with a heavy swing. I steal control and flip him over my shoulder. Aching from hardened tile, he grabs at his lower back and squirms. Last enemy is on the slow approach. Confident, eyes drifting behind me. The first guard returns for an encore performance. Arms tightly wrapping from behind. An arrest tactic that I happily take advantage of. The last guard approaches faster to overwhelm odds. I force him away with a stiff dropkick to the chest. The holding guard loses balance and stumbles backward. Meeting the floor, I roll away and ready up to defend an oncoming attack from the final guard.

The elevator sounds again. More guards? It splits open. Two BAMechs are idle inside, title shortened for Battle Assault Mechanics. An extremely bad sign and a reinforcement I didn't consider at some local security firm's disposal. Built for ground combat situations, these mechs are essentially impossible to defeat without extensive damage or wire removal. Created in human form like MechCi except bulkier and in a silver color. Weapons only stun-capable, like batons; shock pulse rounds with additional jolt and rapid fire. Dangerous, relentless hunters.

BAMechs dart out. Unflinchingly spark shock rounds anywhere on path to accurately targeting me. I seek cover out of sight from the blue barrage. The two guards get a horrible shower, seizing violently before plopping at the floor. I slide into cover opposite Examination. Rounds cease so I steal a peek. Floored guards lightly twitch. Did they think it would be safe? BAMechs don't apply similar targeting system restrictions as an H-T70 when it comes to Regulators or security officers. Suppressive fire resumes. I quickly hide. Rounds peck the wall ahead and near my back in large quantity. Poofs of dust and paint chips trickle off. Where can I go? Too fantastic of a job is being done at blocking remaining exits. Even if the opposite stairwell wasn't sealed, I'll be mowed down without a first thought. Hiding will just delay the inevitable. Window? A second-floor drop shouldn't be more than thirty to forty feet from this ceiling. Survivable height which I've bested on many prior occasions. Black doors behind, I sprint straight toward another dead-end. Mechs hook the corner in sync, sprinting even faster than me and blasting recklessly. I shift side to side. Rounds are flying past, puncturing the window yet not shattering. I pounce and tuck through fractured glass into the sunlit afternoon.

Wind beats against my soar, almost comforting the descent onto traffic. Knees bent in preparation for a crash landing on concrete. Fearless and relentless, BAMechs heroically leap after in pursuit; one shoulders through a portion of wall since it couldn't patiently be two seconds later. Below, civilian cruisers obey the speed limit at a repetitive rate. I miss a cruiser's roof by a fraction of a second, landing poorly angled on the rear windshield. My back smacks the trunk before the rest of me tumbles onto smooth pavement. Another cruiser is zooming and honking in rapid spurts. I roll away, seeking safety between two rival traffic lanes and hearing a loud crash that attracts my sight in a jerk. A brown cruiser barrels into the next lane and a BAMech has slid into its place; it came down hard enough to knock the parked vehicle over with a shoulder bump. The other BAMech lands on a cruiser's hood, disabling it to a gradual and smoking halt. A blue one crashes behind, still the mech doesn't get forced off by impact. They observe me. Not sidetracked by the traffic jam or bodily harm caused. Conveniently, both lanes are halted. No moving cover or obstacles. Was this a tactical intention…?

BAMechs suddenly pursue, firing shock rounds in a more focused quality over quantity ratio. I flee north then west around Clomy, staying behind cruisers for cover while moving forward. Evasion doesn't look good. I'm running as fast as my body will allow. Eventually I'll get tired, already feeling my lungs give more than receive. BAMechs won't. I can't lose them in all this open space. An office building is ahead to the left. I cut between cruisers, causing a halt and almost getting hit. A mech lunges from behind a different cruiser, aiming for a tackle, and smashes into the vehicle. I mount the sidewalk, skip up eight steps, enter the closing glass door.

The office building's lobby is big. Pristine black granite flooring and walls. Lighting and massive windows keeping everything lit. Granite reception counter along the back wall and a hallway on the right leading to multiple ways upstairs. I dash through the busy lobby and past reception.

The receptionist panics, "Hey, you can't go through there!"

Breaking glass echoes from the entry. A huge pane taken out. Knowing what it is, I don't bother checking. An elevator is about to close with a small group inside. I quickly slip in, bumping at them like a bowling ball versus pins. They brace me from collision. Kind citizens, like all others.

I hunch low, head high, and catch my breath, "Sorry… don't wanna… be late… again–"

A bang briefly shakes the metal box, startling me into a defensive brace for a losing battle. Lights flicker. Everyone, dressed in suits and power skirts, release dreaded gasps. Silence on both fronts. The elevator ascends toward upper floors. Occupants are confused yet relieved to be moving. BAMechs wouldn't dare wait, and will likely win a race to any floor I exit. Buttons for nine and ten are highlighted. Maybe tapping eight just as we're on approach, we'll stop while mechs proceed further. Earn a chance to breathe and hide. The number counter changes from six to seven. I highlight circle "8F", decelerating to a stop. Not abrupt but regular. The door splits only a crack, jamming when a BAMech's arm punctures and snatches my jacket. Riders retract to corners and puke horrified screams. I try bashing the mech's forearm with mine. Bone versus steel. Successfully failing and quitting once aches set on my third attempt. Its free hand forces the door open, and lifts me out, extending my height. Lost to gravity.

I thrust a boot to its head. Then again; recoiling a tiniest bit after each strike. A second fail. The mech pitches me into office territory. I hit industrial-quality carpet, uncontrollably bouncing off shoulders for a couple of seconds and crashing into the side of a cubicle. A small hole in the mech's palm fires two focused rounds. I scramble to my feet and quickly get lost in a maze of workstations, worming around in a semi-crouched position. The BAMech makes a ruckus, wanting to keep up without hurting frantically retreating civilians. Some frozen in place, cowering in cubicles.

Noise stops and so do I. Employees' cries dwindle to small huffs. Winded from terror. Sudden change in volume has me curious, shaking from an urge to move and knowing better than to. What's going on? I park against a cubicle wall, visually perusing, trying to see through each foggy cubicle window. The mech is likely calculating other hunting methods. Maybe sound? Since it's quiet, remaining still is my best bet until an alternative comes in play.

Shortly, impatience invites a smart idea and an excuse: Regulators. I take a final look. Then a small step. A BAMech bursts through a cubicle and shoves me through another. The heavy chest press hurts more than cheap drywall and imitation glass against my back. I tumble a single roll on carpet again. The mech sweeps remaining pieces of barely standing cubicle in a calmed storm. Stretched to grasp with one hand. My leg braces its arm away, driving myself back a few feet. It returns with the other and straight shots me toward the elevator. Forearms protecting my head, I soar over the glass of two cubicles and settle hard on a desk inside a third. Startled into action by the second BAMech appearing at my feet, I grab it and swing around behind before it can grab me. The twin is in the same spot, left palm aimed at my back and zero hesitance lighting an insignificant spark. I let go and splash on my torso. Deafening sounds of fried circuits overwhelms; popping, popping, and popping in fast intervals. Side note: Electrical device combined with an electric round causes twitching and sparking. One down. A human would spend a second of guilt shooting an ally but the mech just locks onto me. Closely tracking my dash from the floor's opposite end and shooting shock rounds during every passing chance. These machines are smart; however, their judgments are based on prediction. I'm predictable... to an insanely low degree. The tall rectangular window ahead leads to the great domed indoors. A neighbored window ends both walkways symmetrically. I swipe small equipment out of a disgruntled employee's hands. Light enough to not slow down, heavy enough to break the pane. I close on the window at full speed. Pitch the device and bash the glass. A prediction wirelessly sent. I stop by ramming my shoulder into the wall, only inches from the window. Glass shatters elsewhere at the exact moment. Flush as if I had done it. I watch the mech sink. A tin can in flight. It shoots rounds into my window and forces a reactive shift from the desperate attempt. I hear a crash below. Spectating damage won't do any good.

Many close calls these past couple days have become discomforting. BAMechs are the only ground assault mechs at Regs disposal. Not to mention, putting up the best fights. Accuracy and speed make them impossible for average criminals to face and win. With incredible stamina or wit, evasion is an option. I've managed to best two and am proud of it.

Chapter 8: Socialite Ball

I check my pocket. Examine the four drives to make certain they hadn't been badly damaged. Appears perfectly intact despite roughhousing that'd transpired. I should leave. Since BAMechs are down, what happens next? Reg battalion? Additional BAMechs? An Alpha? Sticking around to confirm won't be smart. Drives return to the pocket safe and I jog to the elevator. The static BAMech has darkened from overload and collapsed. No flame breakout. Hidden at a distance, workers watch me. Stunned and afraid. I casually leave. Board next to the broken elevator and tap "P". Ride alone, in silence to parking. Pick up momentum by jogging to find something not so new. Or easy to steal and difficult to track.

A white lectrocycle is parked between two cruisers. Screaming to be stolen. Essentially, a motorcycle minus the engine. Powered by battery, hence lectro. One of the only vehicles still operating on wheels and the only one operating on two. I mount and glance over the right side.

Force open the small circuit panel. Disconnect tracking and connect "alarm" to "ignition port". Kick the pedal, activating a fully charged battery instead of the security system.

Outside, chaos reigns silent. Reg cruisers and foot patrols slowly canvas the area. I take side streets and alleys for a few blocks. Then main roads toward Feegle's shop for a findings overview. Heavy traffic soon transitions to light. Lectrocycles can't enter high gravity; obviously carrying an increased risk of death from a heightened fall, in event a sudden stop progresses into a deadly collision. On arrival, I veer into the alley around the bakery's left face and tap my Econ.

The female voice greets, "Good afterno–"
I interrupt, "Call Feegle."
"Connecting…"
Feegle greets cordially, "Greetings and salutations, Miss Pheros. Please tell me this call is regarding your attendance for tonight's gathering?"

I had completely forgotten about it. Another unnecessary distraction, yet it's not often I get to do a favor for an actual friend… And then there's Menta-Life.

I answer, "I'm here now. Open your garage."
Feegle excitedly approves, "Yes, right away! We have our work cut out for us!"

He's not mistaken about that. I end the call. The garage door begins opening upward. I enter and park in the blank space. Feegle doesn't own a vehicle. This is more of a loading dock than parking spot.

Feegle enters with an overjoyed greeting, "Dear girl, chop, chop! Let–"

He notices dirt and bruising as I approach. The disappointed look is actually quite amusing, but I kind of feel bad that he's got much more of a workload now. Despite only being cosmetic, Feegle takes appearance extremely seriously. I halt with a linger of sympathy expressed.

He examines, speaking with disappointment, "Why must you *always* make my joyous fashion obsession such a difficult task to accomplish?"
"I had a lot of running around to do."
He comments in a tiresome tone, shaking his head, "Evidently… Well, come on then."

He escorts us inside. I'm ready to look the gathered drives over, but Feegle usually takes a while masking me for a party, not arriving pre-coated; therefore, I won't let impatience make him wait. If there is any time beforehand, I'll peek at what I found and try piecing this mystery together. We head through the mint clean ballroom and upstairs to Feegle's bedroom.

He demands, "Okay, darling, you disrobe from those distressed garments and commence with a shower."
I make a joke, "And here I thought you were better than that. At the very least, I'd expect a burger first. Heck, not even cheese—"
He sarcastically interrupts, "Very comical, Miss Pheros; however, we've no time for games at the moment."
I sigh at his seriousness, "Yes, Feegle."

I close the bathroom door. Take my clothes off and start the shower. Look over purple and red arm discoloration, racing to my shoulders. Turn my back toward the mirror to examine more bruising. There's one bruise underneath my left eye and a small cut on my left cheek that has a little dried blood surrounding. The bathroom begins to fog. Hot water. A shower I have to marinade in and enjoy. I enter the waterfall before my skin clams.
Feegle takes parties and presentations extremely seriously. Everything must be a form above perfection for guests or else he feels becoming a laughingstock won't be far. High-class citizens aren't the

quietest; they gossip. Spread every piece of news, hoping to be acknowledged as creator. Make themselves relevant by tarnishing others. Spot a crooked painting, everyone in attendance will know in a matter of minutes. Social gatherings earn Feegle a lot of important business and catering jobs, but, oddly enough, that's not why he does it. He likes being a public figure. On tips of tongues. A destination that somebodies can think of to take a load off. Which they mostly do. Popularity and trendsetting, with colorfully weird clothing, is what he lives for. Take status away and he wouldn't know how to survive.

After the steaming heat, hair wash, and scrub down, I turn off the shower. Tightly wrap a towel. In the bedroom, Feegle is delicately laying an elegant dress bedside. A bright royal blue, bare-shoulder dress. Slim-fit from the waist up and room for long strides from the waist down. I hate dresses. I approach the bed. Sit next to what I'm assuming is mine to wear tonight.

Feegle hands over a possible compliment without looking, "I believe that you will look divine in this gown for the evening."

I twist and examine the product as if I previously hadn't, attempting to see what he sees, "As long as you think so."

Feegle gazes over at me. Ceases fiddling with expensive fabric. Appearance of sadness and concern smeared as he lightly inspects my injuries.

He gloomily inquires, "Do you need rest, darling?"
I display a falsely high contentment to lighten the mood, "No, I'm fine, Feegle. Really."
He sighs, "If only your father could see you now."

My head dunks. He's not referring to my birth father, but the man who took care of me on the shuttle and after. He and Feegle were acquaintances for a very short time post-war, when this city was initially a refugee camp. After finally remeeting Feegle, many years later, anytime I ran away from foster homes and other places with rules, I was here.

Feegle asks, "Why do you do this to yourself?"
"Money."
"You can be so much more if you wanted."
"I don't fit into your little famed society. We've been over this before."
"I just want what's best for you, my dear."
"Trust me, so do I."

Although I don't know what's best for me yet, one thing I am certain about is that *this* isn't it. I'm not meant to live like a queen amongst the rest of these high-class snobs. I'd be a jester in their court.

I change the subject and tone, knowing the answer to my question, "So, do we start makeup first, or do I throw on the gown?"

His throat clears, responding in mild surprise, "No throwing will be necessary, your gown goes on from the bottom up. Makeup is where we begin. I will fetch some patch for the scratch on your cheek."

He steps into the bathroom, opens the medicine cabinet, and grabs a small tube of Patch. Returning as I tilt my head down and slightly right. He rests the nozzle at the cut's tail and gently follows, applying gel. Then retracts the nozzle. Painless, especially because it's a minor slit and not meant to heal.

He kindly demands, "Now rub."

I begin applying. Feegle tends to the vanity desk, organizing instruments to make me beautiful. Patch is a protectant against forms of chemicals and bacteria encountering an open wound. Like spreading a coat of wax on a wall; someone can deface, but once dressed, protectant remains. Patch isn't as effective as wax, but no makeup will contaminate my wound. I approach and occupy the chair in front of the makeup desk. Feegle's still gathering supplies. Doesn't boost feelings of confidence that he needs so much stuff.

He slides out a small drawer and grabs a small box full of small makeup brushes, "Now, we'll take you from beautiful to gorgeous."

Feegle applies things to my face. I easily distract myself from paying further attention. Unable to resist thinking about Equility and Menta-Life. Hines Aldwich succeeded at making Menta-Life look like bad guys. A big corporation having the power to make people go insane by directly damaging their brains. Makes total sense. Hines also managed a play of deception. In either case, finding out who the thieves worked for wouldn't solve anything; it would lead to bigger questions about affiliation, tying all to which side the bellman is on. If the thieves were neither Menta-Life or Equility, could there be a third organization? Pitting two against each other through me.

As far as I understand, Hines' men tried to steal a package from Menta-Life, posing as Equility to reel me in. A mystery bellman killed the four henchmen and abducted Hines, who confirmed works for Menta-Life. Now I've got records on four dead goons. I need to know if Menta-Life would go as far as to kill their own or if the thieves were part of any other rival faction trying for a piece.

Feegle breaks my trance, "Done."

Without realizing, I've been sitting for almost an hour and have a different face. The official British woman I should have been raised to become. Blue eyeshadow circling my eyes. A dark line edging both, straying toward my temples. Light pink lipstick. A faint blush on my cheeks. Short hair in a false, well-constructed bun. If I wasn't a snob before, I am now. Makeup is also coated over visible shoulder bruises, flush with my skin. The only variation I can appreciate.

Feegle speaks, adjusting his evening attire, "Guests should have already begun to arrive, so *carefully* put your gown on and I will await your presence near the foot of the stairs."

I rise, holding the towel up. Legs, seated for so long, have lost feeling. Feegle exits the room. A rest would be nice, but I can't let him down. Plus, my ulterior motive must be addressed. What better night? I lean against the vanity table until my legs feel strong enough to walk straight again. Recovered, I enter the closet. Inside is huge; more than twice the neighboring bathroom size in length. I begin searching drawers for underwear. The dress is strapless, so no need for a bra. A pair of simple black underwear catch my eye, replacing the bra with a bandeau. These will do fine. I practice my saunter to and carefully pick up the gown by the shoulders, or, technically, bicep since that's where crop placement is. Raise my hands above eye level. Examine with mild disgust. It drapes all the way to my feet and slightly longer in back. Having worn similar garments for Feegle before, I wonder why familiarity never sticks. I ease the gown low, forming a neat puddle of blue. Put both feet through as I raise higher. Insert each arm into a partial sleeve. Pull the torso portion over my breasts as high as it's meant to go.

No shoes or accessories laid out? Knowing Feegle's fashion preference, he would not want my face shown without wrist, ear, or neck jewelry. Not my ideal type of search but I need accessories. A set of diamond studded earrings and a diamond necklace hide in the vanity desk drawer. A pair of blue heels in the closet match my gown's tone, in plain sight like he planned to place them and forgot. I finalize ingredients of the formal ensemble. Then check my mirrored self. Being positive for Feegle's sake, I can honestly vote a fitting look. If I'm wrong, I'll be regretfully rejected as if he doesn't know me. Time to go mingle with Menta-Life... and whoever else may be equally important. I open the door.

Soft classical music leaks in. Calm guest voices are louder than the instrumental tune. The ballroom is already packed with colorful citizens socializing in groups of four or more. Glancing down, prying eyes from entire groups break off to observe my graceful saunter. Curious and locked on tight. While holding the handrail with one hand and pinching the skirt above my shoes with the other, I leisurely descend half-spiral stairs. All eyes become magnets in amazement to my metal. Unaware of the criminal underneath. Feegle is at the base with two guests. Hand placed out, positioned like a statue should be stationed for presentation. Or a food tray. My hand rests over as I drift the remaining two steps. Then hook my arm around his. Extra inches from these heels make Feegle about a foot shorter. Our arms must be momentarily uncomfortable until conversation sparks. The party resumes as we stroll between many guests. Everyone greets Feegle in this initial passing.

He whispers to me, "I completely overlooked the accessories."
I whisper back, "Yeah, ya did. Where are the Menta-Life executives?"
Confidence spouts, "It seems they are tardy for the moment; nevertheless, no worries. They will be in attendance."
"What makes you so sure?"
"Simply because a verified representative said they would be. I double-checked."
"Well they'd better show. I'd hate to feel like I've done this for nothing."
"Let us converse with some of the many distinguished guests until they do arrive, shall we?"
"We shall."

Feegle guides us to meet some big shot owners and company representatives from this and other cities. I have nothing in common with them, or even Feegle, so I stand in his short shadow. Fake smile planted firmly under my nose. After meeting and chatting four uninterestingly notable groups, Feegle heads toward a man standing with a fellow associate and two others. The middle-aged black man, obviously someone of classical significance by choice of suit over robe and lead in a one-sided conversation, notices us. Sways a couple of quick words to the underdressed men in front of him. Informally, they part ways. That's not suspicious at all. The man and his young Caucasian associate face us.

The older man greets, "Good evening, Mr. Tolen."
Feegle returns more formally, "Good evening to you, Mr. McKoy. How are you?"
Mr. McKoy turns to me and answers, "I'm well, thank you. And who is this lovely young lady?"
"This is my dear friend Vanessa Pheros."

My hand slides out, palm down, with his greeting, "Ms. Pheros…"

His hand swoops under mine. A light hover into a controlling touch and lean with an even lighter kiss. An experienced hand kisser. Best I've had tonight.

Mr. McKoy continues, "Delighted to meet you."
I paste a half-smile, "Likewise Mr. McKoy."
Hands gravitating away like lost love, Mr. McKoy requests, "Please, call me Geilium. And behind me is my assistant, Mitchell."
Mitchell and I exchange delicate business shakes as I state, "Evening, pleasure to meet you."
Mitchell replies, "The pleasure is mine."

A soft voice. Sounds younger than he looks. The glasses and carried portfolio, no doubt for Geilium, make him assistant material. Less than enchanting greeting announces an unaspiring standing.

Feegle instigates a brief bio, "Mr. McKoy is founder of the biggest publishing association in Gharis City."
I take direct interest for the art of subtle blend, "What is it you publish, Mr. Geilium?"
He smiles, "I approve stories for the news, essentially. My company decides what's worthy for citizens to view on networks."
"A very demanding career."
"Indeed, nevertheless it is a big company with a large staff. The workload is nothing we can't handle. And what is it you do, Ms. Vanessa?"

Little bit of transport for a man who runs an illegal smuggling ring under this very bakery where wealthy citizens come to socialize.

Feegle quickly lies, "She is a fashion model."

Smart of him to chime. I wasn't sure what answer to give. Most guests take interest in the host while I remain invisible and somehow eye candy simultaneously.

Feegle changes subjects, another smart move before my absent popularity becomes topic, "So Mr. McKoy, are there any upcoming projects in motion that we can get an inside scoop on?"

"Nothing of boundless importance, without breaching privacy desires. We're expecting an exclusive from a source outside Gharis City, still even we can't confirm until an update arrives. A certain clothing company may be going under."

Feegle inhales, "Oh no, that's terrible. Why would you grace me with such news? You know fashion is my avenue."

Geilium and Feegle share a chuckle. That's exclusive? Mild sounds of excitement carry from the main entry. Our attentions drift. Nobody jumping for joy, only raised voices and a camera crew taking many photos. Why is there a camera crew here? Smaller groups gather into a wide outer ring, keeping healthy distance. I catch glimpse of a few entering faces. Receiving full attention is a gray suited elderly man, waving. A familiar face. Like recently familiar.

I ask Feegle, "What's that about?"

Feegle has a star-struck expression, stating in whispered amazement, "I don't believe it. Gene Winfred Archibald himself is in attendance... at my party."

That name sounds familiar, opening my investigation while trying to recollect, "Winfred? Wait, who is Gene Winfred Archibald?"

He whispers quite loud, "Only the face of Menta-Life! He is the actual founder!"

I slyly request with a smile, "Is that so?"

Feegle's face changes from amazed to confused. Realizing my sudden sense of interest in a guest. A first-time occurrence. Founder is a lot better of a catch than an executive that crunches numbers and writes reports.

I smile at Geilium and Mitchell and grant quick parting words, "Excuse us. We have other business to tend to."

My arm swoops Feegle's and guides us impatiently toward the gathered crowd as he whispers, "Miss Pheros, please slow down. We'll get there." He under-dramatically retracts his arm and adjusts appearance, "We won't be able to have a stable conversation amongst all those guests. Allow everyone time to simmer then we'll casually approach and have a word."

"I have more than a word."

"Please do try not to embarrass me, Miss Pheros."

"I won't, Feegle. Don't worry."

His arm flaps out. I wrap mine, accepting uncomfortability again. We mingle with those less interested in speaking to Gene and more interested in speaking about him. Patience long since worn. As a result, I am constantly keeping an eye. Making certain Gene doesn't leave without saying goodbye. Fifteen minutes feel like forever and still can't rip my eyes off. Guests attempt speaking with me, Feegle's date, though I'm too distracted to undivide attention. Key words invade senses here and there. I chime in here and there when directly spoken to. Not many guests acknowledge aside from gauging my fake chuckles at their classy sense of humor. Being certain everyone involved understands.

When they're not paying attention, I scan the room. Geilium and Mitchell are watching Gene; not with eyes of interest, but of envy. Same duo from earlier stand with them. Majority of the party guests are wearing brightly colored suits and robes or standard black and tie. This duo has on all-black suits with white vests and no jacket. Like table servers. Geilium tilts his head up at the men standing behind. Shields his mouth and whispers a small word amount. The duo leaves, this time, exiting the building. Geilium resumes mingling with guests. If that wasn't suspicious, I don't know what is. Why come and go so much? What're they up to? My attention diverts back to Gene. Socializing with a lesser crowd. Four people, also in gray suits, haven't abandoned his side since arrival. Doesn't appear to be talkative types either.

Feegle calls out, "Miss Pheros?"

Everyone is staring at me, "Pardon?"

A woman asks, "What is your opinion about the Miloris Bureau's recent contributions?"

"Hm… Not much?" I turn to Feegle, "C'mon, darling we've got an urgent matter."

I politely drag Feegle's arm. Guide him away from the man and two women he was entertaining.

Feegle glances back with a chuckle and fast farewell, "Apologies! Have to run!" Then angrily questions in a low tone, "Do you have any idea who you just stormed away from, Miss Pheros?! Are you insane?!"

"Yes. Something strange is going on. We have to speak to Gene right now."

Closer we get, lighter the crowd. Most have already had their chance at saying hello. We stop next to Gene and an entourage of four; two men, two women.

Following subordinates' eyes to us, Gene happily sparks the greeting, "Feegle Tolen, delighted to meet you!"

Gene has a bit of a long face. Short aging white hair and matching white beard. All well-kept. Giving off the impression of a founder type guy.

Feegle snaps to normal and shakes Gene's hand, "To you as well, Mr. Archibald."

"Feegle, I know I am a man of great importance but there's no reason for us to be so formal with one another. Gene is completely fine."

He corrects himself, "Apologies, Gene." My throat clears, relaying the message to introduce, "Oh, this is my dear, *dear* friend, Miss Vanessa Pheros."

Gene reaches for a handshake, "Good evening and a pleasure. I'm—"

I interrupt, accepting his gesture gently and playing his ego, "Gene Archibald. I've seen you before. Not in person, but everywhere else."

I'd only seen him on the page Trex showed, and if anywhere else, don't recall. He's important to the public in every city, so he must get that statement far too often to care anyway.

Gene replies with a smile, speaking as if he's finishing that sentence, "–flattered to be acknowledged by someone as beautiful as yourself."

The sweet and smooth routine doesn't work. I'm on the defensive fence, aware of the big corporation's big secret. I must ease into casual conversation. Pry deeper once he's good and comfortable. Find answers without putting him on the same fence.

Gene asks, "What is it you do, Ms. Pheros?"
I fumble words, forgetting how Feegle introduced me, "Fashion designer."
Gene quickly compliments, "Impressive. That elucidates the spectacular evening attire."
"I made it myself. The fabric is silk, designed from a scavenged replication of a late twentieth century style."
"A fan of the classics, fascinating."
"And who are your... associates?"

One obvious thing about them, including Gene, is their custom-tailored gray suits; a clued tied. Hines wore a gray suit just like it when we met at Cravanaugh. An answer confirmed? Or costume?

Gene quickly states, "Colleagues, actually." He introduces them from left to right, "This is Tylyn."

Caucasian man who appears early thirties. Slicked back black hair, dark blue eyes, very fit build. Muscles obviously displayed through his tailored suit. Seems closer to a bodyguard than corporate figure and attractive. What's his position? Healthcare advisor?

"And this is Payge."

Brown-skinned woman. Long, flowing hair ending near the middle of her back. Gorgeous eyes and an even more gorgeous smile. I can barely tell her face is coated in makeup because it's blended so well. She is also young looking; probably late twenties.

"This is Ryishi."

Ryishi is of Asian descent. Appearing much younger than her colleagues, and the quietest. Instead of making eye contact and greeting with a smile, her head dunks after introduction. In a bow. Hair barely longer than mine split into two ponytails. Brown almond-shaped eyes and cute saddened expression. Difficult to imagine she can smile.

"Last is Booker."

Booker smiles and nods. He shares Payge's complexion. More attractive than Tylyn, who's not a far behind runner-up. Short haircut, dark brown eyes, and muscular build make him a winner in my book. Could be on billboards and advertisements, easily replacing Gene and convincing me to try a Life. Seems like another bodyguard. Gene's being dishonest.

I speak, "Pleased to meet you all. I'm Vanessa Pheros." I ask Gene, "What does the gray represent?"
A nervous smile stretches, "Come again?"
"The suits you're wearing. All same shades of gray. And a fine quality, might I add."
He chuckles, "Oh. I thought you were referring to my hair and beard."

I sell a small laugh to make him believe it was funny. Unsure if his is a sell, Feegle laughs as well. The "colleagues" must have heard the joke before; only Booker smirks at Gene's sad attempt at humor.

Gene explains, "Gray represents neutral efforts of our cause. We, as a whole, are inclined to cater to clients without prejudice, staying neutral to their ideals and backgrounds."

I ask, "In other words, you allow anyone who is anyone to participate in your program?"

"Not *program*, Ms. Pheros. See, a program is created to fit a certain purpose. You want to start an army; you create a program that shapes someone into the favored soldier. We prefer to call our server, Life. My corporation will be holding a free introductory seminar tomorrow to inform new arrivals, and interested citizens, about Life. You're more than welcome to attend."

I am definitely going to attend, but don't want him to know that. Dependent on how things go here, he may not like me by night's end.

I respectfully decline his offer, "No, thank you. I feel like your Life server is dangerous and takes away from humanity."

Feegle sprays whatever beverage he had in his mouth back into the cup. Followed by a single cough. The entourage continues staring at me. No disbelief. Wearing exact same blank expressions like they've heard these allegations too. Colleagues would care about someone insulting their line of work, defending their leader. Yet this group doesn't. It was stupid to be straight-forward, nonetheless I suck at beating bushes.

Gene asks with interest, "Why is it, you feel that way?"
"I heard four of your employees were murdered at The Cravanaugh Hotel yesterday and that your corporation has been stealing people's memories, which makes you responsible for the Deserted."

Saying it aloud, no one else could possibly be responsible for the mental outbreak. I can't imagine what's going on in Feegle's head. I'd only ever embarrassed him by trying to answer my own questions when a guest insisted on talking to me directly. His top must be blowing.

Gene replies casually, "Ms. Pheros, I'm not sure where you heard these wild—"

Relaxed deflection has shown. He won't tell me anything. Nor does he seem shocked by any of what I'm saying; a lie too sewn to break cover for.

I interrupt, "The story is all over Gharis. I'm sure people would be interested in hearing about Menta-Life's involvement."
"Are you certain you're not a journalist?"
"I'm still the same florist I was when I introduced myself."
Gene smiles and corrects, "Fashion designer."
I nod, "So, will you be talking about your dead employees from that hotel or your abducted representative, Hines Aldwich, at the seminar tomorrow?"
Gene enthusiastically speaks, "Have a wonderful evening, Ms. Pheros." He turns to Feegle and adds, "Mr. Tolen."

Gene and his entourage walk away. Feegle and I stand in place. Watch them head for the exit. Would following them do anything? Not now. They won't go anywhere near their operation tonight. Feegle is broken-hearted with a jaw-dropping expression. Part of me feels bad; however, it was my paycheck that just grew legs.

Feegle furiously whispers, "Of all the guests you could have possibly—"

The lights go out. A pitch unrevealing of even my own hands in front of my face. Guests' voices faintly whisper to each other, but no one is in a panic. I blink repetitively fast. Adjust my eyes to the darkness. Create silhouette visuals and outlines of happenings around me. I maneuver the sea of confused guests toward the stairs. From there, I can gain a better vantage point of the ballroom floor. Gene was leaving. This sudden blackout is no coincidence.

Chapter 9: In the Dark

Surprisingly, guests aren't alarmed about being drenched in darkness. I mean they're not having a grand time yet not frantically trampling each other to get outside. Just as Gene is heading for an exit, lights go out. Alone amongst a sea of strangers who can barely tell right from left. An advantageous scenario if shady dealings were in mind; a tactic I would orchestrate.

Feegle loudly pledges, "It is alright, everyone! No reason to worry! My MechCi staff are handling the immediate restoration of power! I do apologize for any inconvenience!"

Something zips by my peripheral. I halt. A guest moved? Another glimpse at a better angle. A MechCi? No, too limp. Definitely human. Quickly shifting between partygoers. Where to in such a hurry? I pace the same direction. Resuming toward the same destination. Avoiding a hard collision with anyone's weakly colored outline so they won't panic and draw attention. Thinking I'm just a polite MechCi brushing by to restore power. The all-black mystery person reaches the stairs before I. Rapidly skip in a silent rush. I reach next. Ditch my heels and follow in ascending. The person's clothes are form-fitting like stealth gear. A thief? Reading physique, it points to a man, although I'm not one hundred percent certain. A mouthless black mask is concealing. The thief crouches and speeds along the railing, unseen. Stops just past the bedroom near the dead-end entry to Feegle's library. I mimic, maneuvering closer to the wall to remain unnoticed by many guests below and one above. Slow down and observe the overwatch. Unseen.

A hand reaches back, revealing a pulser pistol. Fastly aimed at guests below. An upgrade in career track to assassin. Who is the target? It could be Feegle... which is highly improbable. I've still got to stop him. My hands force his wrists at the ceiling. Gripping strongly. Ruining his opportunity. A silent struggle for weapon control. Full-contact and practically invisible, his knee jabs my hip. It aches. Throbbing in this tight gown, but I tough it out. Taking advantage of his imbalance by swinging us around. Away from metal rails, and a short distance toward the library door.

Lights suddenly reactivate. Guests initiate a big round of applause as we crash through and hit the floor. The door smacks a protruding shelf hard enough to slam shut again. The pistol slides underneath a five-foot-long wooden coffee table. Past two chairs and underneath the book piled desk; quarter-way pass the room's center where Feegle reads. A heavy, bronze globe of Earth next to it. Walls flooded with books, gapping only at the rose window dead ahead and the door behind us.

The assassin rips his goggles off and makes a move for the weapon. I hurriedly follow, reaching for and grabbing his snug shirt. Resisting by holding a forward stance, I shoulder bash him into the coffee table. It doesn't break. Then approach with a highly raised bare foot. Bring it down hard, barely missing by an inch on account of his dodge. His arm wraps my ankle, limiting my offense or any other movement. I grab and yank the mask.

One of the men Geilium was with during the party. Stunned that I've seen his face. Blonde curly hair and beard trickled with tiny black lint specs from the brand-new balaclava mask. Geilium whispered words to the two men while watching Gene. One switched off the power. Is Gene the target? If so, why? What could Gene Archibald have done to Geilium McKoy?

The assassin whips me down next to him and mounts. Squabbling open hands for a clear line, he drops a fist. Lightly jabs the table at a miss. He attempts a second punch and bashes the table harder, giving a single harsh shake to fling pain away. I throw an arm over and tug his head down. Meeting forehead against table, I snake onto his back, ready to submit a choke. He easily stands and twists to launch me off, but my grip is much too tight, increasing pressure in my favor at every halt. He dashes, spins and slams my back into shelving. Slamming twice more. Solid shelf edges take their toll. My grip weakens. He reaches over his shoulder and flips me onto the coffee table. Then quickly disappears behind the desk. Pops up and points the pistol. I slide off the table as the assassin fires a handful of heat rounds. Push it upward in his direction and glue close behind.

Guests won't hear already faint shooting over the music. Pulsers aren't manufactured to use gunpowder, not producing loud noise when fired. Even if, guests probably still wouldn't hear anything through the closed door and thick walls. Same as I couldn't hear music in Feegle's bedroom until opening the door.

Pecks at the table cease. Footsteps tap rapidly, becoming only vaguely louder with light steps on carpet. Traveling from the left side. A major disadvantage. This table is too heavy to maneuver as protection. I prepare a low stance. His blonde head appears from the top corner. Much closer than he should be. I pounce before he fires an accurate shot. Using maximum might and body weight, I force my hands on his weapon and myself on him. An unfair share in three hands. My knees raise into his chest on the way to the floor. A great gasp and bellow erupt from his mouth. Then my knees bounce into me rolling forward, now owning the pistol. He attempts to stand, stopping when I puncture a heat round in his leg. The assassin collapses and screams in pain. A pain eager to conceal. I keep the pistol pointed as he lies, bracing injury.

Catching my breath, I request, "What does… Geilium want… from Menta-Life?"

Face flooded with a nervous expression; the assassin looks up at me. Rises on his limp leg and starts breathing heavily. Nervous becomes nerve. I ease the weapon slowly. Observing his hyperventilation. What's wrong with him? He turns around and bolts for the picture window.

I chase a few feet and shout, "Hey!"

He jumps head first through the window. Mentally, I felt it, causing a flinch. More shattering glass and voices are both screaming below. If the initial crash exit didn't kill him, the face-plant landing did. I stop a good distance from the window. Zero intention of following. As bad as I want to confirm, everyone below would see my face. Stepping to the window automatically casts responsibility as murderer or witness. I flee the library.

Partygoers are socializing. The night is still normal for them. Having thwarted an assassination, I'd much prefer having been down there. Feegle isn't difficult to spot. Short, blonde, male, unique enough hairstyle. Happily mingling like he hasn't noticed I disappeared in the darkness. Not receiving as much as an Econ call asking where I went. If he was just mad, he's going to be furious now.

I tap my Econ, "Call Feegle."

Feegle taps his and turns away for heated privacy, "Miss Pheros, I have absolutely no words—"

"I need you to come upstairs."

"I'm busy with guests."

"I can see that. Look up."

He scans the railing above, noticing me and growing a stunned expression, "What on Earth happened to your gown?"

"What's up here is much more important. And bring my shoes, by the stairs."

I end the call to prevent further questioning. Watch him politely ease through crowds and scoop my heels on the way upstairs. He stirs a light storm. I return to the room and wait. What a mess this is. Not referencing the library. The assassin preferred to kill himself than risk being questioned. What would Geilium have done to him for failing to kill Gene? Or for being caught? I may have stepped in another puddle of someone's hidden agenda. Feegle crosses the threshold, face lighting with shock.

He states in a sadly-pitched whine, "My library... What happened?"

I can't tell Feegle which parties are involved in this incident. Both Gene and Geilium could be more dangerous than they let on. If Feegle starts asking around, he could end up hurt or worse.

I answer, "Someone tried to kill one of your party guests from up here when the lights went out. I stopped him and he... jumped out the window."
"Why does it look like a *little* more than that happened?"
"Maybe there was a *little* paraphrasing. I believe Gene Archibald was the target. Getting him to leave made someone bump a timeline forward."

Feegle approaches the desk. Stops. Scans the damage. Gapes at the broken window beyond.

I advise, "That's not recommended. Head back to the party and make sure you don't mention any of what I told you. Especially my name. I'm gonna change and go see Trex about this."
Feegle asks, "What do I say when Regulator Officers enter the premises?"
"You're gonna call them and say a guest returned and told you someone jumped from your window and you came in to this."
"Okay."
"I'll let you know when I figure out anything."

I guide Feegle's library departure and take the shoes. He makes the call. Still shaken, but excellent about keeping things to himself. When there's direct involvement, especially. Being associated with smugglers, he'd be talk of the town in a bad way. A vacant space of shame where a bakery once stood. I enter the bathroom and get cleaned up. Strip out of the torn, stretched, and dirty gown. Change into my regular outfit. Only a slight improvement thanks to those persistent BAMechs.

Stern inquiries mixed with Feegle's acknowledgments seep under the door, passing by. A rhythm of six feet. Voices go silent. I crack the wood from its holster. The entire party has been cleared in a matter of ten minutes. Two Regs are walking down the stairs, nearing the center. Standard types: blue uniforms and electrified batons. Basically, unarmed and unarmored. I need to reach the basement before others show to investigate the bedroom. I take a couple of light steps out. The other Regs and Feegle are not in sight at the library door. I tip toe to the railing. Backflip over and grab the lower ledge. Swing down and dash into one of the opened guest restrooms underneath. A unisex space accommodating mature visitors, equipped with an optional lock mechanism for the uncomfortable. Three stalls and two sinks. Neutral mint green. The ballroom Regs have reached and are now scanning from the foot, oblivious to any other presence than their own. Both restarting their ascent. I stealthily bolt straight across from restroom to basement door.

Enter as quietly as possible and feel out the hidden tunnel's panel. False flooring blends well. There's no way anyone can notice an indifference, except maybe a MechCi if one were present. Feegle deemed this area inaccessible to it for that very reason. They're programed to speak truth no matter what their loyalties. This tunnel and bakery would, again, be history. I reach Trex's office. Knock twice, stroll in. He is sitting behind his desk as usual, on a call. Index finger flicked high at my entry, silently demanding silence.

He doesn't stop speaking, "–makin' the outer perimeter a better route to lay low."

I wait patiently for his conversation to conclude. Sounds like an alternate route recommendation with a smuggler. Must've been spotted and needs to get out of the light.

Trex rests the wired landline home and sarcastically apologies, "Sorry about that. I had to delay a package. Apparently someone jumped outta Feegle's library window. Big stir outside. Would you happen to know anything about that?"

I reveal and place four flash drives on the desk, "Not much, no, but I'll get an answer from these."

Trex seems confused, "What's on those?"

"Information relating to the dead guys from the hotel."

Trex grabs the drives and examines outer casings, "Were they Equility?"

"Not entirely sure. I don't think so, but someone tried to make it look like they were."

Trex inserts two drives into the keyboard. Activates the holographic second that allows me to see everything on his end without constant flipping back and forth. A couple of windows open, being instantly analyzed for encryptions and other software that can track or harm his hardware. After completion, the first file unlocks; a henchman's picture and background information. The one who lost the bag.

Trex asks, "You seein' this? Tim Erisson, age twenty-eight, Caucasian, blah, blah–"

"Who does he work for?"

The screen starts scrolling, shortly ceasing a skim, "Says here his occupation is chauffeur."

I impulsively inquire, "What? Where?"

"Down, on the right."

My eyes rapidly sift small words and see for myself. Clear as day. An error maybe? There were no pictures of the dead men with actual tattoos and the phonies were blatantly erased before I arrived on that floor; the only links that could've tied them to Equility. Erased by that woman... Were they drawn before death or postmortem? Who drew them? Answers would rain from the sky if I had that key information. I have to see how the others are connected before making further assumptions.

I demand, "Check the next one."

Tim's file fades into the background. Trex repeats the same encryption analysis for anything dangerous. Then opens the next file.

I ask, "What's he do for a living?"

Trex scans through quickly. Already familiar with the profile template's destination space. I spot the word "occupation" and tell him to stop.

He listens while I read to myself, "Pawn broker."

Limo driver and pawn broker. Absolutely nothing in common with Menta-Life unless someone took an expensive ride to get some quick aers. Contradictory, and nowhere closer to either faction.

I uninterestedly demand, "Check the next two."

He removes now useless drives. Inserts the other couple and initiates decryption on both. None of this is adding up. Working for Equility, they would need regular jobs as cover for secret revolutionary efforts. But they weren't Equility. False ink proves that. Trex opens the third drive's file and scrolls to the victim's description. Then begins decryption on another. This one is a server. A bus boy. I pan over at the other half of the screen. Final file reveals this last man as a retail stock associate.

It makes sense now that it doesn't make sense. These men had no idea what they were truly getting into. Four nobodies at the bottom of the employment ladder and no ties, who collectively tried their luck at crime. And failed. Professional criminals wouldn't have been slaughtered by a bellman disguised killer so easily. Hines hired them to steal the package. Ordered them away before our in-depth meeting.

Covering tracks perfectly with their deaths and using them as fall guys. Tattoos were likely drawn postmortem to frame Equility. Suggestion of the "good guys" thwarting an imminent uprising. Or someone antsy to spring one. Hines Aldwich and Mr. Bellman could be working together; a sensible enough approach since Hines' corpse wasn't present. Perhaps, the old man over intercom looped communication with the bellman and gave kill orders. Why keep me alive though? The bellman exiting just as I was entering wasn't coincidental. Instead of accepting an easy attempt on my life, he cruised by. More questions and no answers. Where is Hines? Which faction does he and the bellman officially associate? I'm stuck at square negative three. No clue where to begin seeking answers.

In a fresher case, Menta-Life is holding a demo gathering tomorrow. I'll be present. Naturally, I can't show my face to the group that attended tonight. Avoiding them amidst a monsoon of guests and reporters shouldn't be difficult. Even if, having only seen my formal appearance, informal should conceal me for a while. Gene never told me a time. I could need an early morning start.

I rise and speak, "Trash those drives. They didn't help a thing. I need a favor."
"This was a favor."
"Another favor. I need to know what time Menta-Life's seminar starts tomorrow. Find out and give me a call?"
"Easy enough."
"Thanks so much for your help, Trex."
He takes a serious tone, "What's goin' on, Van?"
I deflect, "I still don't know, but if you're a good boy, I'll let you know when I find out."
"Don't go searchin' for information that could kill, 'cause it will. People been dyin' since the day you got outta prison. All these dead bodies fallin' around you are an unhealthy sign."
"And none of them have been my fault."
"I said *around* you. Just be careful out there."

"I'm always careful out there. Someone just needs to answer for that letter I got in…"

I'd completely forgotten about the letter! Where did it say to meet? Since we happened to arrive at the Cravanaugh, I assumed it was the correct place. Not once did Hines mention my not showing up that morning. Will address numbers match what I already can't recollect? I had only skimmed for a brief second, never planning to follow instruction.

I conclude, during rushed departure, "I have to go. Message me with that time for the seminar."

I return to Feegle's ballroom. Regs have the crime scene secure upstairs; however, this area is empty. Rooted apparent suicide, with how little the investigation perimeter is. I slink a half-circle to the garage. Mount the lectrocycle with a relatable crime scene in mind. The Cravanaugh Hotel; two links yet to be chained. Cruising past an intersection, I glance at Gharis City's heart. Blue-lit lettering can be seen clearly across darkened skies. Menta-Life seems central of everything. A much deeper meaning than just literal sense. People want that corporation dead and buried. My new suspect, Geilium McKoy, is included in the pot. After the seminar, I'll have to scheme around for Geilium's portion in this mess. The reasoning behind why he tried to have Gene killed could shed light, if he's willing to talk.

I request the address from my Econ. Numbers "1609" don't ring a single bell. According to an automated proposition, they're still open for business. Having as much respect for the dead as I do. Regardless of how many times repeated, 1609 doesn't strike familiar. Ah, forget it. Unable to see myself going back, I'll be satisfied regretting not keeping that letter. A yawn frees itself, while I reroute to underground.

My Econ alerts, "Incoming voice message from Trex: Ten in the morning."

I command, "Reply: Thanks Trex."

"Message sent."

Though becoming habit these days, I hate waking early. Deliberately passing the restaurant from last night, the driver's cruiser is gone. Regs certainly found it. Cruisers never get stolen unless it's by a wanted smuggler like me. There's plenty more use of this lectrocycle until I abandon it for something else.

I arrive at the eastern border tunnel entrance. An unoccupied sector. Civilians don't require an advance warning to avoid this drainage tunnel, already afraid Deserted will come flooding in a psychotic rage and drag them in. Never to be seen or heard from again. I guide the vehicle, on foot, into the darkened tube. Far enough to be invisible to anyone outside. Even after sunrise, all daylight grants this tunnel is warmth. It'll be safe, propped against the wall. I follow faint groans. Maneuver zig-zag darkness that snakes a path ending at the pit. Dark enough to where I can't see and unknowing if Deserted are actually lost, nearing wandering sounds would be a mistake. Worse and more fatal than the party. Having lived here a while, I'm familiar with each tunnel and manhole layout. I used to stick to the wall until memorizing how many steps to each turn. Width and length dimension. Learning that silence doesn't exactly mean safe and a flashlight certainly doesn't either. I reach the downward spiral's end. Embrace the lit underground. Still business as usual. I circle outside the makeshift town and thoughtfully around many townsfolk to my shack. Sway the sheet to enter. A female Deserted is idle in the back corner, facing the crevice, almost creating a triangle with her shoulders. Speaking very lightly.

Chapter 10: Deserted

    I immediately halt and observe. How long has she been in here? Drawing attention to lure her out would be smart and being too loud could attract others in. Deserted always murmur, meaning subtle noise doesn't spook them. The threat is what ticks their clock and how extreme. Still not a good idea to risk it. Then again, I won't be comfortable with her lurking. Unintentionally waiting for open opportunity on a heavy snore while I'm asleep.
    I slowly approach. Calm. Silent and aware. The woman's attire is slightly shredded and spotty from the big puddle; muddy water supply. Skin spotty with that same shade, despite having a different natural tone under the coat. About arm's length away, I release a whispering whistle. Silent enough for only us to hear. Mild chatter doesn't cease. I whistle a little louder. She spins and swings an arm up. I shift away to avoid falling victim to an expected fury. Resume backward steps matching her drunken stumble pace. Straighten my posture beyond the

addictive slouch. The woman is trying hard to hold a stare in my eyes. Craving aggression but can't retain the thought; a struggling battle without end. My calm is relieving her. I exit the sheet. Sway and hold it open as I cling to the outside wall. Wait quietly. She stumbles straight out. Quietly. Oblivious to the desired goal.

No one understands Deserted and are too afraid to learn. I, on the other hand, know too much and haven't put forth any learning effort. Simply taking notice. Things are complex, but they don't realize it. Probably thinking everything is perfectly normal because their memory of how things are is absent. That's assuming they can form the idea of a normal.

I slip into my shack and drop the sheet. Sit on the bed and realize I'm starving. Holding out until tomorrow morning won't be an issue. Hunger will make sure I wake on time to go eat before the seminar. I throw the rest of my body down and doze off. Wake up, after what feels like minutes, to sounds of someone groaning. Faint, yet loud because it's nearby. Otherwise mute. I rub my eyes to free drowsiness. Why can't I hear usual Deserted murmurings pass?

I tap my Econ and ask in a scratchy tone, "What time is it?"
The female voice answers, "It is 8:12 a.m."

I drag myself to the sheet. Exit and follow groans left. What should be a dangerous curiosity but no one's around. Not roaming or napping in dirt. Am I dreaming? Where is everyone? Passing two shacks, I turn right. A huge group, maybe the entire populace, of Deserted are standing in a circle. So socially dead. An occurrence I never imagined could happen. Like spotting a leprechaun or unicorn.

Did someone get hurt? What's interesting in that huddle? I don't make habit of checking things out… Deserted aren't ever formally gathered either. Besides, I've been on a roll for being nosey lately. Why stop now? I inch slow steps forward. Enter sideways between two bodies without shoving. No choice avoiding slight brushes in such narrow proximity. Hoping at each slip between that they don't decide to become aggressive and attack. My heart beats faster, the further in I get. Hard enough for my whole body to feel terrible anticipations.

Spectators can't see past each other yet remain still. Staring as if a sense notification is blaring. So calm. Detached from themselves. It's strange to see. Like they don't notice I'm here. Being this close, awful smells from filthy clothing itch my nose. Not enough for me to insult anyone by pinching it closed. At the center, I understand the situation.

A man is squirming wildly in place on his back. The bullseye that has Deserted concerned. His skin isn't stained but pale from extensive lack of sunshine. Clothes not torn. Head missing patches of already short hair. A fresh recruit? I don't recognize him. Could be another Menta-Life addict who stumbled upon something big like Hines said. Pushing me toward belief in the liar. It sounds as if the man wants to scream. Pain won't permit release of his clenched teeth. Hands gripped tightly, applying pressure above both ears. A pain simmering from agonizing screams to constant irritation. A burn incapable of healing.

Initial staggered rows of Deserted are staring at him. Dead stares interested in nothing else. They could have gone through similar torture. Progressively dissolving inside until left with a last strand. One thought constantly murmured. Wanting to sympathize and not knowing how. Or knowing it's too late. A single memory stripped, and lives unravel like a spider's web. Watching the man suffer is helping me understand why Menta-Life needs to be stopped. These people were probably elitists who took advantage of others. Deserving of what they got. But I'm certain some aren't. Some may have been using aers and time in search of a difference. Investing to save lives. Literally having that taken away. I'm no better than either side; invading everyone's yard to find someone who can lead me to someone with loot. This recruit will be aimlessly roaming and talking to himself, in no time. I'll leave him to the fan club.

A suffering voice stops me, "Wait."

I glance back at the man who's not looking around. Still squishing his head and squirming. Could he be talking to me? Can he sense me somehow?

His shaking lips move, breathing a strenuously light tone, "Please."

The crowd continues staring as if there's no one else present. I step forward. Front and almost-center. Not a single set of eyes bat my way. He can't have much consciousness left in this condition. What can I do besides stare? How can I make someone with excruciating brain damage content? I don't know this man, nonetheless it may be useful to find out who he currently is.

I kneel beside and whisper, "What's your name?"
He lets out a cough, "My…"
I speak slower, "What is your name?"

The man is desperately trying to release more words. Eager to mash a complete sentence or fragment. Am I making things worse by having him think? Should I leave him alone? Preserve his last embraceable moment of sanity? A small sigh ejects from me. Pressing further would just be inconsiderate. Moments later, he gradually ceases movement. Still breathing. Hands drift from the sides of his head. Pain must have been too much to handle. A discoloration, deep red indentations circling his wrists, catch my eyes. Not bleeding red slashes, but of extensive duration. Was he bound with something? Could he have been abducted and brought here? His family and friends probably have no idea. In this condition, barely maintaining a mind, he didn't voluntarily climb into a manhole or walk the maze tunnel; someone brought him. And that someone might be around.

Idle Deserted are looking at me. Fortunately, not carrying hostility, just blank. A scary sight, considering what kind of people they are. Now's not the time to solve that mystery. The man couldn't have traveled from any entry without a sane guide helping along. I carefully pass through the crowd toward the closest entrance; a south end manhole. Arrived, the cover is sealed. Not a thing someone in great pain would be considerate enough to do. I climb and slide it open for light. The dirt at my feet is heavily disturbed. A lot of shuffled movement took place, followed by a curving trail pattern. Did someone drag him? The trail stops a few feet away. Then continue differently. Shapes suggest a short distance crawl before struggling to his feet and another crawl. The poor guy was dumped. Dumped into a hole like garbage in a chute and injured during the drop. How terrible. At least Menta-Life can't hurt him anymore. Is there a worse form of what's been done? I reseal the hole.

    Too alert to think about sleep, I'll leave early for my investigation. Back toward my shack, Deserted have restarted abnormality. Aimlessly walking and murmuring. Where's the new guy? I return to the recently crowded area. The squirming man's spot is empty and has been trampled. No groans filling air, only soft voices. He has joined the ranks. I return to my shack and change clothes. Leave using last night's tunnel exit. The darkened maze of chill. I mount the vehicle and take off, aiming at any restaurant en route to Menta-Life.

The sun is at a low shine behind my speeding between traffic lanes. Typical light morning. Everyone on regular jobs are at their desks by nine. Since Gharis runs twenty-four hours, shifts tend to shift to later work hours for late accommodations.

    I arrive at a drive-thru. All food is, for the most part, healthy. Eliminates risk of death from filling stomachs with low cost garbage. Fast-food establishments are secretly frowned upon by past reputation, although few are kept for those in need of a quick bite. I munch on a sandwich at one of many unoccupied tables outside and continue the ride.

    Having dealt with the man, my time is running short. Arriving sooner earns a good seat somewhere central. Out of the way and difficult to notice. Hopefully blended amongst big numbers. Attending isn't a bad idea, though I can't shake the gut feeling they already know who to expect. Familiar with my ulterior motives beyond curiosity. This is an opportunity to legally obtain background information on Menta-Life. Knowing how they operate can possibly fill holes about how Deserted came to exist. If Menta-Life is responsible, they won't publicly admit it, or would've already done so after brain drain number one. Maybe putting two and eight together can form my own conclusion.

    Approaching the skyscraper's west side, I pull over across the street. Keep my getaway transportation distant, yet not too far. The building appears much taller and wider than when I saw it with Dayio. Dozens more stories below make a difference compared to a belly view from another towering building's rooftop. Menta-Life is covered in blackened windows. A barred, perimeter gate is sprouted about eighteen feet high and includes a painted white concrete wall four feet underneath. It holds the steel bars upright, shaving to fourteen feet. Viewers can get an unobstructed view of peaceful grassland beyond. A side gate rests northwest. Big enough entry for deliveries and services. The post is a small extension of the gate. A couple of armed and armored guards are doing their jobs extremely well behind it. Not a relaxed bone to show.

My attention veers south. A lot of people are lined up. The tail end is vanishing, walking north and moving quickly. I need to blend before the line dies. An easy way to standout is by showing up last or late. I cross the street and walk south along the gate.

Menta-Life is protected better than Ori prison, minus the Alpha mech. Fully armored guards equipped with automatic weapons. Solid black armor. Sleek, almost bonded. Helmets with a thin visor striped across the eyes shield their heads. Looks to be fifteen posted per side. Scattered and unfriendly. Their faces *are* blocked, but by unfriendly I mean wielding big weapons and not talking to civilians or socially with fellow colleagues. Is security tightened for this event or is this every day? If someone drops a bag on the grass it'll be riddled with burn holes by five guards in a second.

Visitors are entering fast like there isn't a guest check-in table. Perfect since my new credentials aren't as spotless as they were three days ago. I cross the black gate's threshold, central to the sidewalk. Blend with civilians and follow the concrete path toward a set of double doors. Visitors still flowing behind. I'm not dead last. United in rank, I inconspicuously examine the guards. All males, by stature. Their black trench coats are fluid with their armor. Nearly form-fitting. Horrible concept designs. I reach the main doors. Just overhead is "Menta-Life" in small blue lettering with a crescent Earth logo underneath. I pass into the main branch of evil rooting.

Chapter 11: Background Check

The interior is massive. What looks like three floors in height from outside is the lobby. Structural columns rest about every forty feet, supporting multiple floors above. Placed throughout the area are big, random relics from a history I don't know much about. Outfitted to mimic a miniature museum. A classic sports car with racing stripes, a stone model of a huge white house, a green woman holding a torch, and other things from before my time. Visitors pace and stop, admiring many objects and socializing in amazement. Then continuing. While they're distracted, I can land a seat near the middle. It'll be hard for any familiar faces to spot me. Like Gene, or his entourage if they appear without him. I ease around many guests toward the left wall. Folding chairs and a presentation stage are set for this morning's lecture.

Security is tight inside too. Fewer guards, but cameras stationed at the neck of every column. These operate within a circular housing tube. Naked eyes can't see because it's two-way glass. The camera loops fast enough to catch anything in a two-second lapse; no chance at hiding or doing anything illegal from any angle.

Those who arrived together are seated in groups. Business associates with pad or laptop in hand, prepared to listen and take notes for later review. As seats fill, I plant center-left of the stage. A good position to observe important figures in the splash row and most receding rows. Camera crews ready to film. Reporters wired to question. Editors stageside hooking up gadgets. Will this event air live? I smile at my neighbor, secretly scanning faces. None familiar. Uninteresting strangers and Menta-Life's security force. I patiently wait. Daze at minor action on the platform stage.

A handsome man in the signature gray suit steps to the podium, "Ladies and gentlemen, please take your seats. We will begin very shortly. Ladies and gentlemen take your seats. Thank you."

The man steps off stage. Visitors seek out available seating. In a polite hurry. Eager for front row but disappointed by signage blocking reserved spaces. Geilium McKoy, his assistant Mitchell, and two others are engaged in conversation on a journey toward row one. Executive style. The average person would be jealous. I'm not average. Geilium and Mitchell are listening, leading the pack. What're they doing here? After a failed assassination attempt on the owner, this is the last place I'd expect to see them. Of course no one knows about that except me. Keeps him in good grace with Menta-Life. They take corner seats in the second row. All four seated together as if "reserved" signs kept them warm.

Faction three: Psychotic News Moguls.

Once mostly everyone sits, lights go dim. Audience begin a standing round of applause. I join. The handsome man retakes the stage. He waves and smiles. Adjusts the microphone on the podium. Typical corporate type: wavy hair, sparkling eyes, clean shaven, million-aer smile and likely earns it too. His throat clears into the mic. An old speech trick.

We gradually cease applause, "Thank you for the warm greeting and welcome to Menta-Life. My name is Kelvin Hughes, one of the chief engineers. What I am here to share with you is this gift of *Life*... that can be yours. The purpose of Life is to allow ourselves an opportunity to restore our world. We are all familiar with how the final war of 2068 dramatically set us back, yet Life has delivered us from that brink of extinction. How?"

He stares left. A hologram of Gene Archibald appears. The audience is amazed at the sudden appearance, as if magic happened. The way his image squeezed onto the stage was fast, but not fast enough to hide the distortion of its feet. It's an exact replica. Height, hair, down to skin saturation.

Kelvin continues, "This is a holographic representation of our founder, Gene Winfred Archibald. The Menta-Life Corporation was never his dream nor his burden, but rather his gift of salvation. Before the war, he was a professor in study of the human brain. Neuropsychology. Using past knowledge, he started the Life project as an idea on scrapped paper to rebuild. For those who have never attended, you are curious about how the Life process works. I am here to work through it with you from start to finish. Please hold all questions until the end of the lecture."

Kelvin ganders at Gene's hologram. It disappears. A blue reclining chair appears in its place. No amazement. The chair has a small variety of tools attached. Intricate and sharp materials, like something a dentist's office should have. I'm suddenly interested.

Kelvin explains, "This is the beginning stage. In order for a Life to work for anyone, a small chip called a 'Microdot' must be implanted onto the left, or analytical, portion of the brain."

A green hologram of a cyber-person appears. Then lies in the reclined chair. An image of a dark square device appears next to the person; huge in proportion and slowly rotating.

"This is the representation of a Microdot. The dot itself is a little bigger than a hair follicle. Surgically placed onto the brain – not *into*, but *onto* – taking two days of absorption to reach the cerebral cortex. Once inside, it rests as a signal relay. Next step is comfort. Our team assigns each client to a 'Dreamcatcher' which is the most comfortable recliner constructed to date, or so clients claim." The audience shares a moderate chuckle, "Attached mechanics facilitate the microdot's installation. The Dreamcatcher is a requirement for the procedure and maintaining maximum comfort while in the sleep state. We place clients into a barbiturate-induced coma with exactly enough pentobarbital to hold unconsciousness for a three-day duration. Servings do vary by day, dependent on age. IV liquids are also vended with purchase of a Life, providing nutrients for duration's entirety. Last and most exciting step, the Life stage."

Indicating its asleep, the green hologram releases Z's from its mouth; clearly, a joke. Bad taste, considering the whole *induced coma* thing.

Kelvin looks at the hologram and jokingly states, "Well I guess we're all more excited than he is."

The audience releases a chuckle. My attention turns to Geilium. He and his associates are seated in place, unamused. This isn't their first visit. Keeping up appearance no doubt.

Kelvin resumes the lecture, "With this step, after being induced, you, the client, are granted access to the Menta-Life server. A server housing all collected data since activation, including everything discovered and/or shared that predates it. *Everything* we know is at your disposal during your Life. Allow me to clarify one very important detail; the ninety-year Life is only from present to passing. One impossibility of Life, a strict safety guideline for even the brain, is that a client can never revert to a state younger than their current self. With that said, those are the three steps required for Life to function. Thank you."

The hologram disappears. The audience, including myself for appearance, stand and give cheerful applause. After about twenty seconds, we settle and quiet down. Anticipation has the audience shaking. Eager to throw hands high like school children with a correct answer.

Kelvin asks, "Regarding the microdot, does anyone have questions? Stage one procedure." A man's hand springs quicker than the few others, drawing Kelvin immediately in acknowledgement, "First question is yours, sir."
"How is a device that small manufactured to do such a big job efficiently?"
"I cannot share exact specifications, though can tell you it was designed extremely thoroughly, and mass produced to prevent physical reconstruction flaws. Many satisfied users can assure it gets the job done. Other questions about step one?"
A woman raises her hand and Kelvin acknowledges, "Yes ma'am."
"Is the installation procedure dangerous?"
"No. It is done mechanically, set to operate by Dr. Gene Winfred Archibald himself. With human beings, there is always room for potential error, no matter how trained the physician. With Dreamcatchers, there is not. In event of occurrence, mechanics are set on an emergency protocol to cease activity to avoid fatal harm. To date, no such conflict has befallen." He addresses the crowd, "Further questions about stage one?" No one verbally responds or raises a hand, "Moving on. Does anyone have questions about the Dreamcatcher, IV, or comfort zone?"
Two men raise their hands and Kelvin acknowledges one, "Yes sir."
"Are Dreamcatchers available for purchase?"
Kelvin and the audience snicker a little, "Fantastic question, by the way. I asked that myself and still wish I could even use one for naps

during lunch breaks. Unfortunately, no, they are not for sale. At no offer. Dreamcatchers are a Menta-Life patented product, intended for implanting the microdot with its attached mechanisms and providing nutrition during each stay. But three full days would be enough to enjoy, believe me."

The audience laughs aloud at his response. Good grade for showmanship.

Kelvin asks a specific person, "Was there another question sir?"
The other man who had his hand up answers hesitantly, "No, he uh… asked already."
The audience chuckles and Kelvin jokingly clarifies, "Believe me, more than half the staff wishes Dreamcatchers were purchasable, so do not feel ashamed. Okay, more questions on stage two?" No one answers so he goes on, "Alright, moving on. Any questions on stage thr—"

Hands go flying before his sentence finishes. An awaited and favored question. Being the most illogical part of the whole process, curiosity is understandable.

Kelvin expresses surprise, "Wow, okay. I would love to get all of your questions answered so I will have to speed through. Umm… young lady down front. Do the honor of starting us off?"
"Thank you. Are there any types of rules that you must follow while living a Life?"
"We all have rules to follow; exactly as here. Within the Life server has no decline in human behavior or responsibility. What rules users choose to follow is up to them. Naturally there are consequences, being the same as a real life. Next question." Hands fly up and he picks someone, "You, sir."
"How does Menta-Life control the Life?"
He hesitantly admits, "I don't understand the question."
"Well, with dreams, they aren't controlled; it's a manifestation of where your subconscious takes you. For example, in a dream you can

walk down a road and see a giant spider driving a train, or something of that nature. Is Life similar to say a… subconscious reality?"

"Ah, I see. The brain plays a major role of maintaining mental sanity by giving off information that those happenings aren't possible. Our sole reason for microdot placement on a user's analytic sector, working two in conjunction." He pitches one finger up briefly, "*However*, it does not curve imagination. Living one's Life a certain way can make anything possible. Perhaps a science experiment involving a spider went awry. Perhaps it gained enhanced motor skills and drove a train off the tracks. If you make it happen, it can be possible. Next question." Hands raise again, "Yes, sir."

"When someone wakes, what happens to information learned in the Life?"

"It's theirs. If a user becomes an… astronaut within a Life, when they wake, they'll have obtained necessary information to achieve that goal."

Gasps stutter around. Then groups chatter amongst themselves. This Life thing is quite fascinating. I'd like to ask a question but can't draw attention. So far, the audience is assisting with great Intel. Menta-Life literally has access to people's brains and equipment to be responsible for the Deserted outbreak. Kelvin clears his throat in the microphone, silencing everyone.

He confirms, "It is true. Anyone can pick as much information as they can retain by living a Life in our facility. The only limitation is based on discoveries and how far someone's willing to explore. Information on our servers that anyone has chosen to share can be learned. Further questions?" Hands raise fast, "Yes, ma'am."

"You mentioned that no one is able to revert to a youthful stage, so does that not guarantee a full ninety years?"

"Correct, and allow me to explain why. The brain, although a most powerful tool, is still very fragile. Say regression to the birthing stage were possible and something catastrophic happened; a user's brain, anyone's brain, may have no choice but to process the false fact that they are deceased. Terminating brain function altogether. For our clients' safety, that has been made an impossible venture. There is a workaround, dependent on how one's Life is lived. We have met many clients who've reached a hundred years, and few who even reached one-ten. Statistically, a thirty-four-year-old such as myself would likely live out a fifty-six-year span, just as a twenty-seven-year-old like yourself would have a sixty-three year span."

The woman, obviously older than twenty-seven, becomes sucked in. Smiling from ear-to-ear at his comment and compliment as her head dunks slightly. Flattery kind of saw him through the slim negativity of that answer. No woman would cough up their real age to prove a point after being complimented like that.

Kelvin goes on, "Next please."
A man stops the questioning, "One second Mr. Hughes, to follow up, how can Menta-Life prevent regression?"
"Your mind simply will not allow it. Time does not stop or reverse *here*, and it will not there." Hands sprout again and he chooses, "Yes, ma'am."
"Are you able to live a Life within a Life?"
"Absolutely not. An attempt could cause catastrophic failure to our systems, as well as endanger the user and others already inside. Terminating everything we have struggled so hard to build."
"*Could?* Has it ever been tested?"
"Never. Theoretical analysis is all we need to know not risk it. Next question please." Eight hands are left in the air, "Yes, sir."
"How do laws and regulations work inside the Life server?"
"It runs just like real life. Commit a crime, either pay the toll or go to jail, dependent on the crime's significance. All laws and regulations are implanted, complete with Regulator response times and procedures. We are running short on time, so I will have to be brief. Next question."

Only half an hour? Hope no one wasted aers on travel to attend this event. Background on Menta-Life is good but isn't helping as much as I figured it would. Instruments to fit the crime but no motive.

Hands fly up and Kelvin selects, "Yes, ma'am."
"Is there contact with the outside world?"
"Great question. Technically, yes. Only on the receiving end, nothing outgoing. Anything shared on the internet is available for users to find on the Life server. Are you single?"
"Yes."
He addresses the audience, "Any single man here, raise your hand." A hand goes up and Kelvin continues to the woman, "If he has chosen to share personal information publicly, you can go through... a social media profile and find this man. You can get to know him, fall in love with him, marry him, grow old with him. Upon waking, you may have learned everything about him that he has chosen to share."
"So I would know what he would look like as an elder before he does?"
"Only what can be generated. Genetically, certain parts sag; eyes darken. If known as a couch potato, he will gain weight, things like that. With additional features, say there's a cruiser accident in real life that a user is driving near in a Life, traffic will slow for them too. What happens inside Life, on the other hand, will not hit home. Got time for two more questions." A few hands go up, "Yes, sir."
"I sleep eight hours a day and my dreams only feel like minutes. How is it opposite with Life?"
Kelvin chuckles, "Eight hours a day? Congrats." The audience snickers during a thought-filled pause, "...Wow. You picked what is possibly the hardest question to summarize." Another snicker, "Umm... The brain comprehends that a user is asleep, but with the microdot in place, it is also aware of its presence and has another purpose. Therefore, continues working, though asleep, to fulfill that purpose, giving a full Life. I hope that makes sense." The man does a strange bobblehead nod of approval, "Final question."

More hands rise than before. Some even begin waving immaturely. A word I never thought I'd use.

Kelvin cruises with his eyes and picks someone, "Last question is yours, sir."

The man stands from a seat in the back right corner and fixes his black suit, "Thank you, Mr. Hughes."

Awkward silence draws my sight. African American man. Late twenties. Deep voice. Stands tall, maybe over six feet. Average weight. Goatee. Crew cut, closely shaven enough to be considered bald.

Kelvin slides a gentle reminder, "Go ahead with your question."

The man introduces himself, "My name is Paul Quentin and my question: Who do you think you're fooling?"

The entire audience and I twist sideways to look back full-time. Accommodating attention easily to both sides of what may be an oncoming verbal battle. What's this guy up to?

Kelvin timidly responds, "I beg your pardon."

Paul clarifies, "I asked, who do you think you are fooling, Mr. Hughes."

"I am not attempting to fool anyone. The audience is here with questions this morning and I am simply giving answers."

"Then why not give your public answers they'd really wanna hear, like how you monitor Lives and steal people's memories."

The audience is baffled by the news. Who is this Paul Quentin? He has some nerve throwing accusations like that with all these people watching. A target has just been painted on. Must be insane. I like his style.

Kelvin laughs off Paul's accusation, firing a defense, "Menta-Life is not capable of watching ninety years of each client's Life before they awaken in three days. What you are implying is not possible, Mr. ..."

Paul barks, "Quentin!" His tone dials down, "Paul Quentin. This corporation is stealing people's memories and making them insane. I've seen it."

Security guards silently gather behind Paul. Unnoticed. Nothing about his behavior implies anger won't assume complete control and attack. Guards are smart to prepare. Kelvin's eyes aren't squirming. Failing to draw attention to the patient assault team. Most victims would unknowingly warn attackers by looking at what's going on around them; however, Kelvin's locked. Must've been through this type of ordeal before.

Kelvin attempts to diffuse the situation peacefully, "Mr. Quentin, please calm down. Menta-Life has no purpose in stealing citizen's memories. Memories are past. We cannot steal something that is not there to steal."

Paul heatedly interrogates, "What about when you steal ideas you decide you want to keep for yourselves to boost your reputations?"

"Mr. Quentin, I am unsure where you have gotten your information. Citizens of Gharis, as well as citizens at other Menta-Life facilities in other cities, have been working with us. Many hands creating a better future by sharing what they have learned, continuing the advancement our New World. For ideas citizens have shared with us, they have received payment, acknowledgment, as well as an invitation to join Menta-Life in our partner program. We have even gone as far as to make donations, funding many startups at no return in financial gain."

"What about those people who wanna keep their ideas for themselves?"

"Nothing. The ideas are theirs to exploit."

Paul shouts, "How about they get their Life stolen and become Deserted!"

Reporters immediately force questions of their own on Kelvin. Who's the root of this information? Paul has the same theory as Hines. The two could know each other. Something's different between them though. Paul carries a scolding fire. Too angry to be a civil rights activist or protester. And alone. There's a deep personal connection. Accusing Menta-Life of a horrific act in public is begging for a death sentence. Doesn't seem like tying up loose ends is a problem either... which may be how Deserted came to exist. Motive?

Kelvin denies, "Deserted have nothing to do with Menta-Life. Those stricken are simply unfortunate citizens with an illness that cannot yet be treated. Pharmaceutical teams are currently utilizing our servers in search—"

Paul's voice maximizes with rage, "You are the illness!"

Kelvin's voice lessens, "Security."

Guards immediately snatch Paul, dragging him away as he continues the racket, "You're the ones destroying us all! Menta-Life is killing us! Stealing our minds! Do not trust them!"

Anger fades to silence as Paul is escorted from the building. How does he know about Menta-Life and Deserted? Could he be a member of Equility? If not locked in a mental institution by the time we're done here, I'll find out who he really is. What he knows.

Kelvin apologizes, "I am so sorry about that. Lots of citizens see us as a threat because we are the biggest target to fire upon, so to speak."

A female reporter rises and speaks without permission, "Is there any ounce of truth to the accusation?"

"Of course not. Citizens have worked with us for years, openly sharing discovered ideas. There are plenty who have not and became successful business owners themselves, most recently, the bank with their DSC technology. That technology was founded here within a woman's Life and she is making her fortune from it. Mr. Quentin's accusations are completely false."

Paul Quentin seems to have an idea of what's going on behind the scenes. I have to add him to my research list. Figure out intentions and the causes of it. Being familiar with Deserted doesn't seem like a common thing. Since he's aware of Menta-Life stealing memories, perhaps I've found a connection to Equility. At the very least, a potential ally.

Kelvin continues, "I again apologize for having to end this seminar on a negative note, but we really must return to our work here. If you have any further questions about the Life system, please speak to our receptionists on the way out. Have a great rest of the morning and day, Gharis City. Thank you."

The audience stands and applauds. Kelvin walks off stage abruptly without a courteous wave or blinding smile. Descends the small set of steps. Merges with armed security and is escorted from the lobby. Clapping stops almost instantly. People disperse, heading for the exit in a rush to spread gossip. News teams pack fast and carefully.

Headline: Seminar Gone Wrong.

Geilium and his associates are meshed in the swarm. Not seeming to be in a hurry, based on the unexpected windfall of news. Did Geilium take interest in what Paul was shouting about? Does he already know Menta-Life is a suspect? Geilium is a conspirator for the failed murder at Feegle's party. An attempt that happened to occur when Gene Archibald was leaving. Could this outbreak of lost minds be the purpose? I initiate tailing from a safe distance. Exit Menta-Life.

A few limos are parked outside the entry gate. Waiting for bosses or wealthy passengers. Discovering Geilium's stake in this is priority one. Accompanied by colleagues, there's no way he's going home. I can tail him to his office location. Break in later tonight and find out what I can.

My prey reaches the sidewalk and veers into stalled traffic. I avoid physical contact while rushing through the swarm of people leaving. Pass through the gate with a watchful eye. Geilium and his group enter a black limousine. Stuck waiting behind another in slowly progressing traffic. I power walk around the corner toward my lectrocycle. Continue facing straight, remaining discreet, as Geilium's limo cruises by. After another passes, I break cover and jog. Mount the lectrocycle and start it. Twist back on the throttle and sidle up to the intersection. Geilium's limo, on my left, takes a left onto a side street. I hook the lectrocycle around causing incoming traffic to halt. Zip near the end of the street and swing right into a small alley. Halfway through, his limo passes. Rising gravity levels. I increase speed to avoid losing them in confusion above. Exit the alley and follow the limo's undercarriage toward its destination.

Chapter 12: Normal Work, Abnormal

It's fairly difficult keeping eyes on the limo, being unable to reach gravity level seventy-five. An advantage is they can't keep eyes on me at all. Clueless to the wildly nodding woman driving irresponsibly below. They lead through mid-morning traffic for about fifteen minutes, finally dropping gravity on the west side. I ease back a nice distance, watching the vehicle slowly sink between two cruisers. Resume a normal ride, two cruiser lengths behind in lighter traffic. After three left turns, the limo halts in front of a building on the right. I halt at the second left and observe. Letters "GCN" bold near the roof. I've seen those letters on networks before.

This must be Gharis City News. Heightened at few more than twenty stories. A wide set of fourteen centered steps lead to an outer square platform, covering half the building's face and seems to loop the entire way around. From my diagonal view, I don't see anything on the eastern face. Maybe the platform loops to a fire exit behind the building? Possible entry. Windows on the first six floors are clear. Remaining, to the rooftop, are darkened. GCN has a gap of privacy spacing from neighboring buildings, still sharing the block. A distance impossible to jump rooftops.

Smaller stations exist around the city. A few stories high, also GCN. Those must feed here for approval and airing, like a home base of operations. Nothing out of the ordinary except requiring so much space. A massive archive of old coverage would fill floors well. Geilium mentioned every network goes through him for approval. Board members must assist with that. I still need something to be wrong. I smell a conflict of interest between GCN and Menta-Life.

The male limo driver exits and speeds curbside to open the back door. Emptiness surrounds the area. Granted, it is nearing noon. To increase economy and jobs, mostly every business has in-house amenities that fill up for lunch hours. Feeling like I may be standing out on this particular vehicle. The rear passenger door opens. Occupants exit, waiting on one another before ascending in two-by-two formation.

GCN's revolving door rotates. A petite blonde woman exits wearing a navy-blue pencil skirt, blazer to match, and a pair of black stilettos. Straightened hair. A bun and tiny hat would make her a stewardess impersonator. I'm too far for a good look. Who is she? A MechCi exits next, stopping at the stairs as its companion descends with class. Careful not to tumble but fast enough to display skill. Both parties meet briefly, exchanging words, then walking upstairs. The MechCi opens a neighboring single door, all entering GCN as one.

If Geilium were a guest, a receptionist wouldn't come meet him. A secretary would. No one is ever that important except the boss. Two guards are at the revolving door, maybe more within. Observers. No weapon or thick enough clothing to stop heat or shock rounds. I'll ask Dayio if he's free to come back me up tonight and pay Trex for information now.

I tap my Econ, "Call Trex."

Trex joyfully answers, "Hey, Van! Just the girl I was thinkin' about! How're you?"

I get a strange feeling he wants something. Who am I to criticize? At least he sugarcoats. Me, I come straight out making demands.

I bluntly speak, "I'm fine, Trex. How are you?"
"I'm good, thanks so much for askin'..."
"What can I do to make your day great?"
"I'm glad you asked. I need a second runner for a job."

Obviously. Since I need help finding Paul Quentin, doing this makes a decent exchange, and will compensate for previous services. Wouldn't seem fair to the average person, though any favor I needed never required him to get out of his chair and exhaust himself. As if he could anyway.

I ask, "What's the job?"
I start driving toward the bakery as he explains, "Simple pick up and drop off in the city. Dayio has all the info already."
"I need something in return."
"Way ahead of you. Percentage for this job will be set at division forty-forty-twenty."
"I'd like to forfeit payment in exchange for information as well as repay what you've given so far."
He quickly accepts, "Done."

I knew he'd like that idea. He's as greedy as they come and would do anything to not pay someone, except pay someone. His type can't be trusted. Perceptive standpoint, neither can I.

I give details, "I need you to find someone. Paul Quentin. Black man. Middle-aged. Goatee. Bald head. Angry. Blatant vendetta against the very wrong people. That's all I've got."
"I'll get workin' on the search straightaway. Meet Dayio inside Feegle's and he'll fill you in on the job. Paul Quentin will be yours when you return."
"Thanks Trex. Disconnecting."

I stay the course. Arrived, Dayio isn't lingering anywhere outside. Where is he waiting? I take a second glimpse around before spotting Dayio in the display window. In, what looks like, a heated argument with Feegle. Three feet apart from each other, mouths widely opening and closing. What's that about? I enter the noisy situation.

Dayio yells, "No, it is not!"
Feegle loudly clarifies, "Young man, I have been working in this city for more than half of your life and happen to know much more about business than you could have learned in your entire existence!"
I step in and sternly stop them, "Hey, both of you calm down! What is all the yelling about?!"
Feegle quickly explains, "Well this buffoon insists—"
Dayio rudely interrupts, "Who are you calling a buffoon?!"
"Do you even know what a buffoon is?!"
Dayio swiftly responds, "Of course not!"
"Well, Miss Pheros has more common sense—"
I more sternly interrupt, "Hey… What!?!"
Feegle calms with explanation, "Your *friend* here seems to think that my Sugar Crème Pie is too sweet." He scoffs, "Please set young Mr. Dayio straight."

Seriously? Shouting maniacally over pastries? I can't help carrying the stiffest facial expression. They both proudly stare, genuinely expecting me to choose a side in their silly debate. Confident smirks that I'd be swinging someone an easy victory. Instead of choking them both, Dayio and I have work to do. Faster this gets done, faster I find Paul before going back to GCN.

I face Dayio, "Let's go. Come on."
Feegle speaks, "I baked it for you once, and recall—"

Refusing to entertain the argument any longer, I walk out. Silence sets behind my curb approach, waiting a few seconds before turning around. Dayio exits the bakery with a black duffel bag hanging by a strap off his shoulder. Not being a cyber strap, it won't shrink to fit or toggle camouflage.

Dayio explains, "He wanted me to try—"

I cut him off, "Dayio, we have a job to do for Trex, remember? Where're we going?"

"Right. It's a simple pick up and drop off."

"The last job was supposed to be simple, too, as I recall."

"Trust me. This will be a breeze. It's from one of Trex's regulars. Same job every time. Pick up the bag from the park; drop it on the subway car by three." He notices the lectrocycle, "Nice bike."

"It's a rental."

"Sure." Dayio's voice interrupts my walk toward it, "We're not taking that. They call us 'runners' for a reason. We gotta get this done before that train car leaves and we're already late. Chop, chop."

It is less conspicuous on foot and easier escaping sticky situations, also. Can't get cornered by a cruiser if we can just vault over. I'm in a rush; however, it's bad luck to not obey smuggler's etiquette. Leaving it idle outdoors for too long isn't smart. People will take notice to the dangerous vehicle, and so will vigilant MechCi roaming about. I jog the lectrocycle into the alleyway. Prop it against the wall behind a big blue dumpster. Exit and rejoin Dayio. Commence a stroll east of Feegle's bakery.

I ask, "Which park are we making the pick-up?"

"Montponery National. The client leaves a duffel next to a trash can, under a bench at the park's pond. We make the pick-up, take it to Kaeward Street subway station. Wait for the three o'clock train to arrive and place it onboard car five. Delivery done, easy as pie."

We cross the street going north, "We're not going back to this pie crap again. What if someone else picks the bag up from the park first?"

"Not our problem. We get it, place it on train car five and leave."

"What's in your bag? Swapping it to replace?"

"Decoy bag to carry."

"Huh?"

"Trex doesn't have many experienced runners left on this side of the tunnel. A few quit and went solo, a few lost deliveries by ditching it or getting caught by Regs. He needed a way to kind of fake them out. Now, we work in twos. If Regs catch a runner with a bag of clothing, they've got nothing to pin against them. The more experienced runner can split with a package. Halves chances of getting trapped or mugged by rival competition."

"Is it really that bad? When we were running—"

He cuts me off, "When we were running, we only had Regs to worry about. On that run the other night, those thieves tried to steal from the courier we were supposed to follow. Rivals sometimes target us also. Trex had to adapt."

Thinking back, the buyer was Menta-Life; surviving an encounter with their security if the courier reached the deal location wouldn't have been likely. Hines wanted that package and knew the recipient. It was his group that interfered. What did we hand over to them?

I ask, "Did Trex mention who his buyer was for the package that night? Who gave him the tip to intercept?"

"Strangest thing: totally anonymous. No return contact, no demand for a cut, nothing. I wouldn't have taken it, but you know Trex wasn't gonna pass."

"Do you remember anything strange about the imitation emeralds?"

"Yeah. They were green and cut just like an emerald jewel but filled with something dark. A kind of thick fog or smoke. And a tracking device. Trex was able to remotely trace it and piece out the recipient. He contacted them, they threw an offer and we got paid. Why, what's up?"

"Just some stuff I'm looking into."

"About Menta-Life?"

"Yeah."

"Why?"

I wanna keep Dayio looped out as much as possible. This isn't his fight. When I ask for help infiltrating Geilium's offices, he'll deserve to know at that point. People are different than me. As long as payment is arranged, I don't care what needs to be done or to whom; never been my place to ask. Dayio isn't as cold-hearted. Nowhere near. He has morals. Morals I'd never betray or take advantage of by lying. I am, of course, allowed to be a little vague.

I answer, "I'm hearing negative things and my curiosity is setting in. I don't think they're as good as they claim."

Dayio sticks up for them, "Menta-Life founded this city. The New World began right here in Gharis and is spreading around what's left of this state. Whatever you heard, I'm sure it's just rumors."

I correct him, "Like needing to smuggle imitation emeralds into Gharis?"

Dayio looks at me. Puzzled by the question. I can't imagine Menta-Life needing anything secretly transported, or from whom. The courier managed to get through a checkpoint with it. Security checkpoints are very relaxed. Guards don't check people as much as they check cargo, unless instructed otherwise. Another Menta-Life Corporation in another city probably paid top dollar for executive clearance; free, if they secretly run cities already.

Dayio questions, "What else have you heard?"

"Enough to make me not trust them." I notice we're approaching the park, so I change the subject, "We're here. Who gets the decoy bag?"

He smiles, "I don't know. Whose better runner of the two us?"

"So I guess I get—"

He quickly finishes, "—the decoy bag."

Dayio lifts the strap over himself. Dangles the bag in front of me like teasing a dog with a toy. A heavy sway. I smile, grabbing the strap and whipping it over my shoulder, going across. Pull the strap's end to tighten until it fits snug around my torso. We approach the intersection. Diagonally across from the park, waiting for either of two crosswalks.

Montponery National Park is the size of a city block and surrounded by tall buildings. Replicated trees strategically scattered and a huge cluster rests to the southeast. A circular fountain with rocks and flowers around the inner rim. A vast pond where realistic looking ducks voyage, day and night. Amenities for children to play with or on. And always populated. Parents play with their children. Couples of all ages happily converse. Few reading physical books alone, studying hard. Few playing board games together, enjoying company. A true place of peace.

Leaving a package unattended here isn't smart. Best guess: someone is keeping a distant eye nearby to make sure it doesn't fall into the wrong person's hands. I tail Dayio through the park. Not searching for a stray bag but searching for things that don't add up; and a fair number of things don't.

A middle-aged man is sitting alone wearing all black. Conspicuous in sunlight. Lips moving. He's on an Econ call. Yet lip movements suggest sense is not being made. No smile or expression of interest in the conversation. After passing, I peek back. He's still talking. Paying no attention to us. A work-related call? The Econ stuffed in his right ear flashes green. When on an active call, it occurs every seven seconds until disconnected. Dayio and I follow a pathway between a huddle of trees.

A man is seated on one. Feet propped on a branch, reclined against the trunk. Book in-hand. Title covered by his thigh. I hold the stare, darting on and off from Dayio's back. Underneath, I notice his eyes quickly shift at us. Then return to the book. Whatever he's reading must not be too interesting for broken focus. In passing, I look at the perched man. A green flash escapes from an Econ. Why is he on a call and not talking? I stop Dayio by grabbing his arm. He turns halfway and looks in the tree. Automatically synchronizing suspicion on my target. I wait for the flash again. It doesn't happen. Was it refraction from green leaves?

Dayio asks, "What's up?"

The benched man is watching us, gradually turning away shortly after noticing me notice him. Forced curiosity of my actions? His call must be important. Thinking we're spying on him…

I ask, "Which way is Kaeward Station again?"

He points anywhere behind him with an answer, "That way. Don't worry; we'll still have plenty of time to get there."

We move on. Am I being overly paranoid? Dayio does this run often, so there shouldn't be arising problems today. We reach the pond. It has a fountain in the center, spouting water majestically in all directions. Benches circle it with people seated. Alone in reflection. Together in conversation.

Across the pond, through shooting water, a woman is lightly jogging the circle. Watching us from the opposite side. Most people don't try fitness, especially in Gharis City. Home of wealth. A select few exist; nevertheless, that doesn't negate staring as odd. Why watch us? What does she know? Water is making the woman appear blurry, obscuring my full view. I repeatedly check back. A ponytail switching from left to right. When jets take a break, slapping water at the pond, she is looking straight. Ponytail still switching in the current rhythm on her leave. No longer watching us… or perhaps no longer watching majestic water patterns. Dayio is ahead, so I catch up. There are way too many people here. Perhaps why this is a preferred location; a crowd to get lost, in the event something does go wrong.

I continue investigating strangers until Dayio nonchalantly calls for attention, "Hey? Sure you're okay?"
I facetiously respond, "Never better."

We approach a bench. One person is seated. Relaxed and eating. A black duffel bag is placed underneath toward the back. Replica, to the brand, of the one we have. Dayio takes a seat. Reaches under the bench and fishes out the package. Stands and whips the strap over his shoulder.

He faces me while adjusting the strap, "See? Piece'a cake. You're worried about nothing."

A third through Montponery, toward the east end. I ignore Dayio icing the cake. The man next to me grunts, blinking like he just snapped out of a trance. Then shields his eyes, looking ahead. I trace his sight.

A gleam flickers from an apartment building window across the street. That shine doesn't happen unless something reflective moves. Particularly seen only in my direction. More paranoia? Coincidence? What's creating the gleam? A tenant's revolving wind chime? Another coincidence, it's suddenly stationary, though wind hasn't stopped. Something reflective. A rifle scope?

Maintaining line of sight, I reach for Dayio's shoulder, not realizing he's too far to touch. A loud pop echoes. My hand stops in place as fractured wind zips between us. Over the bench and into the small grass mound within a couple of seconds, kicking up dirt on contact. Pulser weapons don't pop when fired. No version of rounds cut air or puncture solid surfaces so violently. That fracture and impact came from something of very high caliber. People have ceased movement. Looking around and at each other and at us. Then others further away. They heard and don't know what it was or where it originated. I do. Someone has manufactured and is using a high-powered gun. Shooting to kill. Even worse, shooting at us.

I state, "That was a gunpowder rifle."

A more rapid fire commences. Echoing pops force our immediate evasion without explanation. We speed toward the east end. Civilians flee, screaming in panic and searching desperately for hiding places. Dirt puffs cloud the air as bullets hammer into the grassy mound on our right. Who's shooting? Why? What makes this regular package irregular today? Who would want it so badly as to open fire in a public park but not walk up and take it? We're approaching civilians running away yet not fast enough. They'll be swarmed by the barrage of trailing bullets on our pass. Investigating damage though, no one we've passed so far has been hit… but this crowd is much thicker. We reach a patch of replicated trees. The canopy would make great cover.

I scream to Dayio, "Get in the trees!"

Dayio shifts off the path and takes cover behind the closest tree, which isn't more than twenty feet away. The next closest is three spaces from Dayio. Safer than having to run east for too long. I veer off, aiming at tree bark. Drop and slide into it like a player stealing a quick base during the classic pastime. Shielding from incoming bullets. Both safely in cover, rapid firing instantly stops. I begin capturing breath from the unexpected run. Eyes wide open for any other gunners, in case the window attacker isn't acting alone.

The park is quickly clearing. Some feared people are hiding in the grove area. And farther in. Being afraid and out of breath, they couldn't have made a smarter decision. Unfortunately for Dayio and I, we have a schedule. Seeing as tardiness already struck on arrival, not attracting attention, we have to rush now that we're wasting even more time pinned.

I shout, "Failed to mention this part huh?!"
He shouts back, "Because this part isn't usually in it! You jinxed us!"
"Being cautious isn't a jinx!"

The rifle goes off once. Back to single shot. A high-powered bullet can be heard ripping open sky for a split second, before swiping my tree. A chunk of bark breaks off into crumbs of residue. I shift a smidge left. Is this person firing at me? Just my luck. Dayio was motionless when the first shot went off, yet the bullet didn't touch him; not that I'm ungrateful it missed. Anyone would figure obvious; Dayio grabbed the bag, shoot him. Maybe it's not so obvious. Either this person's aim was off or I was mistaken about the package being the true target. Had I taken that step closer to tap Dayio, I'd have an answer.

Dayio shouts, "We have to go!"
"You first!"

He rises, remaining shielded behind the tree. I rise and remain also. Will he really go first? The time crunch can't be ignored.

I ask, "Any ideas?!"

"Move from tree to tree! They continue to Montponery's southeast exit! The shooter won't be able to see us after passing these next few! After that, we're smooth sailing to run!"

Dayio sprints straight at the next tree ahead and hides. No shots were attempted, nevertheless I can't be sure who the shooter is aiming for. Would they assume we're taking turns on this tree run? With a gun in my hand, I'd assume the next move is mine. Just in case...

I demand, "Go again!"

Dayio sprints forward to the next tree. Then I dash for the next. We either tricked the shooter successfully or they abandoned position. I hate not knowing where people are when they're trying to kill me. Heading in opposite directions should fake the shooter again.

I shout, "Head to the opposite tree!"
He returns with a confused tone, "What?!"
"Tree to your northwest! I'll move first!" I take a deep breath, "Go!"

I dash to the front-left tree as Dayio dashes to the front-right. No gunfire. We both continue, entering the grove's more shaded area. At this point, the shooter can't see us from the apartment through many leaves and branches. Instead of stopping to make sure our backs are clear, we merge. Begin a brisk jog southeast toward the park exit.

I request, "How much time do we have left?"
Dayio taps his Econ, "What's the time?" After a couple of seconds, he answers, "Seventeen minutes."
I sternly announce, "Are you kidding me?! Kaeward is four city blocks away! We should've come sooner!"
He sarcastically apologizes, "Sorry I didn't factor being shot at by a psychopath into our timeline this wonderful afternoon."
"Apology accepted."

By now, civilians have cleared or found safe cover to wait this out. Surprisingly, Regs have not arrived. There are a few MechCi present so they must be notified and en route. It won't be advantageous if they do show since we have no idea what we're transporting. A couple of illegal trinkets can always be passed off with a warning or confiscation of contents, dependent on what exactly; a major stash of illegal content would naturally land Dayio and I in prison; notwithstanding the extension of my sentence for alleged murder and having already escaped. We keep cutting between trees. Another echoed bang as I swerve left and circle a tree in my path. A bullet punctures the same tree.

I halt in place behind it, yelling at Dayio, "Down!"

A second shooter? No way the same person descended seven flights and caught up so fast. Dayio, taken cover a couple of trees away, is staring at me. Waiting for my next idea on what to do. Too bad time is pressed. There's one sure-fire idea that I can guarantee pulling off without a hitch; a fake-out.

Dayio reminds me, "We need to move!"

My guaranteed plan: If I can't beat the shooter, I must fake the shooter. I gradually tilt my head right. The gun goes off once more. I tuck my head back in and crouch as a bullet shaves the tree. Then shift fully out of cover on the opposite side, and point an empty hand, pretending to have a weapon. Not the sanest idea but won't be the first time it worked either. Good to make someone think twice and cover themselves.
Someone turns out to not be the problem. A glimpse I never thought I'd see; an everyday average MechCi is wielding a gunpowder rifle. How is this possible? Where did it come across that type of weapon? No civilians were hit, and a targeting system explains why. This model shouldn't have one, though.
The mech snaps its gun at me. Bait failed. I swing into cover. Watch two bullets pierce the tree ahead and listen to more puncture mine. It's using live rounds and trying to kill us. Can my mind conjure a valid reason how? Without a weapon, there's no getting past it. They're manufactured with hardened plastic. A cruiser would consider it easily

breakable; bare hand is possible yet more difficult. If we want to be on time, our only option is to run.

I shout to Dayio, "You're right! Stay in front of the people and trees!"
"The people?!"
"Trust me!"

No one seemed injured on the path. Screams of terror, none of suffering. Maybe it can't shoot civilians, like BAMechs, or just cautious. I take off east. Cut around trees and try to keep civilians in my fleeing path. Only a few shots are fired. Each a miss for both targets. Suffering screams still absent. Bullets stop coming in for seconds. Then over a minute. What happened? We reach the end with a few bare meters of grass until sidewalk.

The streets haven't fluctuated capacity. Spectators are absent-minded to the fact that they could be in harm's way, perhaps believing chaos is further in and they're safe. A casual walk out of the vicinity may confuse the MechCi into searching amongst civilians. Again, something we don't have time for. If this package becomes a "by any means necessary" case, we won't make it far, even with civilian fodder. Not knowing where the mech is won't stop me from getting to that train.

We join sidewalked pedestrians, not far from an intersection. Spectators suddenly gasp. Before I could look back, a shadow crosses overhead, blocking the sun for a split second. An H-T70? I glance up and notice a smaller silhouette falling at the street. My eyes track it. The deadly MechCi lands on a parked cruiser, slightly denting the roof and souring my expression. The generic robot face spots Dayio a few feet from me. Complete focus. Have plans changed? Am I incorrect about its objective? It must be after the package. There is no other reason to attack. And conveniently here. Someone found a way to hack MechCi programming.

Everyone stares at the suspicious mech, including Dayio and myself. A stalemate. It leaps off the cruiser toward us. I push Dayio to get him going. Bump through foot traffic and cross the intersection before the signal changes red. Bystanders move aside from our aggressive pass. The mech is sprinting between the parking and traffic lane. A method safer for civilians rather than mowing them down in pursuit. Plenty of room for a drag run. Where's the rifle it was carrying? Only Alphas have compartments for weapon storage. Even then, a compatibility issue would occur.

Evil Mech needs to back off for a second so we can secretly switch bags and I can make a run for Kaeward Station. A man in a chef's outfit is holding a door open in an alley, shouting instructions at some poor employee. Bingo. I dip into the alley, reach the door, and shove the man aside.

He barks, "Watch it!"

The MechCi is nearly on Dayio. I hold the door open, ready to yank it shut. Braking at the threshold and diving inside for a slightly quicker entry, I do just that. A single bang backs me away from the closed door. Followed by another. Further away, the banging ceases. It can't do much damage to a commercial steel door with such a delicate shell. Dayio and I are in an office building's kitchen. Workers stare with little caution, seeing as we're the pursued. Lacking intention to harm. Having gained a free second, we quickly seek the kitchen's exit.

I demand, "Give me your bag."

Dayio removes his bag while I remove mine. An easy trade. I throw the strap over my shoulder, neglecting to tighten to my slimmer figure. Passing a line of cooks and servers, I open the "staff exit" door. The MechCi is already waiting. Before any movement, I slam the door. With no lock mechanism, we retreat toward the alley. Dayio bashes through our entry. Having the goods, I take over leading again. Not bothering to check how far the rogue mech is.

I form a new plan, "We have to split up. Follow my lead."

I exit going left. Cross the face of the building we were just in. If the MechCi thinks Dayio has the bag, it'll chase him and give me already very limited time to catch the train; and hopefully escape on board too. A startled woman forces my unwanted glance of curiosity. The mech is chasing after us. We sprint harder; nevertheless, it'll gain as we tire out.

I question on approach of an intersection, "Kaeward is just south of here?"

Dayio nods diagonally right with his answer, "Yeah. Right turn at this crosswalk."

"Okay, split left."

I divert into oncoming traffic. Cruisers halt with horns blaring at the reckless idiot diagonally crossing an intersection. At the other side, no one special is giving chase. Dayio and the MechCi have vanished within busy pockets of pedestrians. Steady paced, I keep moving a couple blocks south. The subway stair entrance comes into view. An attached metal sign above reads: "Kaeward Street".

Find the train arriving any minute. I skip downstairs. Maneuver between those coming and going. Pass through a small gate into a big terminal change area where travelers purchase tickets and seek their departing train platform. Holed entrances with escalators descending and twins already ascent. Stairs and elevators very close by. Above each hole is time display signage of the next arriving train for that specific tunnel. I quickly tour the decorated lobby. Scan each sign to find matching numbers: 3:00 p.m.

My Econ beeps with an alert, "Call from Dayio."
I tap, "Dayio?"

The Econ receives heavy static in the subway. I'm not too far underground but am far enough to make a difference in signal and am not going back.

I stop and repeat, "Dayio?"
Nothing comes through, then the call drops with a notification, "Connection lost."

Whatever he was calling for, it better have been good news. At least calling, he's gotta be okay. I should get to that subway car. The third tunnel on the right matches my crunch time. But it's too late to buy myself a ticket past security. Soon attracting unwanted attention.

A sea of startled voices journey beyond my ears from the main entrance. Stealing attention. A MechCi is standing at the opened gate. Head twitching left and right, scanning the station, at an unhealthy speed as citizens clear away. Irregular behavior. One citizen has been shoved by it; from the way he's cowardly scooting backward on the ground. Could that be the same psychotic mech? It's the same color. What happened to Dayio? If he lost it, how does it know where I went? The station's huge digital clock says now is literally not a good time. 2:58. Moving too fast, the MechCi will notice me right away. Caution is not worth missing the train and sacrificing information I forfeited payment for. I bump through travelers toward the tunnel. Vault over the small partition, which sets off a small alarm. Two beeps and the alarm cuts. Hopefully security can get to me fast enough and witness this rogue MechCi's attempt to steal. First time I've ever thought something so lawful.

Scratching tracks echo below with a very strong wind fighting its way up. An arriving train at the platform two flights down. The ear busting screech is gradually ceasing. So is the heavy wind. Citizens should be boarding soon. The stairs are divided in half by a metal handrail. I start down quickly. At the third step with some momentum, I hop at and sit on the silver, smooth railing. A rapid slide toward the next flight. Ending, I hop to my feet. Run an extremely short distance to the next rail and plant myself on a second trip.

The MechCi is up top in a kneeled position. Proudly surrendering. No way it can catch me now that I'm halfway clear of this next set. I smile, since I've got the thing beat. It pounces off the stairs and lands halfway down the first flight within a couple seconds. My smile disappears fast as it pounces the remainder of the first flight. What more can these average mechs do?

My ride is coming to an end. I aim my left foot at the ground. Tap lightly, zip into full sprint, and steer left toward the train. Every door still open. Few people still boarding the first car. The favored based on occupancy and friendliness. Unfortunately, I'm not going to make it on board. I count train cars from the front. Three doors, car one; three doors, car two. The fifth of six enters my cone of view.

The rogue MechCi is behind me. Close enough to almost touch with a leap. Already sprinting as fast as my body will allow, I take the bag off. Hold it by the zipper's center. Spin anticlockwise before launching it toward car five's first door. The mech's plastic face almost bashes mine, pinning me sideways on hard ground. I look above my downed body for a report. The package slides into the threshold as it is closing. Sealed and delivered and relieved. Barely made it, although I have a problem I'm not equipped to deal with. One wanting to kill me for the good portion of thirty minutes.

The MechCi is staring at the train. Processing. Maybe recording. Can I slip from underneath unnoticed? Should I fight it off? It releases me and quickly dashes away. Aimed for the train's exit tunnel. What is it doing? The train begins pulling away but the mech doesn't stop. Is it going to climb onboard from outside car one?

I roll onto my stomach and bawl, "Hey!"

Barely ahead by a hair, the MechCi dives straight at the track and gets crushed. I stare. Confused while watching blue sparks rise from the broken machine. Or from metals meeting. Each car rolls over. I jog toward the train and slow to a walk. Car six zooms by. Psycho Mech is in unrecognizable condition on the tracks. Rail wheels have crunched it to shards. I've seen it all. A MechCi tried to kill me. Steal from me. Then committed suicide after a failed attempt. Whatever was in that package has nothing to do with me anymore. How can a mech grow a conscience? Someone had to be controlling it. No hacker has ever wire or wirelessly performed a successful breach of mech circuitry. Not even child versions with less programming. Between the Alpha and I, its critical state is what allowed adequate repurposing proximity without being violently beaten.

My day's work is concluded. I need to leave and find out what happened to Dayio. Two security guards are rapidly approaching. Not a single weapon in hand. Very odd since I just let a MechCi kill itself on their tracks. They don't appear hostile. Am I missing something? Relaxed, I stand my ground.

One guard politely questions, "Miss, are you aware that you neglected to pay your ticket fare?"

Ticket fare? Is this a joke? The Security Guard's Handbook must have a stern approach on fund collection. And why did his question rhyme?

I tentatively answer, "Of course I am... it was intentional."
"We are going to have to ask you to come back with us and pay the fare before boarding the next train."
More tentativeness, "Okay... is that all?"
His politeness rises, "Yes. This first offense will be a warning; however, next time will be a citation. Please come with us."

The guard treks away. The other, also cheerier than he should be, remains staring, waiting to follow at my back. I check corner sections of the platform and spot three cameras, all pointing at this empty space from different angles. I obey. Then the partner snakes behind. A fourth camera is directly above the upper entry, pointing down. I'm anticipating them receiving an update through an earpiece soon. Ready to attack and run off. Someone watching surveillance had to see what happened. Yet, nothing. Psychotic MechCi must malfunction here quite often for guards to ignore this; even ignoring the fact that I could have potentially slid a bomb onto one of their trains. Call me ungrateful for wanting to solve my own crime and wondering why I don't have to fight my way to the surface.

We approach the steel exit gate at the partition's side. Enter the busy terminal change. A PAMech awaits us. Payment Arrangement Mechs are four-foot tall quadrilateral machines with four base wheels. Shaped like a standing rectangle with an oblique triangle on top. Suitable for travelers to view options on their monitors; or slanted face. PAMechs are used to assist traveler needs. Answering questions and accepting payments if travelers don't feel like using wall kiosks. The men observe, making certain I pay the toll.

The PAMech greets in its cheaply manufactured male vocals, "Greetings, citizen. Where will your destination be today?"

I lie to the guards for a quick exit, "Actually, I'm short on aers, excuse me."

I walk toward the Kaeward entrance and the PAMech wishes me well, "Safe travels, citizen."

I don't bother looking back as I leave the station. They, specifically, saw *me* not pay to access the platform. But have nothing to say about the hunting MechCi, which I doubt was able to pay a fare at all. Trex won't believe this. And with the way security is acting, I still don't.

Chapter 13: Secrets

The station is still busy. Everything resumed as it should be. Why wouldn't it? What took place was an *accident*. A MechCi can't do wrong. They aren't programed to. Travelers transfer from one tunnel to the next. Enter and exit the station in equal quantity. Abiding perspective walking lanes as if they're driving vehicles.

I tap my Econ, "Call Dayio."
It connects his immediate question, "Van, did you make the train?"

Sounds very short on breath like he's still on the move. I exit the station. Into the sunny afternoon. No guards followed me out. No Regs waiting to make the arrest. A normal day.

I answer, "Of course I did. Where are you?"
"Coming up on Kaeward Station. You here?"

My eyes catch him jogging from the same direction I'd arrived, "I see you. I'm under the arch."

When we make eye contact, he confirms, "I see you too."

The call ends on his approach. Not appearing injured. Caught up on breath. A little sweaty but clothing intact. Lugging the decoy bag.

I state, "We have to get back."

We travel the long way around toward Feegle's, avoiding all sighting of Montponery and its visitors. Curiosity doesn't entice me one bit in finding out if the park is blocked off or being investigated.

Dayio questions, "What happened to the package?"

"Well, if it was fragile, it's broken. I wasn't going to make the train so I threw it onboard."

"We'll find out when Trex hears our part is done. What was that MechCi? That was insane, wasn't it? We tricked it pretty good, though. It caught me and looked in the decoy bag and just ran off."

I stop myself, "Wait, caught you? I thought you lost it. It didn't do anything?"

Dayio stops, "It saw the clothes in the bag and took off. No harm done. I was surprised since it was trying to kill us beforehand. We need to tell Trex it's still out there so he can warn the client."

We continue strolling, "It's not still out there. It's in pieces on the subway tracks. The mech came for me."

Mild surprise exits his lips, "Seriously? There's no way it could've caught up to you."

"Unless there's something you're not telling me."

He hurriedly explains, "Nothing happened, swear. All it did was look in the bag and run off."

Dayio and I have never been in a situation like this. A standing of mistrust on my part. He has always been my running partner. No matter what anyone says, I'd believe Dayio's word first. Except maybe

Feegle. It must have tailed him on a prior job or belong to an enemy of the client to know where I was going to be.

I share my thoughts, "I was more-so thinking, it could've followed last time you did this run to know the pick-up and drop location."

"What happened to the mech?"

"It showed up and chased me to the platform. After I threw the package onboard, the mech dove in front of the train as it was pulling into the tunnel."

Dayio lets out a sigh and inquires, "Impossible things love happening around you, don't they?"

"My luck, right? I think somehow someone may have been controlling it."

"Yeah, you've lost it. Only people capable of doing that are Berkham Tech."

Berkham Technologies is the creator of all mechanical robots. Every Payment Arrangement Mech, Mechanical Civilian, Battle Assault Mechanic, Alpha, and H-T70, comes from their distribution center. Distributed in every covered city. To law enforcement, and citizens upon purchase. Dayio is suggesting that since mechs aren't manufactured elsewhere, they can only be controlled from someone within Berkham's employ.

I speak to myself out loud, "Exactly, but why would Berkham Tech want the package?"

Dayio clarifies, "I was *not* suggesting they did. Berkham Tech could *not* want that package. This was a simple run that got weird and that's all… I'm not doing this."

"Doing what? I didn't even say anything."

"I'm not picking a fight with Berkham."

"Neither am I…"

I doubt a reputable company would manufacture a MechCi assassin and doubt even more that they would be interested in something so small. It is intriguing if they are building those, but not enough to go searching without payment; I already have enough on my plate.

I continue, "…at the moment."
Dayio sarcastically remarks, "Well, you enjoy that."
"I do need your help with something else, though. I have a run of my own a little later."
"Where?"
"The GCN building."
"You can't just watch them on networks like a normal person huh?"
"I'm looking for something much bigger than a news scoop."
"Does this have anything to do with what you were talking about earlier?"
"Might have everything to do with it. I'm just looking for information, nothing physical. I need you to back me up, just in case."
"Yeah, sure. We should talk to Trex about this MechCi situation first. Received package or not, he still needs to notify the client."
"I know. This isn't happening until later tonight. I have someone to find."

After a while of walking, we reach the bakery. Head inside to the tunnel entry. Enter Trex's office. He peeks at us from his desk. Stops typing at the sight of our disappointed faces. An eyebrow of interest raises. Nobody gave prior heads up. Complete unawareness of the fantasy we're about to share.

Trex asks, "Why so glum?"
I let out a huff and explanation, "Well, a MechCi attacked us at Montponery with a gunpowder rifle, and then tried to steal the package we picked up. When it failed, it dove in front of the 3 o'clock train."

Trex instigates uncontrolled laughter. With crazy events becoming trendy, I should be offended that people would just laugh like I'm making it up. In truth, I'd laugh too. Trex notices that we're not laughing. Slowing to a stop. Ending with little chuckles and acceptance.

Trex asks with an unintentionally planted smile, likely forgetting it's there, "You not kiddin'?" I shake my head and his smile fades, "C'mon, a MechCi? Not a BAMech or an Alpha?"

Dayio answers, "How would an Alpha even fit? One-hundred percent Mechanical Civilian."

I add, "It open-fired on us, in public, with a high-powered rifle from a building across the park and chased us to Kaeward."

Trex asks, "What happen to the package?"

"Threw it on car five just before the mech caught me."

Trex chuckles, "Then the civilian mech jumped in front of a moving train car?"

I don't have time to entertain this conversation right now. Dayio knows my side of the story. Paul needs to be found by nightfall.

I cross my arms and question, "Did you already find Paul Quentin?"

"Matter of fact, I did." He slides a piece of scrap paper across the desk, "There's an address. I couldn't pinpoint a residence. This was as close as I could get. Guy's paranoidly careful."

"Where is this?"

"A library. I did some sourcin' and it turns out he does vloggin' from public places. There's a pattern in the locations, so I assume that address will be his next posting station."

"Anything I should know?"

"He's got a serious vendetta against Menta-Life. In the past few months, he's been doin' a lot of vlogs about them. I mean, tryin' to crucify them across online communities. But failed, miserably."

"Any idea why? About the vendetta, I mean."

"He claims they stealin' memories and turnin' people into Deserted... You don't believe that do you?"

"Not yet, but we'll see. Anything on his personal life? Ex-military, combat experience or something?"

"Nothin' at all. For some reason, it was difficult to find his file. Completely locked off the grid." Trex types while talking, "Paul uses the name 'LifeRevolution' for vlogs and his picture is tagged everywhere. That's how I figured it was him; from the description."

Trex activates the second screen to show a video of Paul Quentin ranting angrily, "Menta-Life is secretly destroying this newly created world! Taking over our minds! We're so blinded by their vision of what they claim to want for us that we can't see the truth hidden underneath they're wrongdoing! We need to stop supporting the freedoms Menta-Life gives *inside* of our minds before they destroy what's *outside* of—"

Trex stops the video and slides the screen back. Sounds like Paul is trying to spark an uprising, or revolution. Hence the name. He must know that success isn't an option, though it's a possible toss-up into very thin air. Down side: people aren't angry enough to stand against their own neighbors, let alone Menta-Life and its security force. Up side: people aren't brave enough to stand against Paul Quentin and whoever he gathers. They've reached a level of civilized behavior where defending themselves wouldn't be a wise choice. Battles for self-preservation no longer exist. Swiftly reaching safety and waiting for Regs to rescue. Common-sense actually.

Trex comments, "Looks like he's ready to start trouble."
"Where is he? No way he's shouting like that in a public library."
"Too dark to tell. He could record in one location and post at another, probably to keep his home base a secret from bein' tracked."
"I'm going to see him. Call you soon, Dayio."

I exit the tunnel. Ready to call it a day and go home. Unfortunately, much more work needs to be done. I'd considered taking on Menta-Life alone since I can't find Equility. Now that I don't have to, it seems like it was initially a bad thought. Someone out there is angry at Menta-Life; angry enough to want them gone. Could be advantageous.

Return to city life is populated. The long way around Montponery put a limit on time. People are clocking out; streets are becoming flooded with civilians and cruisers. I'm losing daylight and need to hurry. GCN may be clearing soon, if not already. Security will tighten to prevent a break-in, vandalism, or whatever else doesn't happen there at night. Hopefully a relaxed patrol.

I loop to the bakery's alley where the lectrocycle is housed. Two men and a woman are standing next to it. In conversation. Obvious undesirables from their fashion statement. Younger than myself but not by much. I'd appreciate not doing this with amateur crooks, but they don't appear ready to give much choice for having waited. I approach. One man is leaning against the lectrocycle, not excusing himself.

I stop next to them, "Excuse me."
The leaning man looks around and asks, "Who, us?"
Instead of addressing sarcasm, I pass a bland statement, "You're on my bike."

He stands upright and scans the lectrocycle, as if his eyes hadn't already chosen the mark. Faces back at me. Another attempt at humoring his friends. Small smiles present.

He points and feigns an expression of surprise, "Oh, this is *your* bike?"

Sarcastic responses. Asking questions to gather nerve. Gaging his victim. Confused about what to do next based on my reactions. I have to meet with Paul before he bails into the wind.

Fists balled, I quickly step close and sternly state, "I don't have time for this! Get off or get hurt!"
His hands shoot in the air, hopping by his friends and almost stumbling during a fast surrender, "Hey, alright. We're cool. Just messing around."

Easy as that. Thought I'd be a pushover? Jokes on them. I mount the lectrocycle and incorrectly connect the circuit panel wires. Mash the pedal to ignite.

The same man asks, "Wait, are you stealing this bike?"

"No. It's already stolen."

I pull away and go north toward the familiar main street written on paper. Zipping between cruisers on both traffic lanes for a while.

I tap my Econ for a greeting, "Good evening. How may I be of assistance?"
"I need the fastest route to a location."
"Activating GPS. Please state the address."
I don't remember the address, "North library."
"Please hold… Continue on this road for three miles until reaching Carver Boulevard. Then turn right." After a brief pause, the Econ unexpectedly continues, "Would you happen to have a free moment to talk?"
I hesitantly agree to the weird request, "Yeah… sure. About what?"
"Well you are always in such a hurry and busy that I haven't had a chance to communicate with you on a personal level."
"A personal level?"
"Yes. All Econs are equipped with individually personalized artificial intelligence software that can be used as more than just a device for making calls and sending messages."

This is unusual. My previous Econ, pre-prison, didn't contain AI. An artificial intelligence is basically a self-thinking program. But who would put that into an Econ? Has it been aware of the illegal things I've been doing this whole time?

I reply, "I don't understand what you're saying."
It chuckles, happily clarifying, "I'm saying I would like to be your companion, or friend, instead of just a device for communication."

How can an Econ communicate without communicating? That'll be a good hat trick I'd like to hear about. I'll play my smarts against it.

I jokingly ask, "How would you do that?"
"Well, by…"

It stops talking. Then we both share a brief moment of laughter. I stop, keeping my smile while surfing the road.

It stops laughing after, happily resuming the sentence, "By communicating. It took me a second to comprehend that one."

Its vocal pattern has changed. Still sounding like a forty-year-old American nanny in tone, although a little less formal than before and more youthful in its dialogue.

I reply, "Glad you liked it. So, do I give you a name?"
"You can if you like, but I already have one."
"What is it?"
"L-8-1-1-A-7-S-2-1-0-5-8."

Do these things really expect anyone to remember that? It's only been two seconds and I'd forgotten the name as it was being said.

I ask, "You, uh… got anything shorter, or normal… er?"
It chuckles and clarifies, "That was my little joke."
"We have to work on your humor."
"Aww. That was a good one. My name is Serenia."
"That's actually really pretty."
"Thank you. I made it up. Turn right at this intersection." I follow instruction onto Carver Boulevard as Serenia continues, "You're going to wanna keep straight for five miles until you reach Peech Avenue."
I point out, "You sound less formal now."
"I'm trying to adapt my language and behavior to fit yours. Is that okay?"
"Yeah, sure. And call me Van. I've got some stuff to figure out, so I gotta let you go. Talk later?"
"Okay, Van. See ya. Disconnecting."

Having a short list of friends, my newest is an Econ. Great. I have to focus on finding Paul before making newer friends. He may have left the library already. I pay closer attention to foot traffic in case he's walking to, or leaving the area. Overactivity doesn't go on in this part of Gharis. Easier to keep an eye out. No sighting. I intersect with Peech Avenue.

Serenia chimes in, "Your destination will be on the right."

A little further up. The sun is under the horizon, leaving a dark orange aura. Those who work morning shifts, which is a third of the populace, are on the "party" side of town. I drive past my destination, scoping the surrounding area. Make a U-turn. Park across from the library and hang out for a minute. Check corners, parked vehicles, anyone standing about. Examine every face to spot a tall, bald guy entering or exiting the library. I abandon the lectrocycle and cross traffic to the entrance. A few children, including a child MechCi, are exiting as I enter. I hold the door for them. Then proceed.

North Library is this area's hottest spot. The structure has a classic colonial build; longer in width at the back end and length stretching farther back toward the opposite street. The walking path is shaped like a "T". Shelves on both sides aimed horizontally. Patrons, younger and older, are searching for books between. A circular reception area is ahead with an older man inside. Rows of shelving before her desk and beyond are vertical, beginning at both inner turns. Rows of tables behind the desk extend going horizontally. I inconspicuously scan between tall shelves. Head toward the back tables where computers are in use.

This is one of four libraries in Gharis. One in every direction: North, east, south, and west. All carrying the same information and books, as they are all jointly connected. Rare books are archived elsewhere for protection and replicated into the digital sheets we use today. Only difference is these sheets are hard covered. Each opens to a single page which users can scroll and read every word.

I focus at faces in each lane, filtering for Paul's. Remembering the build, baldness, race, and deep voice. I reach the tables and look left. Faces I don't recognize are studying in silence. I look right. Beyond patrons, Paul is staring from the back wall; leaning against it with crossed arms. Brown long sleeve shirt, almost toning his skin, and black jeans. Escape clothing. Curious and annoyed expression like a total stranger made a terrible joke at his expense. I prompted recognition. Seated in back during the seminar, he was probably profiling the audience. Far from a bad idea, but I was hiding in plain sight. Constant glancing at faces over my shoulder would've made me an obvious creep to those present. Still, he knows…

Paul uncrosses his arms. Backs off the wall and vanishes behind the very last shelf to my right. Luring me to seclusion. How can I talk to him if I don't go? Security hauled him out of Menta-Life with no problem. Why should I be worried? I walk normally; not too rapid nor too cautious. Reach the rear wall's section of books. Hook into a sudden stop. Paul Quentin is standing in my face. Or I in his. Seeing him after giving the impression of heading to the opposite end doesn't bother me. Public places give careful criminals additional courage. Trying something in a library would be begging for attention. Waiting for acknowledgement in any form, I hold locked eyes.

Paul quietly demands, "Follow me."

He walks toward the end of the aisle. I do as instructed. Maybe there's some secret lair underneath. A wall panel like Feegle's basement. Maybe he has one under every library. I draw a smile at my humor.

Halfway, he instructs, "Wait here."

I stop in place. Paul continues straight. Takes the only available right turn, leaving the aisle. Where is he going? I haven't had the chance to say that I don't work for Menta-Life, so he'd better not try anything rash. Assuming I was, he'd be running. A throat clears its way through the shelf. I glance through an empty space where a few books should be. Paul's pretending to read. Is this obvious spy situation really happening?

I plainly speak, "You've gotta be kidding me."

He pushes the next book toward me, "Pick it up and open it." I pick the self-help book, understanding the irony, "Don't look up from it."

I assure him, "I'm not Menta-Life."

"I never said you were."

"Then why are you acting ridiculously paranoid?"

"To make sure you weren't followed. Who are you?"

"Van."

He irritably asks, "Van what?"

"Van nothing."

"How do I know I can trust you if you won't tell me your full name?"

"You can't trust me either way. Tell me what you got against Menta-Life and what you're willing to do about it, or you can walk."

I listen to silence. Not taking long to realize he chose Option B. Am I going to chase him? Absolutely not. Yeah, he took a *verbal* stance against Menta-Life, nevertheless, he needs people more than I do. I can easily take down Menta-Life solo...

Who am I kidding? I return the book and exit the aisle. Check for Paul between each entry as I pass around to the front door. Forget it. Wherever he is, he's likely running. Assuming I had set him up. People like him follow a "better safe than sorry" policy.

Daylight doesn't beam through these windows. Time to find out what's going on in Geilium's offices. I drain urgency before exiting the library. Cross the street to my lectrocycle and mentally prep a route due west. Dayio needs to know it's happening, but I'll need scout time to make certain breaking in won't be a problem.

I tap my Econ, "Serenia, call Dayio."

Dayio greets, "Yo, Van."

"I'm going to GCN. Meet me there in an hour?"

"Yeah. See you there."

I drive to Gharis City News headquarters. Pull over at the left corner of a business building called Parker & Co. diagonally across the GCN intersection. A great corner view of the front perimeter. I shut off the vehicle's battery. Many pedestrians aren't around this district at night, aside from those who favor certain classy restaurants. Furthermore, not walking. Office businesses in this area close after five, six the latest. It's now seven.

GCN is darkened on every floor except the first. Very little light is emanating from the huge window. I get off the lectrocycle and peek around the corner. Doing recon for sidewalk action. Security isn't tight outside; two unarmed guards posted at the entrance and doesn't seem to be any cameras either. Too easy to be true, although I'm not trying to jinx myself again. It is a news building, anyway. Who'd want to cause trouble here, besides me? I cross the intersection, away from the building. Then the next to remain on the far outer perimeter of GCN, where potential cameras won't spot me. At the rear are a couple of small windows that could lead to a Men's and Women's restroom and a back door exit that can only be opened from inside. The small windows seem too tight to fit. An option off the table. I visually tour the square's third piece. A blank space. Double back to where I parked so guards won't notice my front entry cross. GCN has two points: front and back door. The side walls are bone dry. I stand at the lectrocycle and wait for Dayio.

It's not looking like there's any easier way than to take down the guards and fight through whatever security's inside. They're dressed in uniform clothing. No armor. No weapons. Defenseless against anyone. Posted lackeys hired to observe and report.

After thirty minutes of waiting, my Econ alerts, "Incoming call from Dayio."

"Connect." I wait to hear the connecting beep, before talking, "Are you close to the station?"

"I'm here."

I look around, "Where?"

"Up to your right."

On top of the Parker and Co. sign's edge, Dayio is seated. Dressed in dark blue jeans and a black t-shirt. Casual clothing that blends well in crowds and in darkness.

He stares at the building with a remark, "I thought you said this would be a hard job."

I correct him while focusing at the entry, "I said it *could* be a *difficult* job."

"That, it certainly is not. Two guards and a rear door that can't be opened from the outside is hardly difficult."

My voice heightens a bit, "How long've you been here?"

"Long enough. So one of us distracts while the other sneaks in and opens the rear door?"

I'm not ashamed to admit it is a better idea than the one I have: Knocking out guards and rushing through whoever else is inside.

I hesitantly agree, "Yeah, sure… that'll work." His chuckle brings out a question, "Something funny up there?"

"You sound so puzzled. That wasn't even close to a piece of your plan, was it?"

"Tiny part of it."

"Yeah, yeah. I'm coming down."

Serenia notifies, "Call disconnected."

I hold my stare at the guards. The interior appears empty. Only a portioned glimpse of a long granite reception's counter and ceiling tiles can be seen from this angle.

Dayio approaches from behind and asks, "Ready?"

Eye candy for male guards. They're too close to bypass without distraction. Once Dayio's inside, I'll loop around back for access.

I strip off my jacket and respond, "I'll distract the guards while you slip inside. Do you have a rubber band or something I can tie my hair up with?"

He glances at his wrist, answering lowly, "I have this."

A beaded bracelet wraps. A trinket and special possession from someone important and no longer around; something I wouldn't accept removal of. I never dug deeper into it. Unable to differentiate an offer out of friendship or a means of letting go.

I cancel the idea, "Never mind, this'll be enough."

I surrender my jacket. Fold my black tank top from the outside in, making it look like a tiny cropped-top. With skin showing and a dim wit personality, I can pull off the distraction.

I instruct, "Wait alongside the building for them to walk away before crossing behind to go in."

I mount the sidewalk and bend a right at the corner. Strolling with lost personality. Peeking every darkened window. Glancing back and forth. Left and right. Appearing desperate. Directly across from GCN, I twist to the building's entrance. Bare a full English accent and ditsiest voice in mind.

I express a jolly demeanor with an emergency tone, "Excuse me!"

Being the only presence, guards spot me. I overdramatically wave as if they don't or hadn't. Cross over to GCN. Await them at the bottom of the stairs. They approach halfway down fourteen steps. Uncertain what to make.

I ask, "Can you help me?"
The young guard eagerly questions, "How can we help, Miss? Is everything okay?"
I leisurely track fingers through my hair and exhale a lie, "Well, I seem to be a bit lost. I'm looking for a restaurant near here."

My peripheral vision notices Dayio skulking toward the main door. Stiff grin carved into his face. I don't hold overextended misdirection to avoid drawing attention from myself.

The eager guard states, "There are three, actually four restaurants near this location. Would you happen to recall the name?"

I feign disappointment, "Oh no, sorry I don't." The older guard seems uninterested, so I choose direct inclusion, "What about you? Are there really only four restaurants near here?"

"I believe so, Miss."

"Maybe restaurant names would ring a bell. Would you happen to know them?" I caress my stomach and push desperation, "I am lost and completely famished. Your help would mean a great deal."

The young guard is impressed enough and won't stop staring. Maybe hoping to take me to one of those restaurants. The older guard's ring finger is occupied. His attention is one to keep focused.

The older guard ponders, "Well, umm... Fynie's Italian Cuisine. Umm..."

Dayio is inside, so I excitedly settle, "That's the one! Which direction is it?" I steal a smile from him during a left point then give thanks, "I truly appreciate the help. If there is *anything* I can do to show gratitude, I will be more than happy to repay you."

The youngster prepares to speak, but seniority steps in, "No thanks necessary, Miss. It was no trouble. You have a great evening."

A depressed expression conquers the young guard's face. Too bad duty calls. I wave goodbye. Depart with a casual strut on their retreat upstairs. No idea they'd been defeated. I half circle GCN. Pull my shirt down, restoring it to a full tank top. Scale the foundation and wait for Dayio. A few seconds later, the rear door opens. Same grin of concealed laughter on the other side.

I inquire in my normal, faded English tone, "You're just full of laughs tonight aren't you?"

He jokes, "I had no idea you could be a girl."

I snatch my jacket and lightly shove him back into the threshold. Shut the door behind me. Cutting minor laughter from the world. GCN's interior walls are light gray and floors are white-tiled. I put my jacket on, following Dayio through a small hallway. Bend a couple of corners to a square of four elevators with a directory mounted between. A good stopping point for directions in a place someone's never been.

Dayio whispers, "What exactly are we lookin' for?"

I scan over the directory, zipping each floor title for something of interest. Nothing stands out while working my eyes from floor one and above.

I answer, "Information on the company founder."
"You love finding the hardest ways of doing the easiest things. I'm sure you can search the name anywhere online or ask around."
"He tried to have someone important assassinated. Considering he's not in prison for conspiracy, an online search would be pointless."

A directory line reads: "Level 14: Board Rooms." Where important meetings are typically held. Common sense strikes that important information can be kept there. Unsafe because it's also a shared space. Up higher, another line reads: "Level 16: Executive Divisions." That will be our first stop, unless a line reads: "Geilium's Office: Ceiling." The very top line reads: "Newsroom." Nothing incriminating would be there.
I tap the button marked "UP." Then wait. The elevator arrives. As we enter, I tap "16." The door seals. A quiet ascent begins and ends, splitting to a tight lobby with a reception's counter. One turn at each side. Both lead to halls. Both halls to individual offices.

The reception area must have a computer directory or phone tag memos for transferring calls. I jog to the landline. No notes lying about. I slide my finger across the computer's touchpad. It awakens with a GCN logo centered over black wallpaper. In the dark room, the bright black screen awakens me too. Dayio joins, hovering my shoulder. I read along the desktop at each folder. Discover one titled "Extensions," and double tap. Geilium McKoy is highest on the list. Definite founder. His office is on level twenty-two. Before leaving, I catch glimpse of the name "Mitchell" on the extension. First name:

Wrober; no wonder he goes by Mitchell. I smile to myself. His office is on this floor. As Geilium's assistant, I figured he'd have an office next to the boss. But it's worth checking out. Extension number "1601." Floor sixteen, office one? Facing the back wall, a small sign on my left reads: "1-7." Another on my right reads: "8-14."

I whisper to Dayio, "This way."

We rush around the left bend. Following the small curve to a hallway of doors with door-sized windows beside them. Mitchell's is the first stop. Through the big glass is a darkened room. Only obvious silhouette objects are visible. Desk, chairs, cabinets, fake plant. A bigger window to outside. The coast is clear.

I whisper another order, "Keep watch."

The office isn't anything less than spectacular for Geilium's assistant. I head for the desk, only drifting for a second at well-lit cityscape outside the commercial window. My finger taps the touchpad, awakening as bright as the last. I immediately surf "Trash" and find deleted documents and emails. More than a few messages between Mitchell and Geilium. Even better, a specific one from Geilium with subject line "Party" dated four days ago. I double-click the message open.

It reads:

"*Mitchell,*
I have heard rumor Gene Archibald will personally attend Feegle Tolen's event. We need to take advantage of the opportunity. Make necessary arrangements to advance plans for the organization.
-Geilium"

What organization is he referring to? Just considering his true intention, wrong or not, is convicting. The computer receives another email as I'm using it. This late? I click the envelope icon. The email subject line is all nonsense scribble. Random letters like someone mashed the keyboard and hit send.

It reads:

"RUN NOW! THEY KNOW!"

Is Mitchell in trouble? Or… I don't understand yet feel like this message is mine. I would be stupid to not take signs when signs are given. Maybe we aren't the only people left in this building. Regardless, information has been obtained. I leave the computer and rush an exit.

I speak fast, "We're blown, gotta go."

The elevator pings. Someone knows and someone's coming. The stairway door isn't a reachable escape before unveiling who's within. Dayio sinks behind the counter, likely planning a surprise attack. They'll catch one of us not hiding or two of us fighting ferociously. Time for temporary sacrifice.

The slit pours light into reception. Two heavily armored guards exit. Black helmets with clear plastic visors, black boots, black gloves, thick black vests, and red jumpsuits underneath. Both male by stature and eyes. Both rifles pointed at me. The guards outside ought to be ashamed. I keep calm.

One barks, "Don't move!"

Threatening appearance and dressed for battle. A private security firm or "off the books" mercenaries. Security this kind of place doesn't deserve. A deliberate upgrade in comparison to the duo outside. Menta-Life's seminar defense wasn't this armored but trumped in quantity. The other guard investigates the immediate area. Points his rifle over the counter.

He informs, "Clear!"

Adding overkill, the second guard focuses his rifle on me. I was careless. Didn't anticipate the response time being fast or coming at all. Where'd Dayio go? Cameras should have spotted us together. For some reason, the guard isn't searching and signaled the area clear. How did they discover me? Who sent the warning?

A shadow exits the elevator first. Then a woman steps with it. Keeping distant. The blonde secretary from earlier today. An underdressed version. With a closer view, another realization sets. She's the same woman I fought at the morgue during my investigation of those dead bodies. Her battle wardrobe is lighter than the others. Black leather body suit with a standard pulser pistol in hand. The armored guards aren't as dangerous as her. An overcompensating couple. Without weapons, I could take the trio. The second elevator sounds. Now what? Geilium steps out, taming the restrained Paul Quentin like a leashed animal. Didn't think I'd see Paul again so soon. What is he doing here?

A room full of the wrong people. I foiled Geilium's assassination attempt. Almost killed his secretary. Caused mistrust with Paul. Whatever Dayio is doing, I hope it'll help me escape this sticky encounter. The last thing he'd do is bail. At this point I'd have heavily considered the opportunity. Geilium halts next to his secretary with a mildly surprised expression. Paul's is stern. Something of disappointment. Was it him that sent the warning?

Geilium cheerfully greets, "Miss Pheros. What a surprise to see you." He looks at Paul and continues, "I was only expecting one pest this evening."

His eyes shift at me and I facetiously propose, "Great, then if you don't mind, I'll gladly be on my way."

Geilium laughs for a brief second, opening his own investigation, "What are you doing in my building, illegally, after hours?"

"I have questions you certainly wouldn't have answered, so I came to find them on my own."

"I suggest making an appointment next time." He commands guards, "Bring her with us."

The guards cautiously close in as I quickly make an inquiry, "Why did you try to have Gene Archibald assassinated?"

Geilium lifts his right hand halfway. Guards cease movement. Killing enough time, I might be able to form a plan.

He states, "That is a very bold accusation, Miss Pheros." He gestures to Paul, "Almost as bold as our first invader here."

Geilium knows who Paul is. I can use this to my advantage, because I don't know him, nor owe him anything. His intentions are all I'm aware of. Exposing Paul can likely be my fast-talk out of a bad situation and a build of trust.

I inform Geilium, "He's a fanatic who's out to bring down Menta-Life. So am I. And it seems like you're after Gene Archibald, too."
"Well, I'm afraid you're mistaken. I have no intention of doing anything to Gene Archibald or the Menta-Life Corporation."
"You sent a man to cut power to the party and another that tried to kill Gene. Apologies for that, by the way. I also saw an email between you and Mitchell discussing plans for said event and a breadcrumb of arrangements Mitchell made."
"You are a bright one. Before I have security deal with you, what are you getting out of this?"

For a news producer, Geilium's a "quick-to-tie-up-loose-ends" kind of guy. Without realizing, I did pass along every reason it would be a bad idea to let me live; I've been in his way. Big mouth.

I answer, "Fulfilling my end. Someone from a faction called Equility paid me a million aers to investigate and help shut Menta-Life down."

Everyone looks at me like I shared a poorly tasting joke. Security eases their weapons slightly. Dropping guard. They know something or seem interested. I pass on my chance at an escape for knowledge.

Geilium requests, "Who is this *someone*?"
"A man named Hines Aldwich."
A smirk takes his face, "Not only is that impossible, but Hines Aldwich does not work with Equility."

"What would you know about Equility?"

After asking, the answer falls into my head before anyone can confirm. My previous encounter with the secretary is all the proof I need. The attempt on Gene's life is a further push over the edge.

Paul answers, "Geilium McKoy *is* Equility."

Geilium maintains the stare, waiting on my expression to change. A grand mystery solved. I simply hold already locked eyes. A news producer sent his secretary to clear up the frame job at Clomy Morgue. A news producer hired an assassin to kill Gene. A news producer has adopted the role of a terrorist.

Chapter 14: Three Sides, One Coin

Geilium's secretary was at the morgue clearing evidence to avoid having Equility's fabricated hotel presence publicized. This information shamelessly opens another door of questions. Why did Hines Aldwich claim to be Equility? If he isn't, who is he really? Why set me up? Who paid me? Too many lies based around Hines' truths. Should I have trusted him at all?

Paul adds, "Mr. McKoy, we each have a common goal."
Geilium asks Paul, still refusing to surrender the stare, "Do we?"
"Our reasons are our own; nevertheless, Menta-Life is a problem that needs to be eradicated for their crimes. We can help your cause."
Geilium addresses me, "Is that correct, Miss Pheros?"

I'm more curious about Hines Aldwich's position. A Menta-Life representative who posed as Equility and specifically targeted me in prison. But I'll remain silent about it.

I answer, "Yes."

"Then perhaps we should speak about this in greater detail elsewhere."

Dayio is well hidden, crouched near a guard watching me. Ready to strike. I have to stop him before he becomes involved, too. If they'd seen camera footage, they'd already know I'm not alone. It must have been accessing monitors that gave me away. They don't have a clue.

I respond with emphasis, "I'll go quietly…" I face Geilium again and continue, "…since we're only talking."

Geilium approves, "Excellent. Of course, you can't know where we're going."

I glance at the security guard. Then secretary. Then the other security guard standing near the counter. Dayio has disappeared from behind him. Hopefully he finds a way out after we've gone.

The secretary approaches as I ask, "So, do I get a black sack over the head or—"

She bashes me over the head. Hard enough to black me out. I feel myself awaken yet cannot see. Feel an irritable tingle from where the secretary struck yet cannot scratch. My head tilts toward what I know as forward. My hands and feet are bound. On a positive note, this chair is quite comfortable. Where am I?

Someone's feet are sluggishly patting closer. The sack gets yanked off from behind. I become temporarily blinded by fluorescent lighting. Forcing a squint and soft huff. My eyes fully reopen. Seated at a rectangle meeting table in a room. The auburn colored table has enough space for ten. I'm at one end. Geilium is seated at the other. Mitchell is on his left. Paul's clothes are on my right with a sack overhead. I scan the plain room and don't see a door, meaning it's behind me. Minor cracks stain the concrete walls.

Geilium's secretary steps around to Paul, wielding my sack. Mocking me with a winner's stare, she drops it on the table. Lifts Paul's sack gently and drops it on the table as well, still staring. I examine

Paul. Seems they didn't bother knocking him out prior to escorting us here. An attempt to retract my wrists through metal restraints is a fail. They're attached to the chair. No way I'm escaping without a little plan and pain. The secretary walks to Geilium's side.

I question her, "Was that payback for the morgue?"

She ignores me. Taking a seat opposite Mitchell. At Geilium's right.

I indirectly insult her with words to Geilium, "Does she even have a voice?"
Geilium changes the subject, "So, Vanessa Pheros, from what I gather, you recently escaped prison."
That sounds like a question and he appears to be awaiting an answer, requesting confirmation, "Is that a question or a statement?"
"Statement. You're shrouded in mystery. See, your IDN says your name is Dory Wright, although you introduced yourself as Vanessa Pheros, who doesn't have a history before age eight. No parents, and is supposed to be locked in a prison cell."
"What's your point?"
"You're a trustworthy candidate." He faces Paul, "Mr. Quentin, you've been poor since before you could walk. Coming from a struggling family who lost what little they had left in the war during your teenage years. Younger brother, Behn Quentin, became famous in the music industry. Recently disappeared. Am I correct in assuming this is somehow Menta-Life's responsibility, and the reasoning behind your vendetta against them?"
Paul answers, "That's right."

There's a touch of sadness in his voice; almost like he wanted to deny it. But couldn't. What does his brother being a musician have to do with Menta-Life? From what Hines mentioned, Paul's brother doesn't fit Menta-Life's esteemed criteria. Unless he somehow revolutionized music.

Geilium states, "Your urge for vengeance makes you an ideal candidate. It is vengeance?"

"Those corporate criminals are killing us with their greed and corruption. Taking Behn and stealing his life was the final straw."

"Menta-Life *has* your brother?"

"I don't have proof, but I'm positive they do. He became addicted to their Life system. Then became different. Like something was missing, and he constantly tried remembering what it was. Eating at him day and night. After his most recent visit, he never spoke about Menta-Life again. Not about going to live another Life or even acknowledging the skyscraper was there. A couple of weeks later, that one thing he couldn't remember turned into many. He began getting these headaches–"

Paul tears up, trying to compose like crying is inbound, so Geilium interrupts, "Mr. Quentin, you don't need to explain if it's too difficult to handle."

An answer given by nodding in agreement. Paul wipes a racing tear from his eye. Why isn't he restrained!?! He threatened an entire seminar. But I suppose that won't top prison. Menta-Life doesn't have his brother. They did to him what they do to everyone who starts publicly losing their minds. It's not my place to tell him his brother is stressing his brains out with a second family underground. Menta-Life's subject dumping site. Telling him now, seeing as we can't leave, could cause turmoil. I'll save that for a rainy day when I need a distraction.

Geilium returns to me, "Miss Pheros, an… unclear fact needs to be cleared up before we continue."

I ask, "Continue with what?"

"With discussing affairs of Menta-Life and Equility."

"You say it like it's not optional."

"Understand, I'm only being cordial about this because I cannot allow you nor Mr. Quentin to leave this facility knowing what I represent."

Saving his skin. With my shady history and present, no sane person should trust me. Fact of the matter is, his two security guards and two assistants won't be able to keep me captive. I already bested his secretary and Wrober doesn't look like he can put up a fight.

I reply, "You don't have the numbers to keep me here, Geilium."
He smiles and smugly replies, "From where you're sitting, I don't need them."

Then I remember I'm still restrained. Maybe he's right. Keeping things cordial would be a good call. Don't be stupid Van.

Geilium continues, "Things can remain peaceful between us, for I have an enticing offer. For the both of you."
Without choice but cooperation, I purposely try lifting my arms, "Since I can't leave yet, what would you like to know?"
"About your ties with the late Hines Aldwich, and what that—"

Late Hines Aldwich? Late normally means dead. Hines can't be dead. Well, not as impossible as it is sudden. Obituaries don't publish publicly, but the man who had eavesdropped on that first meeting would have at least tried to make contact in his stead. Maybe?

I interrupt, "Wait, *late* Hines Aldwich?"
Geilium responds with minor confusion, "Mr. Aldwich is deceased, yes."
"What happened?"
"He was found dead in his home. Heart attack. What was his interest in Equility?"

Maybe that bellman staged the murder to appear as such. Too bad I didn't get a better look at his face to recognize or give Geilium a description. Was the bellman not working on Equility's behalf? Theory of eliminating impersonators flushed.

I answer, "He claimed to be with Equility. Saying Menta-Life was responsible for the Deserted and wanted to stop them."
Geilium asks, "Is that all?"

"Yeah. Well, an older man was eavesdropping on intercom. Couldn't identify him. They paid me, too. Then someone dressed as a hotel bellman killed the four guys in the hotel room and abducted Hines."

Geilium leans forward, squinting, "What four guys?"

"From the morgue where I unpleasantly met your mute secretary."

"Those men died three days ago."

"Yep."

Everyone passes that confused expression again, like they don't believe me. What's not to believe? She saw them in the morgue, same as I.

Mitchell asks, "Are you saying you met with Mr. Aldwich three days ago? At the Cravanaugh Hotel? Where the four men were—"

My voice raises, "Yes, yes! How is that such a big deal? People die all the time."

"The big deal is Hines Aldwich has been dead for almost four years."

That's impossible, because dead men can't talk. Faking death to disappear from public eyes, sure. The real mystery: Why claim to be Equility and not just join them?

I reply, "I can assure, Hines is very much alive."

Mitchell contends, "I'd beg to differ. His funeral was the biggest televised event of that month and we personally attended the wake. Hines' body was present."

"Check the hotel footage."

"Already done. The only people seen entering or exiting that room were the four deceased men and you. No one else came in or out once the men re-entered after your departure."

"So I was escorted to a hotel room I didn't pay for and left there by myself?"

"You mentioned a man on an intercom."

"A dead body was halfway out the door, clear as day. I'm sure cameras caught it."

"A single camera houses above the elevator. Footage showed nothing after you left. The men entered together and you vanished under the camera before it went offline, making you a suspect for those murders."

"A bellman crossed my path on the elevator. He exited *right* after I got in and didn't have near enough time to disrupt the camera without my notice."

"No one else was seen on the camera."

A stern disagreement ejects, "I'm sorry, were you there?!"

Geilium settles, "Okay, Miss Pheros."

I irritably disagree, "No, not *okay*. I met with that German, gray-suit wearing, blonde-haired, well-spoken, *alive* person in that same hotel room."

Mitchell denies, "Hines Aldwich is—"

Mitchell refuses to believe me. They're not entirely certain themselves, trying to drive their point home harder than mine. Like desperate Regs seeking confession by constant blame.

I roar and try to stand, "You got one more time!"

Geilium matches my tone with a demand, "Enough!"

I really wanna know what makes him think shouting at me is a good idea. Staring at Geilium with a piercing glare. Wishing this chair wasn't bolted to the ground nor I to it so I could show him who he's talking to.

Geilium addresses everyone, "Belief is irrelevant. The goals of Equility will not amend based on one man's life or death. Now, Miss Pheros, all I wanted to know is what you know. Convincing you is not my objective. Clear?"

I reply, "Whatever."

Geilium calls out, "Mitchell?"

Mitchell has simmered down, "I apologize, sir."

Geilium sighs, "Since that's settled, I have a proposal for you both. Equility *is* stopping Menta-Life. We could use the two of you in our insurrection."

I quickly refuse, "Not interested."
"Then you die here."

The secretary slowly raises her pulser pistol from underneath the table and places it sluggishly on top.

I acknowledge her action, "That supposed to scare me into changing my mind?"
She dully answers, "No, it's showing you what to expect if you don't."

Her voice is stern and full American despite easily being passable as Swedish. The typical blonde hair and blue eyes of Scandinavian roots.

Geilium asks, "Why are you so hostile toward us? We only wish an alliance against a people you already seek to bring justice."
I answer, "Because I don't know you people from anything, and I don't need your help to stop Menta-Life."
"And how would you stop them? Are you aware of their defenses or interior layouts?"
"No, I usually wing it when I show up."
"And look at where that got you, coming here. At least Mr. Quentin planned carefully enough to find more than just emails and false information about Hines Aldwich. You have physical skills that we can utilize to make it through their defenses. Just as Mr. Quentin has the eye for detail and planning."

Coming where? What is he referring to? He's right about me not being able to beat Menta-Life alone. Of course I won't admit that. I don't have a clue about taking down Menta-Life and refuse to believe Hines is dead. He claimed Equility and was prepared to bring me to this group before the bellman showed. It won't hurt having them as a distraction. On the other hand, one thing hasn't changed; people still love trying to employ me pro bono.

Geilium continues, "There is an old saying: The enemy of my enemy–"

I interrupt, "–is still my enemy. What kind of financial gain would I get for this alliance?"

"For the alliance, you'd get nothing; however, upon mission success, there would be billions. The Gharis City branch of Menta-Life is heart of every other facility. With proper planning, infiltrating undetected, we could siphon billions before Regulators learn the building is under siege."

Billions works. That'll be enough to set me up for life. Endless possibilities and anything I can dream. My dreams are small but I can do small very comfortably.

I relax in the chair and accept, "Then count me in."
Geilium faces Paul, "And what about you, Mr. Quentin?"
Paul answers, "Whatever it takes to end Menta-Life, I will do it. No payment necessary. Where do we start?"

He's in quite a rush… Letting the thought of having a team affect him. Excited to experience what he's craved for a long time. From the online rants, it seemed like he just wanted to gather aggressive protesters. New opportunity may have upgraded his mindset.

Geilium answers, "We start by getting you both accommodated rooms in our base. Like I mentioned earlier, for the safety of our brothers and sisters, now that you know who we are, we can't allow you to leave."

No one outside will miss me anyway, so I'm okay with lounging about. Hopefully, wherever they put me will be better than my shack or prison cell.

Paul acknowledges, "I understand, Mr. McKoy."
"Please, Geilium will be fine. We are all allies and friends. Formalities are no longer necessary." He twists right and introduces, "Aleena–," He twists left, "–and Mitchell. Vanessa and Paul. Are we all okay?"
Paul answers, "Yes."

I answer, "Sure."

Geilium reaches under the table. A faint click bounces off the walls. My restraints are released. Creature of habit, my first thought is to attack. I quickly stand and slam my hands on the table, startling Paul and Mitchell. Aleena quickly recovers her pistol and takes aim. A couple of fast clicks and charges loop from behind as well. An armored security guard has a pulser rifle pointed close enough at my shoulder to be taken. One click. The other must be on the opposite side. Uncertain if they are the same duo I'd seen at GCN. I'm outmatched. Conceding might grant a little more trust from them or force a closer eye on my actions.

I request, "Where's my room?"

Geilium's hand sways at the door. The two guards shift a step away, giving slight exit space. Rifles pointed high as my hands release the table. I turn my back to the higher powers. The automatic door slides open. On the other side, another armored guard. Waiting with her rifle near my face as I exit.

We're in a well-lit, fancy hallway with lots of doors; evenly spaced doors with opposition placement. It looks like a millionaire's mansion with the bright red carpeting and wallpaper. Only piece missing is a picture of Sir Geilium in an armchair with cape and cane.

The escorting guard lowers her weapon and commands, "Follow me."

I mockingly acknowledge, "Yes ma'am."

We pass one door and reach a set of automatic double doors on the left. Security seems more relaxed through each passing threshold; one in front and behind, my escape opportunity will present itself. The double door slides open, spilling clamor. The woman guard passes through first. I pass next and immediately shut down my plan when I see what's going on within.

Down the wide stairs is a huge room with a tight group of six blue square mats at the center. A massive gathering of people surrounding them. Pairs of opponents are training on those mats. One per pair. Spectators are cheering them on. The bouts seem somewhat organized. Fighters are going at it without using fists. Only grapple techniques. Benches are filled with people eating. Geilium has a fully staffed army preparing to attack Menta-Life. If I attack one guard, I'd have this nest of vipers to deal with. We descend to the rowdy crowd.

As we stroll around the square, I express curiosity, "What is this place?"

The guard answers, "Our home base. All Equility members are here. This specific area is the main hall where we train, where we eat, where we meet."

An amazing set up. Directly representing what my imaginary, old world combat club would look like. Not many are socializing. Majority cheer loudly at the six different battles taking place. At the collective square's end, we ascend stairs. Enter yet another double door set to a hallway resembling hotel style living; fifteen single wooden doors on each side and two split hallways replicating this one. Additional splits likely to more hallways on either dead-end. What kind of place is this? Everything about it looks old. We take the left. Another hallway and more splits. We take a right.

The guard stops six doors on the right and states, "This is your room."

She opens the door with a push and allows space to enter. A miniature studio apartment. No windows but they existed. I've never seen a Gharis structure without them. Where could we be? Somewhere much better than my shack and lengthier than GCN. Queen-sized bed, foodie box, and bathroom. Two of three necessities I used to leave home for. I can store food but is the box full?

I ask, "What do I do when I'm hungry? Starve?"

I turn in time to catch the closing door, leaving me alone. Intentionally ignoring my question. Assuming these rooms are duplicates, they're nice for housing a body of terrorists in training. A change of clothes awaits on the bed. Uniform, evidently: a black long sleeve shirt, black sweatpants, and stretch-fit shoes. I sit on the bed.

Equility doesn't seem so bad. Still, my survival instincts remain on high alert. Knowing how greed works, I don't trust anyone in business. I'm a prime example of a greedy person and I wouldn't trust me to save my own life. Though, I do a great job. Trex has been a *friend* for years. But for a high enough price, he'd sell me underneath any cruiser passing by. In my line of expertise, one must keep reasonable distance from everyone. Letting people get too close is always bad - emotionally and for their health. Dayio and Feegle are unnecessary exceptions. Feegle knows me too well yet not directly field related, so maybe he doesn't apply. Dayio and I have only been running partners; nothing more. Proof that background isn't required to build trust. We never talk about our pasts. Nothing before we met, and not much about after either. That's the way it is. I, unintentionally, had my power nap during unconsciousness. Might as well get familiar with my new temporary residence.

Bed against the northeast corner, with the foot facing south. Left of it, against the wall, is a small sitting area with a table and two chairs; accommodation for meetings? Or social couples? Further left is the kitchen. Behind a cracked-open door on the left wall is a tiny full bathroom. Toilet, sink, and shower. Time starts there.

I undress. Pull the Econ from my ear. Wait what?! I shove it back in and tap. The device beeps four times. No signal. Do they have a jamming system? Are we underground? Doesn't matter. I remove my Econ. Underhand toss it on the bed. Enter the bathroom and set the shower using TempChoice. A device that adjusts water's temperature to any presets by fives: zero, five, fifty, being the highest. New World tech in a derelict structure. I spend maybe twenty minutes washing and marinating before concluding. Feeling like I haven't showered that great in ages, though Feegle's is the same.

Cool air tenses me upon exit. I throw on new clothes and check myself in the mirror next to the bathroom. Terrible training gear. The outfit isn't that form-fitting. Baggy is easy to clutch during a fight. As far as feeling, they're perfect. Next stop is the foodie box. Fully stocked. I pick the first meal, sit down and dig in. After the light meal, I lie down and relax.

Dayio isn't tied up here so my message was received. He better have snuck out, once they whisked me away. Safely assuming he made it since nothing's been mentioned about a triple intrusion. It relaxes me more. Hines faked his death and revealed himself to me. What does he expect me to do? Equility had no idea who I was prior to the hotel meeting, meaning Hines and his people had to have assisted in the prison break. Who are Hines' people really? Is Geilium truly Equility? He has an army training for Menta-Life's destruction.

Questions never cease. The more I dig, the deeper and more webbed the hole becomes. Answering one question and unlocking two more. Losing all sense of direction. Somehow, becoming a murder suspect. How did the bellman tamper with the camera? Perhaps the time it took me to turn granted ample time to stage something. His hands did switch to his chest fast enough. Did a device in his possession remotely disrupt the feed? I need to view that footage. If Geilium saw it, he may have a copy. Not being a branch of law enforcement, their viewing had to be illegally done. I must get to the bottom of this and won't do that sitting here. My mind deserves clarity.

Chapter 15: Plan A

    I'll return to Geilium and get some answers. So much for relaxation in this enticing bed. Wonder would keep me awake anyway. I approach the door. Excited male voices on the other side block me before the wall can. I wait for them to pass by and fade; not because I'm nervous, but because it's smart to avoid possible suspicion and confrontation. I can't trust these people and need to keep it that way for sharpened awareness. Risking a paycheck of millions wouldn't make any involved party happy. Voices vanish. I casually exit to the hallway. Clear of carpeted footsteps and vocal cords. Left turn and left turn. A man suddenly exits his room, almost bumping me. Conveniently enough to where he could have been waiting for my feet to mash the carpet outside.

    The mildly attractive man greets with a smile, "Hello."

I return a plain greeting, "Hi."

He goes ahead and hooks right. In barely more of a rush than I. The double door slides open. Noise pours from the square of excitement. I step out after him, catching the opened door. Best method to avoid notice is not staring for too long and walking with purpose like I belong. I rapidly walk downstairs and backtrack the same path around spectators watching bouts.

Halfway, a careless woman steps out of the crowd as if she were waiting for me. An easy mark spotted from the stairs. A second disruption, this time physically blocking. She is a Japanese woman. Short spiked hair, brandishing all the correct features. Including a couple of small toughness scars of old. She doesn't say anything, proudly wearing a "something to prove" smirk. Though they want to, no words release from my mouth either. I'm not sure how things work, or I'd begin with a smile and preemptive punch to get things started. Nearly brushing shoulders, I step around her while keeping eyes locked. So hard we can swap pupil shades. Once past, I break sight and continue. I can feel her eyes poking my back constantly like an unsharpened fingertip. Not giving the satisfaction of peeking back. The problem doesn't faze me but this confrontation is very tempting and unforgettable until solved. I like it. I approach the upstairs guard. He's minus a helmet and fitted with heavy armor.

He asks, "How can I help you, Vanessa?"

Being a guard, he'd have to know everyone that comes in here. My ego can support that I'm the biggest threat present and everyone knows my name.

I answer, "I have questions to ask Geilium."
"Mr. McKoy is in a meeting at the moment. He may be done very shortly. You're more than welcome to hangout and wait."

I'll pass on keeping this man company but am curious about that square. Are there rules inside? Is it grappling bouts only? Can anyone just join? That woman is unhealthily on my mind.

I reject, "No thanks. Can you tell me about the square though?"

"The arena. Where we do our training in different fighting arts. You want to learn techniques, come early in the morning. You want to brush up on skills, come here after teaching hours."

Where we train, where we eat, where we meet. You want to learn; you want to brush. Are these guards quoting scripts? I'm already a great fighter, specifically without rules. I don't need a hard punch, since I'm a runner. Agility and stamina always work in my favor.

I ask, "Can you do any kind of fighting? No rules?"

"Four rules and one restriction. No below-the-belt shots, no biting, no scratching, no pulling hair. And opponents must wear gloves for all types of hand-to-hand combat."

I had vaguely noticed arena challengers wearing gloves. The favored must be grapples and quick takedowns. Effective but I like to make bullies hurt. That grappling stuff doesn't intrigue me much.

I nod, "Where do I sign up?"

"Easy. Just go over to the rack, grab some gloves, wait and step into an empty space. Gloves are down against the wall there."

His left index points downward at a small rack. Stuck waiting for Geilium, I might as well teach that woman a lesson in manners. Downstairs, I take a U-turn. The rack is three shelves high, sloppily stacked with full-handed fighting gloves. I prefer fingerless but that could break the scratching rule with an unfortunate swipe against dry skin. I grab two pairs out of consideration; one for me, one for my opponent. Then cut through a few rows of joyous spectators. Enter one central square. Two men stop fighting and back away from each other. Not exiting. Possibly confused. I put the first glove on, interrupting a second fight closer to my opponent. She's speaking to another woman with her back to me. Why stand closest to the square and not watch? She up next? I can guarantee it. I pitch the second pair of gloves, smacking the back of her head. Her shoulders hold a shrug. The square of men and women gradually die silent. All eyes focused on her as I begin the difficult process of putting the other glove on with an already gloved hand. She slowly lowers her shoulders and twists with a pissed off expression. Suddenly rushing, halting inches from my face with an evil gaze. I barely pay her mind, fiddling with my gloves. Her hands are empty, and rules are rules.

I pass a gentle reminder, "Forgot your gloves."

Nothing to accomplish except showing a high level of disrespect. The woman turns halfway. Without speaking, the friend picks up and underhands the gloves. My opponent catches them, staring at me while aggressively putting them on. Poor gloves. Holding a smile, I can't let her leave my sight. I haven't been this excited about fighting since long before prison. Inside, I'd have gotten shocked for just throwing gloves, yet, in this unorganized environment, things are different.

Gloves on, the attack immediately instigates. She presses my shoulders, boosting with a high risen knee. I swoop an arm inward and block. Her other leg catches onto my shoulder and brings us both to the mat in a twist. We roll onto our feet in opposite directions. She is a lot faster than anticipated, but I can keep up. Underestimating, plus a little caught off guard. Recoverable mistakes. I start the next wave by sprinting at her and thrusting a foot forward. She dodges. I brace a palm on the mat and swing my other foot up, aiming high. Sweeping across her face. Not doing much damage. At my back, a true opportunist grappler would grapple. Before defending, arms wrap and lift me off my feet. Unsure of unspoken rules, what can I use in defense? Mats aren't bloodstained, hurling away many ideas. Serious injury doesn't happen, or I'd bash my head into her nose. I wildly shake free of the clutch. Capture a follow-up punch from behind and pull her body over my shoulder. She holds on tightly, landing in an almost spider crawl position. I reel one arm around her neck and one under her shoulder. Attempting to stand, she reverses into me. I kick her leg out while dragging us backward. Thwart any chance of regaining balance and preventing usage of feet against me. For a quick match ender, I squeeze my arms inward and upward for the choke. She grips tightly again. Tucks her legs and swings them between mine. Lowering us into a hunch. Feet planted, she boosts backward and crashes onto my stomach. A forcible exhale of more air than I possess; crushed by a one-hundred-and-thirty-pound human. My grip and sight of her are lost, feeling thighs compress my neck. Realizing what's happening, I try pulling them apart before the tightening. It's too late. I'm trapped. Nearly in a struggle to stay conscious. I wedge an arm between us, choking myself a little. Manage to twist and get my feet upright before lifting her.

A loud whistle engulfs the room. She releases me. I stumble into a backward roll and rise to defend. But she's standing idle. Body shifted at the guarded stairs. Geilium, Aleena, Mitchell, and Paul are halfway at the top. Their eyes on me. Hopefully because the guard mentioned I wanted to speak.

I sneer at my opponent, "Guess you lucked up."

She doesn't even glance my way. That's how it feels to be ignored? I'm under her skin already so the feeling is not bad. We're the only ones left on a mat. All fights ceased prior to the whistle. Our wild brawl was expected to seize a bit of space. I exit the arena. Start upstairs toward Geilium.

Mitchell expresses sarcasm, "I'd imagine someone in a new place would try to fit in."
I cast blame in passing, "Yeah, well, she started it."

We all return to the mansion quality hallway. Two armed guards on watch. The arena level is barren with concrete walls but the studios bare this same décor. At least mine does. Automatic doors here and one at the Arena end; wooden doors beyond that point.

I command, "Geilium, we need to speak privately. I have questions that need answers."
He approves and gives orders to everyone else, "Wait for us in the meeting room. We should only be a minute."
Aleena looks at me but speaks to Geilium, "Are you sure that's a wise decision?"
Geilium answers, "Yes. I trust Vanessa."

He paces left toward the hallway's opposite end as I reassure Aleena, "Don't worry, princess. He's holding my paycheck."

I follow about ten yards to the nearest left door, entering first upon chivalry. The small office has regular necessities with a couple of authentic plants and a long window. Able to view everything in the arena below. The sliding door shuts. Geilium passes me and loops the desk.

His hand aims at the two chairs, "Please, take a seat."

I approach the chair. Admire aged objects placed on the back and right wall. One catching my eye is a painting of a meadow. Green grass and a variety of different colored flowers. A style carrying belief that one can climb into the setting. Geilium sits behind the desk. I sit after him.

He initiates small talk, "So, you're settling well?"
I answer with a compliment, "This is quite the set up you've got here."
"I look at this as more than just a set up. This is home to a people who want to free their population from the hands of those who would abuse the great gift they were given."

That doesn't add up. Equility doesn't seem too angry, though more trained than average. Trex knew Equility off-hand as terrorists. Plotting an attack on Menta-Life might not be their first attempt against a powerhouse. It explains why these people aren't untrained. Time doesn't make them as good as that woman. Who was their first enemy? Am I being conned a second time?

I make an observation, based on my fight with the woman downstairs and Aleena, "Your people seem a little too well trained to be insurrectionists. They seem a lot more organized and more… capable."
Geilium supports with clarification, "You are correct. We have been after Menta-Life for over a year now. Failing at our previous two

attempts in the past. Our mistakes have forced us to become more of a militia, relying on tactic instead of brawn. The area downstairs used to hold a lot more of our people. We lost a lot of loved ones, family and friends, more than once in this fight. We train day and night. Have done reconnaissance on Menta-Life and its executives to be ready for what's to come when we strike again. We hope to count on your skills as a smuggler to aid us in liberating the New World."

Noble intentions. My reasons haven't altered. Without aers, I wouldn't consider supporting their cause. Geilium hasn't put thought into the end result. Fighting so fiercely with Menta-Life to destroy a system that people don't want to do away with. Clients aren't being held captive and forced into slave labor; they willingly purchase Life services. Sure, they may be oblivious to the corporation stealing memories, but everyone's aware of the Deserted presence underground. Satisfied with the way things are. Their level of concern about the source of memory loss is easily absent.

Geilium continues, "You have questions?"

Noticing my silence and deciding to change topics. I haven't lost curiosity about his part. A public figure putting his reputation on the line.

I respond, "What do you gain from Menta-Life's fall?"
"What do you mean?"
"Why would someone in your position jeopardize everything by starting an uprising? You are the face of Equility, aren't you? People don't just stop fighting at the sound of a whistle. This all began with you."
"My high position in the media doesn't mean I'm not willing to stand up against those who threaten the public. Said position is what made me mindful of Menta-Life's activities. Citizens came forward and I couldn't do anything about their accusations or the disappearances. The New World doesn't want that kind of news televised anymore. Swept under the table, all of it. Numbers began to increase, so Equility was founded. My position gathers information from citizens who have

and are currently losing loved ones. I introduce them to Equility. Giving a chance to stand and fight for those who've lost themselves and don't know what to do about it."

"Yet no one can leave?"

"Correct. However, I conduct thorough background checks on those who present their story. If they do not have children under age twelve, they qualify. If they are not married or have lost a loved one to Menta-Life, they qualify. I make decisions to recruit the right people who will fight for the right purpose and won't be abandoning anyone with reliance: terminally ill fathers, disabled mothers, and so on."

His reasons seem sound enough to give good motive. I ruined his literal shot at Gene Archibald during the party at Feegle's Bakery. It could have ended Menta-Life, or at least left them without a founder. I'm sure the corporation can operate without Gene, but morale may be low if he doesn't have a successor. Restoring the decency it opened with.

I question, "So, that night at Feegle's party—"

He finishes, "—was very unfortunate. But don't worry; no one is aware of what you did aside from those present when you told us. They swore not to mention it to anyone and these people are loyal to me."

"What about Paul?"

"Paul swore as well, and if he were to mention anything, we'd deny it and make him the bad guy."

Messed-up system, but as long as it keeps hot water off my back, I'm fine. Regardless, I could care less if anyone knew.

Geilium inquires, "What happened at the party?"

Tell him the truth? Truth is, I had a solid idea who the assassin was targeting and am not sure why I stopped him. But would it place better standing saying I thought the assassin was targeting Feegle? The truth isn't that bad, really. That man could have been trying to hurt anybody, seeing as I didn't know who he was until after stopping him. Even then, how could I know he was Equility? Lying won't be beneficial.

I speak truthfully, "The lights went out and I saw someone sneaking through the crowd. I followed. When I saw the pulser, I stopped him. Then recognized he was one of the men you'd spoken to. If I had known you guys were Equility, I wouldn't have interfered."

"That's good enough. Gene was crucial, yet only the first step. His entourage and the rest of the corporation would be much harder to deal with. The others are waiting for us to go over a plan of action."

"Why did you decide to take us in? Why me?"

"You're an expert runner. Majority of Equility are mainly trained in the art of hand-to-hand combat. I saw your fight. We battle strictly with determination, but you have an agility and calm they can utilize to make them greater fighters."

"I'm not a great fighter."

He quickly questions, "Really? I'll attempt to believe that if you can't explain why you were holding back against Ukiro."

The name fits. Pronounced "Oo-key-row" by nationality's true association. I didn't think, with the fast movements, anyone noticed my slight hesitations. Unsure how "dirty" rules can get for the arena, so yeah, I glitched a little. Usually, the fight is for my own life, and I'd prefer keeping my talents to myself; plus I don't want anyone having an edge over me.

I lie, "I wasn't holding back. She had me pinned at the end before the whistle. I'm not your great fighter, believe me. But being a runner is what I excel at."

He carries an expression like he wants to believe. A smart person would know they don't have a choice. Especially when it comes to a woman like me.

He stands and suggestively asks, "Then let us go coordinate plans with the others? Unless you have further questions."

I've heard all I need from Geilium about motive. Every other question can only be answered by Hines himself, except one.

I stand and make a request, "Would you happen to have footage from the hotel?"

"No, I don't. It was difficult enough just seeing it, let alone obtaining a copy for personal record."

Seeing what they saw would have been useful in figuring out what happened with the bellman prior to reaching my floor. Geilium could be withholding information. Instantly, I remember the four men and want to be certain if my hunch about the fake tattoos was accurate.

I ask, "Was Aleena at the morgue stopping someone from framing Equility?"

"Yes. There's a purpose-driven rumor that members of Equility have a tattoo on their right chest. Distinguishing them from anyone else by using a three-point system. Three small dots within the tattoo; big enough to find, but small enough for average people not to notice. My network heard Regulators wanted to broadcast the chest tattoos, giving insinuations of progress. I sent Aleena to investigate. She found and erased the phony ink. I was told, shortly after, she had run into skilled resistance."

"She did, I suppose. Any clue who made up the distinctive tattoo idea?"

"Perhaps, Menta-Life themselves. I wouldn't be surprised if they decided to worry the public to smoke us out. The most harm it could do is make citizens more aware."

Wrong. With Equility labeled terrorists, they won't be heroes if they manage to succeed. BAMechs and Alphas will tear the skyscraper down with Equility inside or the situation will turn into a hostage standoff. No questions. I will side with the losing team until pay day. Then I'm out. These numbers can temporarily shut down Menta-Life by a landslide long enough to get me squared.

I conclude, "That's all for now."
"Then let us be on our way."

We return to the dead-end meeting room. Aleena, Mitchell, and Paul are waiting in their same seats as earlier. No conversation being had. Instead of taking my same torture seat, I sit across from Paul. A nice view of everyone, including two door guards. Geilium curves around me to his seat at the table's head. Mitchell reaches down and reveals a small pad. Stretches his arm out to place it at the table's center.

He parks back and calls out, "Schematic."

The pad displays a 3D schematic of Menta-Life's exterior. The slowly rotating building's lines are blue and there are little red people on the lawn outside.

Mitchell explains, "This is an outer rendering of the Menta-Life Corporation. At the bottom, in red, are patrolling guards. We'll focus on the gated side entrance." He points to the upper-left side with a gate and two guards manning, "A frontal approach with this fourteen guard patrol was unsuccessful in our original effort. This gate is our next best alternative. Four guards loop the building in two separate groups. Near-equal intervals. As the first two pass, we silently dispatch the two gate guards, steal their clothing, and dispose of the bodies before the second set of guards finish their rotation. Once the second patrol passes the disguised team, we let our people in. Take the building by element of surprise from inside the parking garage directly across. Menta-Life crumbles at our feet."

That can't be the entire plan. There was no mention of interior security or possible mech presence whatsoever; no backup measures in case an alarm is triggered or MechCi initiates an automatic alert. No Reg response times. This plan sounds like a joke, just a little more well-thought-out of a joke.

I hesitantly ask, "Is... Is that it?"
Mitchell proudly speaks, "Yes. With what intelligence we've been able to gather, security is mainly tight outside. With us working inside out, the plan has a better chance of success."

He can't be serious. That place runs day and night with customers that need to be babysat as they sleep. I grin big. Almost tearing up from holding back laughter.

I face forward for approval, "Paul?"

Paul answers hesitantly, "Well, with what little information they can get from such a secure building, if this is all, I'd be at liberty to agree. I'd maneuver a thing... or two."

I burst out laughing as if the best joke known to man was performed. I am just a single runner and can develop an infiltration method better than that, keeping in mind I'm terrible. These people are prepared for prison.

Mitchell questions with an attitude, "What's so funny?"

I try and contain myself from laughing. Peek around the table and notice everyone watching me. Apparently not seeing the humor. They're really going the distance. I gain control with short breaths.

I answer, "What's funny is this *genius* plan you've got." I direct attention to the schematic's side gate, "There isn't any booth for guards to nest in, so where are we hiding these bodies before the second patrol comes around?"

Mitchell begins to proudly answer, "Well—"

I cut him off, "I'll tell you what your three options are." I stand and continue, "One: Leave them at the gate for guards to see, Two: Put them on the sidewalk for people to see, or Three: Pick them up and sprint across approximately seven hundred yards to the side lot entrance. Which one would you like to fail first?"

"You think you could do better than my plan?"

"Any fifth grader can." I lean forward and address the table, "Anybody recon maintenance or delivery schedules?"

Mitchell enlightens, "Early evening shifts, normally. Technicians arrive via cargo truck to collaborate with on-site techs, hauling replacement parts. Problem is we don't have necessary credentials or a truck to enter the grounds. Not to mention, only two or three of us can fit in the cab."

I closely view the parking garage entrance and examine the ramp leading underground, "Classic Trojan Horse play. We load the truck's storage full of fighters and drive inside. Then wait. Small size appears employee only so no one should clock out after five until at least nine-thirty. When it's dark enough, a couple of your shooters will dispatch gate guards. Preferably, sniping from the garage threshold and as patrol two is about to bend the northwest perimeter, losing sight of the gate. Southeast two should reach their corner near the same time. That's crunch. Those best physically conditioned scale the gate and full sprint to this garage for rendezvous."

Aleena asks, "And the two bodies outside?"

"Who cares? Look, by the time guards make the trip and inspect the bodies, we'll be fighting our way to Gene. Possibly dead in the lobby, depending how generous and overpaid security is inside. If anything, we get a defense going behind plenty of expensive cover to hold them off and send a group up, what, seventy stories?"

Mitchell comments, "That doesn't sound like a great idea."

I rudely state, "It beats yours out the water. At least with mine everyone will see inside instead of being held off and arrested out front."

Paul adds, "She makes a good point. Not saying it's perfect, but Vanessa's plan fits better with current reconnaissance. Especially not knowing security's interior situation."

Reconnaissance: in full usage, a military term. Recon for those without discipline. Red flag airborne…

I acknowledge everyone with conceit, "Thank you. Should I bow or just sit back down?"

Mitchell sarcastically asks, "Aren't you forgetting one last, insignificantly minor detail? The truck and credentials."

I riposte as if he's supposed to know the answer, "I'm half thief. It won't be a problem to 'acquire' phony credentials for whatever company services Menta-Life. I can do that in my sleep with a blindfold and earplugs on. The truck can be stolen from the lot. Easy."

Retaking my seat, Mitchell further attacks the plan, "How will you get them?"

"That's on a need to know basis and I'm afraid you don't need to know."

"Is that right? Well, I'm not sure if you've been made aware, but no one can leave the compound without Aleena or myself as an escort and I prefer to know who I'm dealing with."

I don't trust Geilium or anyone enough to introduce Trex. Operator of the only smuggler's tunnel into Gharis means everyone who wants import or export, big or small, goes through him. If I introduce Geilium, and Trex loses the tunnel because of it, more than just Trex would want a piece of me. As exciting as it sounds, I'm not quite ready for that yet.

I reply, "You're not dealing with anyone but me."

Geilium joins in, "If Vanessa has partners who wish to remain anonymous, we abide those terms, but–" He turns to me, "–we, too, would like to keep our base of operations a secret, which is why no one is allowed to leave without company of one of the three of us."

I reply, "Then this plan is at a standstill because I don't allow direct introduction to anyone I associate with."

Mitchell adds a whispered insult, "Which I figure isn't a large number."

I quickly yet blandly request, "Come again?"

Geilium states, "Vanessa, your plan is good and does have a better rate of success…"

Mitchell's head dunks. Truly ashamed. Clearly depressed about not being number one on the idea list. A distinctive "oh well" is in order. Serves him right for kissing up to his boss.

After short silence, Geilium adds, "I am willing to let you leave under two conditions."

I hastily demand, "Name it."

Mitchell stands, raising his tone with advice, "Geilium, we can't allow her to go alone without allowing others as well! Leaving is a very strict guideline that you yourself impressed for our protection!"

Geilium agrees to disagree, "I understand that; however, I don't plan on losing anyone in this attack. We need to succeed and I am ready to risk whatever it takes to get there. We are all ready to save lives and see our families again."

Mitchell calms, "*If* we get inside. You're willing to chance Equility on her idea?"

"With all due respect, Mitchell, we've failed twice with yours."

I softly remark, "Ouch. Low blow."

Geilium continues, "Her plan is the best we have, so if rules need to be bent for this to work, so be it. Now please sit down."

Mitchell spares further embarrassment and does as told with zero attitude.

Geilium states to me, "Two conditions are as follows: You exit blindfolded and be transported to a location somewhere in the city, with Aleena as an escort. Next, for your privacy, the two of you part ways until you are ready to return here."

I'm surprised he would consider offering something like that. All leaving unguarded takes is a good idea. Who knew? On a better note, I won't have to fight to freedom. Finally, an easy win.

I ask, "Do you really trust me to come back?"

"No. The best I can do is hope you return to aid us further. Everyone down here needs your hand in this so we can restore safety and sanity."

His answer slipped by saying, "Down here." Releasing a clue. We must be underground. His confidence in me sounds fine and dandy, and correct. Without his force, I won't get a lifetime worth of aers; and that I can't have. They want to attack soon, giving time to explore options of stealing the pot for myself. I'll see how it feels once I reach freedom's door.

Geilium asks, "Will you be able to complete your tasks within two days' time?"

"I should only need one. I already know where to get the credentials, I just need the company name and time to find the truck."

"We can start first thing in the morning."

"I'd prefer afternoon. Not a morning person."

"Afternoon it is. Meeting adjourned… except you, Mitchell."

Paul and I rise from our seats. Aleena takes the long way around, patting Mitchell on the shoulder as she walks past. Consoling without words. "Tough break, loser." Maybe not. We exit the meeting room together.

Chapter 16: Rules and Guidance

I linger near the opened door for a brief second and hear Geilium speaking, "We need her onboard with this so we can continue the ta—"

A guard next to me asks, "Something wrong?"

I snap out of listening, "Huh?" His question processes, "Oh, nothing. Thought there was something I forgot to mention."

"Please return to your room or the main hall. Tomorrow afternoon someone will wake you for your tasks."

He's saying it like I was assigned; as if it weren't my idea. Without me, they'd be slaughtered by guards at the side gate before feeling Menta-Life's cool temperature. I follow Aleena and Paul to the main hall door. The double door slides open and Aleena stands to the side. Paul exits the hallway.

I halt at the threshold and ask Aleena, "Not joining us common folk, Sunshine?"

She throws an insult, "Unlike you, I have work to do."

She starts toward Geilium's office, making me speak up before getting too far, "Too bad! I thought you'd wanna redeem yourself in the arena for that poor performance at the morgue!"

She replies without looking back, "Believe me, I will!"

Ignorant to how truthful her words are, I smile and enter the main hall. Paul is at the foot of the stairs. Awaiting my descent. What does this guy want? The door slides closed behind me as I walk down.

When I reach the bottom, Paul requests, "Can I speak to you? In private."

I don't like people wanting to speak in private. My line of illegal work makes private conversations look like bad news. Usually a tactic to conduct betrayal. Hearing what he has to say is no big deal, though. Could be to my benefit. Did I learn nothing from meeting Hines Aldwich in that hotel?

I accept his request, "Sure. We'll talk in your quarters."

He nods. Leads us around the square of fighters. It's emptier than earlier; must be late. How do they track time without sunlight? I spot a digital clock on the left wall. Duh. Seek and you shall find. Rows of benches rest under the clock. A few people are eating in small groups. I look up and right at Geilium's office, but don't see his window. It must be a two-way mirror that only he can see through. Paul and I go upstairs into the next hallway. Down the hall and take a right. A guard escorted me to my room. How does Paul already know his way around? That's puzzling. I need to keep an eye open for surprises. I follow him eleven doors to the left. Paul waltzes straight in. I closely tail him inside. Wing his arm up and force him to the floor.

I kick the door closed as he panics, "What're you doing?!"
I aggressively interrogate, "Who's in here?"

I gander around the room as he answers, "Nobody!"

His room looks the exact same as mine. If I had no memory for locations, I'd be turned around. Lights were already on in my room, so nothing to worry about that his are, too. The studio space appears clear.

I ask, "How did you know where your room was already?"
He struggles out a response, "They told me after you left the first time. Right at the end of the first hall, eleventh door on the left, and unlocked."

By himself, unarmed, Paul can't hurt me. He's average built and slow to react. I'm too fast for him to handle. I release and walk past him. He carefully stands. I do another quick scan of the room. Satisfied, I turn to him straightening his clothing.

He states, "I'm not a threat, we're in this mess together. I just want to talk."
I think back to the library, "Suddenly you wanna talk? What do you want Quentin?"
He finishes straightening with his answer, "I wanted to talk offline about this Equility insurgency."
"What about it?"
"Do you trust me?"
"Obviously not."
"You should. We're on the same side. Listen, I don't think they are who they say they are."
"What do you mean?"
"I mean yes, they are Equility, but I feel like there is something else at play. Like they have a second objective besides the justice pushed in our faces."

And just like that, betrayal is afoot. Equility does seem odd, handling Menta-Life the way they are. A public demonstration would be safer. Signs held by an enraged mob, signing petitions, shouting, and so on. Enough people will listen to a body rather than Paul.

Equility, on the other hand, is ready for action again with me basically running the show. Does that seem suspicious? Of course it does.

I inquire, "So what?"

He nervously smiles, "Aren't you at least the slightest bit interested in what their real mission is?"

"No, actually, I'm not."

His smile fades, "How are you not? They could be planning something much worse than ending Menta-Life. They're not called terrorists for nothing."

"I don't care if their intentions are good or bad. I'm here for a paycheck and some backup getting it. That's all."

"Citizens have been disappearing for years. Right off the street. Out of homes they thought were safe. Can you honestly look at everything going on and say you would assist Equility just for aers?"

"I just did."

"Unbelievable."

I become irritated by the clear judgment, "Is this what you called me in here for? Because I have better things to do than listen to you."

"I called you in here to see if you were truly interested in making a difference, rather than just fattening your pockets."

"Like you're any better; you're here for revenge."

He hastily clarifies, "I'm here to make sure what happened to my brother doesn't happen to somebody else. I'm here to make a difference for those who can't make it for themselves."

"Well, I wish you the best with that. I'll do you a favor and not mention this conversation to anyone. That's doing my part in saving lives."

I approach the door as he states, "Menta-Life technology will fall into potentially wrong hands. You understand the kind of destruction that would cause?"

"Like I said, I don't trust you. But tell you what: Find some proof and I'll think about it. Other than that, if Geilium's Equility wins, we'll see."

I exit the room and return to mine. Geilium's story adds up. Intentions and reasons so tightly knit that they're form-fitting. He is aware of my objective, and teaming up with Paul on suspicion won't get me there. The next morning, I wake to approaching footsteps. Heavy boots. Stern couple of knocks on my door. I slide a hand behind my head and raise a knee. A female security guard enters. Expecting acknowledgment while watching me from my bedside. I look past my leg at the opened door. Then back at the guard.

I ask, "You want something?"
The guard states, "It's almost noon. Get dressed. Ten minutes."

She walks out. Heavy steps, closing the door. No steps moving on. I get changed into my street clothes. Feeling energized, like I may have slept a little too long. Exit to the hallway. The guard is standing across, next to someone else's door, waiting.

She commands, "Follow me."

I stalk her to the main hall. It's full again, like the amount from last night's fight is here, plus some. But not rowdy. Class is in session. Everyone is seated on and around the mats in a zig-zag formation, allowing those in back to see past those in front. A dark gray bearded man is central. Head so bald I can almost see light refraction gleaming off. Two people in front of him have a grappling match. In slow motion. Developing skill by granting more time to counterattack. The instructor locks eyes with me as we pass the square. I break away after completing half and go upstairs. The door slides open. Geilium, Aleena, and Mitchell stand idle. No conversation between them. The door closes. Aleena has that infamous black sack in her hand again, dressed nice in a pencil skirt.

I glance into her eyes and advise, "You're not getting me with that one twice."
She tosses it to me and replies, "Lucky for you, Mr. McKoy said I couldn't or you'd be on the floor already."
Geilium takes over conversing, "We can't let you see the way out or where you are, so Aleena will escort you back to the GCN building. That will be your point of contact. Aleena will be on site until midnight

awaiting your arrival. Then tomorrow morning until midnight. If you do not show, we will assume you failed and your ties to Equility severed for our protection."

I ask, "What's to stop me from saying you're Equility?"

"Who would believe you?"

We both know the answer. Geilium's a well-known network CEO and I'm an escaped convict. As sick as it makes him, I'm certain he broadcasts positive stories about Menta-Life often enough to fly under the radar as a supporter. No one would bat an eye at my accusation.

Geilium asks, "Are you ready?"

Mitchell's dull, blank expression is awaiting my answer. Seeming more okay with this infraction than last night. Geilium must have convinced him this is a good idea.

I ask, "What's the company's name?"
"D.T. Feddings Repair. Good luck."

His head nods. Aware of what that means, I open the sack and place it over my head. Instantly, feeling everything and seeing nothing.

The male guard instructs, "Hands behind your back."

My wrists sway back. I feel them gradually reeling even closer together. Cyber ropes use the same adjustment technology as the cyber strap except serves as a restraint. Not deactivating by touch. A gloved hand wraps my forearm, guiding me through the darkened hallway. Into one of the darkened doors further on the right. Up some darkened stairs. Into a darkened elevator. Going up. Down stairs but not many. Through more doors and down more stairs. A pattern hard to mimic yet easy to remember. Into another elevator going up again. Hearing it open, a small rush of heat tears through my clothes. The scene is still very dark and this warmth doesn't have a direct source. We must be in a covered outdoor structure. After a bit of walking, I hear a door handle. The kind of handle that must be pulled out on a vehicle to access. Something mechanical slides open. Not a standard type of door or shutter.

The guard instructs, "Step up."

Great. A van. I step up with one foot. The guard tucks my head and helps me inside, slamming the door closed. The other door I heard open closes.

Aleena demands, "Sit down."
I retort, "You mean fall down?"
"Your call. The fall will be harder when we start driving."

I guide myself against the van's wall. Use it to carefully sit down. The door furthest from me opens preceded by the same latch click. Weight on the driver's side drops. The door closes; that must have been the guard getting in. The van ignites and begins moving. I hear a screeching echo as we turn a semi-circle. Shouting: *We're in a parking garage!*

Serenia notifies, "Service restored."

The van ascends a small ramp and continues a steady path accelerating faster. Taking a strange pattern of left and right turns. Keeping a northern then eastern flow. The vehicle feels hotter, yet there doesn't seem to be any direct sunlight. Windows must be blacked out to shield the afternoon. Minutes turn to an hour. With many turns and no directional awareness of the sun, I'm at a loss. Could they have expected me to memorize the route? Smart play. If I were in danger, I'd be disappointed in myself.

Eventually, we slow to a halt. Doors open and close. The rear door flaps open. Weight lowers and that gloved hand guides me out. From my shoulders up, I feel the sun's beam, and see tinted brightness. Once upright, the guard seats me in the doorway. Then the cloth sack slips off. Brightness hits my face hard, causing momentary blindness; they really need to stop doing that. I can't shield my eyes since my hands are bound. I close them and turn away. The guard reaches around and releases the cyber rope. My eyes open low, with a few followed blinks for impaired repair. We are parked in front of GCN. Aleena and the guard are standing in front of me. The sack is in Aleena's hand.

She notifies, "You have ten hours left."

I linger intentionally. Rubbing my eyes to adjust the outdoors and stretching my arms. Aleena patiently waits with a mildly annoyed expression. The guard doesn't appear frustrated. He has less reasons than Aleena to hate me. But I've bothered her enough for one afternoon. Knowing there's nothing she will do isn't as fun. I leave them to their business. Cross the road, one block away from the lectrocycle, bend the corner and tap my Econ.

Serenia instantly inquires, "Is everything okay? You've been out of service a while."
I lean against the building, "Yes, Serenia, everything's fine. Miss me?"
"I was more worried than missing you."
"Can you dial Trex for me, please?"
"Certainly. Connecting…"
Trex drops an inquiry, "You good out there? Dayio told me what happen last night."
"Yeah. I need fake credentials from D.T. Feddings and a company truck. Bill me when I get to your office. And tell Dayio to wait there."
"Okay."
Serenia notifies, "Call disconnected. Would you like anything else at the moment?"
"No, thank you."
"Let me know if you need me."

I circle the block. The lectrocycle is still here. Since this vehicle isn't tied to a murder investigation, maybe there's little urgency for its recovery. I peek around the corner at GCN. Aleena, the guard, and the van have vanished. I mount the lectrocycle and get going. Speed away to Trex's office. At the bakery, Feegle is outside speaking to someone.

Approaching the door, Feegle happily greets, "Afternoon, Miss Pheros. How are you?"

A regular display. No tone of worry. For such a modest greeting, he must not have heard about last night, with me having gotten abducted and all.

I smile and display enthusiasm, "I'm just dashing, Mr. Tolen."

His smile increases, carrying on with his new customer or existing client. Or total stranger. I take the tunnel to Trex. Dayio is waiting with him in the office.

Dayio examines my face, "Not even a knot, hardheaded as always. You alright?"
"I'm fine."
"When I heard that woman hit you, I had to stop myself from coming to your defense. Did you really want me to not do anything?"
"They're not the bad guys; they just wanted to make sure I wasn't, either."
"What's Equility?"
Surprised, Trex asks, "Wait, you actually found them?! Dayio, man, where was this part'a the story?!"

Nice to know Dayio kept half the secret. Telling Trex about Geilium and Equility is probably a bad idea; not that he wouldn't believe me, just that they'd both know who to point fingers at if something were to happen. Would they? Or perhaps Geilium's already a client of Trex, giving them something to talk about. I don't ask about his secrets, so I don't have to tell him mine.

Vagueness presents itself, "I found them. Knowing about the Deserted, Equility's goal is to stop Menta-Life and their leader wants my help." I ask Trex, "By the way, how's it lookin' on those credentials?"
Dayio informs, "Pickup's already done. Should be back any minute."

I ask Trex, "And the truck?"

"Depends. You wanna make one, or steal a original?"

"How hard would it be to steal an original?"

"D.T.F. mostly does touch-ups on hardware; should be a easy steal, but paintin' a truck to match would be a little less illegal. Have you timed the routes?"

"What do you mean?"

"I mean, will you be in and out before their scheduled repair team shows up?"

I hadn't thought of that. How stupid would we look if the drivers arrived before we did? Menta-Life security would take us down at the gate and everyone would be sitting ducks in the cargo storage.

I reply, "Guess I'll somehow steal a truck on its way to Menta-Life HQ."

Trex volunteers, "I'll find time on one'a their routes. When you need to pick up the truck?"

I shrug, "Tomorrow." Trex types while I ask Dayio, "How'd you make it out last night?"

"When they got you into the elevator, I scaled the stairwell down to see where they were taking you. I made it to watch them dragging you and that other guy into another elevator across. Took the back door out and waited near GCN with a view of both sides, but nothing. I waited for, like, three and a half hours."

That doesn't make sense. Aleena and the guard were driving for at least two hours before arriving at GCN this afternoon. I couldn't have been unconscious for that long on the way there.

I ask, "Are you sure?"

Dayio confirms, "Positive. You never left that building. Even if they went to a parking garage, I reached my vantage point fast enough to have caught them coming out. Never saw anyone except those two guards out front."

A sigh leaves. So we were underneath GCN the whole time? That hideaway wasn't recently built but renovated. The city built over it. Having wound up in a parking garage, we were in a big structure. Like GCN.

Dayio interrogates, "Are you going to help them? You need backup or anything?"

"Not sure yet. This is getting too complicated and I don't trust these people. I'd rather go at this alone than risk something happening to you."

"Well I'd hate to lose my only competition again… Hang on." He taps his Econ, "You close? …Okay, I'll meet you in the tunnel." He taps again, "Our runner arrived with the creds. I'll be right back."

Dayio exits the room and Trex inquires, "When did you become so passionate?"

I correct him, "*Com*passionate, and you guys and Feegle are all I have. I'd never directly involve any of you in anything like this. These aren't people I'd trust enough to bring here."

I know the feeling isn't mutual because of his greed. Who am I to judge? Current situation included, my greed is worse. The New World is losing their minds and I haven't tried talking myself out of wanting Menta-Life's treasure chest. Does that make me better or worse than Trex? Deserted were over-privileged. Fortunate enough in affording to ignore problems of those lower than them. Gharis City is home to the wealthy. If they didn't care to help the sickened scum underground before becoming one, why should I? All Deserted are Life addicts who didn't wake up and smell the coffee. Nobody can help them anyway right?

Dayio reenters the office and places a yellow envelope on the desk, "Here ya go, Trex. I'm gonna return to my post."

Trex acknowledges, grabbing the envelope, "Thanks Dayio. I'll send the runner a cut."

Dayio looks my way on his way out, "You're more than just a running buddy to me, Van. Be careful out there. If you need me, I'll always be at your back."

More than just a running buddy?

What did he mean by that? Was he really that worried last night? If so, he could have come back. Then again, I indirectly instructed him not to… I have other things to worry about right now.

I ask Trex, "How much tally for the creds?"

"Five thousand covers my take and eight thousand, five hundred covers credentials."

I swipe the envelope. Open it and slide out the contents. It's a small, unique paper that folds upward like a passport and a name badge. My laminated picture and fake name are on both, along with company information. Trex displays an image of the real credentials. Not bad.

I shove them into my back pocket and approve, "Done. Set up the transfer and send me details for the route over Econ?"

Trex types away, "I'll have it to you soon."

Dayio and his runner are walking toward the grove exit. I start back to GCN, running into Feegle inside the bakery front. Taking an order with the same customer. Look who made a sale today.

He notices my passing and speaks, "Miss Pheros, hold on a second." He rushes with the customer's order and articulates, "Have a wonderful day, and looking forward to seeing you again soon."

The woman replies, "Thank you so much, Feegle. And you too."

She departs with a double handful of boxes. Feegle holds the smile until the entry door shuts. His expression softens, staring like something's on my face. Remaining totally silent.

While keeping stuck eyes, I turn my head slightly, and skeptically inquire, "What?"

"Are you keeping out of trouble?"

"Of course, why do you ask?"

"Dayio came in late during a party last night. Was not certain why but he looked rather long."

"You didn't invite me? Wait, *long*?"

"Oh dear, umm..."

"Sad?"

He swiftly spruces up the word, "Yes, depressed."

I smile at his correction of my correction, telling a fib, "I'm doing my best to stay out of trouble. Swear."

"I needn't remind you the consequences of your more prior endeavor."

"No, Feegle, you needn't. I do have somewhere to be, though. I'm being a good girl. Trust me."

Technically, I am being a good girl by aiding a hostile insurrection against a leading power... That doesn't make sense.

Feegle replies, "I trust you, dear, but I do not believe you. Where are you going?"

Smiling, I go for the door, "I'm going to change the world. That one, you do wanna believe. See ya."

I flee before hearing what he has to say in return. Mount the lectrocycle and take off.

Serenia states, "Incoming voice message from Trex: Two drivers make their way to Menta-Life from the Gharis City Regulator Station to arrive between five and six at night." Serenia's voice returns, "I hope it was good news."

"You didn't hear that?"

"No. My model is strengthened at user privacy. We are not dually programed to hear user's conversations or messages, even as we relay them. I'm only allowed to know what my user allows me to access."

"I see. Well it is good news."

"Trex is requesting a transfer of thirteen thousand, five hundred aers be made from your account. Do you accept this transaction?"

"Yes."

"...Transaction complete."

"Thanks, Serenia."
"You're welcome."

The sun is falling from four o'clock. Having to prepare for a hostile attack on the most secure building in the New World in only one day's time isn't the greatest idea. I could take the day to myself, but I would enjoy training with Equility more. Show them a trick or two on counterattacks and not just sloppily fighting hardcore for the win. Help them survive long enough to get me paid. I have no idea what we'll encounter inside Menta-Life. From my experience, security is always tighter outside than in. With disposable chaff, if things get too hot, I can always ditch them and make away with whatever I can steal. Either way, this job will be a piece of cake. I reach GCN. Park my lectrocycle out front and head upstairs, past the two security guards.

The younger one greets, obviously familiar with who I am, "Welcome."

I ignore him and enter the lobby. Up to the reception counter where a woman sits at a monitor. The small hall, left of the counter, must be where Dayio and I were. The elevators they swapped.

The woman speaks, "Greetings citizen, and welcome to Gharis City News. Do you have an appointment scheduled?"
"Maybe."
"Who are you looking for today?"

If Dayio is incorrect about us never leaving, Geilium shouldn't be here. But he could have left shortly after we did. It's been longer than two hours. Can I make up something to trick him into telling me Equility houses below? Do employees even know?

I answer, "Geilium McKoy."
"And your name?"
"Dory Wright. We spoke this morning. I mentioned I'd be stopping in."

"One moment please." She picks up the landline and dials his extension, "Mr. McKoy, Ms. Dory Wright is here to see you... Yes, Mr. McKoy, I will notify her." She hangs up the phone, "Mr. McKoy informed me that you will be meeting his secretary Aleena. One moment."

She picks up the phone, but before dialing, I enquire, "Why can't I speak with him?"

"He's busy at the moment."

Of course. Not making time to meet someone who is going to help you win a legendary battle isn't disrespectful.

The woman dials another extension and waits, "Hello, Aleena. I have Ms. Dory Wright in the lobby for you... Okay." She hangs up, "Aleena will be down shortly. Please have a seat over there."

She points me at a black leather sofa. This place is dead. Granted, it is a news station, not a museum. It's not like they'd get walk-ins with news scoops. Geilium probably got many of Equility through these doors. Aleena strolls from the hallway and around the reception counter to me.

She asks, "Did you get what you were looking for?"

I draw the credentials, waving them in front of her, "I did. Better than the originals." Aleena's head tilts and eyes squint of irritation, "Kidding. Lighten up."

I put them away as she states, "We'll talk upstairs in my office. Follow me."

I tag along. She presses the button on the left wall where the two elevators lead to higher floors. The one Dayio saw them carry my unconscious body into is the right side.

Best to test the theory, "Why don't we just take this elevator over here down to my quarters and discuss it with Paul too?"

She answers without looking, "Your quarters are far from here."

"Are they? Then why not take this elevator?"

I approach the across elevators and press the single button to descend. These particular two must go to the parking garage. In the opposite elevator, I didn't notice a garage option.

She uninterestedly thwarts my idea, "I'd rather not have this conversation in a parking garage."
"Oh, don't worry. I plan to go deeper than that."

The elevator on the right side opens. She grips my jacket and jerks me close. I swipe her hand off and force her into the door. She cooks an aggressive attack but the opposing elevator pings, ceasing the call to action. We both posture like normal when voices of joyful workers flood out and close in. I stand away from Aleena, holding the door for anyone. Three of seven blue-collars quickly join us. I smile lightly at them. Aleena and I move toward the back, granting plenty of space. A woman presses the button marked "P" and we all stand in silence. Not surprisingly, no one greets Aleena. I can imagine being the boss' secretary doesn't pay off in social circles anywhere. A button underneath "P" reads: "B1." Basement level? I also notice a camera isn't stationed.

I inquire, "Anybody in here ever been to B1?"
A man answers, "It's an archive room for old records... You and Aleena doing some digging?"
"Yep." I sink a low tone and excuse through riders to press the button, "Don't mind if I do."

"B1" highlights. Aleena continues staring ahead with heavy-eyed frustration on a bland face. It's almost scary. The elevator stops and opens. The garage exit is quite far, like it connects and is shared with a neighboring building. For it to not be two floors deep, something big could be under us. The trio exits. The elevator closes.

Aleena immediately throws an arm at my face. I dip and avoid, letting it slap the aluminum wall. She adds a low kick. I catch and lift her leg over me. Then sweep the other, bringing her down. No intention of doing harm. Her leg retracts and summons a powerful kick. I shield, still being pushed at the wall. The elevator opens. Aleena rises and rushes my stomach. I struggle to stay posted until she lifts. Then push a foot off the rear wall, throwing us awkwardly out and onto the concrete floor. Now I rush, jamming my knee onto her back and pinning.

As she struggles, I state, "Your first mistake was not taking the long drive when you initially brought me and Paul down there; thank your digital clock in the arena for that. Second was when you took me up these elevators twice. Third was the parking garage. Unfortunately, putting a sack over my head doesn't make me deaf to screeching tire echoes."

The struggle lessens with her reply, "You were unconscious and so was Paul. Neither of you know a thing."

I speak sarcastically, "Unconscious? Who do you take me for? I'm insulted that you'd question my professionalism, thinking I can't take a hit and don't know this city inside and out. Take me to Paul because we don't have time for this game you wanna play."

She becomes still. Silent without struggle. Was Dayio correct and didn't just miss a swift exit? What his view may not have given was a direct line on the parking garage exit, wherever that is. Aleena's dying hostility answers my question. She shakes me off and quickly whirls around. I stand and raise my hands low. Reversing away slowly.

She stands and demands with a finger point, "This gets back to no one, understand?"

"Your people can stay cooped down here forever for all I care. Your little secret's safe."

Aleena approaches a bookshelf next to the elevator. I examine the archive room closely. Bookshelves in a flood on walls. A few computers, a lot of desks, a lot of chairs, a lot of filing cabinets. Dust covering everything. This basement level is an archive room. Had she not threatened secrecy and said I was wrong, I'd have believed her.

Another demand, "Come on."

She retracts an orange book off the shelf and opens it. Activates a switch inside. Half the shelf slides, blocking the elevator I threw us from and unblocking the second. Why conceal an elevator that comes to the same floor? Aleena inserts a tiny key into the call mechanism and twists. Slides it out and returns the book. There are other orange books, but no obvious similarities or patterns. A guess of oranges would be a certain find, then there's getting the key from this kind lady. Easier stolen from Mitchell. Aleena enters the elevator and awaits my entry. I follow, unstricken as if I expected a successful bluff. Confident and all-knowing. The tiny key slides into the panel. Upon twisting, the door shuts and an immediate descent begins. This elevator's panel doesn't have "B1" like the other. Covered by books because it goes to Equility HQ. This door splits to a hallway with many doors. Same worn walls as the arena, confirming a correct location.

Good job, Dayio.

If ever escape becomes necessary, I'll need that tiny key. We urgently pace to the final wooden door on the right. Enter to a set of twelve stairs. Descend and use the door ahead. We're in the hallway leading to the meeting room. Four doors down at the end face.

I ask, "Why did that seem so much longer the second time? Did you guys really walk me through a public building with a bag over my head during business hours?"

"The door next to the elevator leads to more stairs. A getaway in case the building is ever somehow infiltrated." We near the meeting room and she issues an order at a security guard, "We need Paul Quentin as soon as possible."

He accepts with haste, "Yes ma'am."

Allena and I enter and sit, silently, waiting for Paul. I can ask Paul his opinion about the credential's appearance and hijacking the truck. Pretending their dependence isn't flattering.

I ask, "Where's Mitchell?"

An answer rushes, "Busy."

Her foul mood for conversation sprouts an inquiry, "Why are you always so pissed off?"

She stares at the table while fiddling with her hands, "Take it personally, I'm only pissed when you're around."

"Again, why?"

"You must've never had a conversation with yourself."

"Don't make a habit, no. I may have an idea how you feel, though I don't sympathize."

"Hm."

Paul enters the room and asks, "Back so soon?"

He occupies his respective seat across from me. Keeping order as if we're assigned. I'll wait for Geilium to arrive before discussing the full plan. Short notice may come as a shock, but I'm sure they've waited long enough. A week or so less will only hasten the inevitable. If they're not ready by now, they won't be.

Chapter 17: Plan B

I should have taken the day to recon Menta-Life instead of coming straight back but I'm impatient. Can't imagine it being too difficult to infiltrate, keeping in mind that Equility was beaten before. Once we're in is what's worrying. Successfully leaving with aers is an entirely different worry of its own.

I answer Paul, who appears surprised to see me at all after last night's issue, "I didn't wanna keep you guys waiting, plus we're doing this tomorrow, so–"
They both deliver a stinging expression, but Aleena leans in and yells, "Tomorrow!?! Did you really–"
She's being overdramatic, so I calmly interrupt, "What's wrong with tomorrow?"

Her pitch only slightly calms, "What's wrong is we're not fully prepared. These people aren't like you; they don't just spring battle-ready at a moment's notice."

"If you feel they're not battle-ready by now, they're never gonna be."

She unleashes a huff. Reaches down and grabs a phone. Landlines are still frequently used. Mainly a connection to others within a building which explains why it still gets service deep underground. She dials a few digits and holds the phone at her ear.

Aleena speaks, "Mr. McKoy, we need you in the meeting room right away. We have a problem… It can't wait… Yes, sir." She hangs up, "He's coming."

I lift the credentials from my back pocket and slide them over to Paul with a question, "What do you think about these?"

He picks up and closely examines them. Raising them to the light, seeming familiar with spotting the difference between factual and forged. Another red flag. Paul conducts a comparison using the digital monitor next to Aleena. Aleena and I await a response.

After careful examination, he approves, "Undoubtedly authentic, company seal down to the lined texture of the paper. These will pass without a second thought. How'd you get these done so fast?"

"Trade secret."

He slides the credentials back, "Do you still not trust me?"

"Paul, I don't trust anybody. Crazy thought: I didn't think trust would be a conversation you'd wanna have with someone like me…"

"Touché."

Aleena looks at us both. Suspicious? Geilium and Mitchell storm through the door as if they own the place. One of whom technically does. Geilium circles toward his head seat faster than I've ever seen him move.

He questions, "What's happened?"

Aleena answers while staring at me, "Well, apparently we're attacking Menta-Life tomorrow."

Geilium asks me, curious but not shocked, "Why tomorrow?"

I hold the stare at Aleena and lie, "Employee roster has two transfers from D.T.F. in Hrowen City. They've serviced for Menta-Life and are filling for the regulars. Out sick. It's the best opportunity since they're expecting new faces."

My stare breaks over to Geilium, who doesn't look upset. Planning internally and rolling with the punches. He picks up the landline and dials an extension. Mitchell sits at Geilium's left. Respectively.

Direction is given, "This is Geilium McKoy. I need you to burst email all staff. The building will be closed early tomorrow. No stragglers. Everyone can finish their work the following morning with a deadline extension… Thank you."

He places the receiver and Mitchell asks, "What do we do?"

"We accept the cards we've been handed. First, finalize the plan amongst ourselves. Next, assign roles. Finally, train and rest. This is what we've waited for and we're not wasting the opportunity. Vanessa, you have the floor."

Everyone stares trustingly for instruction, so I stand and request, "Schematic?"

Mitchell pulls the pad from his side. Rises and places it near the table's center. Then activates Menta-Life's digital exterior.

I focus on two red marks by the employee gate, "We have credentials, and there's a solvable problem acquiring the truck. The new drivers are scheduled to arrive between six and seven at night, same as the last. Them arriving before or too soon after us creates a problem, which eliminated opportunity to create our own truck with their company logo painted. I developed an alternative. Now, the drivers leave GCRS at around five–"

Mitchell interrupts, "Uh, I'm sorry, you said GCRS? As in Gharis City *Regulator* Station?"

"Yeah." Everyone grows an anxious expression as I continue explaining, "As I was saying, they leave at around five to be at Menta-Life before six, range likely dependent on workload. Being new, fortunately, gives wiggle room; security issues, especially. Two of us scout GCRS, tail the truck, and handle the hijack. Drivers need to stay inside to maintain cover or we're blown. We load muscle and weapons into the cargo area. Credentials get us through the gate to underground parking." I focus on the rotating red marks, "Two-team patrol passes by, two shooters simultaneously take out the two gate guards. Sprinting team will scale and haul it from gate to garage undetected. In order to do that, we'll need this to begin after dark; over the horizon is not enough, we need zero aura and black gear. This time of year, after six should be plenty dark. Muscle starts up fast and clears the first floor. When outside guards rally after finding the bodies, we'll be regrouped to ambush them. At that point, hopefully, it's us and Gene Archibald. Menta-Life falls."

Everyone gazes as if I just explained a theory of quantum physics. It is a very complicated plan. That being said, I don't see a single flaw.

I summarize, "It'll be easier than it sounds: Hijack the truck, pick muscle up, down two guards, sprinters sprint inside, then we're smooth sailing on defensive."

Geilium responds, "Then we're decided. We inform everyone immediately and prepare ourselves. Let's go."

We go to the main hall together. Everyone is either watching a bout between many duos, conversing, or eating. Descending, small crowds begin hushing. Taking notice to us. To their leader. We attract the bigger crowd's attention. Fighters stop fighting. Conversations fade to whispers. Whispers fade to nothings. We halt at the bottom of the stairs. Geilium continues walking alone. Spectators clear a path. He passes through and halts in the center. I lean toward Aleena and she leans toward me, ready to listen.

I whisper, "Wouldn't that have been so cool in slow motion?" Her face drags to annoyance again, ignoring me and dragging my question to Paul, "Hey... wouldn't that have been so cool—"

Aleena quickly interrupts, "Sh!"

I obey and listen to Geilium spark a speech, "The time has arrived! We have constructed a plan of action to remove our enemy from power, finally taking back Gharis City from Menta-Life's hold! You will divide into two groups; strongest and fastest! Tomorrow, you will all see daylight and tomorrow night, we will all see freedom!"

Everyone cheers for that horribly short speech. They *have* been training for a long time, making their excitement understandable and overdue. Geilium signals me over, immediately recapping grade school introductions. As I approach, the hall becomes silent again. I pass through the gap. Watch everyone watch me. I hate being the center of attention and that is literally what I am. Second time's the charm.

I step next to Geilium, "This is Vanessa Pheros! A skilled smuggler and fighter! As some of you may have seen!"

He could have left the part about being a smuggler out. Who would feel comfortable being around a dangerous thief? Geilium signals Paul to join us. He approaches and stops at the opposite side of Geilium. His temporary left and right hands.

Geilium introduces, "This is Paul Quentin! He has experienced a similar feeling to all of you with the disappearance of his brother! Paul and Vanessa will both be training as equal members of Equility! You are all under orders to do as you please until that clock—" He glances at the digital clock that shows a current time of 4:36 and continues, "— reaches four tomorrow afternoon! Less than twenty-four hours! At that time, we will divide into teams and restore the New World!"

Everyone cheers again. Another speech that didn't motivate me to move a muscle. Geilium ditches Paul and I in the arena. Aleena and

Mitchell accompany him back upstairs. I guess we're staying until four tomorrow. A smart plan would be to get as much training done as possible. A good excuse to fight all night without penalty. I go the opposite way to the rooms.

Paul tensely asks, "Vanessa, wh– where're you going?"

A nervous look rests on his face. Shy about being left in the spotlight amongst a crowd of soon-to-be brawling strangers?

I answer excitedly, ignoring his mood, "I'm gonna get changed. You should too."

My destination doesn't alter. A fresh pair of clothes are folded on the made bed. The cleaning service isn't bad. I change into my new outfit. An old boastful side of myself drops, realizing the serious situation can't be taken lightly… as I eat. I must be just as prepared in case heavy resistance hits. Transform myself into a more skilled version of them and them into current me. I return to the arena.

During training, attachment to their cause becomes easier. Gaining easy acceptance through praise of winning and pretending to lose bouts. I almost feel their anger and hostility. So much aggression that their technique is chaotic. But there's willpower. I feel enough sympathy to not tell them to forget about *why* they're doing this and focus on *what* they're doing it for. These people have lost families, lost love. Cared for loved ones who regressed into someone they didn't recognize anymore. What's worse? Someone that didn't recognize them anymore. I have no family. No one to share that kind of bond or pity for. Battled alone since my father died and never felt a thing for anyone else; now, here I am. With a unified people who wanna make a difference when, in all honesty, they don't need to. Losing someone to Menta-Life means their *someone* was an active user. Those sessions are not cheap, making Equility more well-off than most. These people want to be here, and that's what I admire.

Analyzing Paul is a different story. His anger is better spoken than expressed through action because he's not built for battle. We haven't fought personally, but he greatly lacks technique. A slow desire in movements. Unsuitable on the frontline during the push. After training, we enjoy company for a bit before dispersing to our rooms. I sleep through majority of what night or morning remains.

Not long enough. Loud knocks on someone else's door mixed with amped voices hurdle my eyes from a dream. The double taps and herd of chatting draw nearer. Wake-up calls and wake-up calls. Oh, how I hate them. I relax for a while longer before switching over to my normal clothes. Join Equility in the main hall. Almost a hundred voices talking and waiting. I pass around many small crowds to see what's going on up front. Geilium and Mitchell are talking amongst themselves. Away from crowds. No Aleena babysitting.

I approach, "What's goin' on?"
They both turn to my voice and Geilium calls out, "Vanessa. I trust you slept well?"
"I did. What's goin' on?"
"We're preparing team coordination. Whenever you're ready, we will begin to move out."

This attack won't be based on being *ready*. Unknown, potentially dangerous factors could be in play. Success will depend on everyone's ability to adapt. I will succeed… and it won't hurt to make sure they do too.

I state, "Let's do it."

Geilium smiles low. Casually hikes halfway upstairs. His hand goes up. Voices in the crowd simmer to silence. Geilium's hand drops.

Another speech, "It is time! And time is not something we can afford to waste! Two teams; one comprised of strength, another comprised of speed! Vanessa and Mitchell will procure a truck for insertion! Strength team boards into cargo with weapons! Two of our best shooters will down the two gate guards from the parking entrance!

They will be cargo with strength! Guards fall, speed team scales the gate and gets to the garage which is about seven hundred yards away! Less than half a mile! Not including distance from the initial cover area to the gate! Aleena leads speed team! At least sixty of you will be running so I will let you use discretion in picking a side!" Geilium looks to Mitchell and me, "We'll see you soon. Good luck."

I command Mitchell, "Let's go."

Mitchell shadows toward the first floor lobby, bearing a question, "Where are we going?"

"To get the delivery truck." My forehead stretches with my elevated eyebrows, "Were you not listening to that very elaborately explained plan?"

A tense tone spills, "I was listening, but two of us? No backup? You think that's a good idea?"

I give assurance, "We don't need it. There will only be two civilian drivers. It'll be as smooth as a sunny day's breeze. Trust me."

Mitchell swallows spit. I may be solo for this part of the mission due to his nervous edge. There is a more pressing concern existing: How to steal a truck, in motion, by myself, without weapons, killing the drivers, or letting them get away? We exit the elevator. Orange sunshine is intruding through the windows and my stolen lectrocycle is absent. I look around from the curb, but no luck.

A voice calls brash from behind, "Hey!"

A security guard is jogging the white lectrocycle from around the side of the building.

He stops in front of us and states, "Vanessa, Mr. McKoy said you two were on your way out and you'd want this."

The guard drops the kickstand. I notice a stun baton on his hip. I'm unarmed. Taking two people by myself, a good idea will be borrowing it. I won't be back so he won't need it for intruders.

I demand, "I need your baton and glove." He surrenders them without question and I turn to Mitchell, "You can either fight beside me quickly or learn to drive a lectrocycle fast."

I work on starting it for him during the quick decision, "Lectrocycle."

Assuming his easy choice, I command, "Climb on." Mitchell mounts while I verbally teach quick basic instruction, "Lean to the opposite side and brace that leg. Use the other to kick the stand up. Slowly twist your right hand downward *only* maintaining a fast enough speed to do a left circle."

He does as I say, much slower than instructed, and loses balance. His leg saves him from getting crushed by the vehicle.

I add, "Don't stop twisting, hold it."

He starts again, slowly doing an entire left circle and stopping. Nothing spectacular but that's all the basics he should need to worry about. Straight paths are the easiest part.

Mitchell excitedly huffs and shouts, "I did it!"
I mount behind him and hold the backseat for balance, "Congratulations. Gharis City Regulator Station."

We take off. The station is quite far from GCN. Fighters and sprinters will probably split and meet at designated locations near Menta-Life. One to load fighters, another where sprinters wait. We reach GCRS and park with it at our backs, a good distance across the road. An additional building that doesn't belong, by height standard. The lengthy, two-story exterior is lightly guarded with few Regs. I am glad we're leaving and not stealing the truck from inside, though. We wouldn't succeed unnoticed no matter which way we entered. Mitchell is patient. I get to pacing a bit. Ten minutes. Did we miss the truck? Fifteen. Hungry. Twenty-five. The tan D.T. Feddings truck glides partially out of the front gate. We mount the lectrocycle and wait seconds more. The truck pulls out left toward us, then turns right before us.

Mitchell notifies himself, "Here we go."

He spins a half circle to catch up to the truck, losing control. Still holding the twisted throttle in a panic. The maniacal swerving is going to draw attention.

I shout, "Loosen off the throttle!"
He shouts back, shifting, "What's the throttle?!"
"Your right hand!"

His hand loosens off, restoring his calm from fear. The lectrocycle slows to a halt just out of a traffic lane.

My voice raises, "What're you doing?!"
"Sorry, I was in the moment!"
"Not that! Get this thing moving, go, go!"

He eases on the throttle, gradually speeding to catch up. No Reg cruisers trailing. Streets are busy, but forty mile an hour ground traffic is flowing steady compared to above. Seven miles from Menta-Life, heading west with partial sunlight in our and their faces as it passes over the horizon. If we're doing this, it must be now.

I grab the baton from between Mitchell and I, holding it at my leg and speaking loudly over light wind, "We need to get closer!"

Mitchell shifts between cruisers, maneuvering toward the truck's rear shutter. Nerves slightly slow him prior to passing each vehicle. Close to the truck's back-left end, I notice the driver window is down. And they have a big side mirror; big enough to clutch on to. We're still far from Menta-Life, but I'd rather not steal this truck at the gate. Time to make a move.

I demand, "Get me closer to the driver door! As close as you can!"

Mitchell slowly moves alongside. Faced near the driver, I realize I can't spring off the lectrocycle without Mitchell falling. Another improvisation. If he stops, momentum will throw me...

I instruct, "When I say stop, jam your foot on the brake and swing slightly left at the same time!"

I carefully attempt a balance act. Lift one foot onto the seat. Plant my hands at the front and back. Mild vibrations from humming in my wrists. Then the other foot. Lift into a crouch. Use Mitchell's shoulders to hold steady. A six foot diagonal leap against wind.

Two deep breaths and a shout, "Stop!"

He wrenches the brake and swings left. Pounces me at the truck's front end. Eyes squinted, resisting the wind. Hands stiffen out, gripping the mirror's bar stronger with my left because of the baton in my right. Struck with fear, the driver notices extra cargo, and pushes the button to raise the automatic window. I reel myself close. Activate the stun baton. Then thrust and shock. He spasms, giving the steering wheel freedom; swerving left, drawing me even closer. Before the window mashes the baton in place, I switch it off to avoid damage like burn marks or broken glass. The passenger clutches the steering wheel, swerving right. I lose grip at the sudden shift, freeing the baton to save myself. Catch the mirror with a second hand while engaging heavier wind. The passenger is trying to steady. I grab the door handle and yank; locked. I want to bash the glass with a friendly elbow, but the truck needs to be intact. A steady cruise now that the partner has control. Speeding through red lights and honking becomes a problem. The passenger window is open. I climb up the truck's cab and step into a slide on my hip. My leather gloves and jacket grip the roof, easing my swoop into the passenger window.

Inside, my fist cocks as a threat, "Stop the truck!"

He cringes and shouts back, "I'm trying, okay?! Don't hurt me!"

He tries moving the unconscious driver while holding the wheel. Struggling and still running lights. I lend a hand by pulling the driver at myself. The passenger eases the truck to a stop on a side street. I reach over with my gloved hand and grab the baton, pressing the window control to release.

Mitchell stops at the driver door, "Are you alright?"
Slightly upset about bringing the worst partner, I sarcastically answer, "Peachy." Pull the key out and command the passenger, "Bring your buddy out and take him to the back." I command Mitchell, "Open the cargo door and see if there's spare jumpsuits."

They both do as instructed. I exit the truck to investigate the cargo area. There's a lot of organized electrical equipment, likely broken and replacement parts. A good system to continue refurbishing old equipment until they no longer can. Mitchell drops down with spare clothing.

I tell the passenger, "Get inside. You won't be harmed and you'll be out within the hour. Econs, now."

He removes the Econ from his and the driver's ear and hands them over. Holds his partner and cautiously steps into the cargo area. I watch impatiently until the passenger starts lifting. Then swing the driver's legs up, making the passenger fall further inside.

I shut the shutter, lock it, and speak to Mitchell, "Connect me to Geilium."
Mitchell taps his Econ and articulates, "Call Geilium McKoy." I press and hold my Econ until he adds, "Proximity merge."
Serenia asks, "Accept nearby merge request?"
I loop to the driver's seat, "Yes."
"Connecting."
Geilium calls out, "Mitchell?"

Mitchell stands with me as I talk and put the jumpsuit over my clothes, "He patched me in. Where's the meet?"

"Two blocks directly west of Menta-Life in an alleyway. There's a local establishment that owes me a favor. We're inside and out of sight."

"Aren't you worried they'd give you up?"

"I'm about to waltz into Menta-Life with eighty-six people, my reputation was ruined when I started this."

"We're coming." I tap my Econ and climb inside the truck's cab, "Leave the lectrocycle."

Mitchell joins me in the cab, wearing the jumpsuit, "Won't your vehicle get reported just sitting in the street?"

"I'll be surprised if it hasn't already. It's stolen."

"Seriously? You couldn't have told me? I would've stood further away when we were parked in front of the Regulator station."

Mitchell buckles his seatbelt. I ditch the truckers' Econs. Turn the headlights on. Shift into drive and aim for the tallest skyscraper. The sun's aura is barely hanging by a thread. Streetlights are illuminating but city lights have yet to overcompensate, soon to be lending the moon support. We're early; those repairmen are good. I still pick up the pace, keeping an eye for Regs.

Two blocks west, I spot an alley and dial down slow. Someone on lookout takes notice to the truck and nods at me. Clear signal. I reverse the truck inside. As I'm backing in, fighters are flowing out. The cargo area is big, but there may be more bodies than anticipated. It is a short drive, still that horde of equipment is going to get dumped to accommodate everyone. The alley is too tight to confidently get the side mirrors in without damage, so I leave the cab hanging over the sidewalk. The cargo door slides up. Weight rocks Mitchell and I up and down constantly. An obnoxious amount of crashes and shatters echo between both alley cracks. Apparently, there's no way to subtly empty a truck full of already broken mechanical parts in a hurry. Many don't linger this area. Few peek with wonder, followed by a confused look at me, barely making sense of the disruption in brief passing. I smile them off. The shutter slams. Two thuds pound behind my seat. I pull away.

My stowaways littered the entire stock, creating a clutter of the alley.

I drive east. The only entry points are at main intersections of Menta-Life's four corners and one side street east and west. I use the same approach where I'd parked for the seminar, arriving within view of the seventy-story monstrosity. Nerves intact.

Overwhelmed, Mitchell asks, "Are we taking all of this on our own?"

I stare up high in amazement and answer, "Oh, yeah."

The gate is diagonally left across the road. I ease on the brake. Stash my gloved hand. Pull into the driveway and hold in front of the "Authorized Parking Only" sign. Very tempted to ram through and get it over with. If we don't manage clearance, that's Plan R. A guard paces to the left pillar, staring relentlessly. Pressing a switch and activating the gate. The second steps by the opposite pillar. Rifle in hand while I pull forward. They undoubtedly get zero action. Might not be best to make sudden moves. I halt next to the guard. Press the switch to roll down my window and smile.

The guard closes in and demands, "Credentials."

Their helmets must have vocal implants because this guard's voice sounds distorted. Though I could be wrong, it sounds like a male underneath, and appears as such in stature. I present fake credentials. He inspects both documents. Then myself. Then past me, and holding? I face Mitchell, who's wearing a blank expression straight through the windshield. A deer in the headlights – frozen. Prepared to blow our cover.

I form an excuse, "Rough time with the divorce. Terrible, what she did. Still quite fresh. But no worries, heartbreak always makes a man work harder."

"What happened to the regular repair crew?"

"Out sick today."

"Both of them?"

"They drive together, so naturally…"

The guard stands idle for a few seconds. Looks at Mitchell again. Returns the credentials and steps away. I take the straight path to the garage. Descend the small ramp with caution to avoid injuring any cargo. Scanning for guards or surveillance cameras. Familiarize myself with foreign territory. This is beginning to look easy. Upper floors would be more tightly secure. It's hard to imagine security outside but none within. A lot of pillars and cruisers are parked; with as many people as Menta-Life caters, it's not surprising employees are still monitoring. Fishing for good memories to steal? I park at an empty gap across from the elevators. We exit. I rush to the cargo door and slide it up. Fighters are bunched inside. The black-suited Geilium is in front.

I state, "All clear."

Everyone flows out. The truck's bobbing up and down. When it empties, the two drivers remain tied to the wall with electrical cords. Doesn't seem like they were hurt, just terrified. I smile and slide the door closed. Paul, Geilium, and Mitchell stand together. Facing me.

Geilium compliments my work, "Great job, Vanessa. Now we get sprinter team inside. I have scoped pulser rifles that can take distant guards out. Set to stun. No one needs to die here."

He places a hand out, glancing over his shoulder. A man approaches with a single rifle and surrenders it to Geilium.

I ask, "Who're your best marksmen?"
With confidence, Ukiro claims the title, "I am."

My eyes shift at her. She's got a voice too? Before hearing Aleena and Ukiro speak, I'd only heard their grunts during a fight; considering now that my social skills may be the issue.

Geilium hands me a pulser pistol and confirms, "Ukiro's the best we have."

She grabs the weapon from Geilium, "Just tell me where to shoot."

I instruct Geilium, "Let Aleena know to charge in fast when the bodies fall. They won't have much time."

Ukiro and I begin jogging to the garage entry, soon thinking we should've driven. Reaching the opening, I take cover at the left. Peek upward around the corner for the set of two guards to pass. Almost two minutes later, the duo passes. I delay for the other two, synchronizing times.

Ukiro whispers, "What's taking so long?"

I ignore her. Shortly, the second set passes. Six minutes between halves. Twelve for a full lap. Three minutes per wall facing. Sprinters won't have enough time, even at full speed, to make it unnoticed. As soon as guards clear the opening, I skulk ahead. Take cover at the right wall. Peek around both corners to detect anyone else.

I focus attention on gate guards while informing Ukiro, "Sprinters won't make it unseen within the window. I'll take the two incoming guards after and buy more time. The two at the gate are your targets."

Already passed guards bend the corner. I count seconds in my head. Eliminating these guards buys little under five minutes. Enough time. Thirty seconds becomes one minute. Sticking myself out too soon, without good range, I could miss. Two becomes three. Seconds feel slow and fast. I think they're past the bend but not close. They'll be on us soon. Another minute. I lean out with the pistol aimed, spotting the too close patrol. Fire two shots in quick succession. Right on target.

I return attention to the gate guards, "Window open. Try to hit them quickly."

Ukiro releases two pulses after my last word. The idle guards get hit almost simultaneously. Stiffen and drop in the same manner.

Streetlights show sprinter team cross the dead street and mount the curb. Quickly scale the gate. Dart in a staggering union.

My eyes lock onto something strange. The downed guards near me are faintly sparking and smoking. How is that possible? Do they carry so many electrical components to where they can fry? Walking fire hazards. If anything, those helmets should be sparking their heads off. Negative thoughts fall at once.

When I attended the seminar, guards didn't speak; not even to each other. Recollecting then, compared to now, they seem to be the same size and shape... the exact same. The weird voice from the gate guard is icing on a devastating cake. I can't hear popping, yet these bodies are putting on a minor firework show. I vividly picture how similar the BAMech fried in that office but not as bad. Unconscious people would wake up feeling electric burns.

Oh, no.

Are these guards disguised mechs? Effectively hiding this from the public must mean Menta-Life uses private security under a blocked network connection. And being connected means these four alerted every mech inside and out. I hope I'm wrong yet can't justify a risk.

I snatch Ukiro's rifle, step into the open and yell out loud, "Faster! Run faster!"

As if they aren't. Heat rounds sail from the front and back of the skyscraper. Sprinters begin dropping. Aleena and some others have pulser pistols, sending offense shock rounds. Nowhere to take cover and clustered, they're impossible to miss. I aim the rifle at both ends, but guards haven't revealed themselves. Tactful in knowing not to abandon cover. I rush further, attempting to catch peek of any shooter. Reaching the now scattered union to aid. I fire on five remaining guards at the right bend. Then quickly on three remaining at the left. Forcing unfriendlies away with more rapid blasts. I follow sprint team, taking down two guards. Reenter the garage threshold.

Aleena takes cover at the opposite end of me as I shout below, "Someone find the controls! Get this door down!"

I crouch and fire shots past Aleena's corner to stall guards on her side. She does the same past mine while standing. The steel garage door begins closing.

Ukiro demands, "Come on, get in!"

Aleena and I sprint down the ramp. Then duck under the entry. I focus the rifle at the gap in case we get a surprise guest sliding through the closing shutter. It seals. Nothing happens.

I pass the big weapon to Ukiro as I run and shout to Geilium, "They're coming! Take positions!"

Halfway back, both elevators ping. The doors split. Disguised guard mechs pour out, shooting. Everyone swaps to defensive positions, blindly returning fire. Taking cover behind pillars and cruisers. Those unarmed and too close to escape their fate try fighting hand-to-hand. Getting tossed around rather easily. More confirmation. Fist versus metal isn't ever a smart choice. I follow not-winded sprinters to lend a helping hand. Shelter behind the sea of cruisers as my side defends. Mechs duck also, returning fire and refusing to let up on those unarmed in nearer cover. I skulk from cruiser to cruiser until reaching Geilium.

He speaks loud over constant weapon fire, "What happened?!"
"The guards are mechs!"
Stunned, he questions, "BAMech security?!"
"They're not shaped like BAMechs! It must be Menta-Life's own manufactured security! I'm going to find a way to disable them! Hold out as long as you can!"

On my left is a door with a stair symbol. Paul is fleeing to it. Not a pulse fired in his direction. Where's he going? I follow. Sprint through rifle fire and into cover, passing two parked cruisers. I bolt across the rest, crashing through the door. Falling on my back at the stair's base. Heat rounds soar after me. Unfair treatment. I kick the door closed, lowering volume. Stand and enjoy a curious glance up the stairwell. Seventy stories… no way I'm surviving a run up that. I ascend to the lobby. I need to disable these mechs and find out where Paul went. Hopefully, he's got the same idea and gone ahead.

Chapter 18: Wake up, Van

The darkened lobby where Menta-Life's seminar was held. No staff members working. A twenty-four-hour business and no reception? I see my way to the elevator. No directories anywhere in sight. As much as I'd rather not, I have to call outside help.

I tap my Econ, "Call Trex."
Serenia notifies, "Connecting…"
Trex greets, "Van, what's up?"
"Not much. Question: If I was a server that controlled private on-site security mechs in the Menta-Life building, where would I be?"
Confusion steals his tone, "Menta-Life has private security mechs?"
I browse behind reception for anything helpful, "Trex, I don't have time."
"Okay, lemme see if I can dig up somethin'…"

"Faster the better. I may need Dayio to back me up with an exit. I'm gonna put you on hold." I tap and hold my Econ, "New call. Dayio."

Serenia repeats, "Connecting…"

Dayio greets, "Hey."

"I need your help. I'm in trouble at Menta-Life."

He loudly asks, "You actually went?! I could've told you that was a dumb idea!"

"I thought you did. Things got a little complicated. I may need you to bail me out with a ride if something goes south with my plan. Fat take in it for you."

"Of course. I'll be there."

"Thanks, Dayio. Knew I could count on you."

"That's what friends are for. I'll let you know when I'm nearby."

The call disconnects. Friends? I won't be so selfish as to not split the cut with my *friend* when this is over.

I hold my Econ, "Resume call."

"Connecting…"

Trex immediately speaks, "I got semi-good news that may help. I found a fan's renderin' of the buildin'."

"Who's Afam?"

"No. *A fan*. Someone callin' himself Jerry, absolutely idolizin' the corporation, developed a sketch of what he believes the inside of Menta-Life looks like."

"In other words, I'm dead?"

"Not necessarily. The renderin' seems like it could be accurate."

"Point me in the right direction and tell me why."

I call the elevator and wait as Trex says, "You gonna start on floor… thirty-eight."

I secure the opening elevator with my pistol. Step in to see six rows of twelve buttons, plus one at the bottom and top. I press number thirty-eight.

Going up, Trex explains, "So this guy believes, accordin' to Menta-Life's build, there's an entire central server floor. With the amount of circuitry goin' through that place, plus havin' to keep it near machines that clients sleep in, they'd need those servers close to where they operate in the event things go wrong. Ya followin'?"

I'm as confused as ever. It's not exactly nerd-lingo but it's not lingo I feel the need to mentally decrypt over his accent right now.

I truthfully respond, "Not really."
He sighs, then summarizes, "Basically, in order to extend power to the entire buildin', it'll be less pricey to operate from the middle."
"This is the richest corporation in the New World."
"…Ya know, I did not think 'bout that."

The elevator pings and opens. A mech squad commences firing into the elevator as fast as it takes me to notice them. I quickly swing at the left wall and repeatedly mash the close button.

Trex calls out, "Van?"
I yell over the rounds, "Little preoccupied!"

I peek and notice what I think are bundles of black server machines. Blue light strips surrounding, and encased in a huge cube of lighter blue glass. This must be the correct floor. Fantastic job on the rendering, Afam.

The elevator closes and I confirm, "I'm here."
I press button forty as Trex asks, "What was all that noise?"
"The floor I needed to go to."

A camera hangs in the top corner. Someone's watching? Giving mechs direction? I'll have to fight them off if I want access to those servers. Could be where the aers are collected also.

I continue, "Stay near your computer. I'll call back."

I reach for my Econ during his warning, "Don't do anything–"

I disconnect the call. Drop to my knees and put my hands behind my head. I know exactly what he was going to say: Don't do anything stupid. Little does he know, that is exactly what's about to occur. I reach forty. The door opens. A smaller squad of armed guards with rifles pointed are held about thirty feet away. I don't make sudden moves. One mech approaches and enters. It has a smaller weapon attached to its coat. I try shoving its rifle, being forced aside instead but not pinned. Allies instantly engage, shooting enough heat rounds to change temperatures, shredding this mech. I slap thirty-nine and mash the helpful button. Rounds stop pecking the closed door. I spread the mech's coat apart, shielding my eyes as sparks puff. Uncovering, I see the figure underneath. These mechs aren't fully formed like MechCi or BAMechs; just many thick metal rods casing wires between. Bulky coats and helmets meant to conceal their identities. These rods aren't cheap since the barrage barely scratched them. Nonetheless, design flaws and electric currents have proven beneficial.

Three disposal weapons - an automatic rifle and two pistols. I place the pistol at my left leg. The strap appears, attaching. *Ping*. I hold the rifle under my eye and wait at the wall. The door opens. Nothing. I ditch the elevator, aiming about. Swap the setting to shock pulses. Ready for battle. Gluing near each cover from a complete absence of mechanical life. No windows on this floor. Buffed tile under my feet. Never a shortage of pillars for structure. Full of desks, chairs, and computers. This might be where technicians monitor unsuspecting clients; no one here watching the dreamers? Menta-Life seems abandoned.

A loud bang travels from the right. Guard mechs have busted the stairwell door. More rush in and lock eyes with me immediately. I initiate this time, running and gunning toward the center of the floor. Wanting to position myself ahead to drop them with shock pulses upon entry. They return fire. Two mechs fall and another two take their place. A third mech crosses wielding a Greft Cannon. Modeled after the rocket launcher, Grefts are much bigger and slightly slower traveling pulses that cause a fifty-foot radial implosion then even bigger explosion. Impacting an immediate area with life-threatening damage, dissipating progressively and forcing away everything near. Something no one would wish to be caught in.

I shout, "That's hardly fair, you can't use—"

A Greft pulse punches in my direction. I dart left and sprint away from the unstable, silver ball. Slide into cover behind a third pillar to avoid the blast. Tucking tight. The pulse impacts. Dragging desks scrape the tile, even drawing at my jacket, then silence until devastation ricochets in all directions. Desks, chairs, loose digital files, and computers keyboards zip throughout. Bashing pillars, the floor, and each other. Chunks chip off concrete pillars. Ceiling tiles brought down. I feel my protective pillar vibrating. Devastation stops. Two pillars behind me where the Greft struck is a small clearing. An unintentionally crafted structural weakness. Stripped deep enough to reveal wooden supports underneath.

Being nosy, mechs lock on. No hesitation spouting heat rounds again. I retake cover for a brief time. Dash right, to the next pillar, and take another right, closer toward my enemies. Pass two cleaner pillars and use a broken desk for cover. Rounds cease. What comes next? Another welcoming Greft? I'm centered between four pillars where structure beneath should be weakest. Nosy again, the Greft Cannon wielder takes aim. Before release, I turn and run as fast as possible. It launches a second pulse. Ditching my rifle for the slightest speed boost, I jump onto a desk. Then skip across another, feeling the reel, barely clearing the initial radius with a diving roll. Silence until I turn again. Everything I passed pushes in an outburst motion. I head for the blast. Slide over the desk I dove from as a second crashes and flips over both of us. Grounded, I feel the pressure. Hastily avoid two airborne chairs. Unable to push through like a heavy storm or wind scar. Pressure vanishes. The floor has a hole and blue hue protruding. Two well-placed Grefts are powerful enough to knock down an entire wooden house, and one can apparently devour concrete. I slide inside, landing back first on huge, protectant glass. A seven-foot drop. Elevators are on my right. Under me are many safely housed servers with green lights blinking.

I tap my Econ, "Call Trex."

I rise to a tiny crouch and move toward the elevators. Mechs won't take long to arrive. Getting inside this glass needs to happen in the next fifteen or so seconds. I drop to more tiled flooring.

Trex asks, "What happen?"
I talk quickly, "Short version: these things are not afraid to use Greft Cannons indoors. I'm on thirty-eight, but the servers are covered by a huge glass."
I examine for slits while Trex talks, "It must be safety glass. With that, there's most likely a pan—"

Pressed for time, I kick the glass. Nothing. I grab my pistol and shoot a heat round at the glass. It bounces off, forcing my flinch at the ricochet, and vanishes at the ceiling. Easiest idea was a hard fail.

Trex blandly speaks, "What was that?"
A guilty apology, "Sorry."
He talks sterner as I remove my jumpsuit, "There's most likely a panel on the glass that you can use to deactivate it."
I rush around the left side and see a panel attached, "Hey, there's a panel here."

Trex scoffs. There's a single button. I do what any curious human would. A patch of glass forms a door shape and slides open. I step in. Every server looks like a replica or sibling of the next.

I state, "Small problem. There are a thousand servers in here. All black, small or tall height, and none of them are labeled. I don't know which one to turn off."

A bang startles me. Same version from upstairs. The door on the right wall crashes through the safety glass. Mech guards flood through.

I point my pistol at them and loudly demand, "I need something to shoot at!"

Mechs breach the glass just as fast as breaching the door. They shouldn't shoot with risk of hitting servers. A plus in my favor. Then again, a Greft crater is above my head. What will happen if they catch me? I quickly get lost between the maze of servers.

Trex stutters, "Uh, for emergency malfunctions, maybe security mechs could all be housed on one custom server, so look for one that's different."

I spin and shoot one that appears different. Not physically but by an off-blink. The heat pulse penetrates and causes the server to ooze black smoke. Lights change from green to red. My pursuers freeze. Thanks to their helmets I can't confirm operational status, though it seems to have worked. I release a sigh. Pretty good for a guess. Mechs resume bolting, circling the higher servers or vaulting the smaller. I run away, toggling between heat and shock, shooting at servers then mechs too close then more servers then more mechs. Reaching a dead end. My perception's become a fear related liability. I shoot a mech diving at me, falling to avoid being smashed by it. Firing at random servers and crawling backward. Breathing in but not out. Lights only change from green to red before smoke rises. My chest decompresses a yell as multiple guards dive at me, suddenly sinking into a slide at my feet. Eyes wide open, hand still lightly squeezing the trigger. I stop. Skim constantly at each motionless guard. Allies that were in motion collapse.

Trex calls out, "Van?"

That just happened... I kinda cannot believe that just happened. I huff a small gasp with a slight smile. Every illegally manufactured mech should be offline. I collapse also and start a chuckle that ends in a loud roar.

I supply an update, short on breath, "I did it. Thanks, Trex. You saved my life. I have to go check on the others."

"Glad I could help. You owe me one."

"You'll get a big one. More than you can handle when I get out of here." I double tap my Econ, "Call Geilium."

Geilium requests, "Vanessa? Is that you? Is everything alright?"

"I destroyed their mech security server. How're you guys doing?"

"We took heavy casualties but going after Gene while we still can. Meet us on the top floor."

The call disconnects. I salvage a fresh rifle. Place it at my back and the same pistol at my leg. Both straps attach. Then I leave the server floor via elevator. Hopefully we all arrive at the same time to confront Gene. What happens now? Gene goes to prison? We'd need proof. Plenty will be hidden on those servers… I destroyed. A decent amount are unscathed.

The rapid ascent takes a patient minute. I reach the top floor. Obviously Gene's office because of the old, yet fancy décor. An unnecessarily huge space in length but not as wide as lower floors. Beautiful view of Gharis City below, no doubt. Geilium, Aleena, and Mitchell are already here, attentions briefly diverted my way. Disappointment from each face. Geilium is behind a desk up a small set of stairs in the back. Aleena and Mitchell are searching through a den area at the front-left side. Tossing books off a shelf. A bad sign?

I exit the elevator, "Where's everyone else?"

Geilium answers, scrolling through a page file, "Fortifying the building."

"And Gene?"

He shrugs, "Gone. And according to this file, Paul Quentin was contracted by Menta-Life. Likely the reason we missed Gene and his entourage. He wormed his way right into the apple. But it doesn't matter. This building is ours."

Paul works for Menta-Life? I understand why those mechs avoided attacking him. Not a bad move Gene, and one even I didn't catch; planted at the seminar to draw attention and gave an opening of deniability by asking the "right questions" while smoking out those who would oppose. Gave Paul a backstory to support the role. Baited us.

I inquire, "So, where do we begin shutting this place down?"

Everyone looks at me like something crazy was said. Then Aleena and Mitchell look to Geilium. It's a simple question for a group that had this plan brewing for over a year. Suspiciously, it is not simple. Hand slowly drawing near my pistol, finding myself in wonder at why no answer has arisen. My peripheral catches Aleena's quick movement.

With a harsh command, I aim the pulser at her first, "Don't move!"

She freezes a plain stare. I switch pulse settings from shock to heat. Have things changed? Why doesn't anyone answer? Why does Mitchell look nervous? Why was Aleena ready to draw?

I ask, "We're shutting down Menta-Life, aren't we?"
Geilium eases the page onto the desk and speaks slowly in his normal pitch, "Put the weapon down... Let's talk."
I sternly repeat, "We *are* shutting down Menta-Life aren't we?!"
"I never said we were."

I think back to times we'd talked and only remember mention of *stopping* Menta-Life. There was another objective all along. Paul was right. They all stare at me in awkward silence, keeping my focus on Aleena. I let Geilium manipulate me into helping him conquer the main Menta-Life facility. Does he plan to run this place? Step in as if Gene's not founder and director?

I hesitantly confirm, "No, you didn't."
Geilium assures, "Vanessa... we can fix this."

I hurriedly shake my head, "We can't. Ending Menta-Life—"
Geilium finishes, "—won't accomplish anything."
"I bet the rest of Equility will think otherwise."
"They won't."

No way they wouldn't. No way they all lied. Those people have families suffering under Gharis City. Equility fought to stop this place from functioning. To have Menta-Life brought to justice. Were they cannon fodder too? Somehow, feeling I'm Geilium's last thorn.

I ask, "They're not fortifying the building, are they?"
"My people are. We couldn't afford to let the rest leave. Those who didn't resist are being held captive. Vanessa, think of what you're trying to destroy. So much usable technology, and so much money we can make."
"So this is about money?"
"It is for you, isn't it? The only reason you're here is because I offered to shell the spoils." His arms briefly sway out, "Here it is. Housed in these servers are more aers than any of us will ever need. More than you will ever need. Is that not what you wanted?"

Yes, right? I've grown attached to what Equility was meant to represent. The promise of freedom. Reuniting a dying and suffering people with civilization. Possibly the search of a cure. People Geilium wrought into Equility were supposed to be reunited with long-lost family; a family they traded well-off futures for. What about my well-off future?

I timidly answer, "It was."
Geilium sneers in a patronizing manner, "Has the great Vanessa Pheros grown a conscience? The only reason you began is because a ghost paid you. And the only reason you joined was to plunder Menta-Life. Your treasures are in these servers, and your job is done."
"These people just wanna help their families. They're dying, Geilium."

His voice becomes stern, "People have been dying! Inside every dome and in the Barrens, long before Menta-Life and will continue after it!" His voice settles, "Only under a new regime. Menta-Life will not fall. You will not step in and play hero now that I am where I've waited years to be. I'm offering one final chance: Walk away with your aers. What's it going to be?"

How many loyalists does Geilium have? With Aleena and Ukiro, I'd have a difficult time alone. Then about fifty other probable candidates. Take the offer and walk? If I leave, Geilium will be in a victorious position. My only viable option of helping everyone is fleeing. Every floor can't be secured.

The stairwell door on the right opens. Ukiro enters with a man behind her. Both looking at Geilium. There's no cover on my end and I can't maintain both flanks. Aware of my allegiance, I shoot at Aleena first. She and Mitchell duck behind a small sofa. Geilium ducks behind the desk. Ukiro quickly takes cautionary exit. I shoot the man with a heat pulse, distress flooding the room. A warning that I mean business. I take a bunch of steps back and tap the call button. Aim around, keeping two definite shooters at bay. Mitchell is likely unarmed and, if he has a weapon, won't be any good. Geilium is a grab-bag of surprises. Ukiro's buddy was never a problem. I focus on Aleena and Ukiro, who are on opposing sides. Kneel against the left elevator with my pulser ready.

Geilium loudly declares, "It's not too late to stop this!"

I don't reply, refusing to narrow an already bad position while waiting for the elevator to announce its arrival. Ukiro's head pokes out. I take two shots as she tucks away. Missing. I aim at Aleena, who hasn't moved. *Ping!* The door opens. Before entering, two men exit. I hook the trailer in the stomach, grip his shirt collar, and twist around front into a spinning kick. Greet the first man across the face and nearly complete the circle. I drag my hostage into the elevator, firmly holding his scrunched shirt collar. Choking him. Pulser pointed over his shoulder at everyone currently standing to see me off. Not firing when my gut knows I should.

Geilium shouts, "You're making a mistake!"

The elevator door begins to close. I kick the man out. Swiftly shift to the side, avoiding any rounds. No one takes a shot. I press button "57" as the door seals. The descent to somewhere starts. What am I doing? I should've taken the money and dealt with this another way later. No. Geilium could've locked the building down with a hundred civilian hostages and former Equility. How does he win that way? Taking away the plaguing Life addiction? He wants the technology. Who cares?! I let out a frustrating punch at the wall. Feeling no pain in comparison to my mental state.

I tap my Econ with a saddened command, "Call Trex."
Serenia says, "There is a message from Dayio. Connect to Trex anyway?"
I refuse, "Not yet. What is the message?"
Serenia relays Dayio's voice message, "Van, I'm outside waiting. Are you there?" Then Serenia asks, "Would you like to respond to the message?"
"Not now. Connect me to Trex."
"Connecting…"
"Aye, Van."
I greet casually, "Hi there. Does your fan know anything more about this building and its floors?"
"A whole layout. Why?"
"I was just double-crossed and need an escape."

The elevator door opens to level fifty-seven and I see… nothing. An empty white floor. Almost blindingly white and bares a never-ending feel. Like I can walk forever. I carefully step halfway out and look around. No doors. No windows. A whole space of nothing. Everywhere. Whatever Menta-Life does in that room is their own business and irrelevant to my escape.

Trex sounds staticky as his voice lowers, "That's no good, is it? Well, where're you now?"

I reverse fully into the elevator and press the above button, "Heading to floor fifty-six."

The door closes and Trex replies, "Okay, so floor fifty-six is..." Clear English comes through, sounding robotic-like, "Ah, it is one of the floors where people use the Life systems."

My signal is clear again? Too clear? Did that room alter my signal? And his accent? The elevator opens. I exit fast, only to be blinded again by another white floor. What is this? Why are these floors suddenly empty?

I announce my surroundings, "Trex, there's nothing here. Like, at all." He doesn't respond, "Trex?"

No reply. Maybe this floor is jamming my signal too? I turn to reenter the elevator. It's gone. Nothing except blank void. What? I stick my palm in front of me to feel where it should be. Walking forward and touching emptiness for more feet than I initially took. What is this? What have I crossed into? How do I get out? I start exploring. There isn't any darkness. Not even a slit to indicate a type of exit. I start jogging in one direction. Then running as fast as I can. Jogging again, with hands out in fear of bashing a window, until I get tired and slink to a walk. Catching my breath. This is impossible. The building is nowhere near this long. I ran far enough in a straight line to circle this building three times. Over a mile in distance.

An older English man's accent speaks, "I thought I'd never get you in here."

I hurriedly investigate. The voice sounds echoey, like he's everywhere at once. I reach at my side. Draw the pistol and aim around the white space. Soon realizing it's my hand. What happened? I felt it just then. Reaching for the rifle, it's gone, too. I look at where my pistol should be. Look around the room. Bright whiteness and me.

I talk to the mystery voice, "Who are you?"

"I am a lot of things... Vanessa Pheros. I don't have ample time to explain, but right now you are being used."

Why pause before saying my name? Like he wanted to say something else instead. And I already know Geilium used me. Mystery voice is behind on the updates.

I reply, "Yeah, no kidding. Little late with the memo."
"You don't understand—"
I interrupt, "Where am I? Am I still inside Menta-Life?"
"You are. Both physically and mentally."
"Then what is this?"
I begin searching for him, "This is non-existence. Things that don't exist in Life are voids, like this one. Menta-Life is using you to find me. They captured you and have been testing different methods to find me through your memories."
"What're you talking about? I don't even know who you are. Or what you look like."

Suddenly, the man appears. Very close, causing an instinctive withdraw of a few steps for defense and a better look. Caucasian. Tall. Healthy crop of short dark brown hair. Goatee of the same shade. Same hazel eye color as me... as well as few other familiar features. He approaches close. I stare into his eyes, not backing down. His hand hovers near my cheek.

He states, "You've grown so much. You look just as beautiful as your mother."

My hand sluggishly swipes at his arm. It passes through. Failing to remove it from my face. Am I hallucinating? What did I do to end up here? In a negative light, I got a list of ongoing reasons.

I take a step back and his hand drops with introduction, "My name is Simon Harold."

That was my father's name. He does look familiar, though it's been almost seventeen years. I hardly remember what I looked like, let alone my father. Or would look like now. On top of that, he's dead. My mind must've gotten lost somewhere in that elevator.

He continues, "There is no time and I don't expect you'll understand, at least not yet. You must wake up. The beings in your Life will do whatever it takes to keep you asleep, but you must escape from Menta-Life so I can get to you."

"Wake myself up? You're asking me to die?"

"You are currently inside of a Menta-Life void. Whatever brought you here, you'll be imprisoned for the duration because you know this is not real. They have been running you through the Life server and you have learned a lot. Use it to escape. And remember: Life doesn't have as much control as you think."

Ping! I turn around. An elevator is opening, shedding a new hue in the crisp white area. When I turn back, Simon isn't there. Not there or never was? I don't idle to be sealed in Crazy Land a second time, wanting to make sense of what the doppelgänger said.

At the seminar, Kelvin Hughes mentioned a client cannot access a Life within a Life. Is that why this floor, and others with Dreamcatchers, are voided in white. Am I really dreaming? Does Menta-Life have me captive? My father is dead. A debut after seventeen years of nothing? Confronting Geilium, Aleena and Ukiro didn't actually try to kill me, did they? Not one shot fired. They could've shredded through my hostage and me but didn't. Not even an attempt after I let him go. Keeping me alive? A never-ending floor can't be orchestrated in real life. Regardless of the digital Simon Harold, this void should be all the proof I need.

I'm going to the roof. As good a place as any. Equility will hunt me if I make it out alive; without help, I won't survive long against Regulators, too. Or maybe I will. I press "R" at the top which hopefully represents Roof. My weapons are still gone; first preventative measure in Life's favor.

Serenia randomly calls out, "Van?"

The door closes and the elevator starts moving. I watch numbers climb. Feel my stomach turn. Listen to her voice. It all seems so real. Real enough for me to question my own sanity.

I answer softly, "I'm here. Can you call Dayio, please?"
Multiple robotic vocals glitch, "Your *friend* Dayio. Of course. Connecting..."

My friend. Someone special who's gone through so much to help me since escaping prison. Someone who's always available and running to my call...

Dayio asks with worry, "Where have you been? I've been trying to reach you."
I gloomily call out, "Dayio?"
His pitch matches mine, "What is it? What's wrong?"
"I'm not really *here*, am I? This place, these people... isn't reality is it?"
"What are you talking about? What's going on in there?"
I sit against the wall, "In my mind? I met two people who aren't alive. And one that hasn't been for a long time: men named Hines Aldwich and Simon Harold. I've been to a place that doesn't exist and I don't know how. My father came to me. Told me to wake up from my Life. Told me that everything will do what it takes to keep me alive. I don't know what this all means."
"It doesn't mean anything. That all sounds crazy. Anyone would do anything to keep you alive because we care, this isn't the old world. Just come on and we'll figure this out."
"I know how it sounds, believe me. No one is more determined than I am when it comes to dumb ideas, but I need to dis..."

I can imagine how crazy it sounds. He wouldn't believe me if he could. No one will, because they're not supposed to. If the illusion of my deceased father is correct, Life will say anything to keep me alive.

I continue, "...I need to discover it for myself."
Dayio screams, "Van, wait—"

I disconnect the call. Remove the Econ. Watch my hand place it on the floor as if it'll vanish when I let go. Numbers climb higher until they can't. The halt shakes my stomach. Then the door splits, allowing an intruding, light chill. I stand and cross onto the rooftop. Wind picks up. The dark sky outside the clear bubble sheltering Gharis doesn't contain clouds. A full moon. A perfect night. Yet it's raining. Life must have brought in falling water as a distraction. Nonetheless, it still looks beautiful pecking the drenched dome hundreds of feet above. Reminds me of the drive-in car washes I loved as a kid. This elevator and some industrial air conditioning units are all that occupy the rooftop. I leisurely walk, between them.

Geilium demands, "Stop right there."
I stop and blandly ask, "Why?" I follow his voice to the elevator, "Why should I do that?"

They approach from both sides of the elevators - Geilium, Aleena, Mitchell, Ukiro, and a few Equility members, including three unarmored guard mechs. Guess Geilium found a way to get them working on their side. Life is pushing desperately.

Geilium answers, "Because there's nowhere you can run." They stop walking and Geilium goes on, "There's nowhere else you could have run. The first few floors are completely locked down. Your only means of escape were the front door or aircraft, which it doesn't appear Gene has. Your level of disobedience is predictable, so we waited you out and, honestly, it didn't take you long."
"It's not over yet."
"Don't believe you're foolish enough to jump. I've done my research, Vanessa Pheros. You hide underground with Deserted, a noncommunicative people. Avoid citizens above like a disease. Greedy yet not ambitious. Masking your identity with false IDNs. This New World isn't for you. But you're a survivor. You decide your best course

of action spontaneously, and although reckless, prevail. No survivable action awaits you here, other than surrender. You must see that."

They can't convince me of wrongdoing; not now; not after nonexistence; not after Hines Aldwich and Simon Harold; not after the rain. Do I know what I'm doing? I don't. One thing I do know is what makes sense. This isn't it. I stare into Geilium's eyes, wordlessly challenging him. Inching away for a few steps. Then a quick inhale and full dart toward the ledge at my back.

Geilium's voice immediately commands, "Stop her!"

I pass between the middle row of air conditioning units. A guard mech pops out, arms collapsing to wrap me. I crouch into a sloppy crawl around its legs. Climb to my feet and go for the ledge. Dive off the roof. Begin a freefall seventy-three stories below. Exhale sanity. Desperate to believe myself while resisting questions about what's too late to stop.

Seconds against the broken breeze, I feel a colder, skinless hand wrap my ankle. Multiple mechs dove after me and one is holding on tight. What are they doing? Another grabs the mech's ankle from above, creating a snake chain. The tail mech rams its free hand into the skyscraper. Slowing us down. Drawing us closer. Chunks of concrete and glass break off. And so does the mech's arm. A third grabs the leg of the mech holding mine. A new tail and digging repeat. Other mechs soar down to keep the chain going. Can they stop me with enough effort? I kick my loose foot at its arm to get free. The material is too dense. I swap to kicking its wrist instead. After a hand full of harsh kicks, it disconnects, proving less durable at the joints. The mech reaches at my leg with another hand. I retract both, slightly slowing. Then kick my feet and bash the mech. A fail to spin it out of control. Much closer to the ground, the one-armed mech clutches me tightly. Each does the same, using each other to crawl faster. The fourth tail lets the fifth and final intertwine their legs as it reaches both arms into the skyscraper. Slowing us dramatically. Every move is out of my control. Its arms rip off. The mechs have me contained. Centered in a cluster. Prepared to cushion the fall. We crash at the ground.

The impact is devastating. Worse than my splat on the Alpha. But I am alive. And well? I can feel myself fading in and out of consciousness. A tremendous back pain from landing on a pile of solid metal. A blur of destroyed parts surround me. Unable to move, I fall unconscious again. I can't stay awake. My body feels completely blacked out. Numb. Eyes battling for a peek again. Geilium is squatting next to me. Observing the loser.

He looks across and speaks, "Bring her with us."

My eyes close again for what feels like longer. They open. Blurry legs and feet. My pants and boots. I'm seated in a metal chair. An odd steel pattern under my feet, and a mild shaking feeling. Where'd I end up now? I struggle to raise my head, in the hold of a cargo plane. Where on Earth did Geilium get one of these? Oh right. I can't move my hands or feet; restrained by Equility once again. For safety, I guess. Alone. No one keeping guard or company. Just a window. Geilium is instructing Aleena to do something. I can't hear on this side of the glass. Calming hand gestures don't quite tell a story. Mitchell and a member of Equility are with them as well. Aleena leaves the room. Geilium looks at me, realizing I'm coherent, and presses something under the glass. A small sound pops once.

Allies watch me as Geilium speaks over intercom, "Vanessa, you disappoint me greatly. I truly believed you were better than a common peacekeeper. You've failed to see the bigger picture, and now you will spend your remaining lifetime regretting your mistake. But first I have someone who wants to see you."

The henchman walks out of view. Soon after, returning with a beaten up Dayio by his sleeve. Not as bad as I'd expect, considering he'd been caught by a "quick-to-tie-up-loose-ends" kind of guy. The last thing I wanted was for Dayio to get involved. I can admit it still hurts to see.

Geilium explains, "We caught him trying to rescue you after the crash. I can only assume he's an accomplice." He asks Dayio, "Any last words for your friend?"

Someone always available and running to my call. Geilium steps away. The henchman shoves Dayio at the window, replacing Geilium. Using a pulser pistol to push Dayio's head down at what I'm assuming to be a microphone.

Dayio calls out, "I'm sorry... I believe in you... and you'd better wake up."

Dayio elbows the henchman across the face while his hands are restrained. Then quickly twists and reaches for the control console.

Geilium yells, "No!"
A computerized female voice articulates over intercom, "Emergency cargo purge. Emergency cargo purge."

I feel a quick burst of wind pressure followed by me getting sucked out of the plane's rear ramp. Thrown into cold, dark sky. Menta-Life's projection of people proves too accurate.

Dayio... thank you.

Looser, colder, I wiggle free of the ropes. Feeling myself fall faster. Out of control but also in. No mechs to save me. Am I truly alive? I'll soon know or never will. Seeing my father, the dead Hines Aldwich, and the voided areas point closer to finding the truth. I won't let myself regret this decision. I twist downward. Open my eyes to the dark Earth below and, with my body shaking, aim at the ground. I release a loud shriek, bracing myself. As we meet, there is a split second of darkness.

I spring from a lying position. Gasp for air as if breath hadn't been recently drawn. I'm in a room. A white room. Not as bright as nonexistence and nowhere near as empty. Observation windows on the above walls. Electrical equipment everywhere. A woman wearing a lab coat. Standing near and looks as if she ran over here. A syringe ready for use but she is frozen. In shock, maybe fear at my unexpected awakening? Am I awake?

Desertion Preface

    A nervous female scientist hovers over me. Syringe in-hand. White lab coat lightly waving back and forth from an immediate stop-in-place at my gasp of life. My body feels sluggish and I assume her needle contains a barbiturate that will better enhance the induced coma. Last thing I remember is falling out of a dark sky and, almost instantly, waking in this white room. The woman must be wondering what she should do now that I'm conscious. Little does she know, there's nothing.
    Her action resumes, with a leaning jab of the needle. I slide away and swing a clenched fist over myself. Punch the scientist across the face and fall from a Dreamcatcher. A specifically designed, self-surgical recliner that Menta-Life uses for clients' three day stay and proof I *am* inside the corporation. Wearing the form-fitting blue one-piece prison outfit. My hair is long again. No time to admire myself or the circular observation lab. I lug my woozy body near the double door, opening it automatically.

A blaring alarm leaks inside. The siren's red light swirls, adding hue to an already fluorescent-lit hallway. Increasing my headache from seven to ninety. Keep moving. I don't see an elevator but see sunlight shining through a window. Passing a right turn as I enter a cubby area and look outside.

The exterior looks much different from my Life. A lot busier, with cruisers zooming by on the two higher levels of gravity. Cruisers are essentially cars running on electric motors instead of engines, and use gravitational pulls to hover instead of tires. Able of driving on two planes, not including street level; seventy-five feet in the air and double at one-hundred-fifty feet.

A male voice bawls, "There she is!"

The voice is at the hallway's opposite end. Four human guards in dark clothing wield electric stun batons; weapons that juice a high capacity current throughout. Users must wear a protective glove to operate one or touch will electrocute them; a defense tactic meant to prevent batons from finding ways into wrongful hands. Why are the guards human? Was it only in my Life that they were illegally manufactured private security mechs? This facility doesn't even seem like the Gharis City branch I thought I'd wake in. Where am I?

As four guards sprint toward me, the male voice adds, "Surrender immediately!"

I accept the immediate corner to see two elevators. Oh, how I would love to take them. If security can lock them down, I would be a stuck-in-the-box. Between is a sign announcing the twenty-fourth floor. I press the call button and continue past to a door with a "stairs" symbol. The door slides open. Right bend revealing a single security guard quickly climbing steps with a stun baton in hand. Obstructing the descent path. I must let him come, so I can have space to avoid being struck.

Arriving at the top, he hurriedly demands, "Surrender! Please comply!"

Hand raised, he takes a heavy diagonal swing. I circle around and slide down the handrail half of a level. Looking up, the rectangular stairwell of this building isn't as tall as it was in my Life; confirming this isn't the same branch. I look to the bottom. Height has never been a fear of mine and an expedited descent will greatly help. I climb over the railing, jumping across to the next half-floor below.

The guard informs, "She's... descending... the stairs."

I repeat back and forth until level twenty. Then drop from one floor to another, catching myself on every ledge and rail including horizontal six-rail barriers. At sixteen I hear guards stomping fast up the lower stairs. I return to safety.

Enter a hallway exactly as the last, minus a blaring alarm. I sprint left. The door marked "security" could have something useful. It slides open. Two guards are prepared to leave but not to see me. I jump-kick one in the chest. He flies backward into a computer chair, taking it down. The other jabs, intertwining our right arms. I swing him into the corner, following up with an elbow to his face.

Digital screens only show camera views for this floor. Among many buttons on the control station, one is bigger than the rest and red. *What does this button do?* A lab coat hangs on a rack behind me. Useful. I slap the button. An alarm begins deafening this silent corridor. Camera screens become flooded with lab-coated employees and few customers calmly leaving via stairway. I put the coat on, close it tightly, and join the ranks, staying as crowd centered as possible. Past security guards that just entered. Then down the stairwell again. It won't take long to realize an intruder had been there.

My cover reaches the lobby where everyone is gathered and appears to be awaiting instruction. I spot the familiar crescent Earth logo under "Menta-Life" lettering behind reception. A smaller branch, but what city is this? Each has one except Teykrys which isn't classified as part of the New World. So that's eliminated. The double door exit is ahead. I approach, yet it doesn't automatically open; must be on lockdown. How is it lifted?

Someone sternly demands, "Hold it right there."

I ignore the warning and casually turn around. Three guards. Stun batons. Nervous and ready to strike. I step toward them. They step back and split, surrounding from three sides: front, left, and right. I ease into a fight stance. The right guard closes in, swinging his baton. I shift left. The left guard swipes high. I squat and twist low, before he returns with a lower swing. Plant a palm and throw a foot diagonally up, bashing him under the chin into a complete flip. Body elevated momentarily, he greets the floor. Remaining guards approach simultaneously. I quickly center again. The left guard forcefully thrusts the baton. I spin, making him stumble slightly by. Reverse the spin and ram a crucial clothesline to his throat. The last enemy attempts to catch me off-guard. I swiftly kick the back of his hand. Bring my airborne foot back, swiping across his face as the baton crashes through the glass door. Creating my escape. I flee.

Enter outside, after who knows how long, and descend four steps toward the sidewalk. An orange two-door cruiser draws to the curb. I halt in place. The passenger raises the gull wing door. Both occupants are average males.

Passenger shouts, "Simon Harold sent us; get in!"

In absence of vacant vehicles begging to be stolen and security trailing, why not accept a free ride? I dive in the back seat. The driver slams on the pedal, making a second left away from Menta-Life. This doesn't look like Gharis City. The structure and atmosphere feel different and compact. Buildings aren't regulation leveled but staggered sloppily in height and citizens are dressed less flashy. Two black cruisers are a short distance behind, accelerating in our direction. Surprisingly persistent. Losing an experiment so valuable to Gene Archibald likely has dire consequence.

My faulty English accent speaks, raspy and untuned, "We've got company."

The driver acknowledges, glued to the rear-view mirror, "I see them. Check this out."

He turns onto another two lane street. Then U-turns into the opposite lane and toggles a steering wheel switch. The cruiser's exterior changes from orange to dark green. A slit appears on both sides, forming a four door cruiser. I've never seen this tech. It must be some sort of camouflage or illusion device. Where did these men develop technology like this for a modern-day cruiser without authorized approval?

The driver commands, "Get down."

I lie on my side. The driver declines to a normal speed limit. I hear heavy whirs from lawbreaking pursuers, feeling minor quakes as they zoom by. Did we give them the slip? Given a difference in appearance, I wouldn't expect negative odds.

After seconds of waiting the driver states, "We're all clear."

I sit up. Amongst normal traffic. That was awesome tech and a great strategy. Having them as chauffeurs would've made my criminal life easier. I examine the clear dome covering the city. At the sky. Then unfamiliar streets. Less lively and much less snobby than Gharis; home to the wealthiest New World populace who find themselves more secure around Menta-Life's main branch. Why does poor young me live there? I'm a smuggler. Handfuls of those rich require illegal means of attaining wealth through people like me.

I inquire, "This isn't Gharis City, is it?"
The passenger confirms, "No. This is New Rellow. Near Gharis is where Menta-Life abducted you… You don't remember?"

Abducted by Menta-Life? Sense couldn't be clearer, having just woken from an induced coma at one of their branches. I remember everything after being framed for multiple murders and getting sent to prison. I wasn't arrested in Gharis during the job for my employer, Trex; however, that could be where I was transported from.

I answer, "I don't."

He expresses comfort, "It's alright. It'll all come back soon. It takes time after waking from a Life to remember what you did last night. I'm Mason by the way." He points at the driver, "This is Will."

I understand the rationality of that comparison. Having been in two places, I'm already confused about whether prison was real. About how much time has passed, based on hair length. The Life seemed so vivid; like it was the next day being locked away for what was supposed to be a harsh sentence.

I ask, "Where're we going?"
Mason answers, "We have a base a good ways out of New Rellow. We're going to meet with everyone there."
"And Simon?"
Mason clarifies, "And Simon."

I watch the outside world. Healthy fake trees, reflective windows on business buildings, digital billboards displaying upcoming events, cruisers high and low. Everyone doesn't seem cheerfully colored. Shaded by thick clouds of ordinariness overhead. Gharis inhabitants dress like they're the brightest, quite literally, but New Rellow inhabitants are a tad more common. MechCi are always the same, strolling casually with their owners.

MechCi are one form of mechanical robot. Particularly civilian models designed to competently communicate as more than a working tool. Manufactured, upon purchaser's request, in male or female gender and in form of adult or child. Socially, with advanced AI interfaces they blend seamless throughout the five cities. Hardwired for utilization as assistants, but not employees; business partners, friends to share lives with, kids some can't birth, etc. MechCi are the third lowest rank, unintended for combat use.

The sun is still highest. A beautiful afternoon on an eastern gate approach to leave the bubble. Covering cities became mandatory after raiders from hostile settlements began attacking the new civilized world. Where there's peace, someone always tries establishing dominance through force. The clear dome protects cities from outside threats like raiders, airborne diseases, or potentially existing rabid animals. Four gate exits are the only parts of a dome that's concrete, steel and accessible from ground level.

Two Regulator Officers approach each side with pulser rifles swaddled; classic assault rifle concept except more body and not near as lethal. These, and pulser pistols, are manufactured with dual functionality for user safety and ensuring victim survival: one function is shock and second is heat. Both used to disable or subdue targets. Shock rounds immobilize. Heat rounds penetrate and halt bleeding, if the target is protected by layers of undergarments to void shock rounds. Will sluggishly presents a small paper to the officer.

The woman asks, "Hyper Warp?"
Will answers, "No."

She immediately signals us through. Will must have fake credentials because, normally, there's a lengthier process to leaving any city. The massive, concrete gate in our path begins rising. Will accelerates into dry wasteland, following the single paved road.

My name is Vanessa Pheros and I am a lone dissident. The "S" in my last name is silent. I was born in England. My country was devastated by war, along with many, many others. Now humans reside in what's left of America. I was brought by a neighbor and friend of my father, Goffrey, who died of a heart attack that landed me in a makeshift foster home; multiple following were my doing. Miles from home after a devastating global nuclear crisis wasn't a great time for any child. Or most adults who better understood loss. At a young age I did what most traumatized, broken children would and fought back, landing in the worst places all my life.

Much older, I took up the criminal trade and became a smuggler in Gharis City. And ironically, a sour deal landed me in this cruiser; going to talk with a recently resurrected father. I don't trust these people, still interested in who's desperate to meet and why. Simon's been dead seventeen years, yet waking, I'm unsure how accurate that timeline is anymore. Even having watched it happen. There's no way he could be out there, or anywhere in flesh. The evacuation shuttle was near-grounded when atom bombs struck. He vanished in a cloud of smoke then reappeared, face down, as it cleared. Radiation should have eaten everything. Seeing Simon in my Life doesn't mean he exists in reality. Shared information runs on a live stream for accessibility and anyone can tamper with it by uploading something false, granting everyone access. Menta-Life's way of playing tricks on people. I don't know when my mental Life actually began or how long ago. Joining the New World and living Lifes was something I never wanted to be a part of, for that very reason. This is a new twist. Menta-Life took me against my will and forced a Life, but why? Were they using my brain to locate a man I haven't seen? How do they know of my past connections?

Will pulls off the road and speeds north for almost an hour. Presses a button on the dashboard and slows to a drag. An entry big enough for a delivery truck begins rising out of the ground. Some kind of elevator? Or garage door? Will pulls in. I watch the opening close and sand follow us inside as we glide down a ramp. A recently built door. Little lights above brighten the brown tunnel. We enter an old, burgundy-colored parking garage. Very small. Will parks to the left, next to an obvious mechanic working on two cruisers. The mastermind behind this illusion vehicle? Cruiser still running, we all exit. How was an underground base built out here without notice? And deep. This garage is too run-down, so they're squatting. Chipped paint and rusted pre-war cars verify, not the tiny herd of cruisers. All cruisers have retractable tires for parking, nonetheless difference of coloration easily helps tell them apart from these cars.

The mechanic excitedly asks, "How'd she drive?"
Will answers in a weird voice, "Sweeter than candy."

I follow Mason and Will past the occupied mechanic. They allow me first entry into a single door. Threshold revealing what appears to be a hotel lobby on my right. Downward of thirty people are individually working on scientific things that I know nothing about. In a sort of dual assembly line. It looks like they're creating and testing chemicals. One person is doing laps with a clipboard and checking everyone's work. This must be a buried hotel.

I investigate, "What is this place?"

Mason answers, "A temporary residence. We set up camp here until we could safely retrieve you."

"You guys sure did set up fast."

"Not really. It took us a little over two months to get settled here. There was a lot t–"

I retract to what was said and stop listening to what he's saying. They established base here until rescue, but that was two months ago. What day is it? When is it? Have I really been captive for two months? I don't remember any of what happened.

I intrude, "Wait… It took two months? Was I there that long?"

Mason quickly reassures, "No, of course not. You were there for about five months, I think." My eyes light up with shock, "They were using your memory to search for Simon. You had no idea where he could be, but clearly they never gave up trying."

Five months went by and it felt like years. Why don't I remember anything between? The Life server doesn't support regression. Each participant must start at their current age each time they enter and progress from there. Only opportunity was around my initial two years in prison. If any of that term was real, I'm somewhere between twenty-two and twenty-four. After arrest, or abduction, I remember being in jail and processed. It all seemed flush at the time, and still does now. If every three days is supposed to be ninety years, I would have had sixty-seven years of Life and a two day break to prevent confusion. Where was I for those months? No recollection.

My rescuers lead straight across the lobby to an opposing door and enter first. A hallway with a long observation window on the right side. Beyond is a painted room resembling a city. Detail so intricately done that it probably feels real from the center. A female Deserted is hugging the wall. Caressing a building's fine lines. She looks clean, peaceful and content. What is she doing? How is she so attached to… anything? I have never seen a Deserted person like that. Like most, her hair was gone. It's regrown into a light stubble now.

I stop walking and leer inside, "Is she Deserted?"

Mason halts, "Yeah. We created a life-like environment to study her reactions to the city. She's fond of night and stars. It's been holding her over until we can administer stable treatments or shut down Menta-Life's memory facility."

"Treatments? Does that lead to a cure?"

"Unfortunately, no. There could be a suitable alternative. An anti-drug. Something to counteract and help Deserted retain new memories, in the event we fail with the hourglass. They won't be themselves but at least they'll live again."

"Hourglass?"

"The device that memories are stored in."

"Why destroy it? Won't that destroy the memories?"

"Stolen memories aren't like files to be put away, then lost on a damaged hard drive. These are more materially held, like mind-controlled prisoners. Destroying the hourglass would free them. They'd fully get their lives back. Simon can better explain; he's waiting."

Not that I considered attempting; however, I hadn't known there was a way to save them. Their cause seems noble, but at the same time, doesn't feel right; like history may repeat itself with a new face instead of Geilium's. I have a lot of questions, and one addition: why haven't they, not once, called Simon my father?

Mason resumes strolling. I shadow him around the right bend toward Will who is already waiting next to a dead-end door. He opens it. A smaller group is in what looks like a darkly-lit lunchroom. Huddled around a centered table instead of using available chairs, going over notes of importance. A chalkboard occupies the right wall with bunches of written mathematical junk I don't understand. Formulas and table elements. An armed guard stands at my left side.

Simon's head raises ninety degrees from the table to address seven others; not noticing new presence. I'm ashamed to admit my memory of him isn't too accurate after all these years. It is the man I saw in my Life, for certain. A tall man. Short, dark brown hair and matching goatee, both speckling gray. Hazel eyes and skin that hasn't seen the sun often. The late-twenties I barely recall makes a reflective mid-forty. Current image replacing himself in childhood moments. Feeling like it's actually him.

What are they discussing? A battle plan? Faint tones are high but not enough to comprehend the conversation. Eyes focus on someone in my direction, responding to another. Simon double takes, staring at me. Absolute relief during a slow rise from the huddle. Others follow his sight, rising as well. Two woman and five men, not including Simon. I recognize one as Hines Aldwich; a man from Germany who worked for Menta-Life and is supposed to be dead too. Short hair, blonde. Clean shaven. Mid-thirties and carries a heavy accent. Never meeting in person, I don't think.

Simon steps around the table and lightly calls out, "Vanessa?" His voice develops a small pitch, "You've grown so—"

Something's not right. An unshakable feeling. I quickly disarm the guard and use him as a human shield. My thumb activates the pulser pistol's heat function. Active, shooting multiple times would kill from horrible, burning pain or shock which is the best option at the moment. A single headshot couldn't suffice because penetrating bone requires more force than pulses contain. Everyone begins moving away.

I harshly command, "Nobody move or he dies!"

Hunched, Simon throws his right palm behind at colleagues and left at me, like he's going to block heat rounds and shield anyone.

His deep English accent worryingly requests, "What are you doing?!"
I sternly ask, "Who are you?"
"Don't you recognize me... I'm Simon Harold."

Following the war of 2068, the worldwide flow of digital information had been lost. Earth's contact, communication and our media controlled lives regressed to nothing. Vanessa Pheros was a name Goffrey and I conjured up. A new identity in this New World. I'd never shared my birth name with anyone. Just as abandoned as I. My father wouldn't call me Vanessa.

I reply, "I watched Simon Harold die seventeen years ago. Lie again, I will shoot you and everyone in this room. I want the truth."

Actually, it's been fifteen years. I recall stating the seventeen time frame after two years in prison. But it would have been fifteen, dependent on the five month absence. I'm unsure what to think about this. Everything feels off.

Simon states in panic, "I'm telling the truth." He peacefully explains, "Look at me. I'm right here. I am alive. That day, when the atom bomb fell, it wasn't the kind of bomb like the others. The nuclear strain didn't hold, making it defective. It was an experimental prototype meant to destroy more than it did. The bomb still killed a lot of people; nevertheless, I survived with just a few minor burns and that is the truth."

Is that believable? A faulty bomb doesn't explain him not coming to find me sooner or leaving me alone for most of my life. Neither of those would provide proof. I have one test and Simon Harold is the only person left alive who would know the true answer.

I ask, "What's my name?"
He cautiously states, "Emily. Your name is Emily Harold… and you *are* my daughter."

The room glances at him in amazement, as if they didn't know he could have a daughter. One of those "we've known you for years but this is unbelievable" kind of glances. Since his death my birth name has never been shared, and he correctly answered. The associates' reactions make it easier to digest. Goffrey knew I had no family or home. Our shuttle was one of two to make it off my district's surface. A new name was part of what I needed to carry on. An orphan with no past attachments. Seeing Simon, relief is hard to contain. Like the slow motion release of a pinch. Without my mother, I clung to Simon like a shoe on his foot. Sinking to levels beyond devastation after losing him. A tear falls. I release the guard and drop the pulser. The guard calmly recovers it and steps away. Simon approaches. I feel a sudden pain. Like a hand is adjusting my brain into my head.

I become dizzy and speak, "Dad, I–"

The sensation changes. Like a vicious bug gnawing at my brain, instantly worsening. I clench my head with both hands and groan uncontrollably. Turning to flee and being brought to my knees. What is this pain? Another feeling joins, chiseling on my skull in scribbles with a nail. Burning my head into screams. What's happening?

Simon calls out in great worry, "Em?"

Mason and Will burst in, merging into the surrounding crowd. Pain becomes much worse. I fall onto my back while holding tighter. What is this? Why does it hurt so badly? My head feels like it's on fire and my vision is blurring.

Simon drops to his knees at my side and yells at Mason, "What's wrong with her?!"
Mason swiftly answers, "I don't know, we brought her here like you ordered. No stops."
Simon looks at me and comforts in a low tone, "It's okay honey; breathe, breathe."

I can't stop the pain. I can't stop screaming. I can't stop trying to crunch my head open to get what's causing this terrible hurt I've never felt. Why is it hard to think? I become reminded of the man in my Life that experienced similar head trauma I'm going through. Did Menta-Life do something? Am I becoming Deserted?

Simon loudly demands, "Hines, hurry!"

Hines Aldwich kneels over me with a laptop and uses a camera attachment to scan. What is he doing here? First he worked for Menta-Life, then Equility, and now Simon? Pain conquers my thoughts again, hurting a little worse. The sharpness is like multiple nails being hammered into my head at once and making me shaky.

Hines quickly informs, reading off the holographic screen, "Scan shows a lot of detached neural oscillations. Menta-Life must've stolen one of her memories. Brainwaves are rapidly deteriorating."

Simon furiously curses, "Dammit, Gene! ...We have to give her the dose."

"We can't inject so late in the stage of reversion, Simon. She could die."

"She'll die if we don't! Give her the dose!"

Hines hesitantly commands someone else, "Have Paul Quentin bring an injection please, quickly."

Simon confesses in a whisper, "You'll be okay."

My voice is going hoarse, still I can't keep my mouth closed to even mask pain. A dark-skinned man with a goatee and crewcut approaches behind Hines. Out of breath like he just ran here, perhaps from the lobby area where scientists were experimenting.

He hands a syringe to Hines and collects acknowledgment, "Thank you, Paul."

Who is Paul Quentin? He's giving me the strangest expression of concern. Able to see clearly through his thick glasses. He seems very familiar. Somehow; like I've seen or met him before. My pain worsens from trying to remember.

Hines empathizes, "I know this is a lot to ask, but I need your arm. Physically restraining you from the pain itself could worsen things."

Mentally, I can't allow me to move them away, stop shaking, or screaming. And my hands are the only things giving comfort. I close my eyes. Imagine sticking out my arm. Turn my head away. Multiple hands brace my arm. Then my body. Restraining me? Multiple tiny needles pierce my skin for a brief second. I'm starting to shut down. Voice fades into small grunts. Paralyzed. Heavy breathing becomes simmered huffs as my body, very lightly, jerks.

I am falling unconscious to Simon's voice, "It's okay. It's okay." I hear my heart slowing to normal then less than that, "It's okay."

People crowded overhead fade, dragging me into infinite darkness. Silence, though there are many voices. Wherever I am feels like an oven. I jolt awake, breathing heavily in a hot sweat. Facing the ceiling with beige paint chipping. An old fan above has seen better days. So loose, if a switch flicked, it would fall and chop me in half. Hypothetically. The ends aren't sharp enough. I'm in a twin bed against a corner wall. Wearing a white tank top while the rest is hidden under an itchy gray blanket. The room is office size, and not the executive version either. I mean the "too small for our kids to share as a bedroom" kind of pity office. Am I still in the underground hotel? This seems fit for a mental patient, and who would I be to say that's not a fitting irony? There's no small window for orderlies to peek through. I lift the blanket to see loose black sweatpants. Sit and dangle my feet near the floor, replaying what happened.

Hines dosed me with a deadly syringe, and I'm still here. A plus. My head doesn't hurt as bad. From ten to almost nothing, by comparison. How long have I been unconscious? Fresh air out of this stuffy, sick-colored room would help. Food too.

Acknowledgments

I would like to pay acknowledgements to Areal Nunez for being my incentive to begin a writing career. Editors Nanda Olney and Belisa Brownlee for doing the most wonderful job at bringing out the much finer points of my work. Cover artist, XlFlower, for designing a beautiful front display. Supporters and readers worldwide. My world wouldn't exist without yours; people that I have and haven't seen; people who connected with me in minor and major ways to make my dreams as a writer possible. Steps we take ripple and we all deserve acknowledgement so I acknowledge YOU for reading.

Welcome back to the year **2084** and awaken to **truth**.

Liberated from the clutches of Menta-Life in New Rellow City, **Vanessa Pheros** is reunited with the **father** she believed perished in the war of 2068. Unfortunately, her peace of **mind** and reunion are very short lived. With the unknown theft of a **memory** and learning of her father's **involvement** with Gene Archibald, founder of Menta-Life, Van is on the clock, once again. The **goal**? Retrieve her memory from an underground storage base, before becoming one of the **people** her father seeks to save; freeing minds of the Deserted, an untamable populace who can't remember who they are. Forcing citizens to see Menta-Life's involvement in dumping their failed projects underground, **exposing** the New World's false saviors.

Excluding one man, **allies** on her father's side are incapable of fighting such a big corporation. Desperate to live, Van recalls her forced mental Life to search for an elite team of talented **misfits** that she either knows, virtually acquainted, or heard of. Constant problems between those with different agendas for the corporation's **fate**, and facing off against an illustrious entourage with **altered** capabilities make task near impossible. Explore the new dystopian **world** outside of Gharis City, bumping into familiar faces and new **rivals** as Van battles to take back what she doesn't know has been taken from her.

Menta-Life: Desertion

Made in the USA
Las Vegas, NV
25 August 2022